Books in the NEV

Book 1: Never Say Spy

Book 2: The Spy Is Cast

Book 3: Reach For The Spy

Book 4: Tell Me No Spies

Book 5: How Spy I Am

More books coming! For a current list, please visit www.dianehenders.com

TELL ME NO SPIES

Book 4 of the NEVER SAY SPY series

Diane Henders

TELL ME NO SPIES

ISBN 978-0-9878712-4-4

PEBKAC Publishing
P.O. Box 75046 Westhills R.P.O.
Calgary, AB T3H 3M1
www.pebkacpublishing.com

First printed in paperback November 2011 by PEBKAC Publishing
v.3

Since You Asked...

People frequently ask if my protagonist, Aydan Kelly, is really me.

Yeah, you got me. These novels are an autobiography of my secret life as a government agent, working with highly-classified computer technology... Oh, wait, what's that? You want the *truth*? Um, you do realize fiction writers get paid to lie, don't you?

...well, shit, that's not nearly as much fun. It's also a long story.

I swore I'd never write fiction. "Too personal," I said. "People read novels and automatically assume the author is talking about him/herself."

Well, apparently I lied about the fiction-writing part. One day, a story sprang into my head and wouldn't leave. The only way to get it out was to write it down. So I did.

But when I wrote that first book, I never intended to show it to anyone, so I created a character that looked like me just to thumb my nose at the stereotype. I've always had a defective sense of humour, and this time it turned around and bit me in the ass.

Because after I'd written the third novel, I realized I actually wanted other people to read my books. And when I went back to change my main character to *not* look like me, my beta readers wouldn't let me. They rose up against me and said, "No! Aydan is a tall woman with long red hair and brown eyes. End of discussion!"

Jeez, no wonder readers get the idea that authors write about themselves. So no, I'm not Aydan Kelly. I just look like her.

Oh, and the town of Silverside and all secret technologies

are products of my imagination. If I'm abducted by grim-faced men wearing dark glasses, or if I die in an unexplained fiery car crash, you'll know I accidentally came a little too close to the truth.

Thank you for respecting my hard work. If you're borrowing this book, I'd very much appreciate it if you would buy your own copy, or, if you wish, you can make a donation on my website at http://www.dianehenders.com/donate.

Thanks - I hope you enjoy the book!

For Phill

Thank you for being my technical advisor and the most tolerant husband ever. Much love!

To my beta readers/editors, especially Carol H., Judy B., and Phill B., with gratitude: Many thanks for all your time and effort in catching my spelling and grammar errors, telling me when I screwed up the plot or the characters' motivations, and generally keeping me honest.

To the other Phil, with appreciation: Thanks for all the cold beer and the great stories about your trucking days. That was the most enjoyable research I've ever done.

To everyone else, respectfully:
If you find any typographical errors in this book, please send an email to errors@dianehenders.com. Mistakes drive me nuts, and I'm sorry if any slipped through. Please let me know what the error is, and on which page. I'll make sure it gets fixed in the next printing. Thanks!

CHAPTER 1

I suppressed a curse and furtively shifted the concealed holster to a more comfortable spot at my waist, rearranging my sweatshirt over it. A tension headache pounded sullenly at the base of my skull.

The vibration of my phone made me start, and I snapped a glance over my shoulder before I snatched it up.

I could barely hear the whisper on the other end. "Aydan, can you stall him for a few more minutes?"

"How long?" I hissed. "What's wrong?"

"We just need a few more minutes to get everybody into position."

"I'll try." I punched the disconnect button with more force than absolutely necessary. Why the hell did I let myself get sucked into this?

I knotted my fists in my hair and tugged, but quickly desisted when the door latch released behind me. Trying to look relaxed, I leaned back in the chair and stretched my legs out. The security guard glanced my way and I gave him a quick smile, heart thumping.

At the sound of footsteps, I turned my smile toward my quarry as I stood. "All finished?"

"Yes." He stretched, grimacing. "Long day." He made for the door.

"Hang on a second," I blurted.

"What?" He shifted from foot to foot, obviously eager to leave.

"Um..."

Goddammit, what could I say to stall him? My mind was completely blank. The silence began to stretch. His forehead creased ever so slightly and his eyes darted toward the door.

Think, think, dammit!

Absolutely no inspiration came to mind.

Shit!

I did my best sheepish laugh and slapped my forehead. "Forgot what I was going to say. Sorry, you're right, it's been a long day."

He let out a short laugh and turned away again. "See you."

As he disappeared out the door, I whisked my phone out and hit the speed dial. Still attempting nonchalance, I wandered out of the building, raising a farewell hand to the security guard.

The phone rang interminably at the other end while I muttered, "Pick up, dammit, pick up!" When I finally heard the whisper on the other end, I snapped, "He's on his way!"

"Crap! Can you get here before him?"

"I'll try."

When I was sure nobody was watching, I launched myself into a silent sprint toward my car.

I lunged into the driver's seat and swore violently when the door slammed on my long hair and nearly dislocated my neck. I wasted precious seconds opening and closing the door to free myself. The tires chirped on the still-warm asphalt as I stomped on the gas.

Minutes later, my car skidded to a halt in the gravelled alley and I dashed through the twilight to let myself in the back gate. I spun at the last second to catch it before it banged behind me, then flew across the yard. As I reached the top step, the door to the darkened house opened. A disembodied hand yanked me inside.

My eyes hadn't adjusted to the dimness, and I allowed myself to be towed rapidly through the house. A jerk on my arm made me duck behind the sofa just as the scrape of the front door key sounded, loud in the listening silence.

Light and noise erupted, and Spider recoiled with a shout, his gangly arms flailing in shock.

"Surprise!" Linda flung herself at him, hugging him as he staggered back against the wall. "Are you surprised?"

Spider's mouth opened and closed soundlessly a few times. "Yeah..." he finally quavered. "Yeah... I'm surprised all right." His dilated eyes focused on me. "Aydan! You were in on this all along! I'm going to- "

I raised my arms in mock surrender. "Be nice, Spider. You wouldn't beat up an old lady, would you?"

"Old lady, my foot," he retorted. "I couldn't beat you up if I tried."

"Hey, speak for yourself with that old lady stuff," his mother tossed over her shoulder. "Forty-seven isn't old! That's my story, and I'm sticking to it." She pulled Spider down to kiss him noisily on the cheek. "Happy birthday, Clyde, honey."

"Thanks, Mom." He beamed at the rowdy crowd in the living room. "Thanks, you guys. You scared the heck out of me, but thanks."

Linda tugged at him and he awkwardly stooped from his beanpole six-foot-two to give her a quick kiss. His cheeks turned pink when whoops and catcalls burst out.

Linda shot a devilish glance at the assembled friends and family, and wrapped her arms around his neck as she stretched to her full almost-five-foot height. Pandemonium reigned while her theatrically passionate kiss went on and on. Finally Spider disengaged himself, his face scarlet.

"Isn't there some cake or something?" he mumbled, staring at the floor. Laughter filled the room, and the crowd's attention shifted when one of his sisters brought in the cake. As the discordant chorus of "Happy Birthday To You" rang out, he and Linda sneaked another kiss, their eyes sparkling.

I leaned back against the wall, grinning.

"Talk about the long and short of it. They look just like Ray and me together." Spider's mom smiled up at me. "Thanks for acting as the decoy."

I laughed and rubbed at my headache. "You're welcome. I'm glad it worked. They are cute together, aren't they?" I chuckled again, regarding short, plump Gladys Webb beside me and Spider's tall, lanky dad across the room. Like father, like son.

I accepted my piece of birthday cake and lingered a few more minutes, trying to appear sociable while I sweated profusely. As soon as I could politely excuse myself, I did a fast fade out to the mercifully cool evening air on the back deck.

I was leaning on the railing and sipping a glass of water when Spider came out and leaned beside me.

"Thanks for letting Mom and Linda rope you into this," he said.

"I didn't have much choice. Linda by herself is bad enough. The two of them combined are an unstoppable force."

He returned my rueful grin. "I know. But with two older sisters, I'm used to dominant females. You haven't met them yet, have you? Why don't you come back inside and I'll introduce you to everybody?"

I sipped water, stalling, and he mistook my hesitation. "I know you don't really like crowds. It's okay if you just want to sneak away."

"Thanks, Spider, but that wasn't really what I was thinking. I like your mom, and I'd like to meet your dad and sisters, but I'm cooking in this sweatshirt, and I can't take it off because I wore my waist holster today. Damn October weather, it was cold this morning and then it turned hot."

"Oh." He eyed me uncertainly. "Couldn't you just leave your gun in your car?"

"I could. But I'm not supposed to. And it'd be Murphy's Law that I'd need it the one time I took it off."

"I guess. I hope you won't need it tonight, though."

"I'm sure I won't." I patted him on the shoulder. "Go enjoy your party."

He had just disappeared inside when his father's bony silhouette appeared in the doorway. He advanced on me, hand outstretched.

"I'm Ray Webb, Clyde's dad. You're the only tall woman with long red hair here, so you must be Aydan Kelly."

"Guilty." I shook his hand. "It's nice to meet you."

"Nice to finally meet you, too. Clyde talks a lot about you."

"Spider talks a lot, period. But he's the bright spot of my days at Sirius Dynamics," I added quickly. "He's a great kid. And scary smart."

Ray winked. "Like his dad."

"So I hear."

I knew Ray by reputation only, as a civilian researcher at Sirius. He was brilliant, eccentric, and nowhere close to the security clearance that would allow him to know about my work. I hunched over the railing again, making sure my loose sweatshirt concealed my gun.

"So you do bookkeeping for Sirius Dynamics?" His gaze was a little too piercing, and I felt my eyes slither sideways despite myself.

"Yes," I replied, with perhaps a shade too much emphasis.

"But you work with Clyde."

I could tell he was trying to puzzle out why a bookkeeper would hobnob on a daily basis with a computer analyst.

"Yes... I do some computer work, sometimes, too."

Ray's face brightened. "Really? What's your area of expertise?"

Shit. All I needed was to get into a technical discussion that would reveal how little I really knew about modern computer systems.

"I... help out with some of the network stuff," I hedged.

"In the secured facility," he prompted. "I saw you going in there a few weeks ago."

Shit, shit, shit!

"Uh, sometimes, yeah. But that was for some, um, bookkeeping stuff for one of the special projects. I have to work down there when I'm doing bookkeeping. Um, for the special projects, I mean. Because they can't bring stuff upstairs."

He contemplated me for a few moments. "Don't take this wrong, but you need a better cover," he said at last.

I blew out a breath through my teeth and resisted the urge to yank a couple of handfuls of hair. "I'm just a bookkeeper, Ray, okay?"

"Okay. But you should come up with a more convincing story."

"I wish I could, but I'm really just a bookkeeper."

He opened his mouth and closed it again as one of Spider's sisters poked her head out the door. "Come on inside, Dad. Clyde's going to open his presents."

I sucked in a breath of relief. "I really have to run now. It was nice talking to you. Tell Spider I said happy birthday."

I scuttled out to my car and fell into the driver's seat, groaning and rubbing my pounding temples in the friendly darkness. Christ, I needed to get better at that. Spider's dad was brighter than most people, but it was only a matter of time before others started asking the same inconvenient questions.

CHAPTER 2

Sprawled under my car the next afternoon, I let fly with a few colourful expletives when some of the blackened oil poured over the badly-placed frame member and missed the drain pan. I jerked and barely avoided smashing my forehead on the chassis when a male voice startled me.

"Everything okay?"

"Shit!" I scuffled across the concrete on my back, heart pounding, and peered out from underneath the Saturn at my neighbour, Tom Rossburn.

I blew out a long breath, thankful it was him and not somebody trying to kill me. I'd left my gun in the house when I changed my clothes. Stupid. I should know better by now.

"Sorry, I didn't mean to scare you," he said.

"It's okay. Could you hand me that roll of paper towels, please?"

He glanced at my oil-stained hands and tore off a couple of sheets. "Do you need more?"

"No, that's fine. Thanks." I squirmed back under the car and wiped up the mess, doing a bit of deep breathing in an attempt to dissipate the unnecessary adrenaline.

When I emerged again, he gave me his attractive crooked smile. "Do you need a hand?"

"No, I'll just let it drain for a few minutes and then button it up." I wiped my hands on the paper towel he offered and surreptitiously checked him out, enjoying the view.

The colour of his denim shirt accentuated his sky-blue eyes, and the rolled-up sleeves revealed tanned, sinewy muscle. Even from a couple of feet away, he smelled like sun-baked cotton and sweet, fresh hay. He hadn't turned around yet, but I knew from previous dedicated observation that the rear view of those faded jeans and cowboy boots was drool-worthy, too.

I did my best to project casual neighbourly interest. "I saw you up there with the truck earlier. How's it going?"

"Fine. I just dropped by to let you know I finished loading the bales from your eighty."

"Thanks!" I beamed at him. "I'm so glad you could do that for me. Let me know what your expenses were."

He waved a hand. "Forget it."

"No, we had a deal. Split the expenses, split the profits when you sell the bales. And I still think you should take more than half. You're doing all the work."

"But it's your land," he objected.

I propped my fists on my hips and frowned at him, and his crooked grin came back. "Okay. I'll write it out and drop it off tomorrow."

"Good. Thanks." I wiped my hands again on my coveralls and headed for the beer fridge that was just one of the many things I loved about my deluxe garage. "Do you want a beer?" I pulled out a cold one and waved it in his direction.

"No, I better not. You go ahead though."

I unzipped the hot coveralls and shimmied out of them

gratefully. As I tipped a long swallow of ice-cold beer down my throat, I caught Tom surveying my clingy shorts and tank top with undisguised appreciation.

"How'd you like to go out for drinks tonight instead?" he asked.

"...Um."

In the last couple of months, I'd been more and more tempted to discard my "look, don't touch" policy with him. I gave myself a mental slap to the head. Down, girl!

"I... uh."

Goddammit, what would a few drinks matter? We were neighbours after all. I should at least make an effort to be friendly.

"Sure. That sounds like fun." I regretted the words as soon as they left my mouth, but it was already too late. Tom's face lit up, and he gave me a full-on grin.

"Great, I'll pick you up at six-thirty?"

Still time to back out. Remember some pressing engagement. Do it, dammit. Say no. Say it now.

"Okay. See you then."

Shit. I'm an idiot.

At twenty after six, I locked up the house and sank into the chair on my front porch with a sigh. Several times during the day, I'd stood with my hand poised over the phone, ready to call Tom and cancel. And each time, I'd turned and walked away.

I knew I should have called it off. Never mind that, I knew I shouldn't have accepted in the first place. What the hell was I thinking?

As Tom's truck drove up the lane, I hurried down the

steps and met him on the gravelled turnaround I'd deliberately built outside the range of the surveillance cameras that blanketed my house.

The weathered lines around his eyes crinkled with his smile as I hopped up into the big 4x4. "I'm really glad you could come," he said. "I thought we could go over to Blue Eddy's, if that's okay with you. They have a live band tonight."

"Oh... yeah... that sounds great," I responded brightly, trying to silence the voice in my head that kept repeating, "Bad idea! Bad, bad idea!"

His smile lost a few watts. "We could go somewhere else if you'd rather."

"No, I love Eddy's," I assured him. "The Saturday bands are always good, and the food's far better than the Silverside Hotel."

Which was true. Those were the only two licensed establishments in the tiny town, and Eddy's was practically my second home. That was the problem. We'd be seen together.

Duh. Kinda like a date.

I'm definitely an idiot.

My heart was beating a little faster than necessary when we walked into Blue Eddy's. The band wasn't due to start until eight, so my usual table in the corner was still free. I made a beeline for it and slid into my favourite chair, my back to the wall while I surveyed the rest of the bar. Tom sat opposite me, one eyebrow arched quizzically.

"Hi, Aydan!" The waitress gave me a smile, and her eyes darted between Tom and me. Shit, by morning the entire town would know we'd been out together. I suppressed a sigh. "Do you want a beer?" she asked.

"Yeah, thanks, Darlene."

Her eyes lit up.

Shit. She knew I never drank if I was driving, so now she had proof that we were together. On a date.

Busted.

"Is everything okay?" Tom was watching me with a faint crease between his brows.

I summoned up a smile. "Of course."

"It sounded like you groaned."

I shook off my mood and forced a laugh. "No, that was my stomach growling," I lied. "I'm looking forward to some food and that beer."

He relaxed and smiled back at me, and soon we were laughing and chatting with our usual easy camaraderie. I glanced up as Darlene arrived with our food, and froze.

Tom turned in his seat to follow my sight line, and we watched Kane stride into the bar. Head and shoulders taller than most of the patrons, he was easy to spot. As usual, he wore dark jeans and a black T-shirt that stretched across his broad shoulders and hugged his muscular arms. He made his way through the crowd, seemingly oblivious to the female heads turning to check out his killer body, strong, square face, and short dark hair shading to grey at the temples.

I swallowed hard when his gaze swung over to our table. His face smoothed into an unreadable mask, and he nodded politely in our direction before turning to take a stool at the bar, his back to the wall.

I thanked Darlene and dragged my attention back to Tom. He was frowning again. "That's John Kane, isn't it? The guy who..." he hesitated almost imperceptibly. "...you work with?"

"Yes." I changed the subject and concentrated on Tom, my food, and my second beer. I couldn't help watching Kane out of the corner of my eye, and I relaxed when he finished his meal at last and left soon afterward.

A few beers and some excellent music later, Tom and I emerged laughing into the parking lot. As we strolled away from the lights of the bar, I caught Tom's arm. "Wow, look at that big cheddar-cheese moon! Doesn't it make you think of Halloween?"

He didn't reply right away, and I tore my attention away from the moon to glance up at him. Warning bells went off in my slightly tipsy brain when he smiled at me.

"No, I wasn't thinking of Halloween," he said.

"Oh." I let go of his arm as if it was red-hot, but he caught my hands gently before I could step back.

"I haven't heard a Harley around your place for a while," he said.

"Um. No, not recently."

"Are you still involved with Arnie?"

I ignored the sudden pang and kept my tone light. "Yes, but he's been busy lately."

His callused hands tightened a fraction on mine. "I think you're better off without him."

"You just got a bad first impression. He's actually a really nice guy."

Tom grimaced. "Yeah, there a lot of nice guys nicknamed 'Hellhound'."

"It's just wordplay on his last name." I made a none-too-determined effort to extricate my hands. Standing so close, his clean outdoorsy male scent was threatening to overwhelm my common sense. His grip on my hands was warm and strong.

His voice dropped to an intimate murmur as he looked into my eyes. "My 'friends with benefits' offer still stands. If you're interested."

'Interested' didn't exactly cover the magnitude of what I was feeling. I did my best to hide my internal struggle. I was still trying to formulate a reply when he leaned in and kissed me.

I was fighting a desperate battle against the urge to take him up on his offer right then and there in the middle of the parking lot when the sound of Kane's voice made me jerk away with a gasp.

"Aydan, I'm sorry to interrupt, but we need you at the office." He didn't sound sorry at all. He sounded... dangerous.

"Oh." My gaze ping-ponged between Tom and Kane. They were both expressionless, but I sensed the tension in them as they locked eyes.

"It's eleven-thirty on a Saturday night," Tom said evenly. "I'm sure it can wait."

"It can't." Kane's deep voice was hard. "Aydan, let's go."

I turned to Tom. "I'm sorry, I have to go. Thanks a lot for tonight. I had fun."

I was turning to leave when he caught my arm lightly. "Aydan, you don't have to go with him if you don't want to."

Kane eyed Tom's hand on my arm. The small hairs lifted on the back of my neck, and I pulled away quickly.

"I do have to go, actually." I blurted out the first semi-plausible explanation that came to mind. "We're right in the middle of an audit, and we have a deadline. We've been waiting on some information, and I told John to call me as soon as he had it."

"Oh." Tom's eyes narrowed and his hands clenched into fists as he assessed Kane looming beside me. After a couple of long seconds, he squared his shoulders and gave us a curt nod. "Okay. If you say so. Good night, Aydan." He hesitated. "Call me if you need a ride home. No matter what time it is."

"Thanks." The word came out on a whoosh of breath I hadn't realized I was holding when he turned toward his truck.

I trotted after Kane as he stalked to his black Expedition. We got in, and he sat staring through the windshield for a moment. When he spoke, his normally even voice had a distinct edge. "What the hell was that?"

My temper flared, and I wrestled my voice under control before responding. "A mistake. Obviously."

"I thought you told Rossburn you weren't interested in him."

"I did."

"So what the hell was that?"

"A mistake. I made a mistake, okay? He's my neighbour, he's been doing a lot of work on my farm this summer, I was trying to be friendly and he got the wrong idea."

"You didn't seem in a hurry to tell him that."

I clamped my teeth together on my irritation and concentrated on releasing the fist that I'd clenched unconsciously. "I... He took me by surprise. I would've dealt with it."

"You need to deal with it tomorrow. Tell him you're still scr..." he bit back his first choice of words and continued, "...seeing Hellhound."

I blew out a breath between my teeth. "I did. He knows

Arnie hasn't been around in the last couple of months."

In my peripheral vision, I saw Kane turn to look at me, and I glared straight ahead out the windshield.

After a short silence, he spoke again. "I thought you two were hot and heavy."

"And I thought it was none of your business," I gritted. "And speaking of 'none of your business', what the hell were you doing lurking in the parking lot in the middle of the night anyway? Looking for some cheap thrills?"

"I was doing my job," he ground out. "I'm a spy, not a goddamn voyeur. If you're going to make out in public, you can't blame me for having to watch. And it's a lucky thing I was here. What would you have done when he started getting really friendly and found your gun?"

I was biting my tongue to hold back angry words when he shot a scowl at my snug T-shirt and jeans. "You are wearing your gun, aren't you? Dammit, Aydan, tell me you're wearing your gun! Tell me your judgement isn't that clouded..."

"Jesus Christ! Yes! I'm wearing my gun! It's in my ankle holster. And he wasn't going to get any friendlier because I'm not goddamn *stupid* enough to take a chance like that! And I told you, I made a fucking mistake, which happens occasionally to mere mortals like me..."

I paused only long enough to suck in a furious breath. "...unlike you, who would *never* make an error in judgement, like, oh, I don't know, sneaking into my house in the middle of the night and *fucking my brains out* after we agreed we couldn't get involved..."

Kane tensed in his seat, staring out the windshield, and I realized I'd gone too far. I was about to offer an apology when he jerked around to face me, and I flinched when his hands flew toward me.

One of his fists knotted in my hair as he yanked me close and kissed me hard. My half-raised hands were trapped between us, and I shoved against his powerful chest as I jerked away far enough to yelp, "What-the-"

"Don't fight me," he growled, and pulled me into another demanding kiss.

I made a half-hearted attempt to push him away, but his hands and lips felt too good. The tiny part of my mind that retained some logical thought advised me this was a Very Bad Idea, but I cheerfully ignored it.

I kissed him back hungrily and let hot need overwhelm me while I groped his hard muscles with shaking hands. God, after two months of deprivation, I was ready to combust just from the sizzling memories. I clutched at him as he pulled my T-shirt free of my jeans, his hands burning against the skin of my back. His teeth closed lightly on my earlobe, and I gasped open-mouthed against him, drowning in lust.

Through half-closed eyes, I caught a flash of movement out in the parking lot and moments later Tom's truck roared away.

The heat of anger displaced my desire as I stiffened in Kane's arms.

"You can stop now," I snapped. "He's gone."

CHAPTER 3

Kane released me and drew back, his grey eyes black in the semi-darkness. We stared at each other for a few moments, and I broke the silence first.

"You can be a real asshole, can't you?"

"Aydan..."

The anger drained out of me at the look on his face, and I blew out a long sigh that was half-groan. "Never mind." I slumped forward and pounded my forehead gently against the dashboard. "Christ, what a clusterfuck. I'm such an idiot. I'm sorry."

"You're not an idiot." His voice was soft. "I know how hard it is to do without..." He trailed off. "Everybody slips up sometimes. As you pointed out," he added ruefully. "I'm sorry, too. The last couple of months have been... tough. I overreacted."

"Thanks." I met his eyes tentatively. "Friends again?"

"Always. You know that." He hesitated. "Speaking of friends... I don't mean to pry, and you can tell me to go to hell if you want, but... what happened between you and Hellhound?"

I massaged my aching temples. "Nothing. I just haven't seen him since August, and I don't want to push it. We were... pretty vulnerable with each other when we thought you'd died, and you know how he feels about getting attached."

"The same as you," he said quietly.

I glanced away from his steady eyes. "Uh, yeah." I squirmed a little in the seat.

Since August, I'd been pretending he'd never uttered the L-word. I really didn't want to have that conversation again, especially with my lips still burning from his kisses. Along with the other parts of my body that were still smouldering.

I ignored the subtext and stuck with the stated topic. "I hope he... I hope it works out. He was... he's a good friend."

"Arnie doesn't abandon his friends," Kane assured me. "He's just been busy lately. I called him a couple of times, but I haven't seen him, either."

"Oh." My heart lightened, and I changed the subject to conceal my relief. "Shouldn't we be heading for the office? Were you just blowing smoke, or is there really something urgent?"

"Yes." He started the Expedition, and I eased my stress out in a long, secret sigh.

Relief morphed rapidly into worry as we pulled out of the parking lot. "What's wrong? How bad is it?"

He shot me a quick glance. "Don't worry, I don't think it's life-threatening. If I hadn't already known you were in town tonight, I likely would have left it until tomorrow morning."

My shoulders attempted to climb up around my ears. "You don't *think* it's life-threatening? I told you, if it's urgent, call me. No matter what time it is. You know how I'd feel if something bad happened to somebody because I wasn't there to decrypt a message."

Kane sighed. "Aydan, you can't work 24/7. There will

always be something else that has to be decrypted. You haven't had a full weekend in two months."

"Yeah, but..."

He pulled into the parking lot across from Sirius Dynamics and fixed me with a severe look. "But, nothing. I'm your handler. When I say you need a rest, you need a rest. Stemp will have my head on a platter if you burn out."

"That's pretty rich coming from a guy who hardly eats or sleeps while he's on a mission."

I thought I detected a tinge of bitterness in his voice when he replied, "That's different. I'm supposed to be an agent." He gave his head a quick shake as if to rid himself of a thought, and continued, "You're not. You're a civilian. Aren't you?"

"Yes! Don't start that again. I'm a civilian. I'm not an undercover agent. I'm just saying..."

"Come on," he interrupted. "We're not getting anywhere with this conversation. We need to get this done so you can go home and get some sleep."

I grimaced and hopped out of the truck to follow him into Sirius.

We collected our security fobs from the guard behind the bulletproof window, and Kane made for the heavy steel door that led to the secured area. As he stooped for the retinal scan, I came to stand beside him.

"I'll just come down with you," I told him. "We won't be long, will we?"

The door released with a muffled click, and he straightened and gazed down at me. "When did you get over being claustrophobic?"

"I'm too tired to panic tonight."

He studied me for a second. "No. Go on up to your

office. If you're that tired, I don't want to take a chance."

I shrugged and trailed off down the hallway as he stepped into the cramped time-delay enclosure that always gave me the willies. Not for the first time, I thanked my lucky stars I had Kane for my handler. I'd never take him for granted again.

Up in my second-floor office, I collapsed yawning onto the small sofa. I was hunched over rubbing my temples when Kane's voice startled me. "Are you okay?"

"Fine. Just a headache."

He surveyed me, his brow furrowed. "How long has it been since you *didn't* have a headache?"

"I don't know. Whatever." I held out my hand for the tiny box that contained the world's most secret and valuable technology. "Let's just do this."

Kane frowned down at me. "Do you want some ibuprofen?"

"No, I've tried that. Nothing touches it." I wiggled my outstretched fingers. "Give."

He reluctantly handed me the network key. "Wait," he rapped out as I leaned back on the couch and closed my eyes.

"What?"

"I'll come into the network with you, since Webb's not here to monitor. Just in case you have problems in the sim." He sat in the chair across from me. "Okay, let's go."

I closed my eyes and concentrated on entering the white void of virtual reality. As I stepped into it, Kane's avatar popped into existence beside me, and we strode down virtual hallways to the file repository.

Inside, I scowled at the stack of files. Damn, they were piling up again.

"Do you know which one it is?" I asked.

Kane grimaced. "No. You're the only one in the world who can decrypt any of these. I don't know one from the other. But when I got the call, the analyst said you should look for a timestamp of nine twenty-three p.m."

"Okay, thanks." I flipped through the files, rubbing my head with my free hand as I searched.

"Are you sure you're all right?"

"Yeah, fine," I mumbled, still sifting through the stack. "But I'd be so much happier if I could just go back to being an ordinary bookkeeper instead of a military secret."

"Believe me, I wish you could, too," Kane said.

Something in his voice made me pause in my search. I shot a glance his way, but his face was composed as always. "I guess you must be going a little stir-crazy just sitting around here all the time," I ventured.

He twitched a shoulder, and my attention shifted as I discovered the file.

"Here we go," I said, and plopped into a virtual chair to begin decrypting.

At last, I looked up, rubbing the kinks out of my neck. "Did that make any sense to you?" I inquired.

Kane focused a predatory grin on his virtual terminal. "Yes."

I watched him work for a few minutes, his gaze riveted to the screen while he typed rapidly with his two index fingers. Despite my exhaustion, I smiled at his single-minded focus. He was so dedicated, so ready to lay his life on the line to protect national security. I was proud to be part of his team, and lucky to be working with him.

And he must be hating every minute of it.

Before I came along, he'd been a field agent. Now he'd been stuck behind a desk for two months, with no relief in sight. No wonder he was getting cranky. I sighed, wishing there was a better solution than wasting his talents babysitting me.

He glanced up at the sound. "I'm sorry, I just need to get this tied up, and then I'll take you home."

"It's okay. I'm just going to work on some of these other files while I wait."

I held back a groan and opened the next file in the stack. The encrypted words swam in front of my tired eyes, and I blinked hard, trying to focus. The print crawled on the page. Like bugs.

I sprang up and bit back a yell as hundreds of black beetles skittered over my hands and scuttled under the files that lay on the virtual table. Kane was instantly on his feet. He reached me in two quick strides and his powerful arm wrapped around my waist.

"Let's go," he snapped, already hustling me out the door of the virtual file room.

"It's okay." I tried to get him to slow down, but he continued to rush me toward the network portal. "It's okay," I repeated. "I just lost my concentration for a second there."

"Out." He stopped at the portal and guided me gently through.

Pain slammed through my head. Its familiarity did nothing to diminish its impact, and my violent profanity was edged with an embarrassing whine of self-pity. I shut up as soon as I was capable of controlling myself, but my eyes stayed clamped closed while I breathed through my teeth.

Kane's big, warm hands enveloped my head as he began to massage the pain away.

"Oh, God, I love you," I moaned.

His hands stilled for a bare instant before resuming.

"You love God, or you love me?" he asked.

I couldn't think of any way to backpedal gracefully. I cravenly ignored his question and groaned some more instead, silently berating myself for my poor choice of words.

At last, I straightened and opened my eyes. "Thanks." He stooped to survey my face, and I avoided his gaze by dropping my head forward to rub the back of my neck. "You might as well go back into the network and finish up. I'll stay out until you're done."

"All right. I'll only be a few more minutes."

When I looked up, he had re-entered the virtual reality network and his physical body sat propped motionless in the chair, his eyes staring blankly at nothing. I shuddered, horrid memories replaying while I compulsively watched the rise and fall of his chest. He was only in the network. He wasn't dead.

I glanced at my watch and suppressed a whimper. A quarter to two. My head throbbed slowly and I slid down to rest it against the back of the couch. I thought of Tom, and groaned aloud.

He was such a nice guy. How long would it take before he finally decided I was a flaky, pathetic slut and gave up on me? I knew I couldn't risk any explanation without endangering him, myself, and everyone in Kane's team. Oh, not to mention national security. No pressure.

Tom's lean, honest face and sky-blue eyes floated in front of me, and I smothered another groan of self-pity. If not for the stupid network key and my stupid decryption abilities, I'd be living the life of my dreams out on my new farm, with a handsome cowboy neighbour thrown in as a special bonus. He was my own age. Widowed, like me. And he liked cars. And he was a good kisser. Not in the same class as

Hellhound, but that wasn't really a fair comparison. Arnie was in a class by himself.

My mind drifted, and I smiled up into Arnie's ugly face. As his lips touched mine, I decided it was lucky he wasn't handsome, or he'd be utterly devastating. I found him irresistible just as he was...

He deepened the kiss, his magic tongue teasing me. Heat coursed through my body, and I jerked with shock at the sound of Kane's voice.

"Aydan. Sorry to wake you. Come on, let's go."

I dragged gritty eyes open as he reached a hand down to help me up. Jeez, lucky I hadn't been holding the network key when I went to sleep. It'd be embarrassing as hell to try to explain why I'd apparently been using a top-secret brainwave-driven government network to create porn. Starring me.

I followed Kane down the hallway, silently cursing my life.

CHAPTER 4

The next morning, I bolted upright in bed at the sound of my doorbell. I squinted blearily at the clock as I crawled out of bed, whining. Eight o'clock. God, less than five hours of sleep.

I staggered into the walk-in closet with half-closed eyes and grabbed the first thing that came to hand, an ugly lightweight robe I probably should have thrown out years ago. As I stumbled through the kitchen, I yanked my fingers through my hair, trying to tame some of the night's tangles.

With a yawn that threatened to turn me inside-out, I opened the door, and the wind snatched at my robe. I made a frantic grab and quickly secured it, but not before it became abundantly obvious I didn't own any night clothes.

Heat rushed to my face as I met Tom's paralyzed stare. "Sorry," I mumbled, suddenly finding my floor fascinating.

"Uh," he said. "No... No need to apologize. I'm sorry, I thought you'd be up..." He trailed off.

"It turned into a late night last night..." I dribbled to a halt myself, knowing what he was thinking and knowing that denying it would only cause more complications. I scrubbed a hand over my face, wishing I could shrink and vanish between the cracks in the floorboards.

"I, uh, I brought the expenses you asked for." He held

out a folded piece of paper. I took it mechanically, not meeting his eyes. "Aydan..." he hesitated. "Can I come in?"

"Oh! Um, yeah." I backed away from the door. Jeez, I have all the social graces of an inept chimpanzee. No, wait; chimpanzees actually have a fairly sophisticated social structure...

I tried not to grimace as I dragged my groggy mind back to the subject at hand. "Sorry. I'm not quite awake yet."

He strode in and sat in one of my kitchen chairs without invitation. I closed the door and hovered for a second, looking anywhere but at his face. "I'm, um, I'm just going to go and put some clothes on..."

I fled for my bedroom. Christ, maybe I could find some dignity, too, while I was at it.

I threw on the ratty jeans and sweatshirt that lay on my chair and dragged the brush through my hair, trying not to look at my baggy-eyed reflection in the mirror. God, if I hadn't accidentally flashed him, my appearance this morning would have been enough to make him lose interest on the spot. Too bad he hadn't been looking at my face.

I groaned and considered drowning myself in the bathroom sink, but the logistics defied me. I trailed reluctantly back toward the kitchen instead.

When I arrived, Tom was slouched in the chair, his long legs outstretched, booted feet crossed, arms folded over his chest. He looked up as I entered, and I steeled myself to meet his eyes. He wore a neutral expression, and we regarded each other for a moment before I turned to the fridge.

"I need to eat. Do you want anything?" I busied myself pulling out milk, fruit, bread, and peanut butter.

"No, thanks, I've eaten."

He sat in silence until I took my place across from him at the table and started munching my grapes.

"Aydan, can we talk?"

I suppressed a sigh. "Sure. What's on your mind?" As if I didn't know.

"Are you all right? Are you... safe?"

"Mmm?" I froze, staring at him, before I remembered to swallow my mouthful. "Of course."

His blue eyes searched my face. "Last night you were nervous all evening. When Kane showed up at the bar, you kept watching him as if you were afraid. And then he was waiting for you in the parking lot. Is he stalking you?"

"No, of course not."

He cocked an eyebrow at me. "Then what is he holding over you? Every time he says 'jump', you ask 'how high'. And last night..." He paused. "I came back to make sure you were all right. I saw you in the truck with him. He was so rough with you, and it looked like you were fighting him."

His face darkened, and I did my best not to wince as he added almost under his breath, "At first, anyway..." He frowned at me. "I didn't know whether you needed help or not."

"No," I said quickly, hoping to end the conversation there. "I was fine..."

I fumbled for something smooth and tactful to say, failed, and gave up as heat rose in my cheeks again. Nothing like going out with one man and ending the evening by making out with a different one. Talk about cheesy. Even though I hadn't technically been on a date with Tom. And dammit, making out with Kane hadn't been my idea. And...

Tom leaned across the table and took my hand, interrupting my internal rationalizations. "Aydan, if he's making you do things you don't want to do, you can tell me. Let me help you."

I looked into his earnest face and sighed. "Tom, thanks, but I'm fine. John doesn't have any hold over me."

I saw the disbelief in his eyes and pulled my hand away to rub my aching head. God, I'd been up for less than ten minutes, and I had a headache already. That must be a friggin' record. I was too tired to come up with any convincing lies, so I went with as much of the truth as I could tell.

"John and I... we have a... complicated relationship, that's all. We're attracted to each other, but he wants a more serious relationship than I can give him. It makes things tense between us sometimes. That's all."

"So he was forcing you." His sky-blue eyes turned to ice. "That dirtbag. Aydan, I'm so sorry, I should have..."

"No!" I clutched a couple of handfuls of hair and tugged, trying to salvage an explanation that would reassure him. "Nothing happened between us last night, he... I think he just wanted you to see he was staking a claim..." I shut up, realizing I was reinforcing the 'deranged stalker' label. I tried again.

"There actually was some urgent stuff at work. We drove over there, worked until nearly three, and then he brought me home. That's all. He would never force me or hurt me."

"That's what you said about Hellhound, too, and I don't believe that, either." He frowned at me across the table. "Aydan... You deserve better. Why are you wasting your time with these violent men?"

I swallowed a groan. "I know you're trying to help. But just let me be your dumb, flaky neighbour who makes bad relationship decisions, okay? Just let it go. Please?"

His eyes narrowed as he searched my face. "I know you're not dumb or flaky. And when Kane's not around, you're happy and relaxed with me." He took my hand again. "Tell him it's over. Tell him you're with me now. Let me deal with him."

"Tom." I met his eyes squarely and hardened my heart. "Let it go. I told you months ago there can't be anything between you and me, and that hasn't changed. If we can still be friends, I'd like that, but that's all it can be. You need to let me make my own mistakes with Arnie and John and anybody else I choose. You can't protect me."

He leaned back in the chair and regarded me with obvious frustration. "I can't protect you if you won't let me. Why..."

The sound of scattering gravel made us both glance out the window to see Kane's mean black BMW motorcycle skid to a stop outside.

Tom's brows snapped together. "He's watching you constantly, isn't he? Aydan, you don't have to live like this."

Kane's heavy footsteps thudded on the veranda, and he burst through the door without knocking, wearing an expression as black as his leather jacket. Tom shot to his feet and the two men eyed each other, Kane's stormy grey to Tom's icy blue.

Kane gave me a look from under lowered brows. "Aydan, we need you at the office again. Urgent." His gaze raked over Tom. "Sorry, you'll have to leave now."

Tom's eyes narrowed and a muscle jumped in his jaw. "She's not going with you this time," he said quietly.

Kane's face smoothed into expressionless calm as he placed his helmet on the table. When he straightened, his arms were loose and his posture relaxed, his weight on the balls of his feet. Anyone would think he was completely unperturbed, unprepared for an attack. I knew better.

I put a hand on Tom's arm, feeling the rigid muscle through his soft shirt. "It's okay, Tom, I need to go and work on that audit some more."

"No, you don't." Tom took a step forward, placing himself between Kane and me as he locked eyes with Kane. "I don't like the way you treat Aydan. And I don't want you stalking her anymore. That stops now." His voice was quiet, but hard as iron.

The corner of Kane's mouth twitched up in a small, humourless half-smile. His eyes never left Tom's. "Aydan makes her own decisions. Why don't you ask her what she wants?"

I felt the muscles bunch in Tom's arm. "You're obviously threatening her. She'll say what you tell her to say."

"Tom!" I swung around in front of him and got up in his face. "Stop. He's not threatening me. This is none of your business. Let it go."

He spared me a fleeting glance before meeting Kane's stare again. He spoke without looking at me. "I'm making it my business."

Tom tried to move me aside as he took another step toward Kane, and cold fear pulsed through my veins. He wasn't going to back down. And as brave and strong as Tom was, I knew Kane could destroy three Toms with his bare hands. I'd seen him do it.

Pent-up tension exploded out of me. "Tom! It's none of your business! I don't want your help!" I pushed him toward the door. "It's time for you to go. Now. Goodbye."

He took an involuntary step backward as I shoved him again. "But, Aydan, you..."

"Go," I interrupted. "Goodbye."

My heart wrung as confusion and hurt filled his eyes. Then his face hardened and he gave a curt nod before turning on his heel. The door banged behind him.

Kane's combat-ready posture eased into his normal stance as he surveyed my face. "Are you all right?"

"I..." I stared at him helplessly for a moment before dropping into a chair to let my aching forehead fall onto the table with a thump. "I can't do this anymore," I whimpered into the tabletop.

I heard him pull up a chair beside me, and his arm was gentle around my shoulders. "Tell me what happened. Talk to me."

I leaned into him, taking a little comfort. He brushed my hair back, his fingertips lingering on my cheek. "Tell me."

I determinedly squelched the urge to throw my arms around him and hide my face in his broad chest until everything else went away. I blew out a long sigh and pulled back instead.

"I just can't do this anymore. Ray Webb was asking awkward questions about what I'm doing at Sirius. And I can't keep hurting people like that." A spasm of guilt shook me at the memory of Tom's face. "I just can't."

Kane took my hand and held it gently. "Aydan, I know you can do what needs to be done."

"I can kill criminals if necessary. But I can't... won't hurt innocent people."

He sighed, and his eyes were old and tired as he replied, "Sometimes that's necessary, too." He frowned as I opened my mouth to argue, and spoke over me. "Who's Ray Webb?"

"Spider's dad. I was over at their place on Friday night for Spider's surprise birthday party."

"Oh." Kane regarded me with a troubled expression. "Aydan, I know you're not going to want to hear this, but you need to stop getting so involved with people. You can't afford to get close in our line of work."

His face twisted as he said it, and I knew he was remembering our conversation of a couple of months ago. "I'm sorry, I know you already know that," he added. "But we all need to be reminded sometimes." He lifted a wry eyebrow, and I gave him a bitter smile in return.

"I know. But we need to do damage control. That's twice in two days I've had problems. I don't know what to do."

"What exactly happened?"

I explained both encounters to him in detail, and he sat back in his chair, frowning. "Let me think about it for a while. Just lie low in the mean time."

I suddenly recalled the reason for his visit, and jumped to my feet. "How urgent is the decryption? Do I have time for a shower, or should we go right now?"

He rose, too. "There's no decryption. This time I really was stalking you." He smiled at my expression. "Don't worry, the stalking was in a professional capacity. After last night, I had a feeling you might have problems with Rossburn. I told the analysts to call me if they saw him on the surveillance cameras."

"Oh." I looked up at him, wondering how much of his attention was duty and how much was personal, disguised as duty.

As if reading my mind, he blew out a long breath. "I thought it would be best if I looked jealous. We may have to pretend to be involved as a cover, though I'd like to avoid it if at all possible. It causes too many complications down the line."

"Okay." I followed him to the door, and found myself standing too close for comfort when he turned.

"Don't worry," he said. "We'll figure it out."

"Thanks. See you." I tried to control my face while I ogled him from close range. Those damn riding chaps did it to me every time. A faint whiff of gun oil and leather reached me as I jerked my gaze up from his well-endowed crotch, and I swallowed hard. I could almost taste his skin again, feel that hard-muscled shoulder under my teeth. Could almost feel that magnificent...

"Call me if you need me," I added. My voice came out sounding husky, and I realized I'd licked my lips unconsciously.

I lost what little breath I had left when Kane's eyes darkened. His hand moved as though he would reach for me, but he gripped the doorknob instead, his knuckles whitening. He stepped quickly out the door and closed it behind him without a backward glance.

He revved the bike, and I watched him spray gravel and disappear down the lane before I collapsed into my chair again, knees trembling. Goddamn, he was hot. And if I didn't keep my hands off him, Sirius Dynamics would take him down right along with me when the time came.

Life just wasn't fair.

CHAPTER 5

I trailed into Sirius Dynamics on Monday morning with a significant lack of enthusiasm. When I realized my office was already crowded, I jerked to a halt in the doorway, surveying the occupants.

Kane and Spider were present, as expected. I kept my expression neutral at the sight of Charles Stemp, Sirius's civilian director of clandestine operations.

Stemp looked up as I entered, his reptilian features unreadable as always. "Ms. Kelly, you have a new team member, effective immediately." He indicated the fourth man in the room. "He will be joining your team in an attempt to analyze the unique interaction of your brain with the network key's circuitry."

My cynical inside voice finished the unspoken sentence: "...so we can figure out how to decrypt things for ourselves and kill you as soon as possible." I shrugged off the thought. Same old, same old.

Stemp continued as I reached to shake hands with the newcomer, "This is Dr. Sam Kraus."

A shock of recognition paralyzed me with hand outstretched, mouth gaping. My stunned gaze took in the short, roly-poly white-haired man smiling at me. The red shirt and full, curly white beard. The twinkling, vividly blue eyes and rosy cheeks.

My voice emerged as a feeble croak. "...Santa Claus?"

He laughed, and his belly shook like... a bowl full of jelly...

"Hello, Aydan. Have you been a good girl lately?"

"No *way*! You're kidding me!" I stared at him some more. "Talk about a self-fulfilling prophecy."

He glanced down at his red-clad belly and chuckled again. "I'm sure you planted this idea in my subconscious mind and I fulfilled it," he agreed. "I didn't know if you'd remember me, though."

"I might not have made the connection if you didn't look so... so..."

"So much like Santa Claus," Spider finished for me, grinning. "I thought so, too, but I didn't want to say anything." He eyed us eagerly. "Tell me the story."

"When I was a kid, Dr. Kraus used to come by the house a couple of times a year," I began.

"Call me Sam," the doctor interrupted. "I think we can dispense with the formalities under the circumstances."

I shot him a smile and continued. "I was pretty young. I can't even remember how old I was when we first met."

"You were four," Sam supplied. "You'd started kindergarten a year early."

"And you thought he looked like Santa Claus," Spider prompted.

"No, when I first met Aydan, I was about your age, and just as skinny as you," Sam chuckled.

"Oh. Right, I guess that was a long time ago." Spider flushed. "Sorry," he stammered. "I didn't mean you're old... Either of you. I just meant..."

"It's okay, Spider," I assured him. "No, he didn't look

anything like Santa Claus. But the first time he came, it was right around Christmas, and I didn't have a really clear concept of Santa Claus at the time. So when he told me his name was Sam Kraus, I got all excited and blurted out 'Santa Claus' because I knew Santa Claus was coming soon, and it sounded so similar. It became a family joke, and I always called him Santa Claus after that, even when I was a teenager."

"Talk about a small world," Spider exclaimed.

"Yeah..." A faint thought nagged at me, but it fled as Stemp addressed us.

"You'll carry on with your normal activities, and Dr. Kraus will observe. You'll be working in the secured facility where the doctor has his lab set up."

Spider's head jerked up, his mouth opening, but Kane spoke first. "You know that's not acceptable. Aydan can't work in the secured facility."

Stemp waved an irritable hand. "I realize it's not feasible for the long-term." He turned to face me. "As soon as you begin to have difficulties, we'll find an alternate solution. But I know you can deal with it in the short term, and by then, Dr. Kraus may already have the data he needs."

Kane made as if to speak again, but Stemp overrode him. "This is not open for discussion. You have your orders." He turned and left.

Sam's bright eyes darted from Spider's expression of pure dismay to Kane's scowl to whatever might be showing on my face. Abject terror, probably. I wrestled for calm.

"What's the problem?" Sam inquired with concern.

"No problem," I told him. "I'm claustrophobic, so I'm not very happy in the secured facility, that's all. No big deal for the short term."

"Aydan, the last time you worked in the secured facility, you nearly died! Twice!" Spider sprang to his feet and began to pace, his lanky limbs flailing awkwardly. "He can't make you do this!" He whirled and turned a pleading face to Kane. "Can't you talk to him? Or talk to General Briggs? Make Stemp change his mind?"

Kane twitched a shoulder. His face was composed again, but the gunmetal grey of his eyes gave away his mood. "Briggs won't override the civilian director unless it's military-related. We have our orders. Until Aydan has a problem, we'll follow them." He turned to me. "Aydan, now isn't the time to be a hero. The instant you lose control of the sim, the instant you can't sleep or start having nightmares, you tell me. That's an order. Got it?"

"Got it," I agreed.

Sam's jolly demeanour had evaporated while he followed our exchange, and he turned to me with a crease between his bushy white eyebrows. "You nearly died in the sim? I didn't think that was possible. What happened?"

I sighed. "How much do you know about the virtual reality network?"

"I know the basic structure and operation of the computer side of the network, but my area of expertise is brainwave patterns and frequencies, and their interaction with the fobs that provide access to the virtual reality network. It's my life's work." He eyed me with interest. "That's why I'm so interested in your brain's interaction with this mysterious network key that lets you sneak around undetected in any network and decrypt files that are supposedly secure."

Kane blew out a breath and frowned. "That's part of the problem. Aydan has to use the special key to decrypt files. If she uses a standard fob with a brainwave modulator, she can't do it. And when she uses the key, it hurts her every time she exits the network."

"A lot," Spider put in unhappily.

"And this is life-threatening?" Sam prompted.

"No," I said. "It's just a nuisance. The life-threatening part happens if I get too tired or stressed and I don't control my thoughts inside the sim. If you believe you've died inside the sim, you actually die in real life."

Sam's eyes narrowed as he worked his stubby fingers through his beard. "I'd heard rumours of that. I didn't believe it."

"Believe it," Kane said grimly. "I personally know of three people who have been killed inside a sim. The cause of death looks like a heart attack when their physical bodies are autopsied."

"That changes things..." Sam frowned at me. "But why would you think you were dying inside the sim? And why couldn't someone just wake you? Pull you out of the network? It only takes a touch or a sudden noise to do it."

"That's the other complication," Kane explained. "When Aydan's using the key to access the network, you can't wake her unless you actually hurt her. And if that happens, if she's forcibly woken from the network, she goes through hell."

"It's awful," Spider quavered, his eyes haunted. "It's like she's being tortured. She screams, horrible screams like she's being burned alive, and her whole body thrashes around, and you can't do a thing to help her, and it goes on and on..."

"Anyway," I broke in, thoroughly embarrassed, "I only lose concentration in the sim if I'm overtired. And if I'm in the secured facility when I lose control, my claustrophobic anxieties tend to take over the sim. That's when I have problems."

"Little problems. Like your heart stopping," Kane added.

"Well... yeah. But I should be fine for at least a week before it starts to get bad," I reassured them.

Sam eyed me. "Are you sure?"

"Do I have a choice?"

"Not really, at this point," he said regretfully. "I just spent the last several weeks getting my lab facilities set up downstairs. Some of the equipment can't be moved easily. And this whole operation is so highly classified that it shouldn't be outside the secured facility at all."

I blew out a long breath. "Okay. Well, let's get at it, then." We all rose and trooped down the hallway.

My steps slowed as we approached the heavy steel door. "You guys go on ahead. I'll follow you."

Sam shot me a piercing glance. "It's okay," I assured him. "It's just that the time-delay chamber is so small. It gets pretty crowded."

"Okay," he agreed, and stepped up to allow the scanner to read his retina. When the latch released, the three men entered the chamber, and I hung back in the lobby, breathing deeply.

When the indicator light showed the chamber was clear, I approached the door reluctantly. The secured facility contained nothing but bad memories and despite my best efforts at calm, my heart pounded.

I placed my face next to the scanner and started belly breathing when the latch released. In. Out. Slow like ocean waves.

I stepped into the cramped chamber, twitching when the door locked behind me with a muffled click. I let the next door sensor scan me, then stood with my eyes closed, breathing and counting down the long thirty seconds until the next latch released.

My knees wobbled at the sight of the featureless concrete tunnel of stairs, and I sucked in a shallow breath that tried to turn into panicked panting. With an effort of will, I let my breath out slowly and hurried down, clutching the handrail. At the bottom of the stairs, I snatched the door open.

I managed to contain a jerk and a yelp at the sight of Kane, Spider, and Sam clustered near the door. Kane scanned my face and immediately stepped away, pulling the other two men with him. They stood a couple of paces down the hallway and three sets of eyes surveyed me anxiously.

"Fine, I'm fine," I gabbled breathlessly. "Let's go. Where's the lab?"

Kane eyed my shaking hands. "You don't look fine, you look like you're on the verge of a panic attack," he said. "I told you, don't be a hero."

"I'm fine," I repeated, trying to convince myself. "It's just that damn time delay and the stairwell that gets me. I'm okay down here with all the glass and the air moving." I forced myself to concentrate on the white corridor, the openness of the glassed-in labs, the flow of air from the cooling system. Fine. I was fine.

I took another deep breath. "Let's go."

"This is stupid!" Spider's eyes were dark with distress. "This isn't going to work, we know it won't work, and Aydan's going to end up getting hurt. Or killed..." He turned a beseeching face to me. "Aydan, just say you can't do it."

"I can do it for the short term. And the sooner we get started, the sooner I can get out of here, so let's go do it already! You guys are just making this worse!" My voice came out tight and shaking, and I gulped back my agitation. “I’m sorry, I didn’t mean to take it out on you.”

“It’s all right.” Kane turned to Sam. “We’ll try it. For a while. Lead the way.”

CHAPTER 6

In the lab, Sam ushered me to a chair surrounded by electronic gadgets I couldn't identify. I probably didn't want to know anyway. More adrenaline spiked into my system at the sight of the sturdy straps on the chair arms and at the feet.

"I'm not sitting in that." I backed toward the door, my hand reflexively twitching toward my concealed holster.

Sam made calming gestures. "It's okay. The electronics just look a little intimidating." He eyed me worriedly. "I just need you to sit here while I attach some electrodes to your forehead..."

"I'm not sitting in that. I don't care about the electronics, I'm not sitting in a chair with restraints. No fucking way." I jittered in the doorway, ready to fight or run while cold sweat drenched my armpits.

"Oh! No, I'm sorry, those aren't for you!" Sam's face cleared, and he detached the straps from the chair and tossed them into a drawer.

"Who are they for, then?" I glared suspiciously around the room. "I'm not doing this. I could go into the network and never know you were tying me up until I came out."

"Aydan, I wouldn't do that to you. Don't you trust me?" Sam's brow was furrowed, a sorrowing Santa.

"Fuck, no, I don't trust you. I don't even know you. I haven't seen you in what, thirty years? Why the hell would I trust you?" I could feel my composure slipping as my voice rose, and I held onto it with difficulty.

I twitched when Kane made a move toward me, and he stopped and took a slow step backward instead. "Aydan, if you can't do this, let's go. Just turn around and go out." His voice was deep and soothing. "It's okay. You don't have to do this. You're not trapped here. You can just go."

I brought my breathing under control again and clasped my hands in front of me to still the tremor. "Can I just sit somewhere else?"

"You can sit anywhere you like," Sam replied quickly, his tone suggesting the indulgence one might offer a dangerous lunatic. Appropriate, under the circumstances.

I sidled toward the chair he offered, trying to simulate rational behaviour. As I seated myself shakily, my paranoia erupted in spite of me. "Promise you won't let him tie me up," I demanded.

"Nobody's going to tie you up," Kane reassured me.

"Promise!"

"I promise," he said.

"You, too," I begged Spider.

"I promise, Aydan," he said. "Don't worry, we won't let anything happen to you."

I breathed deeply some more. "Thanks." I turned sheepishly to Sam. "I'm sorry, I'm not usually such a basket case. I've just spent 'way too much time tied to chairs lately."

"It's all right," he said. "I read the reports. I know what you've been through. I'd probably feel the same in your place. Just tell me if anything makes you uncomfortable, and we'll stop right away."

"Thanks." I held myself still while he secured a band festooned with trailing wires around my forehead.

"That's it," he said. "Go ahead and do what you usually do."

"Hold on," Spider cautioned. "Just give me a minute to get set up." He busied himself with his laptop, and turned a worried face to me a few minutes later. "Okay, I'm ready whenever you are."

Kane pulled up a chair beside me, grasping the fob that would give him network access. "Go ahead, Aydan."

I closed my eyes and stepped into the void of the virtual reality network, concentrating fiercely on open spaces.

Sam's bemused voice floated down from the wide blue virtual sky. "What is this?"

"It's not part of my decryption," I assured him as Kane's avatar popped into existence beside me on the mountaintop. "If I'm feeling anxious, I create this sim to keep my mind focused and help myself relax."

My hair whipped around my face and I pawed it into a rough ponytail. I stood for a few long moments, breathing the scent of spruce and gazing down the long, misty valley between mountain ranges, soothed by the ceaseless echoing song of the wind. Kane stood patiently beside me while I took a few final deep breaths.

"Okay, I'm ready now." I dissolved the mountain sim, and Kane and I strode down the virtual corridor to the file room.

Some time later, I folded over in the chair, clutching my head and muttering profanities between gritted teeth. When I finally opened my eyes and straightened, all three men were regarding me with concern.

"Is this normal?" Sam demanded as he slipped the

headband off.

"Yes." Kane stepped behind me and his strong hands began to work out the knots of pain in my temples.

Sam turned to his computer, tapping keys and frowning at the tracery of lines on the screen. "Fascinating," he murmured. "What were you decrypting in this session?"

"Just some tedious, useless emails, as far as I can figure out," I griped. "There's no way to tell whether something's important or not unless we actually have some other evidence that comes in from other sources. I end up wasting a lot of time."

"But you were actually reading those emails in real time. Encrypted emails that are completely uncrackable, as far as anybody else in the world knows." Sam's eyes were alight with excitement. "This is fabulous. This is better than I'd ever dreamed." He turned back to his screen, scrolling through data.

After a couple of minutes of watching his intent profile, I spoke up. "Do you still need me?"

He started as if he'd forgotten there was anyone else in the room. "Oh! No, you can go. Thank you. I have enough here to keep me interested for a while."

"Great." I jumped up and hurried for the door.

When the time-delayed door finally released, I clamped down on the urge to leap into the lobby flailing and shrieking. I took a few steps and stood staring into middle distance, controlling my breathing. Slow and steady. Ocean waves. After a few breaths, I shook myself and refocused on my surroundings, grateful that Spider and Kane knew me well enough to let me have some time. I surreptitiously wiped my sweaty palms on my jeans as I turned to face them.

"Are you okay?" Spider's expression was troubled.

"Yeah, fine." I ignored Kane's sceptically raised eyebrow. "So I guess we might as well go up to the office and get on with some more work."

Kane frowned. "Do you need a break first?"

"No, I'm fine as long as I'm aboveground." I rolled my neck and shoulders, trying to ease their aching tension as I headed for the stairs.

In the upstairs corridor, Stemp emerged from his office as we reached the door to mine.

"How did it go?" he inquired, his flat gaze dissecting me.

"Fine," I snapped.

Kane spoke simultaneously. "Not well."

Stemp looked from Kane's frown to my face. "Which is it?"

"Not well," Kane repeated forcefully. He skewered me with a look as I opened my mouth. "Unless you consider it fine to nearly shoot your way out of the secured facility."

"I didn't!" Indignation made me loud. "I never even drew..."

"I saw you go for your gun," Kane overrode me. "You didn't draw it, but you were ready to."

I glared at him, and Stemp broke the short silence. "Good."

"What?" Spider yelped.

Stemp gave him a cool stare. "Those are the kind of reflexes I want to see." He turned his impassive face back to me. "Always be ready to draw your weapon. Always be ready to shoot if necessary. Good work." He turned and strode back into his office, closing the door behind him.

I gawped down the hallway after him before turning to face Spider's open mouth and Kane's thoughtful expression. "Did I just get congratulated for almost shooting the good guys?"

Kane's laugh lines crinkled. "Not exactly. You got congratulated for being on your toes. And he's right. It's your responsibility to protect yourself. I wish it wasn't that way, but you have to trust your instincts."

I groaned and thudded my forehead against the door jamb. "I hate my life."

"Lunch time."

I gratefully stretched my aching avatar inside the sim when Spider's voice spoke from above the virtual ceiling, and made my way to the exit portal. As usual, my gratitude evaporated when the pain drilled through my eyeballs into my brain.

"Aydan, stop!" Strong hands closed around my head, and I let out the growl I'd been trying to hold back. The grip didn't loosen, and I clenched my fists and rode out the remainder of the pain with my eyes squeezed shut.

When I was sure my eyeballs would stay in my skull of their own accord, I squinted cautiously into the face of Santa Claus, inches away. I recoiled with a yelp, and he drew back quickly.

"Sorry."

I reached up to unwrap Kane's hands from my head. "You can let go now."

He frowned down at me. "That was worse than usual. You were beating your head against the couch."

"Yeah." I rubbed the remainder of the knots out of my forehead. "Just the extra stress, I guess." I rose slowly and cocked an eyebrow at Sam. "Did you need something else from me?"

"No, I was just testing your responses. You really can't hear or feel anything when you're in the network, can you?"

"No..." I eyed him mistrustfully. "Testing my responses how?"

"I tried to stop him." Spider's face was flushed, and his hand clenched and opened as he turned a scowl on Sam. "If you'd pulled her out of the network..."

"But I didn't," Sam countered. He turned back to me and spoke reassuringly. "I was very careful. Your young friend here briefed me on what your reactions have been. I just shouted your name and patted your face. That hasn't been enough to wake you in the past, and it wasn't this time, either."

"Maybe not," Kane grated. "But if it had been... You obviously don't understand the kind of agony Aydan goes through if that happens."

Comprehension oozed into my aching brain and I eyed Kane. "Oh, so that's where you went so fast. You woke up as soon as he started shouting."

"Yes." Kane and Spider hovered protectively, one on either side of me as we faced Sam. Spider still looked angry, and Kane's eyes were hard in his impassive cop face.

With the twinkle gone from his eyes, Sam didn't look so much like Santa Claus anymore. "Well..." He took a step back. "That's all I needed anyway. I'll go back to my lab now." He turned and hurried out, and I blew out a long breath.

"Spider, could you please signal me if anybody even comes near my physical body while I'm in the network? This is just too creepy for me."

"I will. I'm sorry, I should have."

"No, it's okay, Spider, I know you were watching out for

me, and thanks. But I just..." I failed to hide a whole-body shudder. "It's just... like... finding out you've been naked and unconscious in the middle of a shopping mall. You don't know who's been looking at you, who's been touching you, what they've done..."

"That won't happen. Nobody will do anything to you." Kane's voice was edged. "Webb, from now on, our standard operating procedure will be that you signal Aydan and bring me out of the network the instant anybody else enters the room. No exceptions."

"Even Stemp?" Spider questioned.

"Especially Stemp," I said.

"And Kraus," Kane added. "From here on in, we get a full description of everything he plans to do, in advance. Aydan approves it before we go in. If he deviates the slightest bit from the plan, you signal Aydan and wake me immediately."

"Got it," Spider agreed, looking relieved.

"Thanks, you guys." I gave them both a grateful smile. "You have no idea how much it means to me to have you watching out for me."

Spider turned pink. "You're welcome."

"You're welcome," Kane rumbled agreement. "Don't you have somewhere to be?"

"Yes, I'm due over the Greenhorn Cafe at one. Actually, I think I'll head over there for lunch and just stay." I made for the door, feeling the tension leaking out of my shoulders. A couple of hours of sane, normal, non-spy-related bookkeeping was exactly what I needed right now. Thank God for my real life.

My feet dragged to a halt when it occurred to me that this top-secret, dangerous life was actually my real life now.

Except for a few short hours a week when I escaped to my civilian bookkeeping clients, I spent virtually all my time at Sirius.

The thought formed a cold lump in my stomach.

CHAPTER 7

The next morning, I managed a slightly more optimistic outlook. An afternoon and evening away from Sirius Dynamics had helped a lot. And I only had to spend a couple of hours there this morning, before seeing my two favourite civilian bookkeeping clients. I was actually whistling when I strode down the hall to my office.

The tune dwindled into silence when I surveyed its occupants. Kane and Spider were looking grim. Sam Kraus was looking eager. Bad combination.

"What?" I demanded.

Sam's smile faltered. "I'm sorry, Aydan, I need you downstairs again this morning."

"Oh. Shit."

He looked taken aback, and I mumbled, "Sorry," without much sincerity.

"It's all right." His smile returned, sympathetic this time. "I'm so excited about this, I keep forgetting how hard it is for you. I'll try to keep it short this morning."

"Thanks."

I was turning to go when Kane's voice stopped me. "Wait." I turned to face his hard grey eyes. I tamped down my instant defensive reaction when I realized he was looking at Sam, not me.

"First, you'll go over everything you plan to do with Aydan this morning," he commanded.

"Oh..." Sam's ruddy face paled slightly as he sized up Kane's six-foot-four height and massive upper body. I held back a snicker. Yeah, it sure was nice to have Kane on my side. Though I'd rather have him on my front... I jerked my dirty mind to heel in time to catch Sam's hurried explanation.

"I just want to run some tests. Nothing unusual, you don't even have to be in the network." As Kane's gaze continued to bore into him, he fingered his beard nervously and continued, "I'll just put the electrodes on your forehead again and ask you to do some mind exercises."

Relief seeped into my taut shoulders. "Oh, like the ones you used to give me when you came to the house."

"Uh... yes... I didn't realize you remembered those."

"Of course, why wouldn't I? You did them three times a year for what, twelve years?"

Sam finger-combed his beard with what seemed like unnecessary vigour. "Most people didn't-" He clammed up and stroked his moustache.

"Aydan, is that all right with you?" Kane inquired.

"Fine, no problem. Let's get it over with."

Down in Sam's lab, Kane appraised my shaking hands. "Are you all right?"

"Fine," I assured him a little breathlessly. I drew in a deep breath and let it out slowly. Then did it again. Ocean waves. "It's actually a bit better today."

He scowled at me. "You're a lousy liar."

"Thanks. Speaking of which, have you come up with new

ideas about my cover?"

"Why, has Rossburn been giving you trouble again?"

"No." I hadn't even seen him out riding his horse, and I didn't know whether to feel glad or sorry. Glad I hadn't seen him. Sorry I had to avoid him.

Kane glanced at Sam's approaching figure. "We'll talk about it later."

After a couple of long hours underground, I burst out of the time-delay chamber into the lobby, only hyperventilating a little. I handed in my security fob at the desk and tossed a wave over my shoulder as Spider and Kane emerged from the chamber.

"See you." I scuttled for my car.

The sun-warmed upholstery soothed my tense muscles, and I closed my eyes and leaned into it, soaking up the heat. At the tap on my window, my body spasmed and my eyes flew open.

"Jesus Christ!" I rolled down the window with shaking hands. "Don't do that! You scared the shit out of me."

"Sorry." Kane rested a forearm on the roof of the car and leaned down. "Should I come with you to Blue Eddy's?"

"You can if you want. He doesn't officially open for another half hour or so, but he'll probably give you a beer anyway."

"I wasn't thinking of beer. I was thinking of Rossburn."

"I can't imagine why he'd be there. The weather's good, so he'll still be busy on the farm. He wouldn't come into town for lunch, and he doesn't know my schedule anyway." I grimaced. "I really don't think he'll be too interested in talking to me again, under the circumstances."

Kane lifted an eyebrow. "You might be surprised. I wouldn't give up on you that easily. Somehow I doubt if he will, either."

"Oh." I spoke into the short, awkward silence. "I've got to go."

"All right. See you around three."

My heart lifted when I unlocked the back door at Blue Eddy's. Eddy was obviously hard at work. The bluesy notes of his piano curled sensuously around me as I swayed with the rhythm. His face lit up when he caught sight of me.

"Hi, Aydan!"

I grinned back at him, the weight of Sirius Dynamics dropping from my shoulders and washing away in the stream of music. "Eddy, I swear to God, coming here once a week is the only thing that keeps me sane."

He laughed while his fingers continued to dance effortlessly over the keys. "Glad to be of service." The tune slowed to a simple, wistful melody as he examined me, his sharp eyes seeing too much as usual. "Aydan, is everything okay? You've seemed really down lately."

"Everything's fine. I've been really busy with one of my other clients, so I've been tired, that's all."

"Okay." He continued to scan my face, a faint frown creasing his forehead, and I turned away to forestall any other discussion.

"Guess I better get started." I headed for his cramped office, and let the soothing task of data entry calm my mind while the music eased my soul.

After lunch, Linda greeted me eagerly when I stepped in the door of Up & Coming. "Aydan, guess what?"

I grinned down at the diminutive brunette, envying her bouncy energy. "What?"

"Clyde asked me to move in with him."

I laughed out loud. I'd apparently made some incorrect assumptions based on the fact that Spider blushed at the faintest hint of sexual innuendo. "He turned out to be a fast worker. You've only been going out for a couple of months. And move in where? His house isn't rebuilt yet, is it?"

"No, he's still living with his parents. His house won't be ready until November or December. But when it is, I'm going to move in with him."

"Well, congratulations. He's a great guy."

"He is, isn't he?" Her eyes sparkled. "I'm so glad you introduced us."

"I didn't, really."

"Well, no, not really, but he never would have come in here if he didn't have to drop off those papers for you."

"That's definitely true." I chuckled, remembering his scarlet face when he'd stood in the doorway of the sex shop for the first time. I slipped behind the counter and into their office, still smiling. Life was good.

I revised my opinion when I reached the doorway of my office at Sirius and contemplated Sam's enthusiastic grin.

I groaned. "Not again."

His face fell. "Sorry."

I trailed into the office and flopped down on the couch. "What are we doing this time?"

He shot a sidelong glance at Kane's expressionless face. "This time, I need you to go into the network and sneak around. I want to see what your brain activity looks like when you turn invisible. And I'd like to see what happens when you're breaching firewalls, too."

"Our own firewalls in the Sirius network, or external ones?"

"Both."

"So you're just going to hook me up to the headband again?"

"Yes, that's all." I could tell he was trying to contain his excitement, but his eyes were sparkling, and his fingers combed his beard over and over.

I sighed and heaved myself to my feet. Everybody seemed to have excess energy but me. I just wanted to shove my head between the sofa cushions and hibernate. Feeling like a prisoner going into lockdown, I followed the three men downstairs.

Underground once more, I dropped into the chair in Sam's lab with a notable lack of grace when my trembling knees collapsed.

Spider regarded me with concern. "Are you-"

"Don't even ask."

He subsided, looking worried, and my conscience prodded me. "Sorry," I told him. "I'm fine. Thanks for being concerned."

"Don't take this wrong..." He hesitated. "You don't look fine. You're shaking like a leaf, and you're the same colour as the wall."

"I'll live."

Kane glowered in Sam's direction. "How many more times does she need to do this?"

"This might be the last," Sam responded cheerfully. "I just need to gather data from a full range of her activities."

Kane squatted in front of me to look up into my face. "Aydan, can you do this one more time?"

"Yeah, no problem," I lied. "Ready whenever you are."

He eyed me dubiously before rising to walk over to his chair. "All right."

With the crown of electrodes in place, I closed my eyes for what I fervently hoped would be the last time I'd enter the network underground.

I willed myself onto the mountaintop again, unable to control the urge to flail my arms. I caught a bare glimpse of Kane's avatar popping into existence before the chasm opened under my feet and I plummeted.

Blackness and panic swallowed me as I hurtled downward. Rocks gouged my flesh as the shaft narrowed. My arms were pinned to my sides and I jerked and twisted, animal shrieks tearing from my throat. The rocks squeezed more tightly.

Trapped. Buried alive. My throat closed, my screams smothered into rapid, shrill wheezing. My heart hammered, uselessly trying to batter its way out of my chest.

Kane's voice boomed around me. "Aydan, stop! *You control this*!"

Light bloomed as his arms closed around me. Suddenly he was carrying me, and I fought to control my shallow panting.

"Stay with me," he urged. "You're going to be all right."

My breath stopped momentarily at the sight of the blood soaking his T-shirt and smearing his arms. "Stay with me," he repeated. "Just breathe with me. Nice and slow."

"I'm okay! Put me down. Where are you hurt?" I struggled, and his arms tightened around me while he kept up his rapid pace.

"Just lie still."

"No, I'm fine. Where are you hurt?" I ran shaking hands over his blood-soaked shirt, searching for injuries.

"I'm not hurt. It's not my blood."

"Oh." I glanced down. Blood leaked steadily from my

gaping wounds, leaving a crimson trail behind us. The jagged, yellowish ends of a broken bone protruded from the torn, bloody denim over my right thigh. "Oh."

I took a few calming breaths, my panic subsiding when I realized he was unhurt and it was only a sim. "Well, let's just fix that." I waved a hand down my virtual body, repairing bone and muscle and skin and clothing.

Kane stopped and blew out a breath, dropping my feet to the ground and holding me close. "Thank God."

"No, thank *you*. For saving my ass yet again."

He turned me gently toward the exit portal. "Come on, let's get you out of here."

"No, I'm okay now. I just lost it for a second there, but I'm fine. Let's get this done."

"Absolutely not. This ends now."

"We're here. We're already in. I'm fine now. Let's just do it," I argued.

Spider's tremulous voice floated down from the virtual sky. "Aydan, are you really okay?"

"I'm fine."

My knees wobbled uncontrollably, and I pulled away from Kane and dropped to the ground. "I'll just start from here."

Kane stared down at me, and for an instant I thought he might carry me bodily out of the sim. Then the moment passed and he sank down beside me, looking resigned. "Fine. Give me your hand."

"Why?" Sam's voice startled me.

"Because when Aydan goes searching along network paths, she... stretches. I'm her anchor," Kane replied.

"Ooooh..." Sam sounded utterly enthralled. "Aydan, tell me exactly what you're going to do."

"First I'm going to go invisible. Then I'm going to stretch into the network and start tasting data packets..."

"Tasting?"

"Well, yeah, sort of. I don't really know what the correct word would be. I kind of... I don't know, taste? Smell? Listen? Absorb? It's like a sponge floating in a stream."

"This is so exciting..." Sam's voice was trembling. "Can you talk to me while you do it?"

"No. Invisibility itself doesn't prevent me from talking, but once I start sniffing around down network connections, I can't speak. And the further away I go, the less I can hear from this end. That's why John holds onto me. In case he needs to pull me back."

I willed myself invisible, feeling Kane's grip tighten on my hand.

"Wait!" Sam's voice was urgent, and I popped back into visibility.

"What?"

"Oh, good, you're still here. Can you just stay invisible for a few minutes while I monitor the readings? Then move into the network and just stay around here. Then go through some of our internal firewalls, maybe manipulate a couple of files. And last thing, go and breach some external firewalls."

"Sure." I faded away again, but remained seated where I was. After a few minutes, Sam spoke again. "Okay, go and travel the network now."

"On my way." I stretched my consciousness into the swirls and eddies of the Sirius Dynamics network, loitering in the stream and watching the data flow by. I idly sifted through the packets, not paying much attention while I waited for the requisite time to pass.

A sudden familiar flavour tugged at my attention, and I

focused on the string of packets. What the...?

I latched onto the last packet in the burst of data and rode its rollercoaster course through the Sirius firewalls.

At its destination, I shot tentacles of consciousness through the file repository, tracking and tracing all the related information while I wrapped myself around the accumulated data packets like a feeding jellyfish.

Icy chills raced over me, chased by fiery heat as I absorbed the contents in a voracious gulp.

Rage engulfed me, and I flung my consciousness back to the mountaintop. Kane leaped to his feet as I burst into existence beside him and yanked my hand from his grasp.

"Aydan, what...?" he gasped. Seconds later, a fire hose materialized in his hands and he turned the full force of the water on me, his eyes wide with horror.

I barely spared a glance at the blue-white fire hissing from every surface of my skin and licking along the upraised blade of the sword in my hand.

"Get. Out." I could barely form the words. The flames roared to the sky. The water evaporated before it could touch me. "Get. Out. Now! *Go!*"

Soon I would immolate everything. Everybody. Even him. Especially him.

Unable to trust myself, I folded sim space to reach the exit portal between one heartbeat and the next, blazing fire and fury. When I stepped through, the pain goaded me into instant violence. I lashed out blindly, shrieking obscenities. My arms were pinned by a powerful grip, and I redoubled my struggles, incapable of rational thought.

At last, a semblance of sanity returned. Kane still held me tightly, calling my name over and over.

"Let. Me. Go." The words boiled from my throat in a

satanic growl. As his arms loosened, I jerked away from him and stormed for the door.

"Aydan, wait! What's wrong? Are you all right?" I heard rapid footsteps behind me, and Kane's large hand closed on my shoulder. I whirled to face him. "Leave me. Alone," I hissed.

I took the stairs two at a time and glared into the retinal scanner. As the time-delay chamber door released, Kane came up quietly behind me. I stepped into the chamber and shot him a look when he made as if to follow.

"If you come in here with me, I will rip you limb from limb." My voice shook, and he took a slow step back, still holding the door of the chamber open.

"Close the door." My hands ached as my fists clenched. The time delay wouldn't start until the first door was shut. "Close the fucking door!"

"Aydan, what's wrong?" He searched my face as Spider and Sam pounded up the stairs behind him.

"Fuck off!" I roared. "Close the goddamn fucking door!"

Kane shot a quick glance over his shoulder. "Go back down," he commanded, and the other two did a fast fade down the stairs. He turned back to me, his movements slow and smooth, his voice soft. "Aydan, I need you to talk to me. Calm down. Tell me what's wrong."

"What's wrong is you won't close the fucking door! Move, goddammit!" I lunged at him. And the moron wrapped his arms around me and pushed his way into the chamber, the door closing behind him.

He released me immediately and I glared at him from close range in the tiny room, panting and trembling with the effort to keep from attacking him.

"Better start the countdown," he advised mildly.

I wheeled to activate the scanner on the exterior door and stood with my back to him, fighting the compulsion to turn and batter him with my fists.

"You'll be out in a few seconds," Kane soothed. "Just hang on. Just a few seconds more."

The sound of his voice galvanized my muscles like a jolt of electricity. I realized I was growling without words, a harsh keening that rose and fell like the battle cries of two tomcats squaring off in the night.

The door released at last, and I sprang into the lobby. Kane was instantly beside me. "Do you need to run?" he asked urgently.

"Fuck, no!" My feet were already carrying me rapidly toward the stairs. I grappled for control of my voice. "I need... to... talk... to Stemp."

"That's a good idea. I'll come with you."

"No." I gained the top of the stairs and spun to face him. "You stay out of it."

"Aydan..." His forehead was creased with worry.

"I said, stay out of it!" I whirled and strode down the hallway.

I forged into Stemp's office and slammed the door behind me without breaking stride. He began to rise, but I was beside him before he could straighten, my fist knotted in the front of his shirt and my gun grinding viciously under his chin.

He had obviously been a good field agent before he took over as director. His expressionless facade barely wavered.

"To what do I owe the pleasure?" he inquired, his voice slightly distorted by the constriction of his shirt collar and the pressure of my gun.

"You murdered my husband, you motherfucking son of a

bitch!"

CHAPTER 8

His shoulder lifted in a careful shrug. "Not personally. Kane did that."

"You..." I couldn't think of anything vile enough to call him, all my effort focused on not pulling the trigger until I had the information I needed.

"You... fucker! You gave the order. Murdered him. In cold blood. And let me think. I'd killed him. All this time." I could barely breathe. "Two years. I've been living with that." Control shattered, and my voice rose to a shriek. "*You rat-bastard!*"

The door latch clicked behind me, and I caught a blurred glimpse of Kane's shocked face. "Fuck off, John! I told you to stay out of it!" I roared. I shoved the gun into Stemp's throat for emphasis and felt him tense under my grip.

"Kane. Leave," he grated.

"Aydan, stop," Kane implored from behind me.

"Leave. That's an order," Stemp ground out.

Seconds later, I heard the door close again. I slammed Stemp back against the wall and took a few quick backward steps out of his reach. As shreds of sanity seeped back, I realized what a stupid mistake I'd made. I kept the gun trained on him anyway. My hand shook so badly that even if I had the guts to pull the trigger, I'd probably miss.

Stemp straightened his shirt and tie, his face still impassive.

"*Fuck*!" I flung the gun onto his desk. "Just fucking shoot me. Finish this." I threw myself into the guest chair and slumped down hopelessly.

He seated himself behind the desk again, his flat eyes appraising me. "No, I don't think so."

"Because that would be too merciful, wouldn't it?" Bitterness scalded my throat. "Fine. Put me in jail and watch me scream. Enjoy."

"No." He picked up my gun and pointed it at my face, squinting over the open sights. I trembled helplessly in the chair, heart pounding. Fine. Just let it be over.

Stemp sighed and reversed the weapon, holding it out to me by its barrel. "Take your gun."

I stared stupidly at him.

He waved it impatiently in my direction. "Take it."

"No. You're just fucking with me."

He sighed again and laid the gun down in front of me. "No, I'm not. This never happened."

"Why?"

"For one thing, we still need your decryption skills."

I felt my lips twist. "For a little while. Until Sam figures out what makes me tick. Then you'll kill me just like you killed Robert."

He shrugged. "You already knew that. Take what you can get."

"Fuck you." Heaviness descended on me. The heat of rage faded, leaving me icy cold. "Why did you kill him?"

"It was necessary."

"Why? Just to fuck up my life? How long have you been manipulating me?" Fury jerked me upright in the chair.

"You cocksucker! Do you have any idea what I went through? *Do you have any idea how it feels to think you've killed somebody you love?*"

"Yes, actually. I do." Stemp eyed me dispassionately. "I wouldn't have given the order if I'd had another choice."

"Bullshit!" I lunged up out of the chair bellowing, my throat as raw and painful as my heart. "Why! *Tell me why you killed him!*"

Stemp picked up the gun and held it out to me again. "It's time for you to go now."

I leaned shaking fists on his desk and glared into his emotionless face. Nauseating certainty climbed the back of my throat. He wasn't going to tell me. My husband was dead at his hands with no justice, no recourse, no explanation.

I straightened slowly, my spine stiffening with the steel of rage. No. Not dead at Stemp's hands. Dead at the hands of a man I'd trusted. Believed in. Had been willing to die for.

A man who'd been lying to me for months.

The gun felt cold and heavy in my hand when I lifted it from Stemp's desk and made for the door.

"Don't do anything stupid." Stemp's voice froze me with my hand on the doorknob.

"Good advice." My voice rasped like a chainsaw grinding concrete.

I opened the door to see Kane's strained face. "Aydan, thank God." His shoulders relaxed and he slid his gun back into its holster.

I closed the door behind me and glared up at him, violence roiling in my heart. My hand hurt where it clenched around the hardness of my gun.

"Aydan, what happened? What the hell was that?" he demanded, worry dissolving into irritation on his face.

I dropped my gaze to grapple for composure, distantly noticing the glowing white knuckles on my gun hand.

Orders. He had only been following orders.

"Get out of my sight." I shoved my gun back into its holster, releasing my fingers with an effort, and stalked away.

"Aydan! Don't walk away from me." His hand closed on my shoulder.

His touch destroyed the last remnants of my control and I spun, my fist whistling around to drive into his stomach. I knew the blow wouldn't have even slowed him down if he'd been expecting it, but he was clearly unprepared. He grunted and half doubled over, and I used all my weight to shove him back against the wall, my forearm jammed across his throat.

I jerked up on my tiptoes to get as close to his face as I could. "I said, *get out of my sight!*" I spat.

I whirled and strode away.

A moment later, I was pinned against the wall by his hard body while he glared down into my face.

Many people would consider it a bad idea to piss off a martial arts expert. I was far past the ability to exercise that kind of better judgement. I made a zealous attempt to knee him in the balls.

He blocked my attack. His hold on my arm tightened painfully and he crushed me against the wall with his weight.

"Now we're going to talk about this," he said quietly. "Would you like to do it here, or would you prefer to sit down and discuss it like adults?"

"Right fucking now, asshole!" My defiant growl didn't

have quite as much impact as I'd hoped, since I could only inhale enough to manage a breathless squeak.

"Why are you so angry at me?"

I tried to knee him again with no success whatsoever. "No reason. You fucking murderer."

He went very still. "Oh. Aydan, I'm sorry, I-"

"Don't bother. Don't even bother lying to me anymore. I know all about your orders." I snarled up into his face. "Cultivate a romantic relationship with the asset. You show up in my bed and pretend you hadn't planned it. What did you think? I'd just fall into your arms? Well, guess what, you could be the best lay ever, and by the way, *you weren't*, and it wouldn't be enough to make me want a relationship with you."

Rage almost choked me when he pulled back as if I'd slapped him, hurt twisting his face. God damn him, he was still, bloody well *still* trying to make me swallow his act.

"How *dare* you, you... you... prick! All that shit you spewed in the summer. 'Do you love me, Aydan?' What a crock. You killed my husband two years ago, and then you have the sheer fucking gall to pull that shit on me. I can't believe I was feeling bad because I thought you were hurt. Asshole!"

I jerked against his hold again, glaring up at him.

Kane let go and stepped away suddenly, and I barely prevented myself from falling. "Aydan, we need to talk."

"We have nothing to talk about." I spun on my heel and started down the hallway. I couldn't believe it when I felt his hand on my shoulder again.

This time he was ready for the fist I swung at him. He blocked it effortlessly, along with the kick and punch that followed. His face was composed, his body relaxed while he balanced lightly on the balls of his feet. Only his eyes showed his agitation.

Yeah, agitate this, dickhead!

I swung at him again, and again he blocked me. Then I was crushed against the wall.

"I can do this all day long if you want," he said. He blocked my knee. "You have a choice." He jerked his face out of range as I tried to head-butt him. "We can talk, or I'll talk and you'll listen. But either way..." He dodged as my teeth snapped together, barely missing his shoulder. "We will deal with this. Now."

I roared and managed to get one arm loose. In an instant, he had pinned both my arms by the wrists above my head. I caught a movement in my peripheral vision and jerked around to see Stemp's bland face peer out of his office. He and Kane exchanged a look, and Stemp nodded and withdrew again.

I fought harder, humiliation adding to my fury.

"Aydan," Kane snapped. "Stop. Give me a chance."

"A chance to what? Screw me over again? I don't think so," I snarled.

His large hand clamped over my mouth and he leaned into me hard. "Shut up and listen. Your husband was an agent. He went rogue. He was a threat to national security. I had orders to eliminate him. I was doing my job. And I've never lied to you."

Biting a chunk out of his hand seemed like the right thing to do, but I couldn't. My strength drained so suddenly the pressure of Kane's body against mine was the only thing holding me up.

He looked down into my eyes. "I'm sorry."

released me and stepped back. I sank into a huddled

heap on the floor.

My heart thudded in my ears while I memorized the carpet. Gray, with little flecks of blue, white, black and an odd kind of purplish colour. No green. Funny. The ends of the fibres were fuzzy, except at regularly spaced intervals where a loop made a shiny contrast to the plush.

Thud, thud, thud. How could my heart still be beating?

An irritating buzzing gradually intruded. I tried to block it out, but it wouldn't stop. The buzz resolved itself into Kane's voice, repeating my name over and over. I dragged my head up to focus on him as he knelt beside me. He spoke again, and I failed to understand.

"Wha...?"

"Come and sit down for a few minutes. I'll help you if you'll let me." He reached out, and I stared at his extended hand for a few moments before numbly placing my hand in his.

I tottered into my office, his strong hand under my elbow, and he lowered me onto the sofa.

"I'll be right back." He strode out.

I stared blindly after him, my mind still quivering on the threshold of comprehension.

When he returned, he placed a small box of orange juice in my hand. I sipped mechanically. I had been so touched the first time he'd gotten orange juice for me. I had felt so cared-for.

Now I knew he'd just been following orders. Nothing personal.

After a few minutes, the juice did its work and I hauled my trembling body semi-upright. Kane perched in the chair beside me and offered me another box of juice.

I took it from him and sipped some more.

“Tell me everything.” My voice shook along with my hands, and I gulped some more juice.

Kane leaned back in the chair, arms crossed, and sank his chin onto his chest. “I never knew the details.” He stared straight ahead. “We never get details. Just enough to carry out the order. Your husband... Robert had been deep undercover for twenty-four years when they discovered he’d gone rogue. Intel said he would move that day, so I had to act fast. I slipped him a drug at a business dinner.”

He met my eyes then. “I’m sorry, Aydan. We knew his habits. He was supposed to go and work out at the gym like he always did on Tuesdays. The drug would cause a heart attack as soon as he exerted himself.”

The empty juice box collapsed with a hollow crunch in my clenched hand. “But he didn’t. He came home to me instead. We started to make love. And he died in my arms. I’ve been living with that ever since.”

“I’m so sorry.” He opened his mouth as if to say something else, but sighed instead. “I’m sorry you had to go through that.”

“It doesn’t matter. Too late to be sorry about anything now.” I dragged myself up off the couch and wobbled toward the door.

Kane stood quickly and placed a firm hand under my elbow. “Where are you going?”

“Home.”

“You’re in no shape to drive right now. I’ll take you. We still have something else to talk about anyway.”

I looked up into his troubled face. “No, I really don’t think we do.”

“Aydan,” he said urgently. “What we had... this [illegible]. that was real for me.”

I shrugged. "Whatever."

"Aydan, you have to believe me. I would never do anything to hurt you. I've never lied to you."

I pushed down my anger and pain and kept my voice level. "No, murdering my husband wouldn't be likely to hurt me, would it? But I agree, you didn't lie to me outright. When I think back to it, you gave me the whole 'do you love me' speech this summer, but you never once said *you* loved *me*. You just made it sound like you did."

I shrugged again. "That's my favourite trick, too, when I don't want to actually lie to somebody. Tell unrelated truths, ask questions that sound like they're answers. You talked about love, but you never lied to me in so many words. So thanks. At least I don't have to worry about hurting your feelings anymore."

I turned away.

"Aydan..." The rawness in his voice made me turn back to see what looked like anguish in his eyes.

I blew out a breath through my teeth. "Jesus, John, the Oscar's in the mail already. Can the act, okay? It's getting old."

I left him standing in my office and hauled myself down to my car.

CHAPTER 9

I drove home without seeing the familiar road. My mind yammered ceaselessly, trying to find grounding in a worldview that had been completely upended. My Robert, so quiet and unassuming, so dependable. An undercover agent for twenty-four years. Twenty-four years! That was as long as I'd known him.

I slowed to take the corner onto my gravel road, autopilot guiding my hands while I thought back. How I'd met Robert right after I'd begun dating my first husband. The determined way he'd pursued me until I told him I'd already promised to marry Steven. The way he'd hovered in the background for the next miserable years of my life until my marriage ended. How he'd been there for me. How he'd patiently and persistently wormed his way into my heart over the next six years. How I'd finally agreed to marry him, not because I wanted to be married, but because I just couldn't bear to hurt such a sweet man.

How much of that had been lies? Spies lied. It was what they did. But why would he expend so much time and energy on me?

The car skidded, crunching to a halt on the gravel as I braked hard at my driveway. Icy horror slithered down my throat and coiled itself around my heart.

Oh, God. Oh, God, no.

I sat paralyzed with my foot jammed on the brake as the monstrous thought flared into sickening suspicion. Sam Kraus. Working for Sirius all these years. Brainwave-driven networks a specialty. The tests, three times a year since I was four years old.

They couldn't.

They wouldn't.

I sucked in the breath I'd forgotten to draw and stiffly guided the car down my driveway.

The persistent 'recruiter' from U of C, when I was in Grade 12. He'd tried so hard, seemed so irritated when I chose to take drafting at SAIT instead of... what had he wanted me to take? Computer science. And then Robert had shown up a few months later.

I pulled into my garage, hands trembling on the wheel. How long had they been controlling me? Since childhood? *My father died of a heart attack...* Oh, God, had they killed him, too? And what about my mother? I was only seventeen when she died in that car accident. They told me it had been an accident...

I was gasping jerky breaths, hysteria building. Trapped. Utterly controlled by others. No allies left. All my family dead. No way to find the truth.

I clamped down hard on control. Suck it up. Nothing had changed. The dead were long dead, and nothing would bring them back. I was doing valuable work, helping to protect our country. Never mind that I'd been manipulated into doing it. It was still the right thing to do.

Logic didn't help.

I had to know if they'd killed my family. I had to know if they had been controlling me all along. I needed more information, and I knew I wouldn't get it from Stemp.

Idiot. I should have stayed in the network and gathered all the information I possibly could. By now, Stemp would have locked everything down.

I shook myself and peeled my fingers loose from their deathgrip on the steering wheel. I had one faint hope left. One distant family member they'd missed, as far as I knew. It was probably too late, but I had to try. And maybe, just maybe, I could find an ally. If Arnie would help me.

I strode for the house as quickly as my trembling legs would carry me.

My mind whirled while I stuffed my mouth with leftovers, swallowing without tasting. I had to get to my one remaining aunt before anybody else did. I could drive to Calgary tonight, spend the night, and head for the coast in the morning. Sirius owed me some time off, and Kane was always encouraging me to take it. Fine. Their precious decryptions could wait a few days.

I jammed my dirty dishes into the dishwasher and went into the bedroom to stuff some clothes into my backpack. Minutes later, I was on the highway. I stopped in Drumheller to buy some snacks for the road, then hauled out my cell phone to dial Hellhound's number.

"Yeah." His sexy, gravelly voice tickled my eardrum.

"Hi, Arnie, it's Aydan."

"Oh... Hi, darlin'." He sounded wary. My heart sank.

"I'm heading into town tonight. Are you going to be around?"

"Uh... no, I'm tied up tonight. Actually, I'm gonna be busy all week. Sorry 'bout that. Maybe next time."

Shit. I knew the brushoff when I heard it. I held my voice steady as I replied. "Okay. Maybe next time. Take care."

"You, too. 'Bye."

I resisted the urge to pitch my phone across the parking lot. Goddammit! I'd never known Hellhound to turn down a chance to get laid. Now my last hope for an ally had faded, I didn't have a place to stay, and I hated to run up my credit card by getting a hotel room in Calgary. This trip was going to be expensive enough as it was.

I fumed for a few minutes before heaving a deep sigh of resignation. I dialled again reluctantly.

The perky hello at the other end made me wince. I just knew this wouldn't end well. Maybe I should go to a hotel after all.

"Hi, Nichele."

"Aydan!" Her squeal made me jerk the phone a few inches away from my ear. "How the hell are you, girl? I haven't heard from you for so long, I thought you'd fallen off the face of the earth!"

I couldn't help smiling. She had routinely shoved me far outside my comfort zone ever since we were kids, but Nichele's fearless and flamboyant personality still made her one of my favourite friends. And it didn't hurt that her aggressive investing as my stockbroker had made me good money even while it gave me fits.

"Not quite, I've just been buried at work lately."

I pictured her bouncing eyebrows and lascivious grin as she purred into the phone, "I'd stay buried at work, too, if I was working with a hot hunk o' man like John. Did you get it on with him yet?"

"...Uh."

"You did! Aydan, you have to tell me all about it. Oh-em-gee, he's sooo hot! Tell me he was good!"

"Uh..."

"He wasn't? Oh, no, don't tell me he wasn't good!"

"Okay, I won't tell you that. Listen, Nichele -"

"I don't believe you. He had to be good. With a body like that? And what a package that man has, Aydan. You can't tell me he wasn't good, girl. It'll destroy my faith in mankind."

"Yes! He was good! He was fucking amazing, literally fucking amazing, and it's over, and it's never going to happen again! Now can we please talk about something else?"

"Oh, girl, no wonder you're cranky. You come right on down to Calgary, and I'll fix you up with somebody. You just need to get your Eggs Benny heated up again, and everything'll be fine."

I sighed and pinched the bridge of my nose with my free hand, willing the tension headache away. "Skip the fix-up, but that's actually why I'm calling. I'm on my way down. Can I stay with you tonight?"

"Aydan!" I winced again and held the phone at a safer distance. "Girl, you know you don't even need to ask. When will you be here?"

"About an hour and half."

"You just leave it all to me. You're going to be smiling by the end of the night, I promise."

"Nichele, sorry to be a party pooper, but I'm really tired, I have a headache, and I'm pissed off. All I want is a beer and a bed."

"Don't you worry about a thing, girl, you'll get all that and more. See you soon! Bye-bye!"

The phone clicked in my ear, and I scowled at it as I stowed it in my waist pouch again. Already, I smelled trouble.

By the time I'd fought my way into downtown Calgary and paid my pound of flesh to park at Nichele's upscale condo building, my temper was even more frayed and my head throbbed relentlessly. I slung my backpack over my shoulder and trudged to the elevators with a sense of foreboding. I knew better than to believe Nichele would heed my desire for a quiet night.

At my knock, her door popped open, and she flung her arms around me and dragged me inside. "Girl, it is sooo good to see you! Here."

She took my backpack and handed me an ice-cold bottle of Corona, complete with the wedge of lime jammed in the neck. I sank into her buttery-soft leather sofa with a groan and sucked back a long, long swallow.

"Nichele, you're the best friend in the world." I gulped another generous slug as she curled up in the overstuffed chair opposite, grinning.

A few beers and some lively banter later, I lay back on the sofa, sides aching as I wiped tears of laughter from my eyes. The raw tension was gone from my muscles and the headache had miraculously subsided in the presence of alcohol and upbeat company.

Nichele eyed me mischievously. "Do you need another beer, or are you finally ready to act like a human being?"

I let out a cavernous belch, just because I could. "This is as human as it gets. And I'd better quit."

"Okay. Come on, I have something to show you." She grabbed my hand and pulled me off the couch. In the guest room, she pointed toward the bed. "Put that on."

I regarded the sexy brown leather top for a few seconds before shooting her a suspicious glare. "Why?"

"Because that T-shirt won't work for where we're going."

"We're not going anywhere. It's ten o'clock at night, I'm drunk, and I'm going to bed."

"Oh, no, you're not. You're coming out with me, and you're going to meet Dante. And he's going to show you a gooooood time." She bounced her eyebrows. "Trust me, I've already taken this one for a test drive. Talk about Dante's Inferno."

"Nichele, I told you..."

"Girl, shut up and get that top on." Before I could protest, she'd dragged my T-shirt over my head. Lucky I'd worn my ankle holster instead of my waist holster. She eyed my bra critically. "At least you wear sexy underwear under all those crappy T-shirts. Here." She threw the top at me. "Put it on. Or I'll tickle you."

"You wouldn't."

"I would. I'll tickle you until you pee."

"That only happened once. When we were five."

She advanced on me, fingertips wiggling, and I yanked the top on with alacrity. With that much beer in my system, I couldn't afford to take a chance.

"That's better." Nichele surveyed me smugly.

I squinted at myself in the mirror. "Jesus, Nichele, where are we going? A street corner on Third Avenue? This thing's so tight you can see my friggin' pores through it. And if I make a sudden move, the girls are going to fall right out of this low-cut neck."

She put her hands on her hips and glared with mock severity. "If you stop bitching right now, I won't make you put on makeup."

"Okay, okay!"

I know when I'm beaten.

She prattled happily while we zipped to the downtown

club district in her bright-red Mazda Miata. The evening air was still warm, and the breeze from the open convertible top blew my hair around my face. I clutched the armrest as she darted into a tiny parking spot with an airy wave at the horn-honking driver behind her.

"Come on, comb your hair and let's go." Nichele bounced eagerly on the sidewalk, and I smiled despite my misgivings.

"Just hold on a second." I delved into my waist pouch for my hairbrush, and she snorted.

"Do you really have to wear that thing? You're a walking fashion faux pas."

"Bite me. This was your idea, not mine."

She smirked. "You'll be thanking me later."

"I seriously doubt it."

On the sidewalk, I tugged at the tight top, unable to decide whether to pull it up to cover my half-exposed boobs or down to conceal the bared muffin-top hanging over my jeans. I groaned. Definitely hide the muffin-top. At least the top was tight enough to hold the fat roll in place once it was covered.

As I squirmed and pulled at the top, Nichele shot me a quizzical glance. "Aydan, what are you doing?"

"Trying to hide my dinner roll," I gritted. "I hate this top."

"You don't have a dinner roll, girl. And you're totally hot in that top. Come on. Dante's waiting."

I smothered another groan and followed her along the sidewalk, only half-listening to her bright chatter.

"Hey, shithead, cut it out!" My brain re-engaged at her sudden cry as she darted down an alley. Man, that girl was fast on four-inch heels! I pivoted and followed her with a sinking feeling.

Sure enough, she'd found trouble. As she dashed up to him, the clean-cut frat-boy aimed another kick at the huddled figure on the ground.

"Leave him alone!" Nichele got up in Frat-boy's face, still several inches shorter even in her high heels. "You little shit, you leave him alone! He's not hurting anybody!"

Frat-boy's buddy stepped out of the shadows, and I picked up the pace so I could pull Nichele away and place our backs to a wall. Frat-boy shot a glance at his companion, and they both smiled, just two nice all-American boys. Not.

"Chill, lady, that bum was mouthing off," Frat-boy mumbled.

Nichele's fists clenched around her elegant French manicure. "So you little pissants decided to tune him up. Oh, that's really brave. Are you compensating for your tiny dick, or are you just trying to impress your boyfriend here?"

The homeless guy had been edging away during the conversation, and now he clambered to his feet and shuffled rapidly away down the alley. Great. Frat-boy's face twisted in rage, and he took a step toward us.

Adrenaline surged into my veins. I had my gun, but I didn't want to draw it in front of Nichele. And the ankle holster was damn hard to reach unobtrusively.

Nichele practically spat contempt. "What are you going to do? Beat us up? You might get away with roughing up some poor rubbie, but your ass is going to jail for a long time if you assault us."

"'Specially if ya do it in front of a witness." I jerked with shock as Hellhound's solid bulk interposed itself between us and the two kids. They took a quick step back from his ugly bearded face and bulging tattooed arms. Then they exchanged a glance, and a metallic gleam appeared in Frat-boy's hand. Oh, shit.

"Two witnesses." A silver-haired man in a suit materialized beside Arnie. At first glance, I almost mistook him for a typical middle-aged businessman, but something about his face and his bulky, hard-looking body rang warning bells in my brain.

Apparently the two kids were hearing warning bells, too. Frat-boy spat derisively and stuck the knife back up his sleeve as they turned and left.

Arnie turned slowly. "Ya okay, darlin'?"

"Yeah, fine. Thanks for the rescue."

"And thank you, too!" Nichele gazed up at the man in the suit, her eyes shining.

He smiled down at her with interest as he took in her glossy dark hair and the curvy body flattered by her clingy dress. "My pleasure, I assure you."

"I'm Nichele Brown." She extended her hand.

"How delightful to meet you. I'm James Helmand." He took her hand and held it.

Oh, shit. I shot a glance at Arnie's unhappy face.

He blew out a sigh. "Aydan, this's my brother Jim. Jim, Aydan."

"A pleasure." He held my hand a few seconds too long, studying me with striking hazel eyes, and I resisted the urge to pull away.

As soon as he released me, I turned to Arnie. "I thought you were working tonight."

He kicked a booted foot gently at an empty beer can, watching it clatter against the wall. "I am. I was followin' somebody when I saw ya go in here, an' I figured ya were in trouble. I gotta go. Come on, Jim." He turned back toward the sidewalk.

James smiled, eyeing Nichele. "Where are you off to tonight, so elegantly dressed?"

"Right around the corner. Why don't you join us for a few drinks," she invited.

I shot a wide-eyed glare at Arnie. "Nah, we gotta go," he said quickly. "Come on, Jim, let's get outta here."

"On the contrary, I have no particular place to be tonight," his brother demurred. "I'd be delighted to accompany you." He tucked Nichele's hand into the crook of his elbow and they strolled toward the sidewalk, leaving Arnie and me regarding each other sickly.

"What the hell?" I hissed. "I thought you said he was in jail for the rest of his life."

Hellhound scowled. "Thought he was. Bastard's got too much goddam pull, an' he got sprung. He showed up at my place an' I told him to fuck off, but he's been followin' me around for days."

I groaned as I watched Nichele lean into James, gazing up at him. "Shit! Come with me. See if we can break it up before it's too late."

"Can't, darlin'. Sorry." He didn't quite meet my eyes. "I really gotta go."

"Okay." I reached for his hand, but he turned away and headed for the sidewalk. "See you," I said to his receding back.

Inside the club, I leaned close to Nichele to be heard over the thumping music. "Come with me to freshen up." I grabbed her wrist and dragged her to the bathroom.

Inside, I released her. "Nichele..."

"Oh... My... God... Aydan, did you see how hot he is? Did you see that suit?"

"What is it with you and guys in suits? Listen, Nichele..."

"That's Armani!"

"You know I wouldn't know Armani if it jumped up and bit me on the ass. And I don't give a shit if he's wearing a gold-leaf suit with a diamond-studded codpiece -"

"What's a codpiece?"

"It was a piece that covered a guy's junk on..." I cut myself off at the sight of her mischievous grin. "Don't change the subject! You need to ditch him, ASAP!"

"Are you kidding me? I'm soooo gonna hit that!"

"Nichele, you can't. Have a drink with him to be polite, and then blow him off."

She turned a wicked grin on me. "Oh, I'll blow him off, all right. And that's not all I'll do."

I seized her by the shoulders. "Nichele, he's a criminal! He's a dangerous, mean sonuvabitch, he's in deep with the gangs, and he just got out of jail. Ditch him. I mean it."

"Bullshit! Who told you that?"

"Arnie. Trust me, he's not kidding."

She eyed me sceptically. "No way. James is smart and sophisticated, I can tell. Arnie's the mean dumb one, with all his tattoos and leathers. I can see his ugly face in jail, no problem. He's just making that up so you'll stay away from James."

I couldn't help taking offense on Arnie's behalf. I knew he intentionally cultivated his dumb-biker image to hide his intelligence and provide a cover for his activities as a private investigator, but seeing the stereotype in action irritated me. And his face wasn't his fault.

"You try getting the shit kicked out of you for the first

five years of your life, and see how pretty your face looks afterward. Besides..."

"Oh, that's right, he's your booty call, isn't he? Sorry."

"*Was*, apparently. That's not the point..."

"Oh, girl, he dumped you? No wonder you're so bitchy. But it's okay." She patted my cheek. "Dante's my super-hot booty call, and just for you, I'm going to share. Come on, once you get laid, everything'll be all better." She grabbed my arm and hauled me out of the bathroom.

"Nichele, I don't care how hot Dante is, I'm not going to jump a total stranger. And you need to tell James to take a hike."

She had dragged me half-way across the bar and I was still trying to talk sense into her ear when she perked up and waved. "There's Dante! Come on!"

I gaped at the shockingly handsome man across the room. My fingers dug into Nichele's shoulder. "Nichele! Christ, I'm not a cougar! I'm old enough to be his mother! And you know I don't trust any man who looks prettier or smells better than I do. He's gotta be-"

"He's an underwear model. And he's thirty-seven. Ten years younger is juuuust right, trust me."

I did my best to close my mouth when his face lit up and dazzlingly white teeth gleamed. High cheekbones formed breathtaking planes and angles in his tanned face. Longish, wavy black hair, sparkling black eyes, full lips, and a chiselled chin topped the body of a god, tantalizingly displayed in a clinging, silky shirt and extremely well-fitting black slacks.

"...Holy... fuck!"

Nichele grinned up at me. "Oh, you have no idea. Come on."

CHAPTER 10

Apparently I'd been harbouring a few stereotypes of my own. To my surprise, Dante wasn't a self-centred featherbrain. Despite the fact that we had very little in common, he proved to be an intelligent and entertaining conversationalist. And Nichele must have bribed him to be extra nice to me.

I made a few more futile attempts to deter Nichele, but it was clearly a waste of breath. I slammed down another couple of beers and discovered I didn't care anymore. I relaxed with a fresh beer in my hand and let Dante's attentiveness soothe my battered equanimity.

Some time later, I sighed when I glanced over to see James and Nichele in a passionate lip lock. I'd tried. Really, I had.

Dante's gorgeous face blocked my view. "Is everything all right?" His accent was barely noticeable, just pronounced enough to sound exotic. Combined with his deep, mellow voice, the effect was like being stroked with black velvet. In a lot of interesting places.

I took a deep breath and held my voice steady. "Fine, thanks."

He traced a line down my jaw with one perfectly manicured fingertip. "I was afraid you were feeling neglected." His lips were very close.

A second later, his lips were exactly close enough. Cold and smoky-tasting from his single-malt scotch on the rocks. But, oh my lord, they warmed up fast. Dante's Inferno indeed...

I yelped and jerked away when Kane's large hand dropped on my shoulder. "Aydan, I need to talk to you."

"Jesus Christ! What the hell are you doing here?" I clutched at my chest in a futile attempt to slow my hammering heart. His gaze followed the gesture to my exposed cleavage, and I whacked his arm. "Hey, buddy, eyes up here."

His hand closed around my wrist. "We need to talk. Privately." He shot a scowl at Dante. Dante's smooth forehead puckered ever so slightly as he took in the scar that cut across Kane's eyebrow and the slight bump from his long-ago broken nose. Dressed all in black with his massive shoulders straining his shirt, Kane looked almost as dangerous as he truly was.

"I'll be back in a few minutes," I assured Dante, and slid out of the booth.

Kane steered me to a corner where the music was slightly less deafening. He leaned close and growled in my ear, "What the hell are you doing?"

All my irritation flooded back. "What the hell does it look like I'm doing? I *was* having a pleasant evening with friends. What do you want?"

"I want to know why you packed up and sneaked out of your house. I want to know where you're going."

"I wasn't sneaking! Jeez, you're always telling me I'm working too hard. I decided to take a little R & R, that's all."

"Really."

"Yeah, really." I glared at him. "So you can just butt out and... Goddammit!" I exclaimed as comprehension dawned. "You got Arnie to tail me, didn't you? Why don't you leave me the hell alone!"

Kane shrugged. "You should have told me where you were going. I tried to call you, and when I didn't get an answer, I checked the surveillance footage. When we saw you leaving with your backpack, Stemp was afraid you might do something rash, so he sent me to pick you up and bring you home."

"Excuse me?" I glowered at him. "Bring me home? Screw that. How did you even find me?"

"I tracked your cell phone and found out you were in Calgary. I drove out to your place and your overnight things were gone..."

"You broke into my house." My temper flared and I held it back with difficulty. Would've been a lot easier without the many beers circulating enthusiastically in my bloodstream.

He shrugged again. "That's what happens when you don't keep me informed. I set Hellhound up for surveillance at Nichele's until I could get here, and told him to follow you if you went anywhere."

He eyed me humourlessly. "If you're planning to stay under the radar, you shouldn't ride around in a red convertible with the top down."

"Piss off. I'm not trying to stay under the radar, I'm *trying* to have a pleasant evening. It would improve a lot if you'd just leave me alone."

His lips tightened. "Aydan, I'm sorry, I know you're still upset with me, but don't make things worse. Stemp's given me the order to bring you back tonight. Let's just go."

Fury and fear shot through me. If Stemp was willing to

send Kane out to drag me back tonight, I'd never get another chance to talk privately to my aunt. I'd never know the truth...

The beer won the battle.

I leaned forward for emphasis and regained my balance by jabbing a finger into his chest. "You can tell Stemp to go fuck himself! In fact, you can drive all the way back up to Silverside tonight, *without me*, and fuck Stemp yourself for all I care. I'm not going with you. I've been working every goddamn weekend for the last three months, and I'm due for a break. You see that guy over there?"

I wiggled my fingers at Dante, and his brilliant smile flashed through the dim lights of the club. "I'm going to take that home and ride it all night long. And you're not going to stop me."

Kane's face twisted. "Aydan, I know you're not the type to pick up a stranger for a one-night stand."

"Oh, yeah? Well, news flash. I wasn't. But I am now. Because *as you told me*, I can't afford to get close to anybody in my line of work. Tom's off limits, Arnie's taken a powder, and I wouldn't touch you with rubber gloves... or rubber anything for that matter," I amended, ignoring the flash of fake pain on his face. When would the man give it up already?

I smothered a hiccup and went on. "So, yeah, I'm going to go and have very, very nice evening with Dante, and you're going to let me. Because you know damn well I deserve it."

"Aydan, I think you've had a little too much to drink..."

"Fuckin' A."

"Think this through," he urged. "Please."

"I have. We're done here." I got up and went back to Dante.

When I cuddled up to him, he shot a glance over to Kane smouldering in the corner. "Is everything all right?"

Nichele disengaged herself from James to lean across the table. "Hey, girl, isn't that Hot John? I thought you said it was over between you."

"It is. Apparently he's having some difficulty letting go. Ignore him."

Dante eyed Kane worriedly. "Is he dangerous?"

I swallowed a sigh. I'd gotten so used to being surrounded by brave men. But I could scarcely blame Dante for not wanting to get his head kicked in. His face was his meal ticket.

"No," I lied. "He won't cause any trouble. Just ignore him."

"Okay." His dazzling smile came back. "I'm sure he'll get tired of watching soon enough."

Ha. I wish. I shrugged and let Dante's lips drift down my neck. "I'm sure he will."

Some time later, Nichele tottered to her feet. "Aydan, come with me."

I got up and followed as she wove her way to the washroom. Inside, she leaned against the wall and giggled. "What do you think of Dante?"

"The man is pure dark chocolate. Looks good, smells good, comes on sweet and strong..."

"And makes you want to eat him all night long," she finished, grinning.

"That wasn't what I was going to say."

She smirked up at me. "Here's the part where you thank me."

"Yeah, thanks, Nichele."

"No, I mean, here's the part where you thank me,

because...” She paused dramatically.

“What?” I shot her a suspicious look.

Could anything else go wrong tonight? I had no idea how I could give Kane the slip, pick up my things from Nichele’s, and sneak away. Kane had stayed, watching me from across the room, and he was undoubtedly ready to drag me to his truck the instant I stepped outside. Shit, shit, shit!

“Because...” Nichele hiccupped and one eyelid drooped in a conspiratorial wink. “I sneaked your backpack into my car before we left my place. And when James went out for a smoke, I went with him and put your backpack into Dante’s car. So you can have your night of dark chocolate sin with all the comforts of home.”

“You did what?” My jaw sagged as I stared at her impish expression. Any other time, I would’ve been ready to kill her. As much as I was enjoying the flirtation, I had no intention of taking it any further with Dante. But this time...

I flung my arms around her. “Nichele, you’re the best friend that ever was!”

“How drunk are you?”

“Stone cold sober.”

“Bullshit.”

“Okay, sober enough.”

She eyed me uncertainly. “Why aren’t you mad?”

I made an effort to tone down the shit-eating grin that kept tugging at the corners of my mouth. “Because at least once in her life, every woman should get a chance to do a guy who looks like Dante.”

She relaxed, mirroring my grin. “Finally, you’re starting to live a little. About time.”

“You can say that again.”

My mind worked furiously while we made our way back

to the table, arm in arm. Half the problem solved. I had my backpack. Now if Kane would just leave me alone for a few minutes...

James and Dante rose as we arrived at the table, and we headed for the door. I spotted Kane vectoring toward us and sighed. "You guys go ahead. I'm just going to deal with Mr. Creepy Stalker here."

James straightened, his hard eyes measuring Kane. "Do you want help?"

I didn't want to consider the kind of help he might offer. Cement overshoes, maybe. "No, thanks, it's no big deal. I'll just be a minute."

They drifted away as Kane confronted me. "We need to go now, Aydan."

I rubbed the frown lines out of my forehead as my heart rate ratcheted up a notch. Now or never. I summoned up all my acting skills and gave him the imploring big brown eyes.

"John, I..." I broke off and cast my eyes down for a second before meeting his gaze again. "I said some harsh things earlier, and I'm sorry. But I'm just so... you can't imagine what this has been like for me."

That part was true, anyway. Careful, now, don't overdo it...

His face softened. Good.

"I know it's asking a lot, and I know it puts you in an awkward position with Stemp, but..." I gazed up at him and let my voice tremble a little. "Could you... please, just this one time. I just need a bit of time to get over this. Could you just let me go?"

Kane sighed. "Aydan, you know I can't let you out of my sight."

Dammit.

I knew duty came first for him. It always had. I had hoped he hadn't been completely faking his attraction to me, but no such luck. It had all been a lie.

"Fine." I turned away.

Now what the hell was I going to do? I made my way toward the door with Kane trailing me through the crush of bodies. Maybe I could run for it.

His hand closed around my arm. Shit, was the man a mind reader?

"Aydan." He let go and leaned close, his grey eyes searching my face. "I don't want you to go home with that..." He stopped at the sight of my expression and took a breath. "All right. You know how much trouble I'll be in for this. But you're right, Sirius owes you." He blew out a breath. "I owe you. I'll give you the night."

I stared up at him, shocked.

"I'll have to follow you and keep you under surveillance," he continued. "But I'll stay back. We'll leave in the morning."

I clutched his hand. "Thank you."

He sighed. "You're welcome. Just..." His hand tightened on mine for an instant before he released me. "Never mind."

I stepped out onto the sidewalk alone, elation warring with sickening guilt. This was going to work. But I was about to screw Kane royally.

My alcohol-fuelled inner child stamped her foot. I owed him a metric shit-ton of absolutely nothing. He'd murdered my husband, he'd pretended to be my friend, and he'd used and manipulated me. Oh, and he'd screwed me under false pretences.

Bend over, buddy. Payback's a bitch.

Dante's arm slipped around my shoulders, and I smiled at him as he ushered me to his car.

CHAPTER 11

I tried to conceal my nervousness when we pulled up in front of a well-kept bungalow in one of the older neighbourhoods. As we got out of the car, I glimpsed Kane's black Expedition pulling up to the curb in the next block. Damn, he was a good spy. If I hadn't known what he drove, I'd never have spotted him.

I retrieved my backpack and let Dante guide me up the walk with his arm around my waist. At the front door, we shared a lingering kiss while he fumbled for his keys. Despite my apprehension, I couldn't help noting how good his body felt against mine. And he knew what to do with those luscious lips.

Inside, I subtly manoeuvred him in front of the picture window for our next kiss, making sure we'd be visible from outside. This needed to be totally convincing.

My God, speaking of convincing...

Maybe Hellhound had some competition in the kissing department after all. I spared a quick downward glance to make sure I hadn't accidentally stepped into a small bonfire.

Nope.

And anyway, I wasn't feeling the heat in my feet.

I sucked in a breath when he pulled me closer, the sculpted muscles of his arms rippling under my hands. His hot lips traced down my neck, and I twined my fingers in his thick, glossy hair while his kisses burned their way across the top of my cleavage.

God damn, maybe I should stay for a little while. After all, how many opportunities like this do you get in a lifetime?

I refocused with a tremendous effort of will. I only had one chance to give Kane the slip, and this was it. Maybe I could call Dante later...

I ran my fingers down his perfect chest and took hold of the front of his shirt to pull him gently away from the window and further into the house, my small backpack dangling from the fingers of my other hand. From my previous life as a draftsperson, I knew these older bungalows had a predictable floor plan. I'd expected a bathroom and bedrooms down the hallway, and I wasn't disappointed.

Scratch that. I was disappointed as hell that I wasn't going to get any dark chocolate tonight. But at least the floor plan was doing it for me.

"Hold that thought," I whispered as I pulled away from Dante's kiss and slipped into the bathroom.

I closed the door behind me, and heard him move further down the hallway. A few moments later, soft music began to play. Perfect. That would cover the sounds of my escape.

As I'd expected, the house had been built before exhaust fans were common, so the bathroom had a generously sized window. I wasted no time opening it and removing the screen.

I hesitated, swaying slightly in the bathtub while the cool night breeze blew around me. The distant, garbled voice of better judgement suggested I should probably sober up before making decisions like this. A much more powerful and convincing voice suggested that Dark Chocolate Dante would make a scrumptious dessert.

But this would be my only chance to contact my aunt.

And I had to know.

I placed my cell phone on the vanity and sighed. I'd have to leave it behind, or it would give away my movements as soon as Kane started tracking it again. If he wasn't already tracking it.

I tossed my backpack out the window and scrambled up, hoping the thump of my knees against the wall would be concealed by the music. I paused, teetering on the sill. The music was all sensuous horns and throbbing beat. Goddamn.

I jumped out into the dark back yard.

I twisted my ankle on the soft ground and bit my lip until the urge to swear subsided along with the pain. Then I hoisted my backpack onto my shoulder and faded into the back alley.

I zigzagged through the pitch-dark silence of the alleys and scuttled across the lighted streets until the sound of traffic led me to a main thoroughfare. I fervently wished I'd thought to bring my hoodie for warmth and to conceal my hair. The evening air was damn chilly, especially with half my boobs hanging out. I pulled on a baggy sweatshirt from my backpack and made my cautious way out into the lights.

An all-night convenience store beckoned, and I approached its bright lights cautiously. Sure enough, it had an ATM. I hesitated, then shrugged. Whatever. As soon as Kane realized I'd bolted, he'd check my bank accounts, but this withdrawal would only tell him what he already knew: I'd run from Dante's and taken out as much cash as the ATM would allow. He wouldn't know where I'd gone from here.

Cash safely stowed in my wallet, I dove back into the safe darkness of the alleys. I was exhausted, but I had to get clear of the city before the alarm was raised. I'd spend the rest of my life locked down if Kane caught me now.

The last of the alcohol burned out of my system while I hiked along, and I realized I hadn't planned this well at all. Hell, never mind 'well'. I hadn't planned it, period.

I didn't know any of the local transit routes, and I doubted if they ran in the middle of the night anyway. I briefly considered getting to the bus station and taking a Greyhound out of town, but I knew they required ID, and that would give away my destination.

"Dammit!" I leaned against somebody's back fence, trying to pull my thoughts together. How the hell was I going to get from here to Victoria, BC without leaving a trail? I couldn't take any kind of public transportation. I had no idea how to steal a car, and that would attract too much attention anyway. Hitchhiking was untraceable, but it was too dangerous for a woman alone.

I straightened slowly, triumph sending a slow grin to my face. Hitchhiking might be dangerous for a woman alone, but I wasn't alone. I had the best companion a girl could want.

My grin widened as I reached for my Glock in its ankle holster. Hitchhiking wasn't going to be dangerous for me at all. I hauled my waist holster out of the backpack and transferred the Glock to it, arranging the sweatshirt over top. Ready to roll.

My smile faded when I realized I still needed to get to the TransCanada Highway, and I had no idea how to do that at three o'clock in the morning. A taxi would be easiest for me, but I was afraid to try. I knew exactly how dedicated a hunter Kane was. Sooner or later, he'd check the taxi companies. If it was sooner, I'd be out of luck.

I wandered aimlessly down the alley, racking my brain. At last, I drifted to a halt, struck by an idea. It wasn't ideal, but it would work. I headed down the alley with renewed purpose, peeking into each back yard as I went.

Fortunately, October had been unseasonably warm. I had only covered a couple of blocks before I found what I was searching for: a bicycle leaning against a back deck.

I hovered outside the yard, my heart in my mouth. I'd never stolen anything in my life. What if I got caught? I peered around the dark yard, searching for signs of a dog and making sure the bike wasn't chained up. With a last glance around the alley, I let myself quietly in the back gate, hands shaking.

I sneaked across the yard, hugging the fence, and finally stood beside the bike, panting shallowly. Oh, God, I didn't think I could do this.

I jittered there for a moment, trying to screw up some courage. Jeez, suck it up, woman! I'd faced down captivity, torture, and death. Surely I could manage to steal one lousy bike.

But I hadn't been committing a crime with the other stuff. This was against the law.

A dog barked a couple of doors down, and I twitched in the shadows. Goddammit, just do it already!

I offered a silent prayer for forgiveness to whoever might be listening, and quickly wheeled the bike out to the back alley. Then I leaped on and pedalled wildly, leaving the barking dog far behind.

I soon discovered a bike path and shot down it, slamming on the brakes when I realized it was pitch dark down there. Another serious flaw in my plan. I'd hoped to use the network of bike paths, but they were unlit. I couldn't see enough to ride safely.

I got off the bike, sweating and trembling, and leaned against the fence until my heart rate stabilized. Then I turned the bike around and began to pedal the long miles through the quiet streets toward the highway.

It was still dark by six AM. For the last several miles, I'd been fantasizing about dispatching the designer of the bicycle seat to an eternal hell astride a dull carving knife. My butt was screaming agony by the time I finally pulled up beside the highway on the west side of town.

I was shaking with fatigue, hunger, and the knowledge that in a couple of hours, maybe less, Kane would discover I was gone. I had hoped to be out of the city by now.

I didn't even dare go into a gas station or convenience store for a snack. Surely he'd have no way of finding out I'd been there, but I couldn't bring myself to enter a well-lit public place where there might be surveillance cameras.

I leaned the bicycle up against a streetlight and limped away, resisting the urge to publicly massage my aching ass. Westbound traffic was already picking up, and I scanned it for police cars before sticking out my thumb.

To my surprise, a car stopped almost immediately. The passenger window hummed open, and I leaned in to survey the ordinary-looking middle-aged driver.

He gave me a friendly smile. "Where are you headed?"

I hesitated. "Banff," I lied.

"Well, I'm only going to Cochrane, but I can take you to the truck stop at the turnoff."

"Thanks!" I hopped in. The Cochrane turnoff was only about twenty miles out of town, but at least it got me beyond the city limits. And if I could catch a ride with a long-haul trucker from there, it would make for an easy trip.

The driver glanced over as we reached highway speed. "What's in Banff?"

"Um... Just some friends."

He frowned over at me. "Hitchhiking's a pretty dangerous way to get there."

"I know." I hoped he'd shut up. No such luck.

"Don't you have anybody to take you?"

"No."

"Nobody's going to miss you?"

"Um..." I wasn't sure I liked the sound of that question. "No."

"Are you a working girl?"

I didn't like the phrasing of that, either. "No."

"What do you do for a living?"

Jesus, buddy, shut the fuck up. I ignored the question and gazed out the window instead.

"What's your name?"

"Um... Jane."

"Nice to meet you, Jane, I'm Ron."

"Hi, Ron."

Thank God I only had to go a few more miles with this guy. My head pounded and fine tremors of nervousness and fatigue coursed through my body.

"Are you hungry, Jane?"

"Uh... yeah."

"If you come with me to Cochrane, I'll buy you breakfast."

"No, thanks."

"I'll get you something nice. You shouldn't travel on an empty stomach."

"I'll get something at the truck stop. Thanks, anyway."

His left hand slipped down beside his seat, and I tensed. What the hell was he doing?

"Are you in some kind of trouble, Jane?"

"No." I watched him out of the corner of my eye, ready to react. Adrenaline pumped through my body.

"I can help if you are."

"No, I'm fine. Thanks. Actually, why don't you just let me out here."

"We're not there yet."

"I know. I... I've changed my mind. I'm going to go back to the city. Stop and let me out, please."

He slowed the car, still groping down by his left side. I abandoned all pretence of casual conversation and watched him overtly. He smiled as he pulled over and stopped, and I reached for the door handle. The door wouldn't open. Goddamn electric door locks!

I scrabbled at the unfamiliar door panel, searching for the button.

"Wait. Not so fast," he said.

I made a grab for my gun as his left hand appeared, holding a black object.

At the last second I aborted the movement when I realized what he was holding.

"Take this, Jane. Read it. If you're in trouble, if you feel alone in the world, remember that Jesus loves you." He handed me a small Bible, and I smothered a spurt of hysterical laughter. "You're never alone when you have Jesus," he added kindly.

"Uh, thanks." I located the door lock at last and tumbled out of the car, shaking.

He lifted a hand in farewell and pulled away. I stared at

the Bible in my hand and started to laugh helplessly, half sobbing while I braced my elbows on my trembling knees. Jesus Christ.

Literally.

My ass hurt like a bitch, it had taken me all goddamn night to get ten miles out of town, and I was starving, exhausted, and scared shitless. And I had a Glock and a Bible.

Hell, what could possibly go wrong?

CHAPTER 12

I straightened and eyed the Bible uncertainly. I almost left it in the ditch, but I love books too much to abuse them. Besides, it seemed disrespectful. I sighed and stuffed it into my backpack instead.

The sky was brightening, and I stumbled along beside the road, trying to force my burnt-out brain to come up with a plan. I needed a more convincing story. Sooner or later, I'd have to admit to somebody that I was headed for the west coast.

Vehicles rocketed by, buffeting me with their slipstream. I briefly considered walking to the truck stop, but I didn't think I could manage ten miles. A wave of fear washed over me when a black SUV appeared, but it didn't slow as it passed me.

At last, I spotted an approaching tractor-trailer and stuck out my thumb. It barrelled past me without slowing, and I seriously considered relocating my gun back to the ankle holster so I could take off my sweatshirt and show some cleavage despite the chill. I needed a ride, pronto.

I was still thinking, walking backward with my thumb extended, when another semi appeared on the horizon. I put on a smile and waved as it drew closer.

This time, the big diesel snorted and grumbled as the

driver downshifted, and the rig pulled to a stop a couple of hundred yards past me. The air brakes hissed as I trotted up.

The passenger door opened, and the driver leaned out. "Where're you headed?"

"West coast."

"Your lucky day." He pushed the door open, and I clambered up.

We appraised each other as I settled into the passenger seat. He was middle-aged and out of shape, with a generous gut straining a slightly grubby-looking T-shirt. A rip in the shirt revealed a pasty-skinned, hairy belly. Baggy, faded jeans riding too low. Lucky he was sitting down. He'd have a bad case of plumber's butt for sure. Untidy waves made his too-long grizzled hair stick out at odd angles, and a few days worth of grey stubble adorned his face. The cab smelled faintly of onions, or possibly body odour.

His pale blue eyes travelled over my face, politely stopping around chin-level. I must have passed muster, because he smiled and stuck out his hand. "Dave Shore."

"Hi, Dave, nice to meet you. I'm Jane." I shook his hand, and he turned his attention back to the road, winding up through the gears.

After a few miles, I was just starting to relax when he glanced over and spoke as he began to downshift. "Stopping for breakfast. You coming in?"

Shit. The tension slammed back into my muscles. I was doomed to travel this friggin' highway ten miles at a time. I couldn't suppress a jerky glance at my watch. Eight o'clock. Kane would have waited all night outside Dante's place. Right about now, he'd be finding out I was gone.

For the first time, I seriously considered what he'd do. He'd be furious. And he'd be in a lot of trouble with Stemp.

If I didn't get to talk to Aunt Minnie before Kane found me, I'd never get another chance. I found myself leaning over to peer in the side mirror, watching for a black SUV. No, that was stupid. He wouldn't pick up my trail that quickly.

"Jane?"

I started and turned to meet Dave's faded eyes. "Sorry. Um... If I give you some money, can you grab me something?"

He turned his attention back to the rig as we pulled to a halt outside the truck stop. The air brakes hissed, and he turned to study me, his unkempt eyebrows drawn together. "You got a reason?"

"I, uh, I just... don't want to be seen."

"You running from the cops?"

"No!" The word jerked out of me with guilty emphasis as I remembered the stolen bicycle.

"What then?"

"Listen, Dave, never mind. I'm not hungry. I'll just wait for you."

"Bull. You talk now, or you get outta my truck."

I bit back tears of stress and fatigue as I swiped shaking hands over my face. I refuse to cry in public, dammit. "Dave, please." I swallowed hard to get rid of the quaver in my voice. "Look, just..."

He shrugged. "Your choice. Get out."

"I'm running from my ex-boyfriend," I blurted. Closest thing to the truth I could manage. Our friendship had been a lie, and any trust we'd had for each other was shattered beyond repair now. I sank my head into my hands with a groan. "God, he's going to kill me."

"What?"

I looked up at Dave's wide eyes, my sleep-deprived brain

replaying my words. I hadn't meant that literally, although an ugly chill shook me as I thought it through. There might be more truth to that statement than I knew.

I went with it. "If he finds me, he'll kill me. I've been up all night, trying to get on the highway without being seen." This time I didn't try to hide the tremor in my voice. "When he finds out I'm gone, he'll come after me, and I'm only twenty miles out of town. I can't let anybody see me."

"You better not be lying."

I clasped my trembling hands. "I'm dead serious."

"Why don't you call the cops?"

"What are they going to do? By the time they can do anything, I'll already be dead."

He examined my face at length, his eyes boring into mine. Then he eyed my shaking hands and my small backpack, and gave a single nod as if coming to a decision.

"Okay."

Relief flooded me. "Thank you," I stammered as I fumbled into my wallet for a twenty.

"What do you want?"

"I don't care. I'll eat anything."

He paused, one hand on the door handle. "If you want, you can go in the sleeper so nobody sees you sitting here." He gestured to the alcove behind the seats.

"Thank you," I repeated. My trembling knees almost gave way as I stood, and I caught myself on the back of the seat.

"You okay?" I thought I saw a flash of concern on his face.

"Fine. Just tired and hungry."

He shook his head, and I barely heard his mutter as he opened the door to climb out. "I must be nuts."

Through a sliver of view from the sleeper, I watched him stump across the parking lot with the stiff gait of a man who suffers from chronic lower-back pain. He turned once to survey the truck with a frown before turning away and hitching up his jeans to mercifully hide a truly nasty butt-crack. I slumped on the tiny bench seat in the sleeper, gratitude swelling in my heart. He was possibly the most beautiful man I'd ever seen.

Seconds later, I jerked awake at the movement of the cab and the sound of the door. I must have looked panic-stricken, because Dave made a hasty gesture with one of the brown paper bags he held. "It's okay. Just me. Breakfast."

I blew out a breath and relaxed. "Sorry. I guess I fell asleep."

"Guess you need it," he said gruffly. "Here. Eat this and then catch some zees." He handed me the bag and my change, and I slid into the passenger seat again.

The aroma of hot grease embraced me when I opened the bag, and I swallowed hard to control the flood of saliva. I tore into the breakfast sandwich, gulping the spicy, greasy sausage, egg and cheese, hands shaking. By the time I got to the cardboard package of home fries, the truck was in motion, and I finally spared a glance at Dave. "Thanks. This is delicious," I mumbled through a mouthful.

"No problem." He glanced over. "You were starving."

"Yeah."

His brows drew together again, and I braced myself for more questions. Instead, he said, "Didn't know how you like your coffee. Brought you some cream and sugar. Got decaf 'cause I figured you'd need to sleep."

I almost never drank coffee, but his thoughtfulness touched me. "Thanks," I repeated. "That's perfect." And when I sipped the hot, bitter liquid, it cut through the remainder of the grease and warmed me through. It really was perfect.

When I finished, he shot me another quick look. "If you want to sleep, you can use the bed." He jerked his thumb toward the sleeper. "Ain't real safe if there's an accident, but I ain't planning to hit anything."

"Thanks," I mumbled, drowsiness numbing my brain. Safety, a full stomach and a bed. Heaven. I dragged myself back into the sleeper.

Under ordinary circumstances, I'd feel squeamish about sleeping in the bed of a man whose personal hygiene seemed questionable, but I was past caring. When I fell into the narrow bed, I registered brief surprise that the sheets and pillowcase were clean before sleep claimed me.

I woke when the truck stopped. I sat up to peer into the cab, clenching my teeth and heartily regretting the cup of coffee. "Where are we?"

"Revelstoke. Lunch time."

I put on my shoes and slid into the passenger seat, reaching for the door handle.

"You sure you wanna get out? I can get you something."

"I have to," I gritted. "I have to go to the bathroom." That was the understatement of the century. I wasn't even sure I could make it down from the cab without peeing my pants.

"Use the one in the sleeper. I'll get lunch." He swung out of the cab before I could thank him, and I hurried back into the sleeper. Thank God. It had never occurred to me that it would contain a toilet. I opened a skinny door, and there it was, also surprisingly clean.

By the time Dave returned, I'd brushed out my rats-nest

of hair, changed my clothes, and freshened up. I'd also relocated the Glock into my ankle holster and stowed the waist holster in my pack. I had a feeling I'd be safe with Dave.

"Heart attack in a bag," he grunted, handing me another paper sack. That explained the onion scent in the cab. The burger smelled delicious.

"Thanks." I handed him a ten, and he fumbled in his pocket for change. "Forget it," I told him. He shrugged and nodded thanks, and we both devoured our food.

On the road again, we rode in silence until I began to ask questions about the truck. I knew nothing about the big diesels, and apparently I was asking the right person. His taciturn manner vanished as he waxed loquacious over his custom-built sleeper and the inner workings of the engine, and we spent several enjoyable hours discussing vehicles in general.

Apparently the ice was broken, and the conversation wandered to more personal matters. I discovered he was an independent trucker who owned his own rig, and I realized my good fortune when he mentioned he wouldn't have been allowed to pick me up if he'd been trucking for anybody else.

We had been talking about his bitter ex-wife and his adult kids when he shot me a sudden piercing glance. "You really running from your ex?"

"He's not really my ex. But I'm as good as dead if he finds me."

"Who is he?"

"He's... a guy I work with. We... I thought we had something. I was wrong."

"So this nutjob is chasing you. That all you got?" He indicated my backpack.

"Yeah."

He frowned. "You got a place to go?"

"Um..." Now that I'd had a few hours of sleep and a chance to think things through, I realized exactly how ill-prepared I was. Last I'd heard, Aunt Minnie was in a care home. I couldn't stay there. And after I saw her, then what? Keep hiding from Kane for the rest of my life? On four hundred dollars cash?

"I'll figure something out." I hoped I sounded more convincing to him than I sounded to myself.

"You got enough money?"

"I'll manage."

He fell silent, watching the road, and I leaned back in the passenger seat, my mind skittering like a frightened squirrel. I never did anything without a detailed plan. What the hell had I been thinking? And what the hell was I going to do?

CHAPTER 13

By the time we arrived in Hope, BC, I had developed as much of a plan as I could. Dave pulled over for food and returned with another bag of grease, and I began to understand why he had the gut. Under the circumstances, I was surprised he wasn't enormous. I enjoyed the fried chicken, but I couldn't imagine a steady diet of it.

When I offered him another twenty, he turned it down, shaking his head. "Still got change from lunch."

"But..."

He shook his head irritably, and I decided not to push it.

As we approached Vancouver, he kept glancing at me out of the corner of his eye, and his bushy eyebrows merged into a single line across his forehead.

At last, he spoke. "Where're you headed after this?"

"Victoria."

"Why Victoria?"

"There's somebody there I have to see."

He looked me full in the face for the first time in a couple of hours, his expression lightening. "You can stay with them?"

"No."

"Hmmph." He frowned at the road some more. Then he shifted in his seat and shot me another sidelong glance.

"Look, I'm gonna get a hotel in Vancouver tonight. I don't have another load 'til Friday. I could take you to Victoria tomorrow, if you stay with me tonight."

I hesitated, not exactly sure what he was offering. Or asking for.

A dark flush spread up his neck. "I mean, not like stay with me, for... I meant, a double room. Or you could have the room and I could sleep in the truck." He shifted again, rubbing the back of his neck and not meeting my eyes. "I'm not trying to..."

"It's okay. Thanks, Dave, but that's too much trouble for you. If you could just drop me off at the ferry terminal, that would be great."

"You know what time the ferries run?"

"No... but it's only seven o'clock. They wouldn't stop running this early, would they?"

"Don't know. Where're you gonna sleep when you get over there?" he challenged.

"Um..." I cast about for ideas. "There must be... maybe they have a women's shelter or something?"

He stopped at a red light and turned to face me. "Look, if all you got is what's in your backpack, things're gonna be tough. Let me do this for you." His pale eyes held mine. "You might not believe it right now, but not all guys are bums."

"Thanks." I swallowed a lump in my throat. "How... how about if you take the room and I sleep in the truck? I don't want to be seen in a hotel."

He nodded and fell silent while he navigated the big vehicle expertly through the city traffic. At length, he steered the truck into the parking lot of a freight depot. "Better get in the sleeper again," he advised. "Gonna be unloading for a while."

I obeyed, and perched on the bench seat in the sleeper as he backed the trailer into place. He got out, and thumps and bumps signalled that the unloading process was under way.

When Dave climbed back into the cab, he was smiling. "Made a deal to leave the trailer here. That'll be easier."

"Dave, you don't need to do this..."

"I know." He fired up the engine again and pulled out.

The next morning, a rap on the driver's door woke me out of a sodden slumber. I jerked upright with a moment's disorientation. Awareness returned at the sound of Dave's voice. "Jane, you decent?"

"Yeah." I crawled stiffly out of the berth, tugging at the clothes I'd slept in.

Dave poked his head in, accompanied by the smell of shampoo and shaving cream. He looked like an entirely different man, clean-shaven and wearing a clean T-shirt and better-fitting jeans, his wet hair slicked into tidy waves against his head.

I was rubbing the grit out of my eyes when he spoke. "Didn't check out yet. Thought you might want a shower."

The thought of a hot shower beckoned like a little slice of heaven. "Ooh..." I tamped down the desire. "I better not. The longer I stay hidden, the better."

He eyed me sympathetically. "I could let you in the back door. You could wear this. Put the hood up." He held out a jacket.

"Dave, you're a prince."

He reddened and backed out of the cab. "Watch for me at the back door," he said gruffly.

I slipped on the oversized jacket and pulled up the hood. In a few minutes, the back door of the hotel opened and Dave waved. I grabbed my backpack and scampered across the parking lot, my heart pounding foolishly. Who the heck was going to see me and recognize me? Jeez, what a moron.

I breathed again when the door of the hotel room closed behind me.

When I emerged from the steamy bathroom feeling human again, I discovered that Dave had ordered room service. There was a plate of bacon and eggs, but he'd also ordered a fruit cup and some yogurt.

"Thought you might want that," he muttered when I thanked him profusely. "Seemed like a girl thing."

I tried to pay him, but he wouldn't accept anything. After a short wrangle, I gave up.

I let out a deep sigh as we pulled away from the hotel. I couldn't believe my luck in finding an ally like Dave. Even Hellhound wouldn't have been able to help me this much. I wondered if Kane would be watching him in case I made contact. My heart lurched at the thought.

By eleven A.M., we were parked in a quiet semi-residential area across from a low, institutional-looking building. Dave's eyebrows rose. "A nursing home? What're you gonna do in there?"

"I have to see my aunt. I just have to ask her a few questions. Then..." I scrubbed my hands over my face, trying to summon up some usable plan. "I don't know. I'll figure something out."

I perched on the edge of the seat, scanning the building, the parking lot, and as much of the grounds as I could see.

What if Kane was lying in wait for me? Or what if he had someone else in place, someone I didn't recognize? They'd be on me before I even knew it.

Dave frowned at me. "You think he might be here?"

I clasped trembling hands around my backpack. "Maybe. She's the only family I have left. She'd be easy to find."

"Want me to come in with you?"

"No. Thanks, Dave. This is where we part ways. The further away you are, the safer it is for you. In fact," I hesitated, trying to phrase this right. "Don't tell anybody you saw me. And if anybody asks you directly, tell them I threatened you at gunpoint and forced you to drive me."

"What?" He gaped at me. "No!"

"I'm sure it won't happen. But if it does, that's what you tell them, okay?"

"No! I won't lie and get you in trouble with the law!"

"Dave, if it comes to that, it'll be the least of my worries." I surveyed the area one last time and reached for the door handle. "Thanks again. Take care."

"Wait!" He dug into his pocket. "Here." He thrust a crumpled handful of bills at me.

"Dave, thanks, but I have money."

"Not enough to get you by. I saw your wallet."

"No, really, I'm fine." I gently pushed his hand away. "Thanks anyway."

He frowned and dug into his pocket again. "Take this then." He handed me a dog-eared business card. "You call me if you ever need help."

My heart swelled. "Thanks, Dave." I impulsively leaned over and kissed him on the cheek. "You're a great guy. Now get out of here." I opened the door and swung down from the cab before I could have second thoughts.

I scurried into the nursing home, trying to look in all directions at once. The receptionist eyed me disapprovingly, and I sent a silent thanks to Dave for my shower that morning. At least I looked more or less presentable.

"I'm here to see Minnie Kelly."

"And you are?"

"I'm her niece." I resisted the urge to glance around and whisper. "Aydan Kelly."

"This way."

Sweating already in the overheated air, I followed the nurse's bulging posterior down the hallway. The decor was Early Grim, nicely rendered in shades of olive and grey. I tried not to shudder at the smell of over-boiled vegetables and antiseptic as we passed the dining room, where several elderly people already hunched over tables. A bullet to the brain didn't seem like such a bad thing anymore.

The nurse halted outside a half-open door and turned to me. "She's almost blind, and we're not sure her mind is completely sound. She has good days and bad days. She has lunch in half an hour, so I hope you'll keep it short."

I blew out a breath through my teeth as she marched away. Yep, a bullet was looking better all the time. A shudder of claustrophobia shook me.

I took another deep breath and tapped on the door as I stepped into the room. The stringy woman in the bed started and gazed slightly to the left of the door. "Who's there?"

"It's Aydan, your niece."

"Who?"

"Aydan Kelly. Gordon and Nola's daughter."

"Gordon? Is he getting into trouble with Roger again? Those two are incorrigible."

"No, Aunt Minnie, Gordon's dead. Dad and Uncle Roger are both dead."

"You wicked girl, what a vicious lie! Why would you say such a thing?"

I pulled a chair up beside her bed and sat. "I'm sorry, Aunt Minnie, Uncle Roger's been gone for three years. You remember, he had a heart attack?"

"That's a lie! Roger! Roger, come here this instant! Where is that man? Always involved in some foolishness." She hoisted herself up in the bed, her eyes focused somewhere in the corner of the room. I couldn't help twitching when she suddenly jerked around, staring directly at me. "You're covering up for him, aren't you? What is he up to? Spit it out, child!"

"No, Aunt Minnie..."

"Who did you say you were?"

I blew out a breath of tense frustration. "Aydan. Gordon and Nola's daughter."

She peered into my face from close range, turning her head slightly to the side in an unsettling fashion. "No, you're not. You're far too old. Aydan is just a girl."

"I was. I turned forty-seven a couple of months ago. Time gets on."

"Who are you? Stop lying to me."

I sank my aching head into my hands. Time for a new tack. "I'm sorry. You're right. I was just pretending to be Aydan. I'd like to talk about her, though."

"Why?" Her suspicious glare might have been more effective if it hadn't been directed over my right shoulder.

"I'm a friend of hers... her mother's," I corrected myself. "My daughter goes to school with Aydan."

"Oh." She subsided onto the pillows.

"Have you ever met that man who visits Aydan to do some kind of tests? I think his name is Sam Kraus."

"Santa Claus." Minnie chuckled. "She calls him Santa Claus. I can't imagine why. She's old enough to know there's no such thing, and he's a skinny little runt."

"Do you know what the tests are for?"

"I haven't a clue. Gordon says the child is gifted, whatever that means. I was shocked when he stopped farming to take that government job. He says he's making sure Aydan has a future. What's wrong with being a farmer's wife? I'd love to be a farmer's wife. I can't imagine what I was thinking, marrying a Navy man."

"What do you suppose he meant... means by Aydan's future?"

"I'm sure I don't know. But he dotes on that child. He takes her everywhere with him, and never lets her out of his sight. And do you know..." She leaned forward confidentially. "He taught her to shoot a gun. A gun! Can you imagine? What is the world coming to?"

"Why would he do that?"

"Heaven only knows."

"Minnie, do you remember when Nola died?" I held my breath.

"Heavens, yes, it was just last year. What a terrible thing. That poor child, left without a mother. And it nearly killed Gordon, too. I honestly think he would have taken his own life if he didn't have Aydan to take care of."

I managed to speak around the thickness in my throat. "What happened?"

"A car accident. She drove off the road, and the car exploded when it hit an embankment. Her body was burned beyond recognition." She wiped her eyes delicately. "So terribly sad."

"Did anybody see what happened?

"No, there was a driver several miles behind her, but by the time he arrived, the car was completely in flames." She squinted at me. "Who did you say you were?"

"A friend of Nola's."

"Oh, yes. Nola. What a lovely woman. So sad."

"Do you remember when Gordon died?"

"Gordon isn't dead. You must be thinking of Gordon Senior, dear."

I massaged my aching temples. "I guess I was. Sorry. What is Gordon doing these days?"

"He's still working for the government."

"What does he do?"

"Something with the Department of Agriculture, he says. Frankly, I have my doubts." She leaned forward again, her blind eyes alight. "I would never spread gossip, but... I believe he may be doing something... unsavoury."

My heart sped up. Finally, I was getting somewhere. "Unsavoury, how?"

"I'm sure I don't know. I wouldn't spread rumours." Something about the prim set of her mouth made me think she sure as hell would. I'd known Aunt Minnie for a long time.

I leaned forward to whisper. "I heard he wasn't really working for the Department of Agriculture at all."

Minnie leaned avidly in my direction. "He's not!"

"Really!" I didn't have to feign breathless interest. "What's he doing?"

"I think he's a smuggler!"

Shit. Now she was just making things up. I tried to hide my disappointment.

"Really? Why?"

"I caught him unpacking his briefcase one day when he'd been away on what he called 'business'." She paused dramatically. "There was a gun in his briefcase! Why would he need that if he wasn't doing something shady?"

A very good question indeed.

I started as the nurse bustled into the room without knocking. "I'm sorry, but I'll have to ask you to end your visit now. Minnie tires easily, and we have to get her to the dining room." She briskly unfolded the wheelchair from the corner of the room and wheeled it next to the bed. "Come on, dearie, let's take you to the toidy, and then we'll go for din-din."

Gag me.

I fled.

CHAPTER 14

I sucked in the fresh air with relief when I finally stepped out of the gloomy reception area and into the sunshine. I sank down on a bench next to the door and dropped my backpack between my feet so I could massage my temples with both hands. All that effort for a few dubious shreds of gossip.

What the hell was I going to do now? If the information I needed still existed at all, it was probably only accessible through the Sirius network. That was eight hundred miles away, and I seriously doubted I'd be welcomed back with open arms.

I jerked upright at the sound of approaching feet and let out a long breath when I realized who it was. "Dave! I thought you were leaving."

He sat on the bench beside me and surveyed my face. "Didn't go well?"

"No."

I sank my head into my hands again and replayed what I knew. Dad had carried a gun. On "business". Protecting my future. And he'd died of a heart attack, just like Robert. But that had been ten years ago. Surely it was coincidence. Mom killed in a fiery car crash, her body unidentifiable. Cars don't just catch fire and explode when they hit something. That only happens in the movies. And Uncle Roger had died of a heart attack, too...

No, now I was just reaching. Lots of people die of heart attacks. Please, God, tell me I'm just reaching.

I shook myself and sat up straight. I still had boxes of Dad's old farm records and business papers I'd never had the heart to go through. I'd need to go home and dig through them to see if they contained any clues.

But before I did that, I needed to know if Kane was on my trail. By now he might have questioned Nichele and told her I was missing. She probably would've heard from Dante, too. I winced. Try not to think about that.

Maybe Nichele could tell me what was going on, pump Kane for information in the guise of a concerned friend.

Dave's voice interrupted my cogitations. "What now?"

"Now, I make a phone call."

Dave loitered outside the booth while I dialled Nichele's business line, thankful for her toll-free number.

"Nichele Brown."

For a change, I passed up the chance to tease her about the crisp business voice she adopted for her stable of well-heeled clients. I cut to the chase instead.

"Nichele, it's Aydan."

"Hold on."

"Wait!"

Too late. Vapid on-hold music warbled in my ear.

Seconds later, she was back, whispering into the phone. "Aydan, I've been trying and trying to call you. Where are you?"

"In the wind. Nichele-"

"Aydan, you've got to help me, I'm in so much trouble!" Coldness squeezed my heart. Nichele never admitted she was in trouble.

"What's wrong?"

"James."

"Oh, God. What is it?"

"Aydan, he's going to kill me." Her voice came out in a whimper, and fear flooded me. Nichele never whimpered.

"Call the police, Nichele. Right away!"

"I can't. He'll kill me." She drew in a ragged breath. "He must have hacked into my laptop when I took him home. And then he hit me when I confronted him..."

"Goddammit, Nichele, run! Get out of there."

"I can't. He's watching me. He followed me to work today..."

Silence on the line made my heart skip a beat. "Nichele!" I hissed. "Nichele, are you okay?"

When she spoke again, it was in a rapid whisper. "He's drained all my clients' assets into an offshore account and set it up to look like I did it. I saw more transfers today, and I bet he's laundering money through there, too. I'll go to jail if it comes to light. And he swore he'd kill me if I went to the police. Aydan, I'm so screwed!"

"Hang on, Nichele. We'll figure it out. Just keep doing as he says. Stay safe. It'll be okay."

"Don't tell anybody! Promise you won't tell a soul! If James finds out I told..."

"I won't tell anybody, Nichele. We can fix this. It'll be okay," I lied, trying to sound confident.

"But, Aydan, where are you? What are we going to do?"

"We'll figure it out. I'm coming. Just hang on. Don't worry."

"Okay." Her voice was a tiny squeak.

I hung up and beat my head against the side of the phone

booth. It took a moment before I realized Dave was talking to me. "Jane! Jane, what's wrong?"

I looked into his worried face and gulped. "Dave, I need to ask you a huge favour."

Back in the truck, Dave continued the argument we'd begun on the sidewalk. "That's nuts. You just got away."

"I know, but she's my best friend, and he's a dangerous sonuvabitch. He said he'd kill her, and I believe it."

"And your ex will kill you."

"My ex looks like Mother Theresa next to this guy. I've got to get back to Calgary."

"And do what?" Dave demanded. "This is dangerous. Call the police. That's what they're there for."

"Dave, he'll kill her if the police go anywhere near her. And they wouldn't do anything about this anyway. If it was a violent crime in progress or something, they'd respond, but this'll just go through their tips line. Just another thing they might get around to checking out in their spare time between real calls."

"Call them anyway," he argued. "Let them decide."

"I don't dare. And I kind of... can't... anyway."

If Kane was looking for me, he'd have alerted the police. I really didn't want to draw attention to myself at the moment, and I really didn't want to take a chance on endangering Nichele. I racked my brain for a better solution.

A fast-moving black car caught my eye as I stared out the windshield, and adrenaline shot through me. I twisted in the seat to see another black ghost car speeding toward us from the opposite direction.

"Shit!" I dove into the sleeper and huddled on the bench.

Dave's gaze bounced between the action outside and my face. "Thought you said you weren't running from the cops."

"Those aren't cops."

"Stay back there." The big diesel rumbled to life, and he pulled away slowly. "Two guys checking out that phone booth and looking around," he reported. He guided the truck around a corner and slowed. "Road block. Get inside the bathroom. Wait'll I give you the all-clear."

I ducked into the tiny bathroom as the truck stopped. I could hear Dave's side of the conversation, but the voice from outside was blurred by the rumble of the engine.

"Nope. No, I'd remember her."

"Yeah? Jeez, you wouldn't think so."

"Nope."

"...'Kay, will do. Thanks."

The truck began to move again. After several minutes of driving and a lot of turns, the movement stopped and the driver's door slammed. The cab rocked as Dave climbed down. I heard the thump and clink of chains from behind the sleeper, and then movement and the sound of the driver's door indicated Dave's return.

"You can come out now."

I opened the door cautiously, and my heart plummeted at the sight of Dave's hard face. A heavy iron bar slapped against his palm.

"So, Aydan Kelly, let's talk," he said.

"Dave, I'm sorry, I-"

"They said they were cops. They said you were armed and dangerous," he interrupted. The bar described a short arc into his palm again.

I blew out a long breath, attempting calm while my heart tried to escape through my chest. "I'm armed. Not dangerous. Especially not to you."

"Show me your weapon." His knuckles whitened on the bar as I reached down. "Slow."

I carefully grasped the denim just below my knee and pulled up the leg of my jeans. His face paled at the sight of the small gun snuggled in its holster at my ankle.

"Hand it over."

I let the pant leg slide down and straightened slowly. "I'm sorry, Dave, I can't do that."

"Then we got a problem."

"Yeah." I swallowed the quaver in my voice. "You have to decide if you're going to beat the shit out of me or not. Because I won't fight back. I won't shoot you."

"Bull." He stepped closer and shifted to a two-handed grip on the end of the bar. "They said you killed four men. And injured two others."

My knees threatened to give way, and I tried to hold my voice steady. "That's true, but-"

I barely had time to dodge the blow. The bar glanced off my upflung arm and slammed into the door frame beside me. Thank God it was too tight a space for him to get a good backswing. The pain dropped me to my knees.

"It's not the whole story!" I hugged my arm and gazed up at his tense face through watering eyes. "Dave, please!"

I jerked back and toppled against the wall as the bar whistled by again. "Dave, please, just let me go!"

He stood with his feet planted apart, blocking my escape. The bar shook in his hands as he glared down at me, panting. "You got a gun. You just gonna let me beat you up?"

"No, I'm going to beg you to stop and try to get away. But I won't hurt you."

I cradled my damaged arm, pain shooting up to my

shoulder. God, maybe it was broken. I blinked away tears and tried again. My voice came out ragged and desperate. "Please, Dave."

"You just said you killed four guys."

"Will you let me explain?"

The muscles rippled in his forearms as he shifted his white-knuckled grasp on the iron. "Talk."

"The first two men kidnapped me. They beat and tortured me. They were trying to shoot me when I killed them. The third man was trying to rape me while four of his friends held me down. The last man abducted me and took me inside a house and set the house on fire. He was about to kill an innocent man when I shot him."

Dave's eyes widened and his jaw dropped as I babbled.

"What..." The bar drooped and he swallowed audibly. "What about the two you injured?" His voice was a hoarse whisper.

"There were five of them. They'd just shot somebody I..." I gulped as the memory rose up again. "...I cared about. A lot. At the time. I hit one in the face and broke his cheekbone and dislocated another one's knee before they took me down."

Dave staggered back and dropped into the passenger's seat, staring at me. "What the hell...? Heck, I mean. What...?" He stared blankly at the bar in his hands before dropping it as if it had burned him. "Jane... I mean, Aydan, I'm sorry, I..."

"It's okay, Dave, I'll just go now. Remember, if anybody asks, I held you at gunpoint." I dragged myself to my feet.

"Wait!" The hand he placed on my arm was shaking almost as much as I was. "Why are they looking for you? Are these guys going to..." his Adam's apple bobbed as he swallowed, "...rape you and torture you? If they catch you?"

"No, they'll probably just shoot me. I need to get out of here. You'll be safe when I'm gone."

"Will you kill them?"

"No. They're the good guys." I grabbed my backpack with my uninjured hand and tottered forward.

Dave pushed himself to his feet with a sharp gasp, clutching his back. Then he straightened slowly, blocking my way. "You can't go out there."

"I have to." I tried to slip by him, but he grasped me firmly by the shoulders and pushed me down into the passenger's seat, wincing as he bent.

"You need help," he said. "I'll get you out of here."

"Dave, thanks, but you can't." Concern stabbed me at the sight of his grimace. "Are you okay?"

"Yeah. Put my back out, swinging that bar. Stupid." He returned to his verbal campaign. "You can't do it yourself. You can't get off the island."

"I'll find a way."

He frowned at me. "You can only go by air or ferry. They'll catch you in airport security, and there are cameras in the ferry terminals."

"Shit, there are?"

"Yeah."

I squirmed, trying to think of another alternative. "I could hire a boat privately."

"You don't have enough money."

I eyed him hopefully. "You offered to lend me some."

He snorted. "Deal's off. You're stuck. You need me."

"Dave!" I made a fist in my hair and tugged in sheer frustration. "You don't get it. This is dangerous shit. You could end up in jail, or dead, if you get caught in the crossfire. I'm just going to go. I'll figure something out."

I reached for the door handle, but he dropped into the driver's seat with a grunt of pain and slammed the truck into gear. "You gonna jump out of a moving vehicle?"

I sighed. "It wouldn't be the first time."

He shot an avid glance in my direction. "What happened that time?" When I remained silent, he added, "You owe me."

I groaned. "Dave, you're right, I owe you big-time, but I can't tell you anything."

He took the exit for the Pat Bay Highway and studied me out of the corner of his eye while he drove. "You're some kinda big-time spy. Like James Bond or something." He glanced over. "That's why you said your name was Jane. Jane Bond, right?"

"No." I studied the purpling bruise on my forearm and slowly flexed my fingers. Good, not broken after all. The pain was subsiding into a throbbing ache.

"Look," he said. "I'm gonna help you whether you want it or not. So you might as well tell me what's happening."

"Dave, you don't know what you're getting into. Just drop me off and forget you ever saw me."

"Are you kidding?" He shot me a grin, his face alight. "Guns and black cars and Jane Bond? This is the coolest thing that's ever happened to me."

CHAPTER 15

I clasped my aching head. “Dave...”

“Who were those guys? Why are they trying to kill you?”

“I don’t know if they’re trying to kill me or not. They might just have orders to capture me.”

“Why?”

“I can’t tell you.”

“You said your ex was chasing you.”

“Yeah, that, too.”

“Those guys are his friends?”

“Co-workers, probably.”

He threw a frown in my direction. “They really cops?”

“Yeah. Kind of.”

“You said you weren’t running from the cops.”

I scrubbed my hands over my face. “I’m not. Not exactly.”

“Exactly what, then?”

“You’re not going to let this rest, are you?”

“Heck, no.” He grinned at me again. “We got another couple hours before we get back to the mainland. And another twelve hours tomorrow on the way back to Calgary.”

I slumped in the seat and dropped my head back against the headrest. “Shit. Okay. You win.” I tried to organize a story that would answer his questions without telling him anything secret.

"I'm... a witness. They need me for a case. I've been working with them, but I just found out that the guy I've been working with..."

"Your ex?" he interrupted.

"Yeah, kind of. We... I liked him, and I thought he liked me, but I just found out he killed my husband, and he's been lying to me all this time."

"*He killed your husband?*" Dave gaped at me, his eyes round, and I grabbed for the steering wheel as the truck swerved. He jerked his gaze back to the road, blinking rapidly. "But you said he was a cop."

"He said my husband was a criminal and he had to kill him."

"Was he?"

"I..." Somehow, I'd never questioned what Kane had told me. What if he'd been lying about that, too? "I honestly don't know."

"So you think he might kill you, too?"

"He wouldn't have, before. Well, I don't think so, anyway. But he might have orders to now."

"But you said they needed you. You're their witness."

I sighed. "It's complicated. They might have decided they don't need me that badly anymore."

He gave me a sympathetic glance. "That why you ran?"

"No. But..." I swallowed hard. "I think they might have killed the rest of my family, too. I have to know."

"*What?*" He was gaping at me again.

"Dave! Maybe you should pull over."

He gave his head a quick shake and did exactly that, slowing the truck to halt at the side of the road.

"Why in hel... sorry, heck, would they kill your whole

family?" he demanded.

"I don't know, Dave, but I really need to find out. I thought Aunt Minnie might be able to tell me something. She's the only relative I have left. But she was too out of it." I wrapped my arms around myself as a horrifying thought hit me. "Oh, God, I hope they don't kill her, too. She's just a helpless old lady."

Dave's face paled. "They wouldn't let guys with guns into a nursing home."

"They wouldn't use guns. They'd make it look like a heart attack. That's how they killed Robert. And maybe my dad, too."

"Who *are* these guys?" He stared at me. "Cops don't get orders to kill people. And they don't kill them with fake heart attacks. These guys are spies, aren't they? Or mob?" His face went even paler. "And you're running from them..."

"That's why I was trying to get you to butt out. Just go back to your life and forget this ever happened. You'll be safe as long as you don't get caught with me." I reached for the door handle, but he grabbed my hand.

"But what about you?"

I blew out a long sigh. "They're going to kill me anyway, sooner or later. I know too much. I'd just really, really like to know the truth about this before I die. And I need to get back to Calgary and see if I can help Nichele."

"Then I'll take you." He put the truck into gear again and pulled away, his scowl focused on the road.

"Dave..."

"No dice. That's the way it's gonna be."

I gave in. "Thanks," I whispered.

By the time we safely navigated the ferry and landed on the mainland, I'd come up with a desperate idea. I checked my watch. Nearly four o'clock. That would be almost five o'clock in Alberta. Spider would be getting off work soon.

I rolled my head and shoulders, trying to release the aching tension before I turned to Dave. "I need to find an internet cafe or a library or something."

He shot me a quick glance, then turned back to concentrate on driving. "What're you going to do?"

"I'm going to see if I can get in touch with a friend on the internet."

"Sure you want to take the chance?"

"No. But I have to."

He scowled. "Those guys were on that phone booth like white on rice. They'll be watching email for sure."

"I'm not going to use email."

His eyes widened. "You some kind of hacker?"

"Hell, no. I couldn't hack my way out of a paper bag. But I have an idea that just might work."

We stopped at the visitor's centre for directions, and pulled up in front of an internet cafe about half an hour later.

I took a deep breath and met Dave's worried eyes. "Wish me luck." I had the door open before another thought hit me. "If you see me leaving with anybody, or if anything happens to me, just drive away and forget you ever saw me. You don't want to get involved in this."

"But..."

"Really, Dave. I mean it. Promise me, okay?"

He scowled and his lips pressed into a thin line.

I tugged a couple of handfuls of my hair in pure frustration. "Dave, I really need you to do this. I really need to know you'll stay safe. Please?"

The silence lengthened. When he spoke at last, his voice was steady, but his faded eyes were imploring. "Look, I'm just a fat, middle-aged loser with a shi... crap job and a family that doesn't care whether I live or die as long as the support cheques keep coming. I wasn't kidding when I said this was the coolest thing that ever happened to me." He flushed and dropped his eyes. "Just let me help, okay?"

I took his hand in both of my own. "Dave, you're not a loser, you're an amazing guy. You've already saved my life. I don't want it to cost you yours."

He met my eyes. "My decision to make. Get going."

I slumped in defeat. "Okay. But Dave, don't be a hero. A live friend is better than a dead hero any day."

He nodded, and I climbed down from the truck resisting the urge to beat my head against the door. I'd seen the gleam in his eyes. He was going to be a fucking hero.

And the worst part was, I needed one.

Inside, I paid cash for my access time and got settled at a computer to search out the World of Warcraft site. I cursed my lack of foresight in only half-listening to Spider's long-winded descriptions of the game and its interface. At least I knew he used 'Spider' as his screen name, and I knew his character was a night elf, whatever that was.

On the site, I rapidly skimmed the online tutorial, focusing on the chat features. Shit, this was going to take some time. I glanced around, heart thumping, before concentrating in earnest. Thank God they offered a thirty-day free trial. Otherwise, Kane could have nailed me by my credit card activity the instant I bought the membership.

I set up a fraudulent account and debated for too-long seconds over a screen name, then impatiently clicked through the character setup, creating a human female with long red hair. None of the rest of it made much sense, but I only needed to get into the game. Please God, let Spider be playing tonight.

When I completed the setup, my heart sank as I stared at the complicated interface. Realm. That was it. What the hell was the name of the realm Spider was always babbling about? Maybe it didn't matter.

The name of the realm occurred to me just as I discovered how to look for other players online. A surge of triumph filled me when I recognized Spider's screen name. Thank God. I scanned the chat interface. Whisper. There it was.

"Pssst. Spider."

The chat screen scrolled. "who r u?"

"Look at my character. From Dog Star." Come on, Spider, figure it out.

"OMG! where r u??? r u ok??"

"Hiding. I'm fine."

"r u crazy?? dept-wide alert for u dead or alive."

"Need your help."

"i'll call K."

"NO!!!"

"y not? he'll help."

"NO. He killed my husband."

The data stream halted, and I imagined Spider's horrified expression. After a few seconds, another message came through. "WHAT!! pls repeat."

"He killed my husband."

"no way."

"He told me himself."

The scrolling text stopped again. Then, "what do u need?"

I paused, thinking. I really didn't want to name names, just in case. The text window scrolled as Spider demanded my attention.

"r u there? r u there?"

"I'm here." I hesitated over the keyboard, then added, "I was with N on Tuesday night when K came to get me. Do you know who N is?"

"yes"

I breathed a sigh of relief. "N is in danger. She'll be killed if the police get involved. Can you help her?"

Jesus, speak of the devil. Movement caught my eye as two uniformed police officers strode in, scanning the patrons. I hunched down behind the computer screen, praying they wouldn't see me.

I ignored Spider's text response and rapidly logged off, trembling. As I cleared the cache, the officers moved past me to speak to the kid behind the counter. Maybe they weren't looking for me at all.

I stood and meandered in the general direction of the door, forcing myself to stop and examine a display of coffee mugs on the way. Trying not to jitter from foot to foot, I casually lifted one to check the price, then replaced it and made my way out the door.

Then I hustled back to Dave's truck, my bastion of safety. He eyed me with alarm when I scrambled up into the cab. "Those cops looking for you?"

"I don't think so." I took a few deep breaths, trying to stop shaking. "But let's get the hell out of here anyway."

"Did it work?" Dave demanded as we pulled away.

"Yes. I made contact."

"So did you get help?"

"I hope so. But I had to run before I knew for sure. I'll

have to check back with him later." I shot a glance behind us. "At a different cafe."

"Okay." He frowned. "You're still shaking."

"I'm just hungry. I missed lunch."

"Oh." He shifted in his seat and rubbed the back of his neck, not meeting my eyes. "Do you... uh, want to eat something a little nicer tonight? I'll get another hotel room, and we can get room service."

"Thanks, Dave, but I don't want to take the chance," I said. "And anyway, it's too expensive."

"I don't mind," he said quickly. His eyes stayed glued to the road, and a flush climbed his neck. "I owe you, for hitting you. I'm really sorry."

"It's okay, you were just scared. I'd probably have done the same thing in your place."

"I feel bad, though. Let me buy you a nice dinner."

I opened my mouth to argue, but changed my mind. I really couldn't face another greasy meal. "Thanks, Dave. That would be great."

He flushed and nodded, smiling.

Once again I sneaked in the back door of the hotel, enveloped in his hooded jacket. I gobbled a crisp, fresh chef's salad with a delicious garlic baguette, and then leaned back in the chair with a long sigh, stretching out my legs.

The small room was dim and cozy, the heavy draperies drawn, and the peace and safety soaked into my bones and made my eyelids droop.

Dave's quiet voice startled me out of a semi-doze. "Why don't you lie down? You look wiped."

I roused myself and sat up. "Thanks, but I better not." I

checked my watch. "Do you think we can find another internet cafe?"

"Yeah." He held out the jacket, and I shrugged into it again. "Hold on, I'll scout the halls first," he told me, and ducked out the door. He was back within seconds, giving me a thumbs-up, and I scuttled back out to the truck.

Parked near another cafe, I scanned the surrounding area before reaching for the door handle. Dave reached out to stop me. "Wait. Do you have a cell phone? I could just call you if the police show up or if anything weird happens."

"No, I don't have one." I didn't bother to explain why. "It's okay, I won't be long."

I climbed down and made my way inside, finding a table that faced the door. Back in the World of Warcraft interface, I located Spider again and engaged the whisper mode.

"Spider."

"r u ok?"

"Fine. Did you find out anything about N?"

"gone. left work early today, not home, not answering cell. where r u & what r u doing? S thinks ur rogue."

He would. That suspicious bastard. I sighed. I was totally screwed if Stemp decided I'd turned to the dark side. He'd have me shot, no questions asked. At least Spider didn't seem inclined to turn me in. Yet.

"I'm not. I'd never do that. You know that." At least I hoped he knew it.

"i know."

I blew out a breath of relief. Thank God.

"what r u doing tho?" he persisted.

"Trying to save N. Trying to find info about my family." I pressed Send, and then berated myself for telling him that. Then again, somebody had obviously known I was in

Victoria. Somehow. Hmmm.

I typed again. “Was N’s phone bugged?”

“yes.”

That explained a lot. I typed again. “Who else is bugged?”

“everybody. me, K, N, dog from hell.”

Shit. I blew out a sigh. On the upside, at least he was up to speed with Nichele’s situation. Maybe I’d better confirm that...

“Then you know what’s going on with N.”

“yes.”

“Can you save her?”

“i’ll try.”

“Thanks, Spider.” I shot a tense glance around the quiet cafe. I felt like I had a glowing target painted on my back. Nerves seized me.

“Got to go,” I typed.

“WAIT!!!”

“What?”

“how can i contact u?”

“You can’t. Over & out.”

I logged off, cleared the cache, and got out of there.

Dave tried to talk me into sleeping in the hotel room, but I eventually convinced him I’d be safer in the truck. I didn’t know if that was actually the case or not, but I could tell his back was hurting, and it seemed to me the hotel bed was probably better for him than the narrow berth in the sleeper.

Besides, I didn’t feel right about making him sleep in the truck when he was paying for a hotel, and I wasn’t about to propose sharing the room.

CHAPTER 16

The next morning, we hit the road loaded and started the long drive back to Calgary. We chatted off and on, and I tried to encourage him to talk as much as possible. The more he talked about himself, the less I had to tell him.

After I'd deflected his questions for the umpteenth time, he glanced over at me, his brow furrowed.

"You really don't want to tell me anything about yourself, do you?" he asked point-blank.

I sighed. "No, not really. Sorry. The less you know, the safer we both are."

"I knew it. You are a spy."

I clutched my head. "No, Dave."

He gave me a conspiratorial smile and went back to watching the highway. But at least he stopped asking personal questions.

We were on the home stretch when an idea struck me. It was after five o'clock. Maybe Spider had news. And if he still hadn't managed to find Nichele, I might be able to approach the problem from a different angle.

I turned to Dave. "Can we go into Canmore for a few minutes?"

He frowned over at me. "Yeah, as long it doesn't take too long. I gotta have this load in by eight."

"How much time do I have?"

He checked his watch and returned his attention to the road. "Half an hour, tops. You got a plan?"

"Maybe."

"What do you want to do?"

"Find another internet cafe."

After a short stop at the visitor information centre, I gained a new respect for Dave's driving ability as he manoeuvred the huge truck around the cramped streets. When we pulled up near the cafe, he shot me a worried glance. "What are you going to do this time?"

"Same thing." I warily surveyed the parking lot. "Back in a flash."

Spider was in the game again, and I heaved a sigh of relief.

"Spider."

"where r u?"

I knew if he really wanted to know where I was, he'd trace my IP address, so I ignored the question and typed, "Any news on N?"

"no. can't find her."

I swore quietly, trying not to attract attention. Time for Plan B. I typed, "Need to see dog from hell."

"when & where?"

"Tonight, Hotel Village, eleven o'clock. Don't tell anyone we're meeting."

"ok."

"Thanks, Spider. Over & out."

I hoped Spider would have more luck convincing Hellhound to talk to me than I'd had. And I hoped Hellhound would be willing to help me if he did show up.

Back in the truck, I faced Dave's expectant expression.

"I'm meeting my friend tonight," I told him with more confidence than I felt. "I think he'll be able to help me."

"What's the plan?" Dave asked.

I hesitated.

"Come on, Aydan," he cajoled. "Two heads are better than one, right?"

I sighed. "There isn't a plan. Yet."

"Thought you said you talked to your friend."

"No, I talked to a different friend who's going to get a message to him."

His bushy eyebrows met. "So you don't even know if he's coming."

"He'll come."

Apparently I didn't sound any more convinced than I truly was. Dave's scowl deepened.

"You sure he'll be able to help you if he does show up?"

"Yeah. The guy who kidnapped Nichele is his brother. He might know where to start looking."

Dave jerked back in his seat. "Aydan, that's nuts! You're gonna trust this guy? When it's his own brother?"

"Don't worry," I reassured him. "He'd love to see his brother back behind bars."

"*Back* behind bars," Dave said. "So you're gonna go looking for a guy you already know is a dangerous criminal. With the guy's brother for backup."

"No, I'm not going to involve Arnie at all," I told him. "I just want him to point me in the right direction. I don't want to drag him into this."

Dave blew out a heavy breath. "So you're gonna go by yourself. Aydan, that's nuts. I'll go with you. Got a layover for the weekend in Calgary anyway."

"No, Dave, this is the part where it gets really dangerous.

You need to get clear."

"Come on, I want to help."

"I know, and I appreciate it. But I'll be fine."

He continued to argue off and on while we drove. When the unloading was finally complete, he turned to me again in the parking lot at the freight depot. "Look, you're gonna need all the help you can get."

"I really just need you to drop me off."

"Yeah, I'll take you there, but..."

"Thanks, Dave. Let's go. I have to be there at eleven."

He unhitched the trailer and left it in the lot before pulling out to thread the highway tractor nimbly through the light evening traffic, frowning.

In the parking lot at Hotel Village, I spotted Hellhound immediately. He lounged against his Harley Fatboy, the black beast on the back of his leather jacket snarling in the glow of the streetlights.

"Thanks, Dave!" I reached over to squeeze his hand. "I couldn't have done this without you. Take care."

I grabbed my backpack and swung out of the cab before he could protest.

Hellhound turned to give me a quizzical look as I approached, and I jumped at the sound of Dave's voice from behind me.

"*This* is your friend?"

I whirled to see the disgust written plainly on his face.

Shit. Bikers and truckers. Just like oil and water.

"Dave, thanks for all you've done, but you should get going now," I said without much hope.

Hellhound eyed Dave expressionlessly. The streetlights didn't flatter his ugly, bearded face. The leather jacket creaked as his bulky shoulders flexed. "What's up, darlin'?"

he rasped. "I heard ya got a problem. This it?"

"No, Dave's part of the solution. I'd probably be dead if not for him."

"Oh." Hellhound's posture relaxed, and he extended his hand to Dave. "Arnie Helmand. Thanks for lookin' after Aydan."

"Dave Shore." Dave warily shook Hellhound's hand.

"What now, darlin'?" Hellhound asked, turning to me.

"Now Dave leaves, and you and I have a talk."

"Oh." Hellhound eyed me with poorly concealed trepidation.

"Look, does he know the whole story?" Dave broke in.

"Dave, Arnie knows more of the story than you do. But thanks for all you've done. You need to get going now."

"You shouldn't do this alone... he began.

"Dave..." I stopped, realizing the futility of arguing. "Thanks, Dave," I said instead. "Right now, I need you to go so I can talk with Arnie, but I'll hang onto your card and call you before I do anything, okay?"

"Promise," Dave growled, still eyeing Hellhound with mistrust.

"I promise," I lied guiltily. If lying was the only way to keep him safe, my conscience would just have to suck it up.

"Okay. You call me as soon as you're ready to move." Dave squeezed my hand, and limped reluctantly back to his truck. We watched him pull away before I turned to Hellhound.

"Now, darlin', ya know I warned ya," he muttered defensively.

"What?" I blinked at him. "What are you talking about?"

"We talked about this. I told ya not to get attached. We

agreed, no possessive, needy bullshit. Sorry you're upset, but that's the way it's gotta be." He was edging away.

"Whoa! Hold on, not so fast!" I grabbed his sleeve.

"Aw, come on, Aydan, don't make this ugly." He scuffed a boot at the pavement, not meeting my eyes. "I didn't wanna hurt ya, but..."

"Jesus, Arnie, you think I'm upset that you turned me down?"

"You chicks always get all bent outta shape when I don't call," he mumbled. "An' then you're pissed when I say I'm busy..."

"Hey!" I shook his arm. "Hello! Earth to Arnie!"

He jerked startled eyes to my face.

"Arnie, you know me better than that!" I grabbed him by the shoulders to give him a gentle shake, desperate to make him understand. "Jeez, you're talking to the one person on the planet that's more phobic about commitment than you are! You know damn well I don't want to get attached, to you or anybody else."

He gazed at me, apparently unconvinced. I bit back a hiss of frustration and tried again. "Look, we promised not to lie to each other. If you say you're busy, I'm not going to take it personally. I figure if you don't want to see me again, you'll tell me. Otherwise, I just assume we're good."

"Ya mean ya ain't mad?"

"Of course not, why would I be?"

He peered at me uncertainly in the dim light. "Ya said we hadta have a talk. When chicks say that, it's always fuckin' bad news."

"Arnie, you know I don't pull that shit. Just pretend I'm one of your guy friends."

He blew out a sigh as his shoulders relaxed. "Christ,

darlin', ya had me worried there. So we're good?"

"We're good. Same as always. What you see is what you get."

His old teasing smile came back. "I like the sound a' that, darlin', 'cause I ain't been gettin' any lately."

The tension drained out of my body. I didn't want to admit how much his friendship meant to me. Along with the benefits of that friendship. I leaned into him. "We'll have to see what we can do about that."

"Yeah." He pulled me closer and gave me the opportunity to compare his kissing technique with Dante's.

Oh. My.

He was definitely still in a class by himself. And it had been 'way too long since I'd sampled that class.

A few steamy minutes later, he pulled away, his eyes black in the dim light. "So what'd ya wanna talk about?" he asked hoarsely.

"Uh." I refocused with an effort. "Long story." I tugged him toward the buildings. "I don't want to be seen. I shouldn't have been standing out here so long."

"Coffee shop's still open." He jerked his chin in the direction of the hotel.

"No, let's stay out of sight. Have you seen James lately?" I asked as we headed for a darkened corner of the hotel.

He frowned. "Not for a coupla days. Why?"

"He beat Nichele up and said he was going to kill her..."

"Shit!"

Hellhound's yell rang out as I was jerked backward into the shadows. Something very hard ground into my back and a massive arm across my throat crushed me against the tall, muscular body behind me.

"What the fuck?" Hellhound rasped.

I took a shaky breath and pulled cautiously at the arm with both hands. I might as well have tried to wrestle a bronze statue. "Is that a gun in my back, or are you just really happy to see me?" I quavered.

"Don't do anything stupid, or I'll shoot you right now," Kane ground out.

"Ya ain't gonna shoot Aydan," Hellhound protested. He stared at Kane in consternation. "Ya said ya hadta talk to her. Ya said it was a fuckin' emergency. What the hell..."

"Time for you to go, Hellhound," Kane said. "Get on your bike and get out of here."

"I don't fuckin' think so," Hellhound retorted. "What the hell's goin' on?"

"Leave," Kane barked. "Now. That's an order."

Hellhound stiffened. "Come on, Cap, what the fuck?" he demanded.

"Arnie," I said quietly, feeling the tension in Kane's body. "Just do what he says."

"This is bullshit!" Hellhound snapped. "I ain't gonna-"

"Arnie, please, just go!" I widened my eyes at him, willing him to listen. "You don't want to get in the middle of this."

"In the middle a' what?" he asked. "Put the gun away, Cap, an' tell me what the hell's goin' on, an' then maybe I'll think about leavin'."

"I can't do that." Kane's voice was grim.

"What d'ya mean, ya can't? Ya ain't gonna shoot Aydan, so stop dickin' around."

"Arnie, if you push it, he'll shoot me. Believe it. Please, just go," I pleaded.

Hellhound shot an incredulous glance at us. His face darkened into a scowl. "Then he's gonna hafta shoot me, too," he growled.

Kane's grip tightened on my neck. "Arnie, you don't know what's happening. Get out of here, now. I'll explain later. Please."

"No."

I heard the faint but distinct sound of teeth grinding behind me. "Fine," Kane said. "Here's the deal, then. We're going to take a nice, casual walk through the hotel. If either of you makes a sudden move, I'll shoot Aydan. No matter how many witnesses there are. Clear?"

"But, Cap..." Arnie sounded lost.

"Move." Kane released his grip on my neck and nodded forward, his gun rock-steady in his hand. Arnie and I moved slowly in the direction he'd indicated.

When we approached the entrance, he slipped the weapon into his jacket pocket, but I knew it would still be trained on me. And I knew he wouldn't miss.

I walked stiffly down the corridor as Kane directed, half-expecting a bullet in the back.

"That's it. Stop at 210," he commanded.

He held out a cardkey toward Arnie, his gun still held unmoving inside his jacket pocket. "Open it. No tricks, or she's dead."

Arnie took it slowly and unlocked the door.

"Inside. Hellhound first."

Hellhound stepped into the room, and I followed. We stood side by side as the door swung shut behind Kane. He slipped his gun out of his pocket to aim it at me again.

"What the fuck, Cap?" Arnie hissed. "Drop the act. What's goin' down?"

"No act." Kane's voice was as hard as his eyes. "I have orders."

Hellhound made a sudden move, but Kane was faster. There was a tiny flat report and Arnie's body hit the floor with a heavy thud.

I gaped in shock and disbelief for a frozen second. By the time I jerked my gaze back to Kane, I had exactly enough time to glimpse the small trank gun in his left hand before he pulled the trigger again.

My last coherent emotion was fury.

I had just begun to register the yielding surface under me when my left arm was yanked roughly above my head. Cold steel tore at my wrist and my knuckles slammed into something agonizingly hard. The bruise on my forearm seared fire into my bones.

"Aaagh!" My arm jerked viciously and repeatedly, pain hammering through my knuckles all the way to my shoulder. Cries wrenched out of me while I fought to escape the torture, my body flopping ineffectually with still-spastic muscles.

"Stop struggling. You're hurting her." Kane's voice was dispassionate.

"Shit!" Hellhound's voice sounded next to my ear, and the pull eased suddenly. "Ya fuckin' asshole!"

I couldn't suppress a sob of relief when my arm relaxed.

"Shit! Aydan, I'm sorry, are ya okay?" Hellhound's gentle hand stroked my hair away from my face. "Talk to me, darlin'."

I blinked and shook my head, trying to catch my breath and clear my vision. Hellhound's face swam into focus beside me on the pillow.

"Wha..." My tongue didn't want to cooperate.

"Fuckin' prick," Hellhound spat. "Handcuffed us to the bed. Sorry, Aydan, I didn't know ya were on the other end. I didn't mean to hurt ya." He brushed a kiss across my lips. "Come on, darlin', try an' move up a bit. It'll take some a' the pressure off."

I peered up at my left wrist, handcuffed to Hellhound's right. The chain of the manacles passed around a sturdy post in the centre of the bed's headboard. Together, we heaved and squirmed toward the head of the bed. My arm throbbed mercilessly.

"Well." I swallowed thickly and licked numb lips. "Well, this is cozy." I glared at Kane as he loomed over the foot of the bed. "What do you want?"

Hellhound's free arm closed around me protectively. "Ignore him. When he's ready to stop actin' like an asshole, then we'll talk."

"Shut up." Kane glowered at his best friend.

"Don't be a dickhead," Hellhound retorted. "I can't believe you're pullin' this shit on us. What the fuck's your problem?"

Kane turned his scowl back to me. "Thanks for betraying my trust."

I jerked up, momentarily forgetting the handcuff in my rage. "Ow! Fuck!" I fell back on the bed again, clutching my aching arm. "Betraying *your* trust! That's pretty goddamn funny. I've been trusting you all this time. I was ready to take a fucking bullet for you, you *asshole*, and what have you done for me? Murdered my husband, lied to me for months, fucked with my mind, and now this? Fuck you, buddy! You can stuff trust right up your ass! Sideways!"

"Ya killed her husband? What the hell?" Hellhound demanded.

Kane ignored him and fixed his iron gaze on me. "You went rogue. Stemp gave the order. I'm giving you a chance to explain."

"Don't do me any fucking favours," I snarled. "You know damn well I wouldn't go rogue."

"What were you doing, then?" he demanded.

"You undo this cuff, and we'll talk."

"Like hell. You're not getting another chance to lie to me and take off."

"I never lied to you! Let me go." Captivity was starting to have its usual effect on me. My heart pounded and I gasped uneven breaths. "Let me go."

"Come on, Cap. Ya know Aydan can't stand bein' tied up." Hellhound eyed Kane. "It's just a misunderstandin'. Take off the cuffs an' we can talk about it."

Kane crossed his arms over his chest, his expression remote. "The sooner you talk, the sooner I'll let you go. Simple."

"John, please. I was just visiting my aunt in Victoria. That's all." I gave him an imploring look as my hands turned clammy. "Please just take the cuffs off."

"Visiting your aunt. That's a good one," Kane snorted.

"It's the truth. Ask at the nursing home." I clenched my teeth together on panic. Stay calm.

Hellhound shot a worried look at me and turned to scowl at Kane. "Fuck, John, she told ya what ya wanted to know. Let her go. What the hell's goin' on, anyway?"

"I'll let her go when she tells me the truth. And while we're waiting, you can tell me why the hell you were going to jump me."

Arnie glared. "I wasn't. But it woulda served ya right if I did. Ya lied to me. What the fuck was that?"

Kane's lips tightened. "Sorry," he said evenly. "I couldn't take a chance on telling you the real reason I needed to see her. I didn't know what she'd told you..."

"An' ya thought what?" Hellhound interrupted. "Ya thought I'd stab ya in the back after all we been through? That's bullshit, an' ya know it."

Kane blew out a breath between his teeth. "I know the two of you are... close." He shot a glance at Arnie's arm around me. "I thought she might try to turn you against me."

Arnie went still. When he spoke, his voice was quiet. "Ya know goddam well Aydan wouldn't do that, an' ya know goddam well I'd never turn on ya, no matter what anybody offered. But right now you're doin' a helluva good job makin' me wonder why."

"Look, I said I'm sorry, and I am," Kane said. "But Aydan may not be the person you think she is, and I couldn't take a chance on having you caught in the middle. Just tell me what she told you. I'll uncuff you, and you can leave."

"What about uncuffin' Aydan?"

Kane shot me a cold look. "We'll see."

Arnie scowled. "She ain't told me nothin' yet. Didn't have a chance. I got a message on my computer sayin' to be here, an' here I am. That's all I know."

"Bullshit. We've been watching your email. You didn't get any messages."

Hellhound gave him a look that dropped the air temperature by about fifty degrees. "So now you're callin' me a liar an' spyin' on me? We been brothers for forty-some years, an' you're pullin' this shit on me now?"

Kane eyed him, silent and expressionless.

"I already told ya, she ain't told me nothin'. Ya gonna work me over now?" Hellhound grated. "Gonna make me talk?"

Kane flushed. "Just tell me what she told you, goddammit!"

Hellhound's face set like granite. "Helmand, Arnold. Corporal, retired, Canadian Armed Forces, service number-"

"Cut the crap," Kane snapped.

"Helmand, Arnold. Corporal, retired, Canadian Armed Forces-"

"Fine!" Kane threw himself into a chair. "I can wait. She'll crack any time now."

Hellhound turned to face me on the pillow. "Hey, darlin'." His free hand stroked my hair.

"Hey," I responded weakly, trying to control my urge to scream and struggle against the handcuff.

His arm slid around me and he pulled me closer. "Ya got any bondage fantasies?"

I gave him a tremulous smile, and he kissed me gently. I couldn't believe it when his hand drifted down to pull my T-shirt free of my jeans.

He nuzzled my ear, the prickling of his whiskers sending a cascade of shivers down my neck. "Wanna play, darlin'? This bondage thing's givin' me a helluva hard-on." His hand slid under my shirt, caressing my skin while he kissed me again.

"Knock it off." Kane sounded thoroughly irritated.

I suddenly realized what Arnie was doing. Killing two birds with one stone. Distracting me from my panic, and annoying the snot out of Kane at the same time.

Hell, I was onboard with both those goals. I smiled against Arnie's lips.

"Actually," I murmured, "I do have a particularly kinky fantasy involving handcuffs and an audience."

"Oh, really?" He deepened the kiss, his tongue making seductive promises I knew he could keep. Wildly exceed, as a matter of fact. I draped a leg over his hip and fumbled one-handed at the button on his jeans.

"That's enough," Kane growled. "Cut it out."

Hellhound chuckled. "Nah, that ain't nearly enough." He rolled on top of me, parting my legs with his knee while he kissed me hungrily. He pulled away a few inches to smile down at me while his free hand coasted down to fondle my ass before migrating slowly up again. "She's gotta come seven or eight times before it's enough."

"I said, *cut it out!*" Kane barked.

I'd been hoping he'd realize we weren't going to cooperate until he took the cuffs off, but he sounded mad enough to shoot us again instead.

Undeterred, Hellhound's hand slid back under my shirt. "Oh, God, Arnie," I gasped, only slightly over-acting as his fingers slipped inside my bra. Okay, not over-acting at all. Those gifted hands, oh hell, yeah...

He kissed his way across my throat, the roughness of his beard and moustache sending sizzling pulses zipping to all sorts of sensitive places. I let my head fall back, eyes half-closed while I emitted soft, breathless cries.

"Oh... Hellhound... Oh, baby..."

I moaned, giving it all I had. It wasn't much of a stretch. He was making it very easy to be convincing.

Heat radiated through my jeans as his denim-clad thigh rubbed slowly between my legs. When his teeth and tongue found the magic spot near my collarbone, my hips automatically matched his rhythm, and I sucked in a shivering breath. "*Oh...* God, *yes...*"

Kane rocketed to his feet. "*Enough, goddammit!*" His

enraged shout was all but drowned out by the thunderous pounding on the door.

"Police! Open up!"

Kane uttered a word I'd never heard him use before as he yanked his jacket over his concealed holster and paced rapidly to the door. "I'm a police officer. I'm going to open the door now," he called.

Arnie and I froze, watching.

Kane swung the door open. "What-"

His body collapsed to the floor.

CHAPTER 17

Dave stood in the doorway. His face flushed scarlet when he took in our explicit position.

Hellhound snatched his hand from under my shirt and rolled off the bed, looking horrified as he tried to reach Kane without yanking both our arms out of their sockets.

"John!" He threw a wild glare at Dave. "What the fuck did ya do?"

"Stun gun. Sorry," Dave muttered. "Thought you needed help..."

"We do!"

Dave brightened at my response, and he stepped in and swung the door shut behind him.

"Make sure he's breathing," Hellhound urged.

Dave knelt stiffly beside Kane's crumpled body. "He's fine."

"What the hell d'ya think you're doin'?" Hellhound demanded. "Ya just assaulted a fuckin' police officer!"

Dave snorted. "He's no cop. Didn't follow proper procedure."

He started to rifle through Kane's pockets. I suppressed a shudder when the bad memories replayed, and I watched Kane's chest rise and fall for reassurance. Not dead. God, would I ever forget that awful day?

"Here." Dave dragged himself upright, grimacing, and limped to the bed holding a key.

Hellhound was still growling. "This ain't the fuckin' movies, and you ain't Bruce Fuckin' Willis. We're in deep shit now, thanks to you."

Dave shot him a scowl and plied the key. "Like you weren't in deep shit before. Uh, I mean, deep trouble. Sorry, Aydan."

Seconds later, we were free. Arnie and I knelt beside Kane, eyeing each other uncertainly.

"Maybe we should put him on the bed," I suggested.

Dave shrugged. "What do you care? He was going to kill you."

"Well, yeah, but..."

"Hurry up. Take his gun and let's go." Dave shifted from foot to foot, glancing apprehensively at the door.

"We have to leave him his gun. Let's just put him on the bed."

Dave took a step back. "You're nuts. And you're on your own. My back's shot."

"You take his feet," Hellhound directed. He grabbed Kane's shoulders and together we lugged him across the room and manhandled his limp body onto the bed.

We both fussed guiltily, straightening out his arms and legs. I raised his head, and Hellhound stuffed a pillow under it.

"Come on, already," Dave urged. "He's gonna wake up any minute and start shooting."

He was probably right. Kane had been livid before. Now? Yeah, he'd probably shoot us all. Well, Dave and me, for sure.

I turned to Hellhound. "Quick, Dave and I have to get

out of here. Do you have any idea where James might be hiding? He's kidnapped Nichele and he'll kill her-"

"What the hell, darlin'?" he interrupted. "Call the cops. Trust me, ya don't wanna go lookin' for him."

"Arnie, I can't, he said he'd kill her if the police got involved. Just tell me where to start looking." I shot an uneasy glance at Kane. "Hurry up, I have to get out of here."

"No fuckin' way. What the hell's goin' on? Kane killed your husband, an' he thinks you've gone rogue?"

"Arnie, *please*! I have to go! Just tell me where-"

He grasped my shoulders, his grip gentle despite his obvious agitation. "Aydan, I don't want ya lookin' for Jim, it's too dangerous."

"Forget it, Aydan, come on," Dave said. He shot a contemptuous glare at Hellhound. "I told you he'd be useless. I'll help you. Let's just go."

Hellhound stiffened and glowered at Dave. "Ya dumb shit, all you're gonna do is get her killed," he growled.

Kane groaned, and I pulled away from Hellhound, my heart pounding. "Arnie, I have to go before he wakes up. Just give me a neighbourhood to start in," I pleaded.

"Aydan, promise me ya won't go lookin' for Jim," Hellhound demanded.

I turned away. "Let's go, Dave."

"Wait." Hellhound's hand shot out to capture mine, and he stepped in front of me to gaze down into my eyes. "Tell me the truth, Aydan. Are ya still on the same side as Kane?"

"Yes! He's got it all wrong, it's just a misunderstanding..."

"Come *on*!" Dave burst out. He grabbed my wrist and tugged me in the direction of the door.

Hellhound scowled at Dave, who returned a defiant

glare. Hellhound blew out a breath between his teeth and glanced unhappily at Kane before turning back to me. "I'll come with ya, then."

"Arnie, no..." I began.

"Let's go," he interrupted, and I gave up the argument temporarily, my nerves fraying when Kane groaned again. I retrieved my gun from the table where Kane had left it and we hastened for the door, leaving Kane laid out on the bed like a Viking warrior on his pyre.

I was pretty sure he was going to be okay. When I glanced back, he was already starting to twitch and mumble profanities I was almost certain he'd learned from me. My steps slowed, my conscience nagging me. It just felt wrong to leave him there helpless, despite how much he'd pissed me off. Oh, yeah, and threatened to kill me. There was that.

"Aydan!" Dave hissed. "Hurry up!"

I quickened my pace and we followed Dave out the back door of the hotel to clamber into the idling truck. I strapped into the passenger seat while Hellhound stood in the alcove of the sleeper, bracing his outstretched arms against the cabinets. I couldn't make out his expression in the dim light, but tension rolled off him in waves.

Dave glanced over as he pulled onto Crowchild Trail and ran rapidly up through the gears. "Where to?"

"We need to hide," I blurted out, then gave myself a mental slap upside the head for stating the obvious.

"Christ, ya gotta know fuckin' stun guns are illegal in Canada. What the hell were ya thinkin'?" Hellhound burst out. "You're gonna be in a shitload a' trouble."

"Doubt it," Dave grunted. "He doesn't know who I am."

"He woulda seen ya when ya dropped Aydan off. He never misses anythin', an' ya got big motherfuckin' signs on the sides a' the truck."

Dave shrugged. "Oh, well."

Hellhound snorted. "Ya got no fuckin' idea what a world a' hurt ya just walked into. Head for the Forest Lawn Industrial Park. I know a guy there with a big bay, owes me a favour or two."

"Got a better idea," Dave said. "Think he got the tag?"

Hellhound considered for a few seconds. "Probl'y not. Ya parked out front, an' he was right by the hotel. He couldn'ta seen your plates."

"Good." Dave steered the truck down a side street.

I couldn't contain myself any longer. "How did you find us? What happened?"

Dave grinned. "Circled around back and parked for a few minutes. Saw you walking through the lobby. The big guy looked mad, and you looked scared. Followed and watched what room you went into. Looked like he had a gun, so it took me a few minutes to come up with a plan. Lucky I sneaked that stun gun over the line the last time I was down to the States."

I didn't know whether to kiss him or kick him. I really wasn't sure whether Kane would have killed me or not. A few days ago, I would have put my life in his hands without a qualm. Now I wasn't so sure. Dave might have just saved my life. Or he might have just sentenced me to certain death.

Shit.

Dave stopped in the shadows next to a small park and rose painfully to shoulder past Hellhound into the sleeper. He withdrew two large rolls from a tall, narrow cabinet. "Give me a hand," he said, and we followed him out of the truck.

The rolls proved to be self-adhesive decals that

completely covered the 'Dave's Trucking' logos on the doors. Hellhound shot a suspicious glare at Dave as we applied 'Rosie's Custom Transport'.

Dave shrugged. "It ain't what it looks like. I do a regular hitch for Rosie, couple times a month. She likes having her logo on the truck when I do, so she got me these removable signs."

"This still won't help, though," I argued. "If Kane saw your truck earlier, he'll track you down through Dave's Trucking."

"Worry about that when the time comes." Dave winced his way back into the cab, and we followed suit.

"Arnie, you should go now," I said. "I don't want you to get involved."

We peered at each other in the semi-darkness. "Involved with what? What the fuckin' hell's goin' on?" Hellhound demanded.

"Arnie, never mind, just go, okay? I want you to stay safe."

"Fuck that, Aydan, I wasn't gonna leave ya with a fuckin' gun in your back, an' I ain't gonna leave ya knowin' you're plannin' on lookin' for that fuckin' asshole Jim! Tell me what the fuckin' hell's happenin'! Now!"

I gave in, taken aback by his uncharacteristic harshness. "First things first. Have either you got a cell phone?"

"Yeah," they agreed in ragged unison, groping in pockets.

"Turn them off, and then we need to get out of here. They can track those."

"*Fuck!*" Hellhound flung his phone at the floor with a violent sweep of his arm, and I flinched as pieces ricocheted around the cab.

"That's one way to do it," Dave observed. He continued

to excavate his pockets, stepping up the pace as he went. At last, he threw up his hands. "Must have lost it at the hotel when I jumped out of the truck. Shi... Crap. Well, guess it's no problem, then."

He put the truck into gear and pulled away.

"Sonuva*bitch*!" Hellhound grabbed at the tiny counter for balance as the truck swayed, and kicked savagely at the cracked phone case. "This is so fucked up!" He wedged himself into the tiny bench seat and scrubbed his fist roughly against his beard.

I turned sideways in the passenger seat, trying to make out his expression in the fluctuating illumination as we passed under streetlights.

"Are you okay?" I asked, concern gnawing at me. I'd seen him sleep-deprived, in agony and facing death, but I'd never seen him lose his cool like that.

"Yeah," he muttered. "Sorry, darlin'. It's just this thing with Jim's buggin' the shit outta me, an' now Kane's got some wild hair up his ass. I never thought he'd ever..." He bit off the sentence. "What the fuck's goin' on?"

I sighed and tried to formulate a reply that would explain enough about the situation with Kane without giving away classified information. "You knew my husband died about two and a half years ago."

"Yeah. Heart attack, ya said." Hellhound leaned forward to study my face in the dimness. "Ya were in bed with him. So how the hell could Kane have killed him?"

"He slipped Robert a drug that caused a massive heart attack as soon as he exerted himself. It was just my bad luck that he decided to come home to me instead of going to the gym as usual."

"That's crazy. How d'ya know that?"

"Kane told me."

"Fuck." Arnie reached for my hand and held it gently. "Sorry, Aydan. That's gotta be tough. But why would he kill your husband?"

"It seems Robert was in the same line of work as Kane," I said carefully.

"What?" He jerked upright. "What the hell..."

"And..." I swallowed. "I think... Robert might not have been the only member of my family who didn't die a natural death."

He stared at me. "Ya mean..."

"They might have killed my parents, too. And maybe my uncle. That's why I was flying under the radar. I needed to talk to my aunt in Victoria. She's the only one left."

Hellhound sat in silence, and I knew the wheels were turning in his keen mind. "But there's more to it than that, ain't there, darlin'?" he asked finally. "Back at the hotel, ya said he'd been lyin' to ya for months, fuckin' with your mind."

"Yeah." I knew I shouldn't say any more, but the anger and betrayal burst out of me anyway. "My mind wasn't all he fucked with. That asshole."

"What... Oh. Shit! No wonder he was so pissed when we were gettin' it on. Sorry, darlin', I didn't know the two a' ya were..."

"We aren't. And I don't think that was why he was mad. He didn't do me because he wanted to. He had orders."

Arnie gaped at me. "What the... That's the sickest fuckin' thing I ever heard. Why the hell would he have orders to bang ya? No offense, darlin', I know how good ya are, but it just ain't that important in the big picture."

"No, you're right. It was part of a bigger plan. He was

supposed to fake being in love with me so he could manipulate me to keep working for them. So he said all this mushy shit, and I turned him down because you *know* I don't want to get attached..."

My throat was tightening, and I took a deep breath to hold my voice steady. "...And I felt so bad because I liked him and I thought he was hurt, but he's just a lying scumbag and he's been playing mind games the whole time and I can't *believe* I wasted any sympathy on that *asshole*, and then he has the fucking nerve to say I betrayed *his* trust..."

My tirade was muffled by Hellhound's shoulder as he knelt on the swaying floor of the truck beside my seat and pulled me into a hug. "Shh, darlin', it's gonna be okay. He really cares about ya, I know he does."

I pulled away. "No, you don't get it. I don't want that from him, or from anybody. It's a relief to know I don't have to deal with it. But he didn't have to pull that shit on me. He could've just told me the truth. I would've done whatever they needed anyway. I can't believe he didn't trust me enough to know that."

Hellhound sat back on his heels, frowning. "Yeah, I can see where that'd hurt. He tranked me, for fucksakes. What the fuck was that?"

"I don't know. Do you think he's got something else going on that we don't know about?"

"Hell, yeah. That's gotta be it."

We eyed each other uneasily for a few moments. "Are we just bullshitting ourselves?" I asked finally.

He blew out a long breath. "I dunno, darlin'. D'ya think he really woulda shot ya?"

"I don't know. I don't know him at all anymore. Shit, who am I kidding? I never knew him."

"I do. 'Least I thought I did."

"Do you think he would have shot me tonight?"

Arnie rocked to his feet and reseated himself on the bench in the sleeper. "Tell me what's goin' on with Jim an' Nichele."

I made fists in my hair and tugged. "I warned Nichele that James was bad news, but she wouldn't listen. She took him home, and he hacked her laptop and stole her clients' money." I paused as a new thought occurred to me. "Shit, my money, too."

I sighed. "Now he's forcing her into a money-laundering scheme. He beat her and threatened to kill her if she told. He's making it look like she's the one doing it all, so it's her ass on the line either way."

"*Fuck!* That asshole! I knew things were gonna get ugly as soon as he showed up. Fucker's just like the ol' man. Waste a' fuckin' skin. I kept hopin' somebody'd slit his fuckin' throat while he was in jail."

"Arnie... he's your brother."

His clenched fist jerked as though he would punch the cabinet next to him, but he controlled the motion. Even in the dim glow from the dashboard, I could see his shoulders bunched with suppressed anger.

"No, he ain't," he said quietly, and the edge in his gravelly voice made me shiver. "I only got one brother. An' he just knocked me out an' handcuffed me."

CHAPTER 18

I stared at Arnie helplessly, getting angrier at Kane by the minute. He'd had orders to screw me over, literally, and I could probably forgive him for that, if he let me live. He'd only been doing his job. But betraying Arnie was above and beyond the call of duty.

"We need a plan," Arnie said, his voice controlled.

Dave spoke for the first time since putting the truck in motion. "Got one."

Hellhound and I both stared at him in the dim light. I'd been so absorbed in our conversation I'd forgotten Dave was listening, and I did a quick mental review to make sure I hadn't said anything he shouldn't have heard.

I shook my head and tried to focus. God, I was so tired, I couldn't even remember what had been said. I'd have to ask Hellhound later. Not for the first time, I wished I had his photographic memory.

"What's your plan?" Hellhound inquired sarcastically. "Ya wanna cram in a few more criminal offenses tonight while you're on a roll?"

"Got your sorry a... butt out of there, didn't I?" Dave retorted.

"Guys!" I shot a warning glare at Hellhound, and he slouched back on the bench, arms crossed. "What's your plan, Dave?" I asked.

For the first time, I registered our surroundings. Total blackness around us, with the highway unrolling ahead and fading away at the limit of the headlights. "And where the hell are we?" I added.

"TransCanada, westbound. Plan is, we get some rest. Can't keep running on empty, something's gotta give. I'll pull in at the truck stop. Good place to blend in."

"But, Dave, we have to figure out a plan."

"Yeah, we will. First we sleep. I've been driving since seven this morning. Way past my legal limit." He flicked a glance toward Hellhound. "Think we all need to cool down anyway."

I opened my mouth to argue, but Hellhound spoke first. "He's right, darlin'. Sorry, Dave, I was outta line."

"No problem."

The lights of the truck stop glowed ahead, and I suddenly realized what a bad idea this was.

"Shit!"

Dave jerked in his seat. "What?"

"Go north here!"

Dave swerved onto the exit ramp, braking and downshifting in a flurry of motion. Hellhound braced himself in the rocking sleeper, arms jammed against the cabinets. "What the hell?"

"Yeah, what the hel... sorry, heck?" Dave echoed as the lights receded behind us.

"Sorry. I didn't mean to panic everybody, but it just occurred to me. They'll be watching the truck stops."

Dave shot me a sceptical glance. "You sure? Out in the middle of nowhere?"

"I wouldn't want to chance it. By now, Kane'll have run

Dave's Trucking through the system, pulled your plates, your phone numbers, your address, and what you ate for dinner last night. He'll have given your plate number and a description of the truck to the city police and the RCMP, and they'll all be watching for us. I can't believe we even got out of Calgary without hitting a roadblock."

Dave's eyes were wide in the dashboard lights. "You mean he really is a cop?"

"Fuck, yeah, he's really a cop," Hellhound growled. "What part of 'He's a cop' didn't ya get?"

"But... No way," Dave argued. "Cops can't get away with stuff like that. That's like... police brutality or something. He didn't even show you a badge."

Neither Hellhound nor I responded to that, and Dave peered over at me. "What are we going to do now?"

I groaned and sank my head into my hands as another thought hit me. "I have no idea. We used up our margin of safety getting out of the city when we should have been hiding *in* the city. Because now we can't go back. We'll get caught for sure. Every cop will be on the alert."

In the disheartened silence that ensued, I leaned my aching body back in the seat and pummelled my forehead gently with the heel of my hand. God, I was too tired to function...

"Dave's right." Hellhound's vote of confidence made both Dave and me throw a surprised glance back at him. "We all need sleep. An' there ain't any point in tryin' to get back into the city tonight. Time to lie low an' let things settle down a bit." He turned to Dave. "Just get off the highway on one a' these back roads an' park somewhere. We'll figure somethin' out in the mornin'."

"...'Kay. You got somewhere in mind?"

Leather creaked in the darkness as Hellhound shrugged. "No fuckin' idea. Just pick somethin'."

Some zigzags on the back roads brought us to an overgrown crossing off a gravel road. An embankment on one side and a few acres of scrubby trees on the other provided a bit of concealment. Dave pulled onto the crossing and shut down the engine. We all sat in silence for a few minutes, our eyes adjusting to the darkness.

A faint glow of moonlight provided enough illumination for me to identify the shapes of the truck seats and my companions. Finally, Dave spoke. "Aydan, you can have the bed. We'll take the seats."

Hellhound muttered agreement and stood.

"No, Dave, you'd better take the bed," I disagreed. "If your back hurts as much as I think it does, you'll need to stretch out. We don't want to take a chance on you not being able to drive."

"It's fine," he countered.

I took a different tack. "Okay." I stood up and stretched before moving uncertainly into the sleeper alcove. "Dave, sorry, I'm disoriented here in the dark. Can you point me to the bathroom?"

"Yeah, hold on." He started to rise and let out a gasp of pain as he froze half-erect, bracing himself on the steering wheel and the back of the seat. He was straightening by slow degrees, hissing through his teeth, when Hellhound and I each took an arm and steered him to the bed. As we got him settled, he spoke through clenched teeth. "Must've twisted it again getting in and out at the hotel. Really starting to stiffen up now. Might be a better idea to stay in the seat."

"I doubt it. Hang on." I fumbled in my waist pouch and extracted my tiny LED flashlight.

"Lights are on the switch over there," Dave said.

"Never mind, I don't want to turn them on," I said. "Here, hold this." I handed the flashlight to Arnie, and he trained the spot of light on my hands while I fished out my pill container. I shook a couple of ibuprofens into my palm and handed them to Dave.

He swallowed them gratefully, and I surveyed his face in the feeble illumination, feeling responsible. "Would massage help? I'm no pro, but I could rub it for you and see if it eases the stiffness."

Hellhound snorted laughter in the darkness. "Usually things get stiffer when ya start rubbin'."

"Wise-ass. What do you think, Dave?"

"I dunno." He eased himself over onto his stomach with a grunt. "I'll try anything right about now."

"Tell me if I hurt you. I don't really know what I'm doing."

He groaned as I started to gently knead his back, and I snatched my hands away. "Did I hurt you?"

"No. That's great." He let out another ecstatic groan as I resumed working the muscles.

"Jeez, Dave, ya need to be alone for a while?" Hellhound made his way to the passenger door. "I gotta take a leak an' stretch my legs. Don't do anythin' I wouldn't do."

I laughed. "Carte blanche. Sweet."

He chuckled and swung out of the cab.

For a while, I worked in a silence punctuated only by Dave's blissful moans. Eventually he spoke, muffled by the pillow. "Are you and Arnie, um...?"

"Friends."

Silence.

"You seem pretty... friendly."

"Friends with benefits."

"Oh."

About the time my arthritic thumbs began to complain in earnest, Dave heaved a huge sigh. "Thanks. That feels a lot better."

"Good." I rose slowly, straightening out some kinks of my own after spending so long contorted over the narrow berth. "I'm going to go outside for a bit, too."

I lowered myself down from the passenger door and bit back a cry when I turned and bumped into Hellhound in the darkness. His arms closed around me. "Ya get Dave tuned up?"

"I hope so. He was in rough shape."

"I'm in rough shape, too. I could use some rubbin'."

"No doubt." I snuggled closer in the chilly night air. "So could I."

"That could be arranged." His hands drifted down my back.

"Sorry, your opportunity to indulge in the audience fantasy has passed. And it's too damn cold outside." I kissed him and pulled away. "I've been cooped up in that truck for days. I'm just going to walk for a few minutes. And if I don't sleep soon, I'm going to puke."

"I'll walk with ya."

We meandered down the middle of the deserted road, his arm around my shoulders, listening to the country night noises and the crunch of our own footsteps.

Out of earshot of the truck, he spoke. "We gotta have a talk."

"Uh-oh. Any time a guy says we have to have a talk, it's nothing but bad news."

"I ain't kiddin' around. I need the whole story, Aydan."

I blew out a long breath. "You know I can't do that."

"I know. But ya can tell me more than when Dave was listenin'." He stopped and turned, tilting my face up to study me in the moonlight. "How long have ya been an agent?"

"I'm not. I never was."

He sighed. "Darlin', ya been workin' with Kane for seven months. Ya got a license to carry a concealed weapon, an' I know ya know how to use it. An' back at the hotel, Kane said you'd gone rogue an' he had orders to shoot ya. I ain't stupid."

"Arnie, I know you're not stupid. But I'm not an agent. I'm just an asset. You remember that thing I was carrying back in the summer?"

He nodded, and his hand closed on mine. "Thought we were both gonna bite the big one that time. So that's what ya been doin'? Usin' that thing? Workin' with Kane?"

"Yeah."

"Must be pretty high-level, considerin' they brought in Special Forces choppers to pull ya out this summer."

"Yeah."

"So if you're that important, why'd they decide they wanna kill ya?"

I hung my head. "I ran. They got the wrong idea."

"Why'd ya run? Ya found out Kane killed your husband, an' ya figured you were next?"

"No. I..." I squeezed my eyes shut and tried to force my sluggish brain to work. "They're going to kill me anyway. As soon as they find a way to replace me. I thought Kane was going to shoot me this summer..."

"What?" Arnie seized me by the shoulders. "What the hell? That can't be right, darlin', he wouldn't..." His voice trailed off as his hands tightened. "Would he?"

"Yeah." The word came out as a long sigh. "Yeah, he would. Orders. That's how dangerous I am when I'm using the... thing. If they think I've gone rogue, I'm toast."

He let go and took a slow step back, peering at me in the darkness. "But... ya wouldn't..."

"No, I wouldn't betray them. But they're all spies. They don't believe that. And in a way, they're right. If I get captured... Well, you know. Everybody breaks under torture, sooner or later. I'm no hero. It wouldn't take long."

I dropped my head, feeling a hundred years old. "But that's not why I ran. It's because... I think they've been manipulating me since I was four. Killing whoever got in the way." My voice shook, and I shut up, swallowing hard.

"Aw, darlin'." Hellhound's powerful arms closed around me, and I buried my face in his shoulder. "That can't be right. We'll figure out what really happened." His rough-edged voice caressed my ear. "Don't worry, it'll be okay."

The exact promise I'd made to Nichele. I choked and wrapped my arms around him, huddling into his reassuring bulk. "I just want to make sure Nichele's okay before they kill me. There's nothing I can do about the rest of it," I mumbled.

"Aydan, nobody's gonna kill ya. They gotta come through me first."

"Thanks, Arnie, but you know what I'm up against. Don't put yourself in the line of fire. All that'll do is get you dead. It won't change anything else."

"Lemme worry about that. You just concentrate on stayin' alive, an' it'll all work out in the end." He leaned down to kiss me, and even though I knew otherwise, I let his words comfort me.

Fatigue descended like a lead blanket, and I steered

Arnie into an about-face to retrace our steps. By the time the truck loomed up in the moonlight, I could barely keep my eyes open.

A buzzing sound made us pause outside the passenger door.

"Shit, he snores." Hellhound blew out a sigh and climbed up.

"So do you." I followed him into the cab.

"Not like that. He sounds like fuckin' ruptured bagpipes or somethin'."

I stifled a giggle. The rattling drone did sound a lot like bagpipes, punctuated by a staccato snort at the end of each breath.

Some time later, my urge to giggle was a distant memory while I squirmed in the passenger's seat, trying to find a comfortable position. Dave was still sawing logs in the sleeper, and Hellhound contributed his usual quiet, rhythmic thrumming from the driver's seat.

At last, I blew out a frustrated breath and gave up on the seat entirely. I tiptoed into the sleeper and stretched out on the cold, hard floor. Dave's snoring was only marginally louder there, and at least my legs weren't cramped. I stuffed my backpack under my head and drifted into a miserable doze.

I woke in the early grey half-light, aching and shivering. The duet of snores continued unabated, and I scowled at the two sleeping men with the particular brand of caustic irritation that can only be achieved while freezing one's ass off at oh-dark-thirty.

I curled into a ball and wrapped my arms around myself, but the penetrating chill of the floor sucked every vestige of heat from my body.

Fuck this.

I eyed Dave. He was on his side. There was a little space at the edge of the narrow bed. And he had blankets.

I eased the blankets up and insinuated myself onto the few inches of bed as slowly and smoothly as I could. I was clinging to the edge and wondering whether it was worth the trouble when Dave erupted in a huge snort and a sigh. His arm fell heavily over my waist, and he pulled me against him spoon-fashion.

I froze, but his snoring continued, ruffling my hair. Blissful warmth enveloped me.

I woke to a weight on my chest and a suspiciously hard something jammed against my butt. My eyes flew open. Dave was still spooning me, his snoring heavy and regular.

Awkward.

I was easing his inert hand off my left boob when I caught sight of Hellhound's grinning face in the dawn light. I shook my head at him in warning.

The movement roused Dave, who let out a snort. There was a second of silence as his hand cupped my breast, and then he yelped and recoiled against the back wall of the berth with a thud. I tumbled off the edge of the bed and turned to look back at him while he pressed wide-eyed against the wall, the blanket bunched protectively in front of his crotch.

"Sorry," he stammered. "Sorry... Uh. What...?"

Hellhound guffawed. "Funny, that ain't my reaction when I find a hot chick in my bed."

Dave glared at him, a dark flush climbing his neck.

I hastened to intervene. "Dave, I'm sorry, I got cold in the night and I needed a blanket. I hope you don't mind."

"Uh, no... it's okay." His gaze darted around the sleeper as if seeking a place to perch. He released his grip on the blanket with a convulsive movement, his face still red.

"I'm going to go out and stretch my legs." I made for the door.

By the time I returned, Dave had recovered his composure except for a tendency to avoid meeting my eyes. We took turns going for "walks" outside the truck to allow each other a modicum of privacy to use the tiny bathroom, and at last reconvened for a planning session.

"We've got to get back into Calgary," I said. "We've got to find Nichele."

Hellhound frowned. "Are ya sure we hafta? Don't ya think that's a job for the police? Or for Kane?"

"We can't call the police. And Spider's been looking for Nichele for two days now."

"Darlin', let them deal with it," Arnie advised gently. "Ya need to figure out how you're gonna save your own ass, never mind anybody else's."

"I think my ass is past saving. I just want to make sure Nichele's okay. That's why I wanted to talk to you in the first place. I thought you might know how James thinks, and where he might be holding Nichele. But I wasn't planning for you to end up on the run with me."

Arnie eyed me and sighed. "Ya ain't gonna let this go, are ya?"

"No. And we need to get back into town so we can start looking." I smothered a sigh of my own, internally cursing Dave's initiative. If he'd just listened to Hellhound last night and driven to Forest Lawn...

As if reading my mind, Dave turned an apologetic face in my direction. "Sorry. I screwed up. Should've stayed in town last night."

"No, it's okay, Dave. It seemed like a good idea at the time."

We all fell silent. It was just too risky to take Dave's truck back to Calgary. And we needed wheels no matter what we planned to do. Wheels. Hmmm.

"What?" Dave demanded eagerly.

I looked up to discover both men eyeing me with hope. I grinned. "I think I have an idea. Lucky it's Saturday."

"What's that got to do with it?" Hellhound asked.

"Hey, Arnie, did you ever mention Kelly's to Kane?"

He stared into space for a few moments, and I knew he was flipping through the mental file cards of his phenomenal memory.

"Nah."

"Thank God. Neither did I. I think I can get us a car. And once we have a car, we can get back into the city."

"What's Kelly's?" Dave asked.

"A bar."

"Oh." Dave regarded me uncertainly, but apparently decided not to pursue the subject.

"Uh, Aydan, ya gotta get back *into* the city to get to Kelly's," Hellhound pointed out.

"I have an idea for that, too. I think I can do it if I go by myself. Then I can get the car and come back and pick you guys up." I turned to Dave. "Where's the best place to hitch a ride with a trucker? Besides a truck stop?"

He considered for a few minutes, his brow furrowed. "There's a pullout off the number two highway where a lot of the guys stop."

"Good. Because you're going to get me a ride."

"Don't know if that'll work. Most of the guys aren't allowed to carry anybody."

"Could they be persuaded?"

Dave hesitated and flushed slightly. "Maybe. There are some lonely guys out there."

I grabbed my backpack and stepped into the tiny bathroom. When I emerged, I took stock of Dave's stunned face. Yeah, that's right, he'd only seen me in baggy sweatshirts.

"Do you think this would be persuasive enough?" I asked.

Hellhound gave my tight leather and half-exposed boobs a slow, lascivious once-over and leered. "It's doin' it for me, darlin'."

I grinned. "Yeah, but you'll screw anything that moves."

He straightened with an affronted expression. "Ow. That ain't true. Ya know it's gotta be female. An' human."

"Picky, picky."

He grinned. "Ya got me all wrong, darlin'. I ain't gonna screw any ol' skank that crawls up on my doorstep. I'm a man of taste. I just happen to have varied tastes."

Dave had been following our exchange open-mouthed. "You're nuts," he blurted out. "You'd sleep around when..." His gaze teetered precariously on my cleavage, struggled up to my chin, and then flitted up to the corner of the sleeper as his face reddened. He cleared his throat. "Yeah, I think you'll get a ride. Let's go."

He made his way stiffly to the driver's seat and eased himself into it with only a quiet in-drawing of breath through his teeth. Apparently my massage had helped.

As we approached the highway, I scanned anxiously for

any sign of police cars. By the time we pulled off behind three other tractor-trailer units, I was perched on the edge of my seat, heart pounding.

Dave eyed me unhappily. "You sure this is a good idea?"

"It's the only idea I've got."

CHAPTER 19

"Okay, we need this to work the first time," I said. "I don't want to be seen by any more people than absolutely necessary." I turned to Dave. "You need to convince one of these guys to take me into Calgary."

He shifted uncomfortably in his seat. "What should I say?"

"I don't know. Tell them whatever they want to hear. Tell them I'm a trucker groupie and a great lay, I don't know, whatever it takes."

Dave flushed. "I ain't gonna say that."

"Would it work?"

"Probably," he muttered. "But I ain't gonna say that about you. It ain't respectful."

"Hell, Dave, I don't care. Do you have any other ideas?"

He scowled at the floor. "No."

"Then let's do it. Make sure you pick an older guy without a wedding ring."

Hellhound laughed. "Trust me, darlin', the way you're bustin' outta that top, it ain't gonna matter."

We left Hellhound hiding in the sleeper and wandered across the asphalt, covertly surveying the other truckers.

I nudged Dave. "What about that guy?" He was practically a clone of Dave, but with a little less gut and a lot less hair. Same nondescript jeans and T-shirt, but his elaborately tooled cowboy boots made a strong fashion statement.

"Okay," Dave mumbled. "Hey," he greeted the other man as we approached.

"Hey," Cowboy responded. His face brightened as his eyes veered in my direction. His gaze travelled up, down, up, and reluctantly back over to Dave when he spoke.

"This is Jane. She needs a ride to Calgary."

Cowboy stuck his thumbs in his belt loops and rocked back on his heels. "Would if I could, but you know, regs."

I shot Dave a look and drifted away, watching out of the corner of my eye. He leaned confidentially toward the other man, his face reddening as he spoke. Cowboy gave a bark of laughter and punched Dave on the shoulder, eyeing me with interest. A few minutes of conversation later, Dave shrugged and turned away. "Your loss," he threw over his shoulder.

Shit. Time for desperate measures.

I oozed up to Dave, giving him my best sultry smile. I captured his hand in both of my own. "Dave, you're such a sweetie," I purred. "And I'm so sorry I put your back out last night, but you were just sooo good, I got carried away."

I pressed his hand into my cleavage and pulled him into a hungry kiss. Lots of tongue.

He froze, and I tightened my hold on him, transferring my lips to his ear to whisper. "Come on, Dave, work with me here."

"Urgh," he said. I pulled back a fraction to look into his paralyzed face.

Shit.

I kissed him again and he finally reacted, his free arm closing around me while he removed his hand from my chest to run his fingers through my hair instead. His stiff lips relaxed, and he took the initiative on the next kiss. A plain vanilla kiss, but at least he didn't look so terrified.

At the sound of the throat clearing behind him, Dave turned, still holding me.

"Yeah?"

"Uh." Cowboy rubbed the back of his neck. He tore his avid gaze away from me to meet Dave's eyes. "I could take her. It's only a few miles. Nobody'd ever know, right?"

I gave him a hungry smile, blatantly looking him up and down. "Would you?" I breathed. "That would be... wonderful."

"Yeah." He bobbed his head and his ears turned scarlet. "Yeah, I could do that. Jane."

"Oh, thank you!" I turned back to Dave. "Dave, sweetie, you take care of that back of yours, and save up your strength. Call me next time you're in town, you hear? We'll go for another little ride."

"You bet I will, Jane, honey." He pulled me closer and kissed me again. The merest touch of his tongue, quickly withdrawn. He was blushing when he stepped away. "See you soon."

I watched him walk away before turning to Cowboy. "What's your name?"

"Rick."

It took only a little persuasion to get Rick to agree to drop me off near Kelly's. I wasn't sure what Dave had said to him, so I babbled for most of the drive about how wonderful Dave was. By the time we arrived in Calgary, Rick had apparently figured out that whatever Dave might or might not have gotten from me, it wasn't being offered to him. He looked thoroughly disappointed when I thanked him profusely and hopped down from his cab.

As soon as his truck was out of sight, I pulled my baggy sweatshirt on again. No need to attract any more attention than necessary.

I checked my watch and made for the back door of Kelly's. I was light-headed with hunger and adrenaline, and my hands trembled finely despite my best efforts to still them.

Please let this work.

Inside, I stood for a few seconds, waiting for my eyes to adjust to the dingy corridor. Then I moved quietly toward the bar and peeked around the corner. At the sight of the group sprawled on the broken-down couches in the corner, I drew a huge breath of relief.

I plastered on a smile and strode toward them.

"Aydan! Hey, long time no see!"

"How are you?"

"What, we're not good enough for you anymore, you snob?"

"Here, grab a seat."

My friends called out greetings and reshuffled themselves to leave a position open on the couch with its back to the wall, my usual spot. I sank into it, gulping back unexpected emotion at the warmth of their reception and the sheer heavenly normalcy.

The waitress stopped in her tracks. "Aydan! Where have you been? How are you?"

"Great, Alanna, I'm great. Good to see you."

"Corona?"

I sighed. "You have no idea how much I'd like a beer

right now, but I can't. I'm 'way too hungry, and I have to drive." I glanced around at the food-laden table. "Can you just bring me my usual?"

"Sure, no problem." She hurried away, and I appropriated a chicken wing from Bruce's basket before leaning back, glancing nervously toward the entrance of the bar when a couple of patrons entered. They took seats at the front of the bar, oblivious to us, and I relaxed again.

I took stock of the assembled group. "Hey, where's Nichele?" I kept my voice as casual as possible.

Jean laughed. "You know Nichele. She told me on Monday she'd be here, but she probably met some hot guy and decided to dump us."

"Yeah, probably," Brenda agreed. "I was supposed to go for coffee with her Thursday night, and she stood me up. When I phoned her, she said she was sick. But she was on her cell. I'd already tried her at home and got no answer. In bed, sure, I believe that. Sick? Not so much."

Everyone laughed. They all knew Nichele. I did my best to join in with the ensuing banter, fear twisting my gut.

"Try her now," I urged Brenda. "Maybe we can convince her to come anyway."

Brenda dialled, listened, dialled again, listened some more. "She's not picking up. That's weird. She always answers her cell."

"Definitely in bed," Jean grinned, and I tried to conceal my concern while the conversation veered to other matters.

After a decent interval, I turned to Bruce. "Hey, Bruce, have you still got the Caprice?"

He grinned. "Of course. Why? You want to borrow it?"

"Actually, yeah, can I take you up on that?"

He gaped theatrically at me. "You're kidding me, right?"

"No, not this time."

"Get out of here. You're cheating on your beloved Saturn?"

"My beloved Saturn is on its way to the shop." I crossed my fingers, silently begging the car gods to forgive my lie. "The tranny started slipping a bit once I got into city traffic, and I didn't want to take a chance. They'll probably have it for a few days, and I could sure use some wheels."

"Well, sure, no problem," he agreed. "We can go and pick it up right after we're done here."

"Bruce, you're a lifesaver."

"I know. Stop eating my wings."

Under other circumstances, I would have enjoyed the lengthy bullshit session with the convivial group, but my head was throbbing and my shoulders were wracked with tension by the time everybody straggled out of the bar. They lingered agonizingly on the sidewalk, and I resisted the urge to grab Bruce's arm and hustle him over to his car.

At last we drove away, and I relaxed a fraction in the safe anonymity of traffic. Bruce chatted cheerfully, and I did my best to hold up my end of the conversation, fervently wishing he lived a little closer to Kelly's. When we finally stood in his garage, I breathed a silent sigh of relief.

"Here you go." Bruce swept off the car cover with the grandiose gesture of a man unveiling a priceless treasure.

I grinned at the sight of the clapped-out 1980 Chevy Caprice. "I like what you've done with the rust," I complimented him. The half-eaten holes in the rear quarter panels had been plastered with several criss-crossing layers of duct tape, lifted and frayed along the edges.

He grinned. "Thanks." He tossed me the keys. "Have fun. Don't take too many pink slips."

"I'll try to restrain myself."

I turned the key and listened to the velvety rumble with a smile.

My spirits lifted as I steered the car out into traffic. Phase One complete. My smile faded at the thought of Nichele's no-show and the fact that she wasn't answering her cell. That was definitely bad news. Unlike the others, I knew that wherever she was, she probably wasn't enjoying herself. I really needed to find out whether Spider had made any progress.

I steered the car toward the nearest public library. I knew they had free internet access, and on a Saturday afternoon, Spider would almost certainly be online.

When I went inside, though, I was dismayed to discover they required a library card before they'd let me use a terminal. I almost gave it up there and then, but decided at the last minute to simply renew my expired card.

Hoping fervently that Kane wasn't monitoring the library computer system, I paid the small annual fee in cash. But why would he monitor the libraries? What fugitive in her right mind would renew a library card?

My hands were shaking by the time the renewal was complete, and I determinedly suppressed the urge to glance over my shoulder every ten seconds. At last, I made for the terminals, only to find them all occupied. Tension wound up in my gut while I spent nearly twenty minutes roaming through the stacks waiting my turn.

Approximately an eternity later, one of the terminals opened up, and I slid into the still-warm chair, already reaching for the keyboard.

I'd just brought up the World of Warcraft site when a quiet voice spoke behind me. "Hold it right there."

CHAPTER 20

I tried to gulp down my heart, which suddenly seemed inclined to vibrate frantically in my throat, and turned slowly. Wild escape plans jostled through my mind.

I locked eyes with a wizened man who was so short, we were of a height while I was seated.

"Hold it right there," he repeated softly but indignantly. "You're at my station. Use that one." He made a shaky gesture with his cane toward another station that had just been vacated.

My heart resumed beating with a thump that made me gasp. "Sorry," I stammered, and tottered over to the other computer as quickly as my shaking legs would carry me.

Jeez, wouldn't that have been a disaster. Attack some poor little old fart who just wanted to surf midget porn or something. My hands shook so much I could barely type the website address.

In the game, I rapidly scanned for Spider's character. There was no sign of him, and the mouse creaked under my frustrated grasp. He must be working overtime, trying to keep up with the demands of the teams that were undoubtedly searching for me right at that moment.

I threw an involuntary glance over my shoulder as my stress level ratcheted up another notch. Nothing but the usual hush of the library. I willed the tension out of my shoulders and tried some yoga breathing. In. Out. Ocean waves.

Too keyed up to stay any longer, I ran one last quick search before I left. And glory of glories, there he was. Whisper...

"Spider."

"where r u?"

"Any news on N?"

"no."

Several heads turned as I swore slightly louder than I'd intended. "Sorry," I muttered, and returned to my keyboard. The chat window had scrolled, and Spider had typed another message.

"listened to recording again. who's J?"

Shit, I didn't realize he didn't know who James was. I'd just assumed Kane would know.

I thumped my forehead. Jeez, idiot. Kane didn't know we were doing this.

"r u there? r u there?"

"J is dog's oldest brother," I typed. "Has gang connections."

"thx, i'll check it. r u & dog ok?"

"Yes."

"come in b4 it's 2 l8."

"Not until N's safe. Thanks, Spider. Over & out."

I ignored his scrolling demands in the chat window, logged off, and cleared the cache before I left, trying not to draw attention by scuttling furtively.

I hoped Spider was still on my side. If Kane had told him about our run-in at the hotel and convinced him I'd gone rogue, I'd be sunk. I knew he'd be able to use his űber-geek skills to trace the computer's IP address back to the library in no time flat.

I hurried out to the car and slid in, mentally thanking Bruce one more time.

Back on the road, I shot a quick glance at my watch and groaned. Three thirty already, and I still had an hour's drive to rejoin Dave and Arnie. My stomach growled, and I suddenly realized they must be starving. I didn't think Dave had any food in the truck.

I blew out a sigh, trying to release my tension along with it. One more stop.

At the strip mall, I flew through the grocery store. As I crossed the parking lot carrying my bags, another idea occurred to me. I dumped the bags in the trunk and headed back toward the buildings.

Twenty minutes later, I was the proud owner of a baggy, nondescript hooded sweatshirt. I pulled the tags off and slipped it on before I left the store, hood up.

When I reached the city limits, I huddled deeper into the hood. A layer of tight leather, two layers of warm fleece, and a layer of sheer panic made the sweat trickle down my back while I carefully maintained the speed limit past the eagle-eyed police officers at the edge of town. They'd constricted traffic into one lane, and as I watched, they flagged down a tractor-trailer and waved the driver over to the side of the road.

Lucky they weren't looking for a dull-blue, rusted-out junker of a Caprice. I drove on by, eyes riveted to the road.

After an hour of driving, I bit down rising panic. I was lost. I hadn't been paying attention to where Dave had gone in the dark of the previous night, and in the morning we'd driven north and east instead of retracing our original route.

Goddammit, that road had to be around here somewhere.

After another fifteen minutes of futile zigzagging on the back roads, I slapped my forehead hard enough to rattle my teeth. Retracing my route to the highway, I headed north until I found the road where we'd joined up in the morning. Then I followed the route backward. Duh.

Dave's truck was a beautiful sight when I crested the gentle hill at last.

As I nosed the Caprice into the crossing, Hellhound swung out of the truck and hurried over while Dave climbed stiffly down from the driver's side. Arnie's arms closed around me the instant I stepped out of the car.

"Jesus, darlin', it took ya that long just to pick up this piece a' shit?" he teased, but his eyes were worried and he ran a gentle hand over my hair.

I pulled away to grin at him. "Watch your mouth. You should know better than to judge a book by its cover. Look at this."

I popped the hood and enjoyed the sight of two astonished faces. "Sleeper car," I told them with satisfaction. "It's the 350 with the four-barrel carb that came with the original police package. It made over two hundred and fifty horsepower before Bruce even started tinkering with it. And it's got all the drive train and suspension upgrades. Bruce picked it up at an auction and did everything but the body. And look at this."

I grinned as I opened the trunk and pointed out the blue-painted steel bottle and braided steel lines.

"Nitrous boost. Sweet," Dave breathed. "And is that a Hurst shifter I saw? Got a racing tranny in her?"

"Yep. She's done to the tits." I beamed at them. "This

car's taken more pink slips than you can count. Bruce used to make some good coin selling off the cars he won in bets, back before they cracked down on street drags."

I savoured the happy memories for a few seconds longer before reaching in to hand them the grocery bags. "You guys hungry?"

"Darlin', I love ya. Will ya marry me?" Hellhound grabbed the package of pepperoni sticks and tore the plastic off with his teeth.

"Not a chance," I assured him, and we exchanged a grin.

Dave selected a package of deli roast beef and ripped into it with equal enthusiasm, if slightly more decorum. For a while, the only sound was the crackling of plastic wrappers while we perched on the trunk of the Caprice and ate.

At last, Arnie blew out a long sigh and leaned back, reclining against the rear windshield with his arms folded behind his head. "Shit, I needed that. Don't s'pose ya got any beer."

"No, sorry. That would go down nicely right now, wouldn't it?"

I leaned back beside him, enjoying the fading sunset and letting the day's tension leak out of my muscles.

Dave straightened slowly and turned to regard us. "Now what?"

I blew out a sigh of resignation and sat up. "Now we need a plan. Spider still hasn't been able to find Nichele."

"Ya talked to him?" Arnie sat up hastily. "How? Isn't Kane watchin' him, too?"

"Not when he plays World of Warcraft. That's how I got in touch with you the first time. I contacted Spider inside the game, and he contacted you."

"Shit, I wondered about that. I was just doin' a report for

a client an' all of a sudden, this message popped up on my screen, 'Aydan, Hotel Village, eleven PM, emergency'. I couldn't figure out what it was, 'cause it wasn't an email or anythin', just a little message box." He scowled. "An' then I called Kane right away. Fuck."

I rubbed his shoulder. "It's okay, you couldn't have known."

"Who's Spider? Is that a code name?" Dave peered at me eagerly.

"No, just a nickname," I said, to Dave's obvious disappointment. "His real name is Clyde."

"Oh. So..." he hesitated. "That's bad news about your friend. Do you think she's... uh..." He gave me an apologetic glance. "Already dead?"

I scrubbed my hands over my face, trying to hold back despair. "I don't know. She was still alive Thursday night. One of my other friends talked to her then. But she was on her cell, not at home, so maybe James is holding her somewhere. I hope."

I looked over at Arnie's rigid face. "You're the private investigator. What do you think?"

"I think I'm gonna kill the fucker myself if I find him."

"Arnie..." I laid a hand on his arm, feeling the unyielding muscles through his jacket. "I know you're not a violent man."

"Then ya don't know me very well."

I hid a shudder at the sight of his eyes. I didn't know how to respond. I knew he'd dealt death in combat, and I knew how much violence he'd suffered as a child. But he'd always been so gentle with me.

I took his face in my hands and looked into his eyes. "Everybody has a violent side. I know you choose not to be that person. You don't have to let James change that."

His face softened, and he pressed his cheek briefly against my hand. "Thanks, darlin'."

"So what do you think we should do?"

He sat for a few moments, absently running his jacket's zipper up and down while he stared into the gathering dusk. "We gotta find Jim. No point lookin' for Nichele. He's prob'ly got her stashed somewhere." He reached over to squeeze my knee reassuringly. "Don't worry, darlin', I doubt if he's killed her. Jim's a smart sonuvabitch, an' I bet he still wants to set her up to take the fall for this launderin' scheme."

"So how do we find him?" Dave asked.

Hellhound scowled. "*We* don't. I do. I got a few markers I can call in. Might take me a while, but I know where to start lookin'."

"Do we go back to Calgary tonight?" Dave persisted.

Hellhound and I exchanged a look. "Can you think of any place we can hole up?" I asked.

"Yeah..." he replied slowly. "But I don't wanna stay there any longer than we hafta. We're prob'ly better off stayin' here tonight. It's gettin' late anyway. Better to sleep here an' get an early start tomorrow." His eyes glinted with his wicked grin. "Mosta the guys I'm gonna see tomorrow ain't much for early risin'. They'll be easiest to find in the mornin'."

"Okay." I slid off the trunk of the Caprice. "I have to go for a run. I've been cooped up and on edge for so long I'm ready to explode." I grabbed my backpack and headed for the truck to change.

Later, shoehorned into the miniscule bathroom in the sleeper, I realized my mistake when I peeled off my sweaty clothes. God, when had I washed my hair last? I ran a brush through it, shuddering. Not for the first time, I blessed my coarse waves. Even when my hair was nearly crawling off my head, it still didn't look too bad. I freshened up as best I could in the tiny sink and put on the last of my clean clothes.

When I emerged, Hellhound eyed me enviously in the dim illumination of the dome light. "Wish I had a change a' clothes, too," he said.

"Thought you'd never ask," Dave snorted as he opened a cabinet door and tossed a T-shirt at Hellhound's head. "Here. You smell like the south end of a northbound bear."

Hellhound reddened. "Didn't think it was that bad," he mumbled as he rose.

"It's not, Dave's just rattling your chain," I assured him.

He peeled off his shirt, and the sleeper seemed suddenly smaller as I admired the play of his bulky muscles. Dave offered him a deodorant stick with slightly more deference, possibly impressed by the extensive display of colourful tattoos.

Arnie nodded thanks and wedged himself into the bathroom to wash up as well. When he stepped out, he pulled the clean shirt on and flexed his shoulders carefully. "Ain't sure if this's better or not."

Dave's T-shirt strained across his chest like a second skin, and his biceps stretched the sleeves. His solid abs were clearly defined under the taut fabric, and I nearly suggested to Dave that it was time for him to go for a walk. A nice long walk.

"It's doing it for me," I purred.

Hellhound grinned, his eyes hot on me. "Ya think this's

doin' it, gimme a few minutes alone with ya."

Dave flushed and shuffled toward the door. "Uh, I think I'll go for a walk."

"It's okay, Dave," I said quickly, tearing my eyes away from the skin-tight cotton. "We're just kidding around. We all need to get some sleep."

"Speak for yourself, darlin'." Hellhound leered. "I don't need sleep that bad."

"That's because you were snoring your head off last night while I lay here and listened to you," I retorted. "You might not need sleep, but I do."

"Okay," Dave agreed hurriedly. "You can have the bed tonight."

When I started to protest, he raised both hands and took a step back, flushing. "No, really."

"Why don't we take shifts," I suggested. "That way, we can all get a bit of sleep."

"Nah, I don't need the bed," Hellhound disagreed. "It's prob'ly too small for me anyway. The two a' ya can trade off. I did fine in the seat last night."

"You can have it for the first half, Dave," I said. "I didn't get cold until later in the night anyway."

"Okay..." he said hesitantly. "Promise you'll wake me up when it's your turn, though."

"I will."

I had hoped to fall asleep before Dave, but he was snoring within minutes. I sighed in frustration while I squirmed in the passenger seat again. Arnie seemed to be having difficulties, too. In the cloud-bound blackness, I heard him shift a couple of times before he blew out an irritable breath. Dave snored on, a raucous one-note solo.

I wrapped my jacket more tightly around me and tried to find a comfortable position, not quite shivering, but not quite warm enough, either.

I heard movement from the driver's seat again, and a moment later, Hellhound whispered, "Can't sleep, darlin'." Leather creaked, and I felt him kneel beside my seat. Warm lips and rough whiskers trailed down my neck. "I been thinkin' about your leather top, an' it's keepin' me up."

My hands found his chest in the blackness, and I leaned close to nibble his ear. "I've been thinking about your tight T-shirt. And what's underneath it. And what's south of it." I slid my hand a little lower.

His growl raised the small hairs on the back of my neck. "Oh, yeah, darlin'. Down an' to the left."

His lips found mine as his hand glided over my breast. I encountered the bulge in his jeans and fondled it, tasting his lips with the tip of my tongue.

He groaned and pulled me closer, dexterously unfastening my jeans one-handed.

I grabbed his hand and pulled away a fraction to whisper, "We can't. Dave's right there. And there's not enough room anyway."

Hellhound's hand slid under my T-shirt to begin a persuasive campaign, teasing me with feather-light touches. I found myself clutching at his firmly-packed cotton as his gravelly murmur tickled my eardrum. "It'd take a bomb to wake Dave up. An' there's always a way if ya wanna get creative."

He kissed me deeply, his tongue sending shivers of hot desire to places that were already begging for his touch. He slipped an arm around me and stood, pulling me out of the seat.

He kissed me once more, then spun me around to pull my back against his front. His beard and moustache woke electric tingles under my skin as he mumbled against my neck.

"Did ya like spoonin' with Dave this mornin'? How'd ya like to spoon with me now?"

His hand slid under my shirt and into my bra, and I drew in an unsteady breath when his fingertips transformed into a teasing mouth, nibbling and sucking. His other hand drifted to my undone jeans, easing them down.

I made a grab for his wrist in an effort to keep my pants on. "I'm not going to get naked, not with Dave right here," I hissed. "If he opens his eyes, we're the first thing he'll see."

Hellhound's deep chuckle vibrated my neck. "It's dark. He couldn't see his hand in front of his face. An' ya don't hafta get naked, darlin'."

His fingers dipped inside my panties and I gasped as he began to do all the right things in all the right places. My God, the man was a virtuoso. And it had been two goddamn long months.

I pressed back against him, trying not to soak up the delicious sensations shooting through my body. Dave was only a few feet away. This was totally inappropriate. Any minute now, I'd make Hellhound stop... doing... ohmigod... *that...*

My hips moved against his hand without my permission, begging for more despite the distant protests of the tiny remaining part of my sensible mind.

"You're all hot an' slippery, darlin'," he growled against my ear. "Ya like the danger, don't ya? Ya like knowin' ya might get caught."

My denial somehow got lost on the way down from my brain, and all that emerged from my lips was a breathless moan when he got truly creative with those magic fingers.

My jeans slid a little lower. He wrapped an arm around my waist, holding me while his hands momentarily ceased their mind-melting work. A zipper whispered behind me, and I recognized the sound of a condom wrapper. I tried to seize the opportunity to pull away, but lost the will to complete the movement when his hands went back into action seconds later.

Hot, stiff temptation pressed against my ass, and a wave of hungry lust dragged me under.

I tried. I really did. One last feeble attempt. "There's not enough space..."

"No problem," Hellhound whispered. He sank into the passenger seat and pulled me toward him. "You're gonna sit on my lap an' tell me what ya want for Christmas, little girl. I think ya been naughty." He hooked a finger into the crotch of my thong, pulling it aside as he guided me down. "This's what naughty girls get for Christmas."

I lost my breath as he slid inside me, and his hand began to work its magic again. I had a moment of sheer appreciation for his strength and flexibility when he began to thrust unhurriedly, and then sentient thought melted and puddled in the luscious heat.

"What d'ya want for Christmas, naughty girl?" he whispered, pulsing slowly, so slowly. "Ya want this?"

"Harder..." My plea came out louder than I'd intended, and Dave's snoring was broken by a sigh and a suspenseful pause before it resumed, louder than ever.

"Shhhh. Don't wanna wake Dave." Hellhound continued his smooth, leisurely rhythm, driving me wild with need. I rocked in his lap, trying to make him quicken the pace, but he wrapped an arm around my waist to hold me firmly. His strong abs flexed, the feel of all that controlled power beneath me making me hotter still.

"Ya want this?" His fingers increased their tempo between my legs while his slow, sensuous thrusting continued.

"Please..." The word came out on a rising moan while the wicked pleasure expanded and radiated through my body.

He removed his grip from my waist to clamp his hand over my mouth instead. "Shhh, darlin'. Remember, Dave's right there."

He nibbled my neck and kissed his way up to nuzzle my ear, stroking more heat into me all the while. "Dave could wake up any minute an' catch us. He could open his eyes right when you're comin' your brains out." His rough-edged voice stimulated my eardrum with the same erotic texture as his whiskers on my skin.

God help me, I didn't think I'd been harbouring any audience fantasies, but the illicit excitement spiralled out of control. Little whimpers escaped me while my body begged for release, and I struggled again, trying to urge him on. Oh, God, almost there...

He held me tightly, controlling the pace while my pressure built. Tremors of tension shook me, and he reduced his tempo still more while his touch lightened, prolonging the exquisite finger torture while those slow, slow thrusts pumped in more ecstasy than my body could hold.

"What d'ya want for Christmas, darlin'?" he muttered breathlessly.

A few more measured strokes...

I gasped an uneven breath, the first of the contractions rolling through my body at last. I arched back against him with a strangled cry.

"HardOhGodHard*Please*..."

His body tensed. "Don't... wake... Dave..." he rasped. His grip tightened convulsively, and he pounded up into me. Once. Twice...

My orgasm ripped through me, the intensity redoubling with each powerful thrust. His body was like iron under me, his arms locked around me while I bucked mindlessly against him.

His hoarse whisper jerked out in time with his hard, deliberate rhythm. "Ah... God... darlin'... Nnnngh!"

He slammed home one last time, and our bodies strained against each other to the sound of our ragged gasps.

CHAPTER 21

I sprawled limply in Hellhound's lap, trying to catch my breath. Dave snored on, undisturbed by our panting. Sweat trickled down my back, and when I made an attempt to sit up, my entire body trembled.

Hellhound's breathless chuckle rumbled up from beneath me. "Sure glad I ain't Santa Claus."

I fell back against him, setting up the straight line for the old chestnut. "Because..."

"I'd only get to come once a year." His arms tightened around me and he pumped suggestively.

"Uh-huh. Old joke." I twisted around to give him a sideways kiss over my shoulder. "Help me get up. My legs won't work."

"An' ya think mine're gonna? Hell with that. Sleep right here." He cuddled me closer and faked a snore.

"No, thanks. I don't want to get caught with my pants down." I struggled away and stumbled gracelessly to my feet. "Shit. That was my last clean pair of underwear."

I heard the grin in his voice. "Everybody needs a purpose in life. Mine's makin' sure panties get wet." A pause. "Shit."

"What?"

"I think ya creamed on the front a' my jeans, too.

They're sticky."

I let out an evil chuckle. "Everybody needs a purpose in life. Mine's getting your jeans sticky."

I woke to gray dawn light, a kink in my neck, and scratching sounds from the driver's seat. I yawned and squinted over to see Hellhound scrubbing at the crotch of his pants. He grinned at me as I sat up. "How're your panties this mornin'?" he inquired.

"About the same as your jeans." I yawned again and stood up to stretch, realizing as I did that Dave wasn't snoring. He met my eyes and glanced away quickly to study the ceiling of the sleeper.

"Good morning," he mumbled. "You, uh, didn't want the bed last night?"

"Um, no, I fell asleep in the seat and just woke up now." I felt heat rising in my face, and turned back to the passenger seat to fumble in my backpack for a fictitious something.

Hellhound rose from the driver's side and finished brushing off his jeans, completely unabashed. "Ya might wanna go for a walk, darlin'," he advised. "I gotta take a dump."

"On my way." I reached for the door handle.

"Jeez, too much information," Dave protested.

As I swung out the door, I heard Hellhound's retort. "What, like ya weren't gonna notice me takin' a shit two feet away from your head? Just givin' ya fair warnin'..."

I was pacing back and forth, shivering and watching my breath plume in the cold morning air when Dave climbed stiffly down from the cab a few minutes later.

I shot him a grin. "Decided to vacate?"

"Uh... yeah." He reddened, and I followed his gaze to the used condom peeking out of the tall grass. We both turned away hurriedly. He scuffed a toe at the gravel. "Aydan... why are you with a bum like him?"

"He's not a bum. And I'm not *with*," I made air quotes around the word, "...him. Arnie's a good friend. I trust him more than... anybody..." I trailed off as the memory of Kane's betrayal sneaked up and sucker-punched me.

Dave frowned. "You should find a guy that won't sleep around on you. Somebody who'd always be there for you. Somebody with some manners at least."

I heaved a sigh. "I don't want that kind of commitment. And Arnie's completely genuine. What you see is what you get. That's worth more to me than any fancy manners."

"But... don't you ever want..."

"No, I don't," I interrupted gently.

"Oh." He stared at the ground. "Well, guess I'll stretch my legs a bit." He turned and limped away, and I resumed pacing, trying to stay warm.

Shortly after, Hellhound swung out of the cab. "Better give it a minute," he advised when I started toward the truck.

"I'm freezing my ass off," I complained.

"Ya need some breakfast," he nodded sympathetically. "Come here, darlin'." He unzipped his jacket and folded me in, wrapping his jacket and arms around me. I snuggled close, soaking up his body heat.

The sound of the truck door made me look up, and Hellhound shrugged. "Looks like you're last in line this mornin'. Might as well get breakfast." We rummaged through the remainder of the previous night's groceries, and by the time Dave emerged, I was feeling much better. I dawdled over the last few bites before taking my turn in the truck.

I hesitated over the tiny sink for a few moments, contemplating the dirty clothes in my backpack and trying not to look at my hair. Clean clothes and a shower were beginning to take on an attraction of mythic proportions. I rinsed out a few pairs of panties, cursing my lack of foresight. If I'd done this last night, they'd be dry by now. Dammit.

I regarded the cold, wet handful with irritation. They were clean, but I didn't know whether we'd be coming back to the truck or not. No point in hanging them to dry here. I pondered for a few moments before sticking my head out the door. "Hey, Dave!"

"Yeah."

"Have you got a tool kit?"

"Yeah, what do you need?"

"Wire, if you've got it." I climbed down as he extracted a box, and we surveyed the contents together. "There, that'll do." I pointed to a small roll.

"What's it for?" he asked as he handed it to me.

"Don't ask." I popped the hood on the Caprice.

Naturally, both men ambled over to take a look. Hellhound guffawed and Dave blushed when I strung my panties on the wire and carefully secured them in front of the radiator.

"Is that a good idea?" Dave mumbled.

"It should be okay. It's a cold morning. They don't take up too much area, so it shouldn't overheat on the highway. I'll take them off before we get into city traffic."

Hellhound leaned against the bumper, still grinning while he surveyed Dave's red face. "Maybe the car won't overheat, but Dave might. 'Specially when ya show him your skimpy panties an' start talkin' about takin' 'em off. Ya tryin' to get his jeans sticky, too?"

Dave scowled and his flush deepened as his fist clenched.

"I was talking about taking them off the radiator, smartass," I said. "Just ignore him, Dave."

Dave seemed disinclined to let it go. His normally cheerful face was hard as he turned to Hellhound. "Time you started showing Aydan a little respect."

Arnie sobered and heaved himself off the car. "Ya know I respect ya, don't ya, darlin'?" he asked, eyeing Dave.

"Of course. Dave, it's okay, he's just joking around." When he didn't respond immediately, I laid a hand on his arm and made the most convincing appeal I could think of. "Dave, I really need you guys to get along. You're all I have right now."

He glanced down at my hand and covered it with his own. "Okay. For you." He shot another hard look at Arnie. "Clean it up from now on."

Hellhound's shoulders seemed to expand. Leather creaked ominously.

I hastened to intervene. "Dave, I know you're looking out for me, but Arnie and I have been friends for a long time, and I like him just the way he is. If you guys turn this into a pissing match, I'm going to end up dead. So stop, okay?"

Dave dropped his gaze. "Okay. Sorry," he mumbled.

"It's okay." I turned quickly to intercept Hellhound's expressionless stare. "We need to get going. Arnie, what's your plan?"

He eyed Dave for a second longer before turning to me. "Head into town. I'll tell ya where to drop me off, an' we'll set up a pickup point."

We got under way with only a brief moment of tension when the two men faced each other beside the passenger door. “I’ll need Arnie in the front to give me directions,” I said, trying for a casual tone. Dave grunted and got in the back, and Hellhound remained impassive as he slid into the front seat.

Once in Calgary, I followed Arnie’s directions and pulled over beside the curb in one of the seedier neighbourhoods, thankful for the camouflage provided by the rusted-out Caprice.

Arnie nodded. “Pick me up here at one. If I ain’t here, keep comin’ back every hour. If I ain’t back by four, leave without me.”

“But...”

“Trust me,” he interrupted. “If I ain’t back by four, I ain’t comin’ back.”

Anxiety chilled me. “How dangerous is this for you, anyway?”

He shrugged. “Dunno. Guess I’ll find out. See ya.” He got out of the car.

“Wait!”

He paused on the sidewalk. “What, darlin’?”

I hopped out of the car and came around to hold him. “Don’t go. It’s not worth it. We’ll find another way.” I tried to guide him back to the car, but it was like trying to move a boulder.

He leaned down to drop a kiss on my lips. “It ain’t gonna be a big deal. See ya at one.”

Fear squeezed my heart, and I wrapped my arms around his neck to hold him when he tried to pull away. Discomfort flickered in his eyes, and I understood immediately. I quickly pasted on a grin before I kissed him thoroughly and groped his ass with both hands. “Get your ass back here in one piece. I’ve got plans for it later.”

He grinned and relaxed. "See ya, darlin'."

I made myself turn away and get into the car. He was vanishing into an alley by the time I turned to look again.

Dave climbed into the passenger seat with a grunt and surveyed my face. "He'll be fine," he said gruffly. "Let's go."

I put the car in gear and drove blindly away, my mind racing. God, what if something happened to him? Because of me. I endangered everybody. Everywhere I went. Everyone I met. The horrible responsibility crashed over me.

I hadn't realized I'd whimpered out loud until Dave's hand closed over mine. "Hey, Aydan, it'll be okay."

I looked into his faded, concerned eyes and felt even worse. Because of me, he was on the run from the law and his livelihood was parked out in the middle of Bumfuck, Nowhere. He might end up in jail, or dead, just because he was a nice guy who was trying to help.

"Jesus, Dave, I'm so sorry," I choked.

He frowned. "Pull over for a second."

I obeyed, steering into a convenience store parking lot. When I put the car in park, he took my hand and looked into my eyes. "What're you sorry for?"

"I'm sorry you're involved in this. You're in deep shit because of me, and I feel so bad, and I don't know how we're going to get you out of this..."

"It's not your fault," he protested.

"Dave, it's *all* my fault. You could end up in jail, or dead, Arnie could get killed..." I tried to swallow the tremor in my voice. "Nichele might die because I was too damn stupid and selfish to warn her off..." Guilt suffused me as I remembered my drunken decision to give up trying to convince her to dump James.

"Hey." His hand tightened on mine. "Hey, Aydan, this

was my idea, remember?"

"I know, but you didn't know what you were getting into..."

"Yeah, I did," he said firmly. "You told me right from the start. Look, we're in this together, okay?"

"Yeah, that's the whole problem..."

"It's okay." He pulled me into an awkward hug and patted me on the back. "It'll be okay."

I dropped my forehead onto his shoulder in resignation. He thought I was exaggerating. He thought he was being a hero, and he didn't have a punched-out clue.

The smell of ripe armpits brought me back to practicality, and I pulled away. Too late to worry about what we couldn't change.

"Thanks, Dave. We've got a few hours to kill. Let's go get a shower." A flush crept up his neck. "Separately," I added.

"Where?" he asked. "Thought you said we couldn't go to a hotel or a truck stop. Campgrounds are all closed by now, too."

"But the gyms aren't. If you were hunting for a fugitive, would you think to look in a gym? Who in their right mind would go and work out when they were on the run?"

"Guess you're right. Good idea."

At the YMCA, we paid our cash drop-in fee and parted ways in the lobby. The bored clerk paid us no attention, and I strode into the women's change room trying to look nonchalant, backpack in hand.

When I emerged blissfully clean from a long hot shower, I poked through the contents of my pack with distaste, selecting the cleanest of my dirty T-shirts. At least I had clean underwear.

I hesitated for a few moments, then shrugged and tossed my remaining T-shirts into the sink to wash. If I spread them out in the car, they'd dry eventually.

It was nearly noon by the time I stepped out of the change room again.

I spotted Dave immediately, in conversation with a heavyset, balding man at the edge of the lobby. Both men looked up as I approached. Dave gave me a nervous smile, and the other man eyed my snug T-shirt and jeans with interest when I joined them.

"Jane, this is Randy," Dave introduced me. "We drive for the same outfits a lot of the time. Randy, this is my girlfriend, Jane." He slid an arm around my waist, and I leaned into him and tried to act natural as I greeted Randy. Shit, what were the chances that Dave would be recognized here of all places?

"You're putting me on, right?" Randy demanded. "No way you're going out with him."

I felt Dave stiffen, and I ran my fingers through his still-damp hair. "Of course I am."

I kissed Dave, and he pulled me closer and took his time. Apparently he'd had a chance to think about the tongue action. He was considerably bolder, and he was only blushing a little when he pulled away. We were smiling at each other when Randy snorted.

"Nice try, Dave. How much did you have to pay her?"

Dave reacted so fast I didn't even have a chance to stop him. He bunched Randy's shirt in his fist and shoved the other man back against the wall. "Now you're going to apologize to Jane," he snarled, his scowl inches away from

Randy's alarmed expression.

"Jeez, relax," Randy stammered. "I was just kidding around."

"Apologize," Dave grated, jerking Randy's shirt for emphasis.

"Sorry, I'm sorry, Jane," Randy babbled. "I didn't mean anything by it..."

"Dave, sweetie, it's okay, let's go." I glanced around at the interested bystanders and the clerk, who was reaching for the phone.

Shit, shit, shit!

I pried Dave's fingers loose and tried to drag him away as unobtrusively as possible while he glowered back at Randy.

"Dave, come on," I hissed in his ear. "You're attracting attention. We've got to get out of here."

Dave shot one more venomous glare at Randy's pale face before he turned and put his arm around me again. "Nobody calls my girlfriend a whore," he spat.

I hustled him out the door. "Calm down," I whispered. "And hurry up."

Once in the car, I drove rapidly, taking as circuitous a route as possible. With a safe distance between us and the gym, I pulled over, shaking, and blew out a long breath. I stared through the windshield for a few moments, trying to summon up some tact.

"Jeez, Dave, what were you thinking?" I burst out. "What if that clerk had called the cops?"

Oops. Failed at tact. As usual.

He scowled and crossed his arms as he slouched down in the passenger seat. "Nobody calls you that. Nobody."

"Dave, I don't give a shit. They can call me frickin' anything they want. We can't afford to attract that kind of attention."

He gave me an obstinate glare. "Not gonna apologize for that. You don't talk that way about a lady."

I stared back at him in frustration, teeth clenched to prevent me from saying something I'd regret. It wasn't worth the trouble to point out that I was about as far from being a lady as I was from being his girlfriend. He clearly wasn't in the mood to listen to reason.

"Just don't do that again, okay?" I gritted finally. "No matter what."

Dave said nothing, just stared out the windshield with his lips pressed together.

I blew out another breath and steered the car toward our pickup point.

CHAPTER 22

I shifted impatiently in the seat and looked at my watch for the sixth time in about ten seconds. The clanging of the warning bells at the train crossing matched the jangling of my nerves while the train dragged its interminable ass across the road.

I looked at my watch again. "Jesus Christ!" I burst out. "Could you go any fucking slower, buddy?"

Dave shot me a worried look. "It's okay, we're only a couple of minutes late."

"Yeah, but what if he needs us? Or what if he's waiting, and he decides we're not coming, and then he goes away for another hour..." I realized my voice was rising rapidly and bit off the rest of the sentence. And glanced at my watch. Again, for chrissake.

At last, the train cleared the crossing and the guard-arms lifted. I bumped over the tracks a little more quickly than absolutely necessary. "What the hell were they thinking putting a train track through the middle of a residential neighbourhood, anyway?" I muttered.

Dave wisely made no response.

I pulled in at the curb, gazing anxiously around. There was no sign of life except a ragged elderly man shuffling along in the next block, pushing a shopping cart full of bottles and cans.

Heart pounding, I glanced at my watch, then around the neighbourhood again.

"How long are you gonna wait?" Dave asked.

"Just a bit longer. Just in case he's running late." I caught sight of my glowing white knuckles, and peeled my fingers off the steering wheel.

"We better go," Dave muttered after a few minutes.

I was just reaching for the shifter with a shaking hand when a bulky figure limped out of the alley toward us.

"Oh my God!"

I bailed out of the car fast. Hellhound swiped a hand across his eyes and squinted at me. "Hey, darlin', let's get outta here," he mumbled.

His face was a mask of blood, and his hands and shirt were so blood-caked I couldn't tell whether he had other injuries or not. Dave opened the back door, and I guided Arnie toward it. He pulled his arm away from me impatiently.

"Get drivin', darlin'," he muttered as he stumbled to the car and fell into the back seat. Dave and I exchanged frightened glances, and I dove back into the driver's seat and got us out of there.

Hellhound hauled himself upright and slumped against the door.

"Where are you hurt?" I demanded. "Dave, look him over, find out where he's hurt."

"I'm fine, darlin'," Hellhound mumbled thickly. "Just a busted nose. No big deal."

I eyed him worriedly in the rear-view mirror. "That looks like a gash in your forehead, too."

"Yeah, I got a couple little bumps and bruises."

Dave peered over the seat at him. "Head for the hospital," he advised. "Gonna have to get that nose straightened out."

"Nah," Hellhound disagreed. "Don't wanna attract attention, an' I been able to fix that since I was a kid." He wiped some more blood out of his eyes and scrubbed his hands against the torn T-shirt before reaching for his nose.

"Since you were a kid?" Dave demanded.

"Yeah." Hellhound snorted, sending a fine spray of fresh blood over the grisly T-shirt. "First thing I ever remember about Jim, that fuckin' asshole. Him tellin' me to shut up an' yankin' on my nose. Learned how to do it myself after that."

He positioned his hands, and Dave and I both flinched at the unpleasant crunching sound that followed. A fresh cascade of blood poured down. Arnie wiped his hands on his T-shirt again and extracted a switchblade knife from his jacket pocket, flicking it open to slice strips from the cleaner part of his shirt.

I chose to ignore the illegal weapon. "How old were you?" I asked.

"Dunno. Mom was still alive, so maybe three or four."

"Jeez, how many times did you break your nose when you were a kid?" Dave gaped at him, eyes round.

"Coupla times." Hellhound began to methodically pack his nostrils, stopping to swipe away the steady trickle of blood from his forehead as it ran into his eye.

"Didn't your folks take you to the hospital?" Dave persisted.

"Nah. Mom tried to fix my face..." He shrugged and smeared his hand through the seeping blood again.

I pulled the car into an alley and parked so I could get into the back seat beside him. "Where else are you hurt? Let me see."

"Told ya, I'm fine," he muttered. "Keep drivin'. We gotta get ya outta here, fast." He cut off another chunk of T-shirt and pressed it against the torn skin of his forehead. I winced at the sight of his swollen, gouged-up knuckles.

"We go nowhere until I'm sure you're okay."

"Aydan, get in the goddam seat and get fuckin' drivin'! Jim's got a fuckin' contract out on ya. No tellin' who's after ya now. Move!"

A fresh wave of fear washed over me, and I swallowed it with difficulty. "No. The sooner you let me look at you, the sooner we'll get on the road, so cooperate."

"Fuck, Dave, take over!" Hellhound commanded. "Get us the hell outta here."

Dave swung out the passenger door with alacrity and froze, half doubled over, hissing through his teeth.

"Aw, for chrissakes!" Hellhound snapped. "Don't tell me ya put your fuckin' back out again!"

"It's fine," Dave gritted, and hobbled around to the driver's side, still canted over. He sank slowly into the car, the muscles in his jaw bunching as he clenched his teeth. Seconds later, we were in motion.

I turned to Arnie. "Now, tell me where you're hurt. Or I'll strip you naked and find out for myself."

His teeth flashed in a lopsided grin through the gory mess. "Sounds good to me, darlin'. Come an' get it."

"You asked for it." I leaned close and pulled his hand away from the gash on his forehead. "You should probably have stitches."

"It'll heal up."

"But not well."

He shrugged. "It ain't gonna hurt my modellin' career

any."

I examined the rest of his head and face. His left eye was swollen half-shut, but the skin didn't seem to be broken. Hard to tell under the layer of drying blood.

"Okay, let's get your jacket off."

"I'm fine. Just lemme be."

"Now, soldier!" I rapped out, and he started.

"Jeez, darlin'..."

"Move it!"

He blew out a half-sigh, half-groan, and painfully leaned forward to remove his jacket. I helped him work the sleeves off his arms, and reached around behind him to lift it away. I froze when my hand contacted a hard shape at the middle of his back.

"Arnie...?"

He shrugged and pulled out the gun. "Just bein' prepared."

The car swerved slightly as Dave peered at us in the mirror. "Where'd you get that?"

Hellhound shrugged again. "Found it."

"Where?" Dave demanded suspiciously.

"A guy kinda gave it to me."

"Kinda?" It was my turn to fix him with a sceptical eye.

"Well, he didn't object," Hellhound mumbled, not meeting my gaze. "Don't think he'll report it missin'." He stuffed it back into the waistband of his jeans.

I opened my mouth to admonish him, realized the futility, and sighed instead. A once-over of his upper body revealed only bruises, providing an unflattering background for his tattoos. I stopped again as I worked my way down his legs.

"Just leave 'em there," he muttered when I drew a

wicked-looking knife out of each boot and examined them.

"Nice." I tucked them back into place. "Rambo."

He laid his head back and closed his eyes. "Ain't takin' any chances. Ya still got your stun gun, Dave?"

"Yeah."

"Good. Aydan, ya got your gun, too?"

I sighed. "Yeah. But I'm the only one who can use a weapon and get away with it. You guys are going straight to jail if you do."

Hellhound shrugged and said nothing.

Dave shot me an avid glance over his shoulder. "I knew it. You have a double-oh-seven license, don't you?"

I winced. "No, Dave."

"Then how'd you get away with killing those four guys?"

Hellhound's eyes snapped open. "Four?" He regarded me sharply. "Ya only told me about one."

"Um, yeah," I mumbled. "Sorry, need-to-know. And anyway, Dave, I told you, it was self-defence. It wasn't James Bond stuff. Pull in here!"

Dave slammed on the brakes and took a hard right into a strip mall. "Where?"

I pointed. "We need some first-aid stuff, some more food, and Arnie needs a couple of shirts."

He parked, and I started to get out of the car. Arnie grabbed my wrist. "Wrong, darlin'. Let Dave go. Ya got two separate bunches a' guys tryin' to kill ya. You're gonna stay here where I can keep an eye on ya."

"Right," Dave agreed. He eyed Hellhound. "What size do you need?"

"Extra-large. Double-X if they got it."

"Get some frozen peas or something, too, if you can," I told Dave. "A couple of bags. One for his face and one for his hand. And some bottled water and a towel so we can get him cleaned up."

"Got it." Dave swung the door open. He eased one leg out of the car before stiffening into immobility with a gasp. I could hear the faint grinding of his teeth as he lifted his other leg out with both hands. By the time he had his feet on the ground, I got around to the door and helped him stand while he straightened by degrees.

"Guess I twisted it again messing with Randy," he grated. "Back in a bit." He hobbled slowly across the parking lot.

"I'm gonna get in the front," Hellhound mumbled around his packing. "He's gonna need to stretch out. Come an' stand in fronta me so nobody sees the blood."

He got out of the car with slightly more grace than Dave, but I could tell he was feeling the effects of all those bruises. As he sank into the front seat, he transferred the gun to the front of his jeans and pulled his jacket over top. He eyed me for a moment. "Ya might as well get in the driver's seat again. An' then we gotta have a talk. While Dave's in the store."

I got back in the car and shot him a look. The wound in his forehead was still oozing steadily, and his beard and moustache were so encrusted with clotted blood that he looked barely human. "Are you really okay?" I asked before he could speak. "Tell me the truth, now that you don't have to put on a front for Dave."

Hellhound made a noise that probably would have been a snort if not for the packing in his nose. "I don't give a shit what he thinks," he growled. "I got nothin' to prove. An' I'm fine. But we gotta talk about Dave. Who's Randy, and why's he messin' with him? What'd ya do while ya were waitin' for me?"

"We went to the Y and had showers. Dave ran into this guy, Randy, that he knew from work. Randy made some crack about me, and Dave grabbed Randy and threatened him. Made a scene, and I had to drag him out before anybody got excited and called the police."

"Fuck. The guy's a fuckin' walkin' mid-life crisis," Hellhound spat. "He ain't thinkin' straight, he's got a giant hard-on for ya -"

"Oh, I don't know," I interrupted. "It was big, but I wouldn't say it was giant."

Arnie snickered. "Hope it ain't bigger'n mine."

"I'm not sure. Let me get my calipers." I rubbed my fingertips together and reached for him, bouncing my eyebrows.

He laughed out loud, the sound incongruous with his horror-show face. "Glad ya got your priorities straight. But seriously, darlin', ol' Dave thinks he's in loooove, an' he wants to be a fuckin' hero. He's gonna get us all killed."

I sighed. "I know. Any suggestions?"

"Drive away. Right fuckin' now."

"You know I can't do that."

"Why not?"

"Arnie, you know I can't. You wouldn't either. He's trying to help, he's put his ass on the line for us, and we can't just abandon him."

"He put his ass on the line for you, not us." I glared at him, and he blew out a sigh. "Yeah, I know, darlin', you're right. I just don't wanna see him puttin' ya in any more danger than ya are already. He's just a dumb civilian."

"So are we."

He eyed me thoughtfully, working his fingers through his crusty beard. "I don't think so, darlin'. Four guys?" He frowned, winced when the wound in his forehead opened up, and surveyed me levelly as he pressed the sodden wad of cotton against his brow again. "Why'd ya tell Dave that?"

"I didn't. The guys that were trying to capture me in Victoria told him. They were pretending I was an escaped criminal, and they told him I was armed and dangerous. That's how I got this." I flashed the black and purple bruise on my forearm.

"Wondered about that. What happened?"

"I was hiding in the bathroom in the sleeper. After they told him I was dangerous, he picked up an iron bar for self-defence. I had to let him hit me to prove I wasn't a danger to him."

Hellhound jerked upright, his face twisting with fury. "He hit ya? That fucker, I'm gonna twist his fuckin' back so he never fuckin' walks again!"

"No, you're not." I glared at him until he subsided. "He was scared. They told him I'd killed four guys and that he was in danger. You would've done the same thing."

"No, I wouldn't," Arnie said flatly. "I'd never hit a woman. Never. No matter what."

"I'm sorry." I took his uninjured hand and stroked it, smearing the half-dried blood. "I know you wouldn't. I'm sorry."

We sat in silence for a few moments before he met my eyes again. "Yesterday, I thought ya were just bein' nice when ya said everybody had a violent side. Seems like ya know more about that than I thought. Ya wanna tell me about the other three guys?"

"It was self-defence. I shot two on the way out of the warehouse in March, right before you picked us up."

"Those fuckin' assholes," Hellhound growled. "After

what they did to ya, shootin' was too good for 'em."

I sighed. "And you remember the fire at Spider's house a couple of months ago? There was a guy... He was going to kidnap me and leave Spider in there to burn. I had to shoot him so I could get Spider out. That was... hard. Personal. I... I'd known the guy for a while, and I liked him... before. I thought he was a nice kid. But it was all lies. Just more lies."

His arm closed around my shoulders, and I leaned my head against him. "Ya okay, darlin'?" he asked gently.

"Do I have a choice?"

He sighed and his arm tightened around me. "Nah. Just askin'."

"I'm okay."

"Good."

"There's Dave." I straightened up as I spotted him limping toward us, a couple of large bags in his hands. "That's got to hurt his back, carrying those bags."

I reached for the door handle, but Arnie's hand closed on my wrist. "Wait for him to get to the car. Ya can help him then."

I waited until he drew closer before getting out to take the bags from him and hand them in to Hellhound. Dave eased painfully into the back while I did my best to support him, and at last we got him half-reclining across the seat while Arnie rummaged through the bags.

"Lotta stuff in here," he observed. "Ya need more cash?"

"No," Dave grunted. "Used my plastic."

"What?!"

"Shit!"

Hellhound and I let out simultaneous exclamations of dismay, and I leaped for the driver's seat.

CHAPTER 23

"What?" Dave demanded as I slammed the car into gear and peeled out of the parking lot.

"Slow down, darlin', don't attract attention," Arnie said tensely.

"Right. Dave, stay down. Arnie, get cleaned up if you can." I slowed the car to the speed limit and tried to look everywhere at once. "Where should I go?"

"Forest Lawn. Use some back roads," Arnie snapped, scrubbing roughly at his face. He slopped some water onto the already scarlet towel and twisted around to look behind us before continuing his efforts.

"What? What's wrong?" Dave repeated.

"They'll be watchin' for credit card activity, dumbfuck," Hellhound grated. "Ya might as well've put up a big fuckin' neon sign, 'Here we are, come fuck us up the ass with a dead chicken'. If they catch Aydan because a' you, I'm gonna -"

"Arnie, cut him some slack, he didn't know..." I begged.

I jumped as Hellhound overrode me with a sudden shout. "Fuck, Dave, don't ya ever watch the fuckin' movies? Ya thinkin' with your fuckin' dick, or what?"

"Arnie, don't! Please!" Stress nudged my mind into overload. "Wait... what did you say?" I faltered as the car slowed along with my brain. "Isn't that '*like* a dead chicken', not '*with* a dead chicken'...?"

"Like, with, whatever!" Hellhound yelled. "Drive the fuckin' car, or we're all gonna be fuckin' dead chickens!"

"Don't talk to her like that!" Dave blazed from the back seat. "You big dumb ugly bastard, you're not worth the dirt on her shoes..."

Hellhound spun to lunge over the seat at Dave. "Ya fuckin' little-"

I slammed on the brakes.

The car jerked to a halt, accompanied by two heavy thuds and yells of pain as Hellhound slammed into the dashboard and Dave crashed into the back of the front seat.

Hellhound dragged himself slowly up from his contorted position in the foot well of the passenger seat, holding his head. I squelched my spasm of guilt at the sight of the gash in his forehead bleeding freely again.

"What the hell did ya do that for?" he inquired mildly.

"Speak for yourself," I told him. "I'm not fucking any dead chickens."

"Say what?" He held the towel to his brow and gaped at me.

"You said we were all going to be fucking dead chickens. I'm not fucking any chickens, dead or alive, and that's final."

He stared at me for another instant before letting out a roar of laughter. An irritated driver laid on the horn behind us and swung out to pass, giving us an aggressive middle finger as he went by. Arnie laughed even harder, holding his sides and bellowing.

Dave joined in with a feeble chuckle from the back seat, and within seconds, the car was rocking while we guffawed helplessly. A chorus of angry horns from behind us made me wipe the tears from my eyes and take my foot off the brake, still giggling feebly.

"Dead chickens," I repeated, and we all snickered some more.

I sobered as a police car sped toward us in the oncoming lane, lights flashing but no siren. "Better put on your seatbelts, guys."

I took the next right turn and zigzagged sedately through a residential neighbourhood to emerge on another main road. We had a quiet and uneventful trip to Forest Lawn.

At the industrial park, I followed Hellhound's directions to a large overhead door in a nondescript brick building. As we pulled up, Hellhound shot a wary glance around the deserted parking lot. "If anythin' happens to me, just drive away."

"No." I pulled my gun out of my ankle holster. "I've had enough bullshit today. If anything happens to you, I'm shooting the guy who made it happen."

He eyed me for a second before the uninjured corner of his mouth quirked up. "Okay, darlin', that works, too."

He climbed stiffly out of the passenger seat and approached a keypad beside the door. After another furtive look around the lot, he punched in a code and quickly stood back against the brick wall as the door began to roll up.

He glanced into the opening and nodded satisfaction, motioning me forward. As soon as the door was high enough, I drove the Caprice into the cavernous space. Arnie ducked in behind and immediately punched a button to roll the door down again. As the crack of light disappeared, I turned on the headlights in the pitch darkness.

A few seconds later, ceiling lights blazed to life, and I turned off the headlights. Arnie headed for the front of the bay, looking pleased. "We're good, darlin'," he tossed over his shoulder. "Ya can get out now."

I scanned the bay, recognizing autobody and welding tools. I was just beginning to wander away from the car when Dave's tight voice stopped me.

"Need a hand."

I turned back to the car to find him still crumpled in the back seat, half on the floor. "Can't move," he said apologetically.

Fear rushed through me. "Can you feel your legs?"

"Yeah. Wish I couldn't, though." He grimaced and struggled to sit up. Sweat sprang out on his forehead, and he froze again, panting through clenched teeth.

I heaved a sigh of relief. "Be careful what you wish for."

"Yeah, guess you're right. I'm okay, just need help to swing my legs around."

"I'll get you out." I leaned in, surveying the situation. "What do you want me to do?"

"Don't know. If I could get up on the seat, I'd be able to use my arms. Just can't get ahold of anything here."

"Okay, I'll try to get you onto the seat."

"Don't wreck your back, now, too," he admonished.

"I'm not planning to." I placed one foot carefully beside his legs in the foot well. "If you just put your arms around my neck, I'll be able to push off the seat with both hands and drag you up. Hold on..."

I got my other knee braced on the seat, one arm on each of the seatbacks. "Okay, put your arms around my neck."

"No," he objected. "You can't hold my weight with your neck."

"Arnie!" I called.

"Yeah."

"We need help."

"Be right there."

"What if you put your arms around my shoulders?" I suggested.

"Might work." Dave clasped his arms around me, and I heaved upward.

I managed to raise him a few inches before my shaking arms collapsed under an overdose of adrenaline and an under-dose of blood sugar. The impact wrenched a cry out of Dave when our combined weight landed on the seat. Panting, I tried to squirm carefully off him before I hurt him any worse.

"Jesus, no kiddin' ya need help," Hellhound chuckled. "You're doin' it wrong. Ya gotta take your clothes off first."

I struggled up from my straddled position over Dave's body and backed out of the car to see Arnie leaning against it, a beer in his bloodcaked hand.

"What are you doing?" I demanded.

"Raidin' the beer fridge," he said smugly. "Weasel owes me."

"We need to get Dave out right away." I took a deep breath, trying to slow my racing heart.

"Awright, what d'ya wanna do?" He poked his head in. "That's gotta hurt."

Dave grunted. "Just get me out of here."

"Okay. Aydan, if ya go around to the other side, can ya lift his shoulders? I'll get his legs."

"I'll try."

Arnie eyed my trembling hands and blew out a breath. "When did ya eat last, darlin'?"

"Breakfast." I went around the car.

"Fuck, this ain't gonna work. Ya gotta eat first."

"No, I'll be okay. We've got to get him out."

Dave was the one stuck in the car, but I was feeling panicky on his behalf. Trapped, in pain, unable to move... I shuddered and got into the car beside him, switching to yoga breathing. Stay calm.

"You okay?" Dave eyed me with concern.

"Fine. Come on, Arnie, let's do this." I slid my hands under Dave's arms and locked my hands over his chest while Hellhound reached in the other door, one arm under Dave's legs while he braced himself against the seat back with his other arm.

"Pull him toward ya. Just get him on the seat," Hellhound directed. "On three. One, two, *three*!"

I heaved on Dave's shoulders and a hoarse cry burst out of him as his body flopped onto the seat.

The nightmare flashed in front of me. The unending raw-throated screams of agony. The smells. My own pain. The terror of being trapped.

I squeezed my eyes closed, breathing carefully. In. Out. Ocean waves. That was long past. Breathe.

"Aydan?"

I jerked with shock, my eyes flying open when Dave touched my face. Trapped. I clamped down hard on my urge to leap out of the car and run screaming.

"What's wrong?" he asked, wide-eyed. "You're white as a sheet."

"I'm fine." My voice didn't seem to be working right.

Hellhound opened his mouth to speak, his eyes worried, and I shook my head. "I'm fine. Let's get Dave out."

"I can sit up. Just help me a bit," he said, still eyeing me with concern.

I sat beside him and pushed him slowly into sitting position, trying not to listen to his grunt of pain. My heart hammered and long tremors shook my body.

"Okay, I'm gonna pull him out now," Hellhound said. "Just stay up against his back while I pull."

I nodded, and together we shuffled Dave across the seat. When his feet were on the ground, he drew a long breath. "Should be fine now."

He grabbed the door and hauled himself up inch by inch, muscles working in his jaw. When he finally stood almost upright, I scrambled out the opposite door and clung to it, trying to calm my breathing.

Dave took a few faltering steps, leaning heavily on the car, before straightening another couple of degrees and limping ahead with more confidence.

"Couch over there," Hellhound suggested, pointing to a broken-down sofa so begrimed I hadn't even noticed it skulking in the shadows.

Dave nodded. "Later. Gonna walk a bit." He hobbled down the bay, and Arnie turned to me with a frown.

"Ya okay, darlin'?"

"Fine."

"Bullshit. Sit." He steered me over to one of the grubby upholstered chairs beside the sofa.

"Arnie, I'm fine. You should sit, you look like hell. Let me-"

"Sit," he interrupted, and pressed me into the chair that had the least amount of duct tape holding the upholstery together. "Stay."

"Woof, woof."

"Funny girl." He strode to the car and returned with the grocery bags, then sank slowly into the second chair. "Here." He handed me a cellophane-wrapped chocolate snack cake.

I shuddered, my stomach twisting. "I can't. If I eat that

sugary stuff, I'll throw up."

"Shit, no orange juice." Hellhound dug through the bags. "I shoulda told Dave to get some. Wait, here's some bread an' peanut butter. An' some beef jerky."

"That'll do." I accepted the food gratefully. I paused with the open peanut butter jar clamped between my knees, then shrugged and rolled up a slice of bread to drag it through the peanut butter. Hellhound grinned as I stuffed in a mouthful.

"I was gonna offer ya a knife for that," he observed. "Guess ya don't need it."

"Got one of my own. Later." I wolfed the slice in a few bites and stole a swallow of his beer to wash it down.

"I'll get ya a beer," he said as I tore into the beef jerky, but I grabbed his sleeve and shook my head, gulping my mouthful.

"Can't. I have to be able to drive." I swallowed a few more bites before turning back to him. "Hold still."

I wrung out the bloody towel and poured fresh water over it to clean his face more thoroughly. The wound in his forehead still bled sluggishly, and I dug into the shopping bag. At least Dave had gotten a good selection of first-aid supplies.

Taped and bandaged, with most of the blood cleaned away, Arnie looked marginally better. He took the wet towel from me and scrubbed at his beard and moustache.

I pulled two packages of half-melted peas out of the grocery bag and handed one to him. "Put this on your face, and give me your hand." He slouched down in the chair with a sigh, leaning his head back and draping the bag over his nose, cheek, and forehead. I cleaned his hand and bandaged it, then gently applied the other bag to his swollen knuckles.

"Arnie, I'm so sorry."

He shrugged and mumbled from under the peas. "No big deal. Price a' doin' business with these guys."

"Tell me what happened."

"Nothin'. I found a coupla guys, talked to 'em, found out what I needed to know."

I blew out a breath of frustration. "I meant, what happened to you?"

"Nothin'. Some a' these guys, ya just gotta talk to 'em by hand."

I gave up. "So what did you find out? Did you find out where Nichele is?"

He lifted the peas off his face and squinted at me. "Kinda lost interest in that when I found out Jim's tryin' to kill ya."

"Arnie, we need to find Nichele."

"I know, darlin'. None a' the guys I talked to today knew anythin', but I put some feelers out. Should have somethin' in the next day or so."

"Why would James want to kill me?" I asked. "Unless... he's trying to get rid of anyone who can connect him to Nichele."

"Yeah, that's what I was thinkin'," Arnie agreed. "Guess I'll be on the list, too, then." He lay back and stretched out his legs, replacing the cold bag on his face.

I bolted upright in horror. "Oh, no, Arnie, he wouldn't. You're his brother. He wouldn't..."

"Hell, yeah, he would." Hellhound shrugged. "I told ya he ain't on my Christmas card list."

I clutched his hand. "Arnie, I'm so sorry, this is all my fault..." I froze as another ghastly thought hit me.

"Oh, no! And Dante will be on the list, too! Poor Dante,

he doesn't have a clue, this has nothing to do with him..." I wrapped my hands over my head and curled into a ball, rocking in sheer misery. "Oh, God, Arnie, how many innocent people have to suffer and die because of me?" I clenched a couple of fistfuls of my hair, still rocking. "Everything I touch, everybody I meet..."

"Shhh, darlin'." The peas hit the floor, and Arnie's arms were warm around me as he knelt beside my chair. "Shhh. It ain't your fault. Who's Dante?"

"He was at the bar, too. He's a friend of Nichele's. That's how I got away from Kane, I pretended I was going home with Dante, and now he's going to die because of me, just like you and Nichele and probably Dave..."

The peanut butter and beef jerky attempted to climb the back of my throat as my stomach clenched. "Arnie, I can't do this anymore! I'm going to call Kane. Maybe he can still stop James. Where's the phone?" I pulled away and staggered to my feet, nausea searing my gut.

Dave limped toward us, looking anxious.

"Slow down, darlin'." Arnie rose to take me in his arms, holding me firmly. "Ya ain't callin' Kane. He's got orders to shoot ya, too, remember?"

"Arnie, I don't care anymore! I'm not going to get out of this alive, anyway. If that's what it takes to save innocent people, then the sooner I'm dead, the better. Just let me call him and get it over with." I tried to twist away from him.

"Aydan, stop!" Hellhound's voice was like the crack of a whip, and I froze in shock.

"We're bustin' our asses here to keep ya alive," he snapped. "I didn't get the shit kicked outta me so ya could lie down an' die. Dave's fuckin' crippled, an' screwed outta his next haul, too, if he don't end up in fuckin' jail over this, 'cause he's tryin' to keep ya alive. The least ya can do is try."

I stared into his swollen, battered face, sick with guilt, and swallowed hard. "But you'd both be fine if not for me," I whispered.

I felt Dave's hand on my shoulder, and he came around to stand beside Arnie as he looked in my face. "Aydan, it's not your fault."

"It ain't, darlin'," Arnie agreed. "This's my fault for leadin' Jim to ya in the first place. I shoulda tried harder to shake him. This's my fuckup, not yours."

"We knew what we were getting into," Dave put in. "We're gonna help you."

"Guys, you can't..." I looked from one to the other and gulped back the urge to burst into tears. "Thanks. You're the best."

CHAPTER 24

I turned away to hide my emotion. "So is your buddy an autobody guy?"

"Yeah, kinda."

"It's a chop shop, isn't it?" Dave demanded.

I turned in time to see Hellhound's eyes dart sideways. "I wouldn't know," he said virtuously.

I manufactured a grin. "You mean you haven't asked the question."

"That, too."

"I wondered why you were so jumpy coming in here," I prodded.

"Yeah, well, sometimes if he's busy, he don't like to be interrupted." Hellhound studied the ceiling. "Ya know how it is when you're workin' on somethin'."

"Yeah. Any chance he'll be getting any... work... in the next couple of days?" I asked.

"I dunno, hard to say. Ya know how it is when ya got your own business, ya don't always work regular hours."

I snorted. "Well, at least we won't have to worry about him calling the police."

"Nah, prob'ly not. Wanna beer, Dave?"

I smiled at Arnie, recognizing the peace offering. Apparently Dave was willing to give it a chance, too.

"Yeah. Maybe it'll relax my back. Thanks."

Hellhound headed for the front of the bay, and I turned to Dave. "I'm sorry I slammed on the brakes that way. That must've really hurt."

He shrugged and shuffled his feet. "It's okay. You had to do something. Sorry. Really sorry about the credit card, too," he mumbled. "Should've known better, I just wasn't thinking."

"It's okay. Do you want me to rub your back again?"

He looked up hopefully. "Would you? That'd be great."

"Come and lie down on the couch." I looked at it a little more closely. "Ew. Maybe you don't want to put your face on that."

"I don't care."

He started to lower himself onto the couch, and I shuddered. "Wait." I grabbed my hoodie out of the car and spread it out. "There."

"Thanks."

He eased into prone position and buried his face in the jacket. I perched beside him and began to knead his back to the sound of his rapturous groans.

Hellhound returned and placed Dave's beer on the floor beside the couch before sinking into one of the chairs with a fresh bottle of his own. "Jesus, Dave, d'ya mind? Ya sound like a fuckin' porno movie."

Dave grunted. "You don't know how good this feels," he mumbled into the jacket.

"Christ, if it gets any better, you're gonna need a smoke after," Hellhound groused.

I got up to drop a kiss on the undamaged part of his face. "You're just jealous."

"Hell, yeah, darlin'. When're ya gonna make me groan

like that?"

"No time soon." I laid the cold peas over his grin. "Keep these on until I say you can take them off. And here." I placed the other bag over his knuckles. "Now behave."

Some time later, Dave sat up slowly while I rubbed my aching thumbs as unobtrusively as possible against my thighs. "How's that?" I asked.

"Better." He stood and stretched tentatively. "A lot better. Thanks."

He made for the grocery bags, and I turned to Arnie with a pang of concern. He was still immobile in the chair, his face obscured by the soggy bag of peas, and he'd been silent the whole time. Not a single smartass remark. That couldn't be good. I lifted the bag off carefully.

"How are you doing?"

"Fine."

"You're very quiet."

"Just thinkin'."

"You should eat something, too."

"Yeah." He sat up and took the grocery bag from Dave. "Sit down, darlin'. Ya need to eat somethin' more than a slice a' bread."

I eyed the contents of the bags without enthusiasm. Chips, pepperoni, snack cake, beef jerky, and pop. Not a scrap of fruit or anything resembling nutritious food. Guy heaven. At least there was peanut butter and the loaf of whole-wheat bread. I was touched that Dave had remembered my breakfast of choice.

"Thanks for the bread and peanut butter, Dave," I said, and he flushed and nodded, looking pleased when I helped myself to another slice.

I drank the last of the bottled water and sighed,

unsatisfied. I got to my feet. "I'm going out. I should be back in about an hour and a half."

"Not so fast, darlin', where ya goin'?" Hellhound rumbled.

"I need to find a library or an internet cafe. I need to tell Spider to protect Dante. Oh." I stopped as a thought struck me. "Oh, shit."

"What?" Dave demanded.

"I... uh... just thought of something. We have to warn Kane."

Hellhound rose, frowning. "Aydan, ya promised ya wouldn't call Kane."

"I... won't... But, Arnie, he was at the bar, too. James saw him, and Nichele knows who he is. If James is cleaning up, Kane will be on the hit list, too. We have to warn him."

"*Shit!*" His fist clenched. "Goddamn sonuvabitch shit! Who else was there? The fuckin' Pope, too?"

I sighed. "No. That's it. Nichele, James, Dante, Kane, and me. But I don't know how Spider can warn Kane without telling him about us. If Kane finds out he's been holding out on him, Spider will be in deep shit, too." I groaned and made fists in my hair. "Christ, I'm fucking Typhoid Mary. One more innocent bystander bites the dust because of me."

"Don't fuck Typhoid Mary," Hellhound said solemnly.

"...What?" I caught sight of the twinkle in his eye and gave him a feeble grin. "Wiseass."

"An' anyway, ya ain't goin' anywhere. Let Dave or me go."

"I can't."

"Why not?"

I turned to Dave. "Do you know how to play World of

Warcraft?"

"Uh, what's World of Warcraft?"

I turned back to Arnie. "You?"

He scowled and kicked his heel at the concrete floor. "Okay," he growled. "Lemme change, an' then we'll get going." He extracted one of the new T-shirts from the shopping bag and yanked the tags off.

"No, you guys stay here. I'll just go."

"Not a fuckin' chance." Hellhound shrugged stiffly out of his jacket, held it up briefly to examine the drying blood, and tossed it on the chair. The tattered rags of his T-shirt followed, and I took a moment to appreciate the view before he pulled on the clean shirt.

I trod carefully. "Um, I don't think it's a good idea for you to come with me. You and Dave both need some recovery time."

Hellhound eyed me with unconcealed exasperation. "What part of 'ya ain't goin' out alone' ain't ya gettin', darlin'?"

"I'll attract less attention if I'm by myself."

"Aydan, for chrissake," he began.

I abandoned subtlety. "Arnie, you can't come with me. Look at yourself. You're a mountain of tattoos and leather, your face looks like you just lost an argument with a Mack truck, and your jacket and jeans would be cleaner if you'd dismembered somebody with a dull axe. If anybody sees you, they're going to call the police just on general principles. I can't afford that."

"Well, ya ain't goin' out alone." He glowered down at me.

"Fine, I'll take Dave."

He started to speak, scowling, and I shot him a warning

glance. We locked eyes for a couple of long seconds before he blew out a breath. "Okay. Tell me exactly how long you're gonna be. If you're gonna be even a second late, call the shop here. I'll give ya the number. If ya call from a pay phone, nobody'll know to trace it."

He turned and limped to the front of the bay, disappearing through a grubby door that presumably led to an office. In a couple of minutes he was back, bearing a scrap of paper with a number scrawled on it.

"Now tell me where you're goin'. An' if ya don't check in on time, I'm comin' to get ya."

I gazed around the empty bay. "With what?"

"I'll find a way. Where're ya goin'?"

With our itinerary established, Dave winced back into the passenger seat, and I backed the car out of the bay and headed for one of the free internet terminals downtown.

We'd driven for a few minutes when Dave turned to me. "Uh, Aydan, can I ask you something?"

"Sure."

"What was wrong? Back in the car there? Were you sick?"

"No. If I get too hungry, I start to shake, that's all."

He eyed me uncertainly. "Yeah, I figured that out the first day I picked you up. But this was different. You looked like... I dunno, like you were seeing a ghost or something."

"Oh." Embarrassment flooded me. "I was in a bad accident quite a few years ago." I shrugged, watching the road. "It was just a flashback. No big deal."

"Are you okay now?"

"Yeah, fine." I hoped he'd drop it, and he mercifully did.

I kicked myself for my stupidity as I shoved four dollars into the parking machine for a lousy half-hour. Note to self: Next time, find a place with free parking.

I approached the computer kiosk in the mall warily, Dave trailing a few feet behind. I glanced back to see him swivelling his head back and forth, looking nervous.

"Dave."

He caught up to me, and I leaned close to whisper. "You look like you're about to shoplift something. Try to look casual."

"How?" He gazed at me imploringly. "Tell me what to do so I don't screw up again."

"Come here." I put an arm around him and guided him to the counter. "Just lean against the counter beside me and pretend to be bored waiting for me. Stare off over my shoulder so you can watch my back."

He placed an elbow beside the keyboard and propped himself up stiffly, still looking anxious. I patted his cheek. "Relax. Think happy thoughts."

I turned my attention to the terminal and got in the game.

"Spider."

"r u OK?"

"Yes. Did you find N?"

"no"

I swore without much surprise, and Dave jerked beside me, his worried eyes glued to the screen. I squeezed his hand. "Dave. Watch my back. Look casual." He nodded and cast a nervous gaze over my shoulder, and I returned to the chat screen to find Spider's text scrolling.

"r u there? r u there?"

"Yes. J might have a contract out on Kane."

"u mean a hit?"

"Yes. Make sure he's careful. And he needs to protect D. Might be a contract out on him, too."

"who's D?"

Shit, of course he wouldn't know who Dante was. I racked my brain for Dante's last name and came up completely blank. Surely Nichele had mentioned it, but I hadn't been sober at the time. I hissed frustration through my teeth.

"Dante. Sorry, don't know his last name. Friend of N's. Underwear model." I felt a pang as I imagined Spider's blush, wondering if I'd ever see him again.

My fingers trembled over the keyboard for an instant before I added, "Find out if D's still alive." I couldn't bear the thought that he might be dead, but I had to know. I swallowed hard and pressed the Send key.

Dave's arm settled around my shoulders. "It'll be okay, Aydan," he said.

"Thanks." I swallowed again and turned back the screen where Spider was again demanding my attention.

"r u there?"

"Yes."

"u need anything else?"

I was just about to type 'no' and sign off when a thought occurred to me. I took a deep breath. If anybody could find out, it would be Spider.

"Can you find out," I hesitated, afraid to ask the question, afraid to hear the answer. Dave's arm tightened around my shoulders as I took another deep breath, hands frozen above the keyboard. I let the air leak out between my lips. "...if S killed my parents and Uncle R, too?"

"WHAT??"

I saw no need to repeat myself. "I'll check back later. Over & out."

I logged off and cleared the cache, then stood staring at the screen for a few seconds. I barely prevented myself from jerking in shock when Dave pulled me gently to him and kissed me. A soft, vanilla kiss.

He stroked my hair back with a tense hand and leaned close to whisper in my ear. "There's a guy watching us."

"Thanks, Dave, let's get out of here." I pulled away and smiled at him, and he slid his arm around my waist as we turned to stroll back to the parking lot.

Inside the car, I shot a look around. "Do you see him?"

"No. He didn't follow us." Dave's hand closed over mine as I reached for the ignition. "Aydan?"

"Yeah?" I turned to face him.

He flushed. "Uh... Could I, uh, could I... kiss you for real?"

I felt heat rising in my face as I gawked at him, wondering what to say.

"Sorry, never mind," he muttered, blushing scarlet. He turned to stare out the window, his ears fiery red. "Forget I said that."

"Dave..."

"It's okay, forget it. Let's go." His fingers closed convulsively on the hem of his T-shirt, bunching it in his fist. The muscles in his forearm rippled as he worked at the fabric.

Oh, God.

"Dave, you have been kissing me for real."

"I meant..." More abuse of the T-shirt. "...Like maybe you'd kiss me because you want to, not because you have to."

I spoke to the back of his head. "I've never *had* to kiss

you. If I didn't like you, I wouldn't let you within ten feet of me. And I sure as hell wouldn't be tongue-wrestling with you."

His fingers stilled, but he didn't turn. "Oh. Uh." A long pause. "But you're not really, uh... enjoying it. Are you?"

I grimaced, resisting the urge to pound my forehead against the steering wheel. Tact. Summon up some tact, for once in your life.

"Dave, I've been too shit-scared to think about enjoying it. This isn't the movies, and I don't get off on danger."

My conscience twinged as I flashed vividly back to Hellhound in the passenger seat. I bit my lip and ploughed on. "I'm sorry, I know I've been giving you some really mixed messages. I really do like you, but..."

He turned at last and met my eyes briefly before dropping his gaze to study the torn carpet on the floor of the car. "But not that way," he finished matter-of-factly.

"I..." I stared at him, struggling for something kind to say. But not too kind. Complimentary and encouraging, but not... encouraging. Goddammit...

"It's okay. Just had to ask." He shrugged. "We better go."

"Dave..."

"Forget it."

I watched him for a few seconds, but he didn't look up. I sighed, reached to guide his chin to me, and leaned over to kiss him. Plain vanilla. I didn't rush.

When I pulled back, I met his puzzled eyes. "I wanted to do that," I told him.

He smiled. "Thanks."

I fired up the car and listened to its smooth, soothing rumble for a few seconds. I love cars. They're so uncomplicated.

"How are we doing for time?" I asked.

"Forty-five minutes before we have to call Hellhound or get back there."

"Good. I want to stop and grab something for supper. I'm starving."

I chose a large, busy grocery store and gave Dave the mission of raiding the deli while I grabbed some apples, cereal bars, and juice. When we met at the checkout, he eyed my basket. "Sorry, guess I didn't do so well with the groceries earlier," he muttered.

"No, you did fine. I just like to have the juice in case I need a quick blood-sugar boost, that's all."

"Is this okay?" He held his basket out for inspection. My stomach growled audibly.

I clapped a hand over it and grinned at him. "Gets my seal of approval."

I dug into my waist pouch for my wallet, feeling Dave's eyes on my dwindling sheaf of bills. Back in the car, I consulted my watch. "Good, we've got enough time to get gas. I don't want to let the tank get too low."

"What'll we do when we run out of cash?"

"Worry about it when the time comes," I told him with more confidence than I felt. "Maybe Arnie has some."

"Yeah." He fell silent as we pulled onto the road.

Back at the industrial park, I waited for a couple of trucks to vacate the parking lot before I parked in front of the overhead door and trotted over to the keypad. I punched in the number and relaxed when the door began to roll up.

I was turning back toward the car when I caught a flicker

of motion in my peripheral vision. I sprang back, twisting to face the movement, and tripped over my own feet.

CHAPTER 25

My butt hit the pavement as a tire iron whistled by inches from my nose. I yelped and rolled, vaguely aware of Dave's shout as he started to scramble from the passenger seat.

My short, skinny assailant swung again and I scuttled crabwise on my knees and one hand, scrabbling for my ankle holster with the other. He might not be big, but those sinewy arms could sure swing.

I jerked away from his next attempt, and the iron swished through the ends of my hair where my head had been seconds before. Rolling frantically, I managed to fumble my gun out of its holster. Dave was hobbling toward us, yelling.

Everyone froze when I swung the Glock up.

"Drop it," I gasped, and stood carefully, trying to keep the gun steady. "Back in the shop. Slow."

God, where was Arnie? If this asshole had harmed him...

The asshole's prominent Adam's apple bounced as he gulped and dropped his weapon.

I steadied the Glock with both hands. "Back up. Nice and slow, into the bay."

I panted open-mouthed, trying to catch my breath and slow my pulse. As he backed away, hands in the air, I followed, maintaining our distance.

"Dave, pick up that tire iron and drive the car in. Don't get in my line of fire."

I didn't spare him a glance, just kept my eyes locked on my target. I registered movement out of the corner of my eye and heard the car door close. The Caprice eased forward at the same pace as I did.

When my captive reached the door of the bay, his eyes flicked sideways.

"Try it and die," I barked.

He paled and swallowed again, and I took stock of him while we continued our slow progress inside. Grubby sleeveless T-shirt. Skinny legs encased in dirty jeans. A skull-patterned black do-rag that didn't conceal the strands of greasy hair that drooped to his shoulders. Bad skin and a weedy moustache. Ground-in dirt on his hands. Blotchy blue tattoos on his forearms. And now I knew the true meaning of 'shifty eyes'.

A LeSabre convertible was parked in the middle of the bay. Dave snuggled the Caprice up to it and got out slowly.

"Close the door, Dave."

I heard the door roll down behind me. My arms were beginning to tire with the strain of holding the gun steady while my heart tried to hammer its way out through my backbone.

"Where's Arnie?" I snarled.

Do-rag's eyes widened. "Jesus, lady, why didn't you say so? He's in the shitter."

"Dave, go find him."

Dave was spared the trouble when Arnie appeared through the grimy door at the end of the bay.

"Fuck, Weasel," he snapped. "What the fuck're ya doin'?

I told ya they were comin'."

"What do you mean, what the fuck am *I* doing?" Weasel protested. "This crazy bitch pulled a gun on me, man!"

I blew out a breath of relief and let the Glock down.

"Don't you dare call her that!" Dave stumped furiously over to shove his glare into Weasel's face. "She should have shot you, you scumbag!" He turned to glower at Arnie. "He tried to kill her!"

"Ya tried to kill her?" Hellhound loomed over the other man.

"Jesus, no, I wasn't trying to kill her!" Weasel's gaze darted between the three of us, looking for an escape route. "I was just -"

"Swinging at her head with a tire iron," Dave finished grimly.

"I wouldn't have hit her," Weasel denied. He turned to Hellhound with a self-righteous expression. "It wasn't my fault. She didn't say she was with you."

"Ya fuckin' dumb shit," Hellhound said with resignation. He turned to me. "This's Weasel. In case ya didn't figure it out already."

I eyed Weasel. "I'm Jane. This is Dave." I moved to the car and pulled my waist holster out of my backpack, then made a show of putting it on and stowing the gun in it.

Weasel's gaze skittered to the LeSabre and back to my gun. "You're not a cop, are you?"

"No."

He relaxed visibly. "Want a beer?"

"Yes."

He hurried toward the front of the bay.

"So. Jane." Hellhound raised the eyebrow that wasn't obscured by bandages.

"Yeah."

"Weasel's a slimy little shit," he said. "But he'll keep his mouth shut."

"Just playing it safe. What happened to your pants?"

"Wet. Tryin' to get the blood out."

I gave him an up-and-down look, grinning. "Nice kilt."

He did a slow three-sixty, and I admired the way the thin material of the former T-shirt showed off his assets as he turned. He plucked at the crusty, tattered fabric and gave me a lopsided leer. "Like it?"

"Uh-huh."

Dave groaned. "Didn't need to see that." He limped over to one of the chairs and lowered himself carefully into it as Weasel returned with the beer.

"You're lucky," Weasel said. "When I came in, he was balls-ass naked. Like I wanted to see that. Jesus."

He strolled over to pass a cold one to Dave. "No hard feelings?"

"I'll think about it." Dave shot him a dark look and accepted the beer.

I tottered over to the chairs, too, knees quivering with my massive adrenaline overdose.

Dave glanced over as I sank down beside him. "Need to eat, don't you?"

I took a shaky swallow of beer. "Yeah, probably."

He was beginning to hoist himself up when Arnie limped over. "I'll get it." He reached for the grocery bag lying beside the chair.

"No, we got better stuff," Dave said. "In the car."

Arnie nodded and leaned in to extract the new batch of groceries. "Good." He nodded approval as he handed me an orange juice. "Here, darlin', drink this first."

"Thanks." I sipped at the juice while he unpacked the roasted chicken and tubs of potato salad.

"That's more like it," he said as he tore off a drumstick and took an enormous bite. "Got forks?" he mumbled through the mouthful.

Dave and I exchanged a sheepish look. "No."

Hellhound shrugged. "No problem." He pulled a knife out of his boot and scooped some potato salad out on the blade. He tipped the salad into his mouth and offered me the knife.

"I'm good." I delved into my waist pouch and pulled out my own sturdy folding knife.

Dave eyed me with askance as I tore off the other drumstick and dug into the potato salad. "How many weapons do you carry?" he asked diffidently.

"Just these." I carefully ate the salad off the razor-sharp blade. "Oh, and I have another jackknife with some tools in it."

He nodded, looking uncertain, and dug into his pocket to come up with a penknife. Hellhound shot him a pitying glance and pulled the knife out of his other boot. "Ya want a real one?"

Dave's gaze tracked from the boot, to the knife, and back to the boot again. "No. Thanks."

Hellhound shrugged and stowed the knife again, and we all settled in to devour our food while Weasel hovered, apparently fascinated.

"Any luck, darlin'?" Hellhound inquired at last.

"Made contact." I reached over to wipe my greasy hands on the cleaner part of his makeshift kilt, nobly refraining from leaning over a little farther to sneak a peek between his widespread knees. I took a deep swallow of beer. "I'll need to go back later tonight."

"Shit."

We finished eating, and when I drained the last of my beer, Weasel took the empty bottle out of my hand, his grubby fingers brushing mine. "Another?"

"No, I have to drive later."

"What time're ya gonna go?" Arnie asked.

"Around ten, I think. That'll give Spider enough time to find out what I want."

Weasel rested his elbows on the back of my chair and leaned into my personal space to eye me inquisitively. "Spider? Friend of yours?"

I kept myself from recoiling from the miasma of stale cigarette smoke that surrounded him, and gave him my best dead-fish eyeball. "Yeah."

"Oh." He leaned a little closer. "Damn, you smell good."

Hellhound shot him a menacing glare. "Back off."

Weasel straightened and shuffled his feet. "Uh, guess I've got work to do." He meandered toward the LeSabre. "I could use a hand," he threw over his shoulder.

"The less we know about what you're doin', the better," Hellhound growled. "All I know is, you're workin' on a car. Let's leave it at that."

Weasel bobbed his head. "Okay. That's cool, man."

We turned our backs on him as the din of pneumatic tools filled the bay.

Several hours later, my head was pounding. The air was polluted from Weasel's chain-smoking. Conversation was sporadic between the bouts of noise from his efforts, and there really wasn't much to talk about anyway.

Both Dave and Hellhound had helped themselves to a couple more beers, so I was reasonably certain they were enjoying themselves more than I was. Other than the fact that they were both probably in quite a bit of pain. I didn't envy them that.

When the hands on my ancient watch finally dragged around to ten o'clock, I got to my feet gratefully. "Time to go."

"...'Kay." Dave tried to struggle out of his chair and failed. He frowned, shuffled forward in the seat, and hauled himself onto his feet, his back still bent.

I took his arm and helped him straighten slowly. Furrows of pain etched his face, and he rested a heavy hand on my shoulder, staggering sideways a half-step.

I grabbed him around the waist, and he turned in my grasp, his eyes unfocused. "God, you're byoo'ful," he slurred. "Th... think I love you..." He staggered again and wrapped his arms around me. "Le's go..." he muttered into my neck. "Le's go an'... an'..."

His knees buckled, and I jerked my arms tighter to keep him from falling. His back popped under my grip, and he cried out in agony.

"Help!" I strained against his dead weight as he slithered toward the floor.

"Got him! Get him to the couch." Hellhound jerked his chin in that direction, and together we half-dragged, half-carried Dave over to it.

As we laid him out, he peered up at us through half-closed eyes and giggled. "Beauty... an'... an' the Beasht..."

"Fuck, Dave, how much did ya drink?" Hellhound demanded.

"Didn'... Jush a couple..." Dave blinked and screwed

one eye shut, apparently concentrating intensely. "Took... some pills... Oopssssh..." His other eye slid closed and he started to snore.

Hellhound glared down at him, fists on hips. "Shit."

I did a quick inventory of the empty beer bottles beside Dave's chair. "He really did only have a couple. The pills must've been pretty strong to knock him out like that. Maybe it's some prescription for his back pain. We'd better check and find out what it was."

Hellhound shrugged. "Well, I sure as hell ain't gonna put my hand in his pocket. That's more than I wanna know about him."

"I'll do it. We might need to phone Poison Control or something." I knelt beside the couch and gingerly slipped my hand into the nearer pocket of Dave's jeans. He snorted and sighed, but didn't wake. I came up empty, and reached across him for the other pocket.

This time my fingers contacted a jumble of change and other unidentifiable objects, and I groped through them, hoping I'd be able to recognize the shape of a pill container.

Dave let out an aborted snore. "Yeah, honey..." he mumbled. "Lower... Don' shtop..."

Hellhound snickered, and I froze until Dave's snoring resumed in a few seconds. Some more careful exploration yielded a small pill bottle. I let out a breath of relief at the sight of the label.

"They're just over-the-counter muscle relaxants. He should be fine. He'll just have a really good sleep."

"An' really good dreams," Hellhound snorted. "Lucky bastard. Well, darlin', guess we better get goin'. Lemme go get my pants."

He turned to go, and I stopped him with an outstretched

hand. "Same logic applies as last time. I really don't want to attract attention."

He frowned at me. "Well, Dave's outta the picture."

"It's no big deal. I'll just go by myself."

"No."

We eyed each other for a few moments, and I could tell I was going to have to come up with an alternative.

"Could Weasel come with me?" I suggested finally. "You trust him, right?"

Arnie's scowl darkened. "I trust him not to rat us out. That's it. I ain't sendin' ya anywhere with him."

"Well, it's him or nothing." I gave him my best don't-mess-with-me face.

He blew out an irritable breath. "Weasel's slime. He's got some kinky tastes, an' he doesn't know how to take no for an answer. He just finished doin' time for sexual assault."

I turned to stare in Weasel's direction, revulsion crawling over my skin. "He's a rapist?"

"Nah. He just doesn't know how to keep his hands to himself, an' it got him in trouble."

I blew out a breath of relief. "Well, that's no big deal, then. I can deal with roaming hands."

Arnie frowned down at me. "Darlin', I know ya can take care of yourself, but-"

"Look," I interrupted. "I need to get going. I don't know how long Spider will stay online tonight. You decide whether you want me to go by myself or take Weasel, but I'm leaving now."

He scowled and said nothing. I was turning away when he bellowed, "Weasel!"

"Yeah." Weasel's head popped up from the other side of the car.

"Need ya to do somethin'."

"What, like drinking all my goddamn beer isn't enough?" Weasel complained. "Come on, man, what do you think, I'm made of money or something?"

Hellhound shot him a hard glance. "Yeah. That's what I think. An' I know a coupla people that'd be interested in findin' out how ya get it."

"Aw, come on, man," Weasel whined. "Lighten up. I was just yanking your crank."

"Like I'd let ya touch my crank," Hellhound retorted. "Not. Get over here."

"Jeez," Weasel griped as he came around the car. "What got up your ass? What do you want?"

"You're gonna take Ay... Jane wherever she wants to go tonight. You're gonna watch her back the whole time. You're gonna keep your filthy fuckin' hands to yourself. An' you're gonna bring her back here, nice an' safe an' sound. Got it?"

Weasel eyed the half-stripped LeSabre before turning back to Hellhound. "How long is this gonna take?" he muttered. "I got work to do."

"An hour, hour and a half tops," I said.

Weasel tossed his wrench onto the floor with a clatter. "Fine." He shot a contemptuous glance at the Caprice. "We'll take my ride. Come on out the front."

As he turned to go, Hellhound stepped in front of him, looming threateningly. "Just wanna be clear. Ya do whatever it takes to keep Jane safe. Anythin' she says, ya do. Anythin' happens to her, an' ya ain't gonna live to boost another car. Got it?"

"Jeez, man, chill. I got it."

Hellhound stepped back, then added, "An' we need cash.

As much as ya can get."

"What?" Weasel yelped. "Come on, man. What the fuck..."

"I'll pay ya back." Hellhound glowered, and Weasel eyed him uncertainly, obviously wondering whether that was a threat or a promise.

"Okay," he muttered, and made for the door as if afraid Hellhound would add more demands to the list.

"Wait."

Weasel stiffened at the sound of Hellhound's rasp, and we both turned.

"Here, darlin'," Hellhound said, and held out my hooded jacket. "Better put this on. Ya forgot it last time."

"Thanks."

I took it from him in exchange for a kiss, and he leaned down to mutter in my ear. "Don't let him get to ya. Don't react, just ignore him if he gets started."

I pulled away. "I can handle him. I'm armed, remember? See you later."

He opened his mouth as if to admonish me further, but I gave him a reassuring smile and left before he could say anything else.

CHAPTER 26

Weasel's ride was a pimped-out Tiburon, lowered to within an inch of the pavement. I shot a look at the ultra-low-profile tires and slid into the car, wondering how many rims he went through. He'd need new ones every time he hit a dimple in the road. Then again, acquiring new parts probably wasn't a big deal for a guy like him.

Weasel lit up another cigarette and started the car. The stereo boomed to life, making me flinch. The bass resonated in my chest cavity, and the legs of my jeans quivered under the assault. Some part of the car vibrated with an irritating high-frequency buzz on each beat. I dug into my waist pouch and extracted my earplugs.

With earplugs in place, the noise was tolerable. I pulled the hood of my jacket over my head and slouched in the seat. At least nobody would think to look for me in a car like this with the stereo blaring. Talk about hiding in plain sight.

Weasel's hand skimmed the air from my knee to high on the inside of my thigh, mere molecules away. I started and jerked around to lip-read him over the din.

"Where to?" he asked.

I gripped his wrist and pushed his hand back over to his side of the car before reaching over to turn the volume knob down. "Do that again and I'll cut your hand off." I pulled out my knife and turned it back and forth, letting the light run along the blade.

His eyes widened. "Jeez, you're one crazy bitch. I never even touched you. Chill, already."

"Get the cash first. Then take me to an internet cafe. Somewhere far from here."

"All right, all right." He cranked the volume again and pulled out, bobbing his head in time to the music and grinning when car alarms went off in the vehicles parked beside the road.

After a stop at an ATM, Weasel drove south and eventually pulled up in front of a strip mall. When he turned the car off, the silence echoed. I gingerly removed the earplugs.

"There you go," he said, waving an expansive hand toward the small cafe.

"No, there we go," I corrected. "You're going to come in with me. You're going to watch my back and tell me if anybody is looking at me. You're going to stay with me until I'm done, and then we're going to come back out to the car together. If anything goes wrong, we'll split up, and I'll meet you at the car later. If you take off on me, I'll cut your nuts off and shove them up your ass. Got it?"

"Christ, lady, I said I'd help. You don't have to make such a big fucking deal about it." He paused. "You're thinking about my nuts?"

I ignored his last question as I folded up the knife and tucked it back in my pouch. "Just making sure we don't have any misunderstandings. I don't like misunderstandings. Now give me the cash."

"I'll give it to Hellhound when we get back." His eyes didn't quite meet mine.

"You'll give it to me right fucking now, or I'll ventilate your spleen." I lifted the bottom of the jacket to display my gun, channelling Hollywood gangsters for all I was worth.

He eyed me with an utterly unconvincing expression of wounded innocence. "You don't trust me."

"Hell, no, I don't trust you. Give me the goddamn cash."

He hesitated for a second before giving me a nicotine-stained grin. "I like you. You're fucking batshit crazy. And you wanna touch my nuts. That's totally hot." He handed over the roll of bills, his fingertips brushing my palm intimately. I hid my twitch of revulsion with an effort.

"Let's go." I got out of the car and waited for him to precede me into the cafe, making sure he didn't decide to bolt.

I sidled into the dimly-lit space and chose a terminal in the corner. Weasel hovered, and I nodded over to the counter. "Pay for it. I'm only going to be a few minutes."

He gave a martyred sigh and wandered toward the counter. I pulled my hood closer around my face and slouched while I logged in. I found Spider with no difficulty this time. Whisper.

"Spider."

There was a pause before his response appeared on the screen. "finally. r u okay?"

"Fine. Sorry, I got delayed. Any news?"

"nothing good." My heart plummeted, and I clenched the mouse until it squeaked. His text continued to scroll.

"no sign of D or N. all info on u redacted." I let out a breath that sounded like a whimper as Weasel meandered back. I ignored his questioning look and took a couple of deep breaths. At least they hadn't found any bodies.

"Is K all right?"

"yes."

Small mercies. "Thanks, over & out," I typed.

"WAIT!"

I ignored his text and logged out of the game. As I cleared the cache, I racked my brain. I had to do *something*.

Weasel offered me another yellow-toothed smile and drifted closer, and I realized I'd been staring blankly at him. I averted my eyes from the unedifying sight as an idea occurred to me. I might not have any family left, but my dad had lived on the farm most of his life. Maybe he'd confided in one of his neighbours. Or maybe one of his school friends from long ago.

As the names occurred to me, I searched them on the internet, scribbling contact information on the scrap of paper I'd extracted from my waist pouch. My heart pounded with tense hope. Thank heaven people of my dad's generation rarely bothered with unlisted phone numbers.

A movement at the doorway caught my eye, and I froze at the sight of the handsome young man who strode in. There was no mistaking the dimple in his chin and the thin scar that sliced across his cheekbone, visible even in the dim light.

Shit, shit, shit!

I dropped my head and logged off, clearing the cache again with shaking hands as I mumbled, "Create a distraction."

"What?" Weasel leaned closer.

"Create a fucking distraction. Now!"

There were definite advantages to associating with criminals. Weasel oozed away with movements as smooth and unobtrusive as his namesake, and slid into a seat at a terminal on the opposite side of the cafe. I kept my head bowed and watched from under my brows.

Suddenly, he smashed his fist onto the table. "Fuck! Fucking cheater!" he yelled as he rocketed to his feet. All eyes jerked toward him.

He dealt the table another vicious blow, shouting obscenities and alternately punching the air and the table. I moved unhurriedly for the exit, heart hammering.

Weasel kicked his chair against the wall, then swung around and grabbed it, brandishing it above his head as he bellowed. Nice work. He had everybody's full attention. I faded out the door and made a beeline for the car.

The locking system chirped as I approached it, and I realized with a surge of gratitude that Weasel was actually thinking. And looking out for me. I slid into the back seat and wedged myself as close to the floor as I could manage in the tiny space, wishing the streetlights weren't so bright.

About thirty seconds later, I heard Weasel's voice approaching the car. "Yeah. Sorry, I just got carried away. Sorry."

Another male voice rumbled, but it didn't sound like it was getting nearer.

"Yeah, I'll just go now. Sorry for the disturbance." Weasel slid into the driver's seat and whispered, "Jane?"

"Go," I replied.

The stereo blasted out its thumping beat again, and I felt the car accelerate.

I stayed hunched in my uncomfortable position for long minutes while the bass mule-kicked my eardrums and my protesting knees ground into the hard floor. I leaned forward on my elbows, stuffing my fingers in my ears in a desperate attempt to preserve some vestiges of my hearing. At last, the volume dropped from brain-pulverising to merely painful.

"I said, you can sit up now," Weasel shouted.

I uncurled, groaning, and hauled myself up onto the seat. "Thanks," I yelled over the music.

"What?"

"Turn down the goddamn music!"

"What?" The volume dropped again. "What did you say?"

"I said thanks."

"You're welcome. Want to fuck?"

I couldn't have heard that right. Loud music. "What did you say?"

"I said, you want to fuck? I got a massive boner thinking about you squeezing my balls. Mmmm."

Yeah, I'd heard that right. Unfortunately.

"No."

"Jeez, why not? I'm good. You'll like it."

"I'll pass."

"How about giving me a blowjob then? As a thank-you?"

My residual adrenaline morphed into irritation, making a potent cocktail. I kept my voice flat. "How about I give you a handjob with my knife? Last one you'll ever need."

"Kinky shit. Now I'm really hard." He reached to turn up the music again, then caught my eye in the rearview mirror, grinning as his hand slid into his lap. His elbow began to jog vigorously, and I developed a sudden keen fascination with the largely invisible scenery in the darkness outside the tinted windows.

Back at the industrial park, I climbed out of the car, resisting the urge to drop to my knees and kiss the ground. I settled for a couple of deep breaths of clean, quiet air while we walked across the parking lot.

Weasel sidled over, and I sprang away as his hands hovered inches from my ass.

"What?" he asked with pained innocence. "I didn't even touch you." He stepped close again, his face almost skimming my hair. "Damn, you smell crazy good. Sure you don't wanna fuck? I'm so hard I could drive nails."

My temper snapped as I dodged away again. "I wouldn't fuck you if you had the last dick on earth. You try that again, and you won't even have a dick. I'll rip it off and stuff it down your throat. We clear?"

"What? I didn't do anything." His eyes drifted half-closed, and he cupped his crotch. "You wanna pull my cock. You wanna squeeze my balls," he singsonged. "Goddamn, you're one crazy hot bitch. I'm gonna jizz in my pants right now." He rubbed himself through his jeans, moaning.

I breathed slowly through my teeth, wrestling with the fervent desire to pull out my gun and shoot him. At last, I convinced myself that being slimy and disgusting was, unfortunately, not an offense worthy of death. I turned and walked away instead, nerves twitching and sizzling.

The front door was locked. Of course.

"Sonuva-fucking-bitch!" I pounded violently on the door.

My skin crawled when Weasel spoke from too close behind me. "I got the key. Want me to slam my key into your hot, wet keyhole?" His hands appeared in front of me, tracing the shape of my breasts without actually touching me. His stale smoker's breath ruffled my hair. "Yeah," he crooned. "Oooh, yeah. Bend over. I wanna see your sweet ass in the air-"

The world went red, and I spun. My fist made a creditable attempt to reach his backbone through his solar plexus. The air barked out of him as he doubled over, presenting a marvellous target for the knee I hammered up into his face.

He said, "Urmfp," and started to fold. I was just winding up for a ball-crushing kick when powerful arms closed around me from behind and dragged me away.

I roared with pure rage, stomping down with one heel while I slammed my head back. The grip released when I made contact with a foot and a chin respectively, and I belatedly recognized Hellhound's yell.

"Darlin', stop! Ow! Fuck! Jesus! Fuck!"

I spun around, reaching for him in horrified remorse, and he took a quick step backward, his hands flying up defensively.

"Sorry, I'm so sorry!" I babbled. "Are you okay? I'm so sorry!"

He relaxed and gave me a lopsided grin, rubbing his chin. "Fine, darlin'. Thought ya were gonna kick the shit outta me, too, for a minute there."

"No, I'm sorry." I caressed his bruised face with quivering fingertips, panting with reaction. "I'm so sorry. That must've really hurt."

"It's okay, darlin'. What's goin' on?" He eyed the groaning heap on the pavement. "Weasel get outta hand? I'd offer to tune him up for ya, but it looks like ya got it under control."

"Yeah." I turned to look down at Weasel, my conscience already beginning to niggle at me. "I... kind of overreacted. He was just coming onto me. Usually I can laugh that stuff off, but I was really on edge..."

Weasel slowly uncurled to reveal a bloody nose. He groaned and clutched his stomach, and guilt suffused me. "He actually saved my butt."

I stepped forward and started to kneel beside him, but Hellhound took my arm. "Don't."

I let him pull me back, alarm trickling into my veins. "Is he going to be really mad?" I whispered. "Do you think he'll rat us out?"

"Hell, no, darlin'. Ya prob'ly made his night. If ya go near him, he'll just provoke ya again so you'll hit him some more. Hold the door, an' I'll drag him in."

Hellhound seized Weasel by the shirt and hauled him through the door one-handed, dropping him unceremoniously just inside the office. He stepped over Weasel's prostrate body to lock the door before turning to put an arm around me and guide me into the back bay.

"Was he doin' that thing where he almost touches ya?" he asked.

I blew out a long breath. "Yeah. What the hell is that?"

"Just his way of pissin' ya off. Most women take a swing at him sooner or later, an' that's just what he's lookin' for. He got charged last time, though, 'cause the chick jumped the wrong way an' he accidentally touched her. I was tryin' to warn ya, but ya left too fast."

"You're kidding me. He actually likes women to hit him?"

Arnie shrugged. "Yeah. Come on, darlin', let's get ya a beer an' ya can tell me what happened."

I threw a glance back at Weasel. "Shouldn't we..."

"Nah. He'll be okay." Arnie placed an ice-cold beer in my hand. "Now, what happened?"

"Mark Richardson almost caught me."

Arnie paused fractionally, and I knew he was accessing his memory banks. "Kane's Calgary guy? How the hell would he know where ya were?"

"I don't know if he did. It might have been sheer coincidence. I saw him first, and I got Weasel to cause a ruckus so I could sneak out." I swallowed another pang of guilt along with my beer. "He did a really good job, too. Richardson would've seen me for sure if not for him." I half-turned back. "Maybe we should-"

Hellhound's arm tightened around my shoulders. "Forget it. Trust me, darlin', the only way ya coulda made Weasel any happier tonight is if ya screwed him while ya beat the hell outta him. An' I'm thinkin' ya prob'ly don't wanna do that."

I shuddered. "No."

He guided me back into the bay, where Dave still snored on the couch. We sank into the chairs, and he leaned back slowly, holding his cold beer bottle against the bridge of his nose.

"When are you going to take the packing out?" I asked.

"Tomorrow."

"That's a horrible first memory you have of James."

He shrugged. "Whatever. He's an asshole. Always was."

"Do you think he really always was? Or do you think he got that way because your dad-"

"I don't call that sonuvabitch Dad. All he ever gave me was his fuckin' shitty genes an' a busted-up face. An' a few other busted bones. Asshole. Doug Kane's the only dad I got."

I shut up and took his hand. My parents had loved me and protected me. My dad was my hero. I couldn't imagine the kind of pain Arnie had lived through.

His voice interrupted my thoughts. "Did ya find out anythin' from Webb?"

"Yes and no. Still no sign of Nichele, and Dante's disappeared."

His hand tightened on mine. "Maybe he went somewhere. A trip or somethin'."

I swallowed hard. "Well, they haven't found any bodies yet." After a moment, I added, "At least Kane's still okay."

Arnie studied my face. "Ya still pissed at him?"

"Yeah. I mean, not that I'd want anything to happen to him or anything, I know he was just following orders, but... I thought we were friends, you know? I guess I should've known better. Spies don't have friends."

I took a long swallow of beer and slid down lower in my chair. "I'm probably more mad at myself for believing his bullshit than I am at him for shovelling it at me. I'll get over it. If I live."

"What about your husband?" Arnie asked carefully. "If it was me, I'd have a hard time forgivin' that."

"Actually, I'm not mad at Kane for that."

"Bullshit. Ya don't just get over havin' somebody ya love killed like that."

"I didn't say I wasn't mad. I'm just not mad at Kane. He didn't know me or Robert at the time, he was just doing his job." I gulped some more beer. "I still can't believe Robert was a spy. And I can't believe he'd ever go rogue. He was so..." I trailed off. "Well, what the hell do I know? If he was a spy, it was all lies anyway. Nothing but fucking lies."

I upended the bottle and drained the last of the suds down my throat. "I need another. How about you?"

"I'm gonna quit, darlin'. Think I'll take a coupla pills tonight, too."

"Back in a flash." I headed for the dark front office.

I'd just closed the fridge door, beer in hand, when the sudden motion of a shape in the semi-darkness made me spring back against the wall.

CHAPTER 27

I recognized the dirty-ashtray smell immediately, along with a wet sound and an amorous moan from inches away.

"Fuck off, Weasel," I said tiredly, and pushed past him.

"Why didn't you hit me?" He sounded disappointed. "That was no fun."

"Not tonight, dear, I have a headache." I turned and left.

He followed. "Hey, I saved your sweet ass. You could at least slap me around."

"No."

"Come on. Please? I know you wanna leave bloody teeth marks on my big, hard cock. You wanna squeeze my balls while you whip my ass so hard..."

"If you're trying to piss me off, it won't work." I kept walking and let the door go in his face.

"Ow." He trailed me out into the bay. "See, that was okay. You could do that again."

Hellhound shot him a deadly look from under lowered brows. "Go work on your car."

Weasel sent a disinterested glance toward the car. "Nah. Your crazy bitch's giving me a boner that won't quit. Think I'll go home and jack off." He turned a hopeful face toward me, his nose still red and puffy. "Or I could spank the monkey right here while you watch. That'd be so hot." His hand drifted toward his crotch.

"No," Arnie and I chorused.

"You're no fun." He shuffled out, and we heard the front door close and lock behind him. Seconds later, the muffled thump of the bass faded away.

I dropped back into the chair and swallowed a generous slug of beer. "What a piece of work. Where do you know him from?"

"He's one a' my sources. For my P.I. business. I don't deal with any a' the hardcore assholes, but I got a few little slimeballs like Weasel that're tapped into the grapevine. Known him for a long time. He's bent to shit, but he won't rat us out."

"Does he ever actually manage to get laid?"

"Don't even wanna know, darlin'."

"Good point." I drank some more beer. "What's the plan for tomorrow?"

"I gotta go back an' talk to my contacts again, see if they found out anythin' yet."

I hesitated. "Arnie, I don't think that's a good idea. You're so beat up already..."

He waved a hand. "No big deal. The guys that messed with me today ain't gonna mess with me tomorrow."

"How do you know? What if they come back with a bunch of their friends?"

He grunted. "They ain't got friends. An' they ain't gonna be outta the hospital yet."

"Oh." I couldn't prevent a sidelong glance at his injured knuckles. I was having a hard time reconciling the gentle, good-natured man I knew with the reality of the battered, scowling giant in the chair beside me.

As if reading my mind, he leaned forward and stroked

my hand with gentle fingertips. "Ya know you're always safe with me, don't ya, darlin'? Ya know I'd never hurt ya."

I took his hand and brushed my lips over the skin that wasn't covered by bandages. "I know."

Dave let out a particularly robust snore, and Hellhound shot a glare in his direction. "Must be fuckin' nice, sleepin' on the only couch without a fuckin' care in the world. I should go kick his sorry ass off there an' let ya have it for a while."

"Don't bother. Maybe it'll help his back if he spends the night stretched out."

Hellhound grunted. "I don't give a shit about his fuckin' back. He's been hoggin' the bed every night. Ya need a decent night's sleep, too."

Weariness washed over me in a sodden wave, and I drained my bottle. "I'm so tired, it's not going to matter to me tonight. But maybe you should wake him in a few hours and take the couch for the rest of the night. You must be hurting like hell."

He shrugged. "I'm okay." He stood and stretched carefully. "Where ya gonna sleep tonight, darlin'?"

I eyed the filthy chairs. "I think I'll sleep in the Caprice. Do you want the back seat? There's probably a little more room there than in the front."

"Nah. Go ahead an' take the back. I ain't even gonna try. If I get crunched up in there, I'll never get out again." He wandered over toward the LeSabre. "This'll be better."

Weasel had left the rear bench seat lying on the floor, and Hellhound dragged it away from the car and arranged the cushions from the chairs at the end of it. He lowered himself cautiously and settled with a long breath. "That'll do. 'Least I can stretch out."

"Where's your jacket?" I asked as he wrapped his arms over his chest.

"Left it hangin' in the shitter with my jeans after I cleaned the blood off it."

"I'll get it." I ducked into the revoltingly dirty bathroom and grabbed his jacket.

When I leaned down to spread it over him, he rolled against the back of the seat and held out his arms. "Come here, darlin'."

I knelt beside the seat and eased down, stretching out on the few remaining inches. His arms closed around me, and I snuggled into his warmth.

I woke with a start when I rolled off onto the floor.

The lights still blazed overhead, and the men were enthusiastically competing in the Snoring Olympics. Ordinarily, I found Arnie's quiet buzzing as soothing as the purr of a big cat, but the packing in his nose forced him to sleep open-mouthed, snoring like a spavined chainsaw.

Combined with Dave's bagpipe imitation, the echoes bounced through the high-ceilinged bay, amplifying instead of softening.

I groaned and squinted at my wristwatch. Quarter to two. Another friggin' long night.

I opened the door of the LeSabre so the dome light would stay on before turning off the overhead lights in the bay. Then I crept through the darkness into the back seat of the Caprice, and thankfully closed the door on the racket outside.

"Fuck!" I threw an arm over my face in an attempt to block out the insufferable light, and tried to squirm away from the seatbelt buckle grinding into my hip.

I heard the sound of the rear door opening, and a whiff of dirty ashtray reached my nostrils as Weasel sang out, "Good morning, Jane-Crazy-Bitch!" He inhaled deeply and groaned, "Goddamn, nothing like the smell of hot pussy in the morning."

I realized I'd draped one leg over the driver's headrest and the other on the back deck when I pried open one eye to see Weasel's face inches away from the crotch of my jeans.

In sheer reflex, I jerked away and kicked both heels into the middle of his chest. I caught a glimpse of his wide eyes and open mouth as he toppled backward.

Blind, brainless rage overwhelmed me. The rude awakening after a too-short, shitty sleep obliterated everything but the primal urge to find the source of the irritation and eliminate it. Permanently.

When I woke fully, I was astride Weasel's motionless body. My knuckles hurt and my arms were pinned behind me. Dave knelt beside me, his eyes wide and frightened while he called my name. When I snapped my head around to look at him, he jerked back.

"Aydan!" Hellhound's strained voice came from behind me. "Calm down, darlin'."

I realized I was gasping for air, my heart hammering. I sagged in Hellhound's grip, and he slowly relaxed his hold. "Ya okay? Ya know where ya are, right? Ya know you're safe?"

"Yeah." I couldn't catch my breath. "I'm. Okay. What...?"

Dave reached slowly for Weasel's neck and pressed trembling fingers against the pulse point. There was a lot of blood. What little breath I had went out of me.

"Oh... God... is... he...?" I doubled over, panting, afraid to hear the answer.

"He's fine." Dave's voice was full of relief. "Guess he's just got a glass jaw."

"Oh..." I slumped back into Arnie's arms. "Thank God."

He held me close for a few seconds. "Ya scared me, darlin'. I thought ya were gonna kill him."

Dave rocked back to sit on the floor, his face ashen. "I thought you had killed him. Jeez. What kind of martial arts was that?"

"I don't know any martial arts. I don't even know what I did. I'm not even awake yet."

"If I let ya go, will ya hit him again?" Hellhound asked.

"No. I didn't really mean to..." I trailed off as Hellhound released me.

"Come on, darlin'." He offered me a hand up. I winced when his grip crushed my aching knuckles, and he let go hurriedly and examined my hands. "Shit. You're gonna need the frozen peas this mornin'. 'Cept they ain't frozen anymore."

He looped an arm around my waist and helped me totter over to the couch. Dave handed me an orange juice and hovered while I attempted to free the straw from its cellophane with shaking hands. After a second, he took it away from me, inserted the straw, and handed it back.

I sipped slowly under the weight of two sets of worried eyes. A groan from behind the car signalled Weasel's return to consciousness, and a couple of minutes later he staggered toward us, smearing the sleeve of his jacket through the blood on his face.

"Jesus, Jane-Crazy-Bitch, you know how to get a guy up in the morning," he mumbled. "I shot two massive loads last night, and now you got me hard all over again." He pushed his hand inside his jeans and fondled himself.

Dave gaped at him in frozen outrage for a split second. Then he shot to his feet, his face contorting with fury as he lunged at Weasel. "You scumbag pervert! You..."

Hellhound and I both leaped to intervene as Weasel snatched up a tire iron and swung it in a whistling arc. "Right now, old man! I like it from the bitches, but I ain't gonna take no shit from no fat old fart."

I flung both arms around Dave and dug my toes into the concrete floor, trying to shove him backward. He made an equally determined effort to push past me, and we struggled against each other for a few seconds until I found my voice. "Dave, stop!"

I got a close-up view of his scowl as he panted, "Filthy. Scumbag. Pervert. Gonna..."

I wrestled with him a few more seconds before I finally brained up and let out a pitiful cry. "Ow, Dave, you're hurting me!"

He backed off so suddenly I almost fell. His arms closed around me. "Sorry, I'm sorry. Didn't mean to hurt you, are you okay?"

"Dave..." Hellhound's rasp held a world of menace, and I turned quickly to see him holding the tire iron in one large fist and the front of Weasel's shirt in the other. Weasel's toes were still touching the ground, but barely. His eyes bugged out while he gurgled desperately.

"I'm fine," I said quickly. "I just hit the bruise on my arm."

"Ya sure you're okay, darlin'?"

"I'm fine. Don't kill Weasel," I added.

Hellhound grunted and half-shoved, half-tossed Weasel

away. He landed hard on his butt and sat gasping and massaging his throat. "Look who's talking," he croaked. "You were all over her like slime mould last night, you fat old fuck."

Dave tensed and shot an anxious glance at me. A slow flush climbed his neck, and he let go of me abruptly. "Uh..." He studied the floor, his face flaming, and then dragged his gaze up to my eyes. "I owe you an apology."

"No, you don't," I assured him. "You had a reaction with your painkillers and some beer, and you kind of fell against me. It might have looked as though you were groping me, but you weren't. We just put you on the couch, and you fell asleep."

"I remember being on the couch..." He blushed even more furiously. "I might've said some things, um..."

"No, you were just snoring," I lied.

"Oh." He sagged with relief. "Good. I mean... uh, my back's good today. Muscle relaxants must've helped."

"Your back cracked when you fell last night. I was afraid I'd hurt you worse."

"No." He stretched and twisted tentatively. "Feels as good as if I went to the chiropractor. Thanks."

"Time we got outta here," Hellhound growled. "Ayd... Jane, get some breakfast, an' let's roll."

Dave surveyed me with concern. "You're shaking like a leaf," he said, and ushered me back to the couch. "Sit down, and I'll get you something to eat."

He turned to head for the car and stopped when Weasel climbed to his feet. The two men locked eyes, glaring until Hellhound stepped between them.

"Back off, both a' ya, before I rip your fuckin' heads off and shove 'em up your asses," he advised.

Dave and Weasel surveyed his blackened eyes and the blood-stained packing that still protruded from both nostrils. I could track the progress of their inspection over his bulging arms and shoulders, down to the ludicrous tattered skirt drooping over his hairy, muscular legs and heavy boots.

Neither man seemed inclined to laugh. Or to argue. Weasel turned back to the LeSabre without another word, and Dave made for the Caprice.

Hellhound raked them both with an expressionless stare before turning to me. “Be right back. Gonna put on my pants an’ take this packin’ out. Yell if the gonad twins start up again.”

“I will. Wait,” I added as he turned.

“What?”

“What about Hooker? I just realized it’s been three nights. Will he be okay?”

Dave made a slight detour around Hellhound with the grocery bags. “Who’s Hooker?”

Arnie eyed him impassively. “My cat.”

Dave let out an uncertain laugh that trailed away as Hellhound’s deadpan scrutiny continued. After a few seconds, Arnie turned to me. “I called Miz Lacey yesterday mornin’ right after ya dropped me off. She’s handlin’ it.”

“Oh, good. You’re lucky to have her.”

Arnie’s face softened. “I know. She’s gonna gimme hell when I show up lookin’ like this, too.” He chuckled and turned away, his good humour obviously restored by the thought of his feisty, elderly neighbour.

As he vanished into the front of the bay, Dave leaned closer. “Does he really have a cat?”

“Yes.”

“A real cat. Not like some perverted joke, like hooker...”

He flushed and whispered, "...pussy..." His flush deepened. "You know."

"His cat's full name is John Lee Hooker. He's named after a famous blues musician."

"Oh." He busied himself getting out the bread and peanut butter. "Sorry. He, uh, doesn't seem the type."

"There's a lot about Arnie that you don't know. He's a very talented blues musician himself. He plays the guitar and harmonica."

"Oh."

I let him chew on that while I dug into breakfast. A few minutes later, Arnie reappeared. Most of the bloodstains were gone from his jeans, and his face looked a little better without the packing. He dabbed carefully at his nose with a bloodied wad of toilet paper.

"Are you okay?" I asked.

"Yeah. It's just bleedin' a bit 'cuz I took the packin' out a few minutes ago. It'll be fine." He inhaled cautiously. "That's better. 'Least I can breathe now."

"Breakfast?" I offered him the bread and the peanut butter jar.

"Nah." He dug into the grocery bag and extracted a couple of handfuls of beef jerky and a snack cake. "Shit, I'd kill for a coffee. Weasel!"

"Yeah."

"Ya got coffee here?"

"No."

Hellhound blew out a sigh. "Guess we'll hafta catch a drive-through. Ya ready to go?"

"I guess." I surveyed his bruised face, feeling guilty. "I really don't want you to do this."

"It'll be fine."

I waved them toward the Caprice. "I'll be right there," I told them as I started toward Weasel.

"Darlin', don't..." Hellhound cautioned.

"It'll be okay." I stopped well outside Weasel's groping range. "Hey, Weasel. Thanks for letting us crash here and drink your beer. And thanks for looking out for me last night at the cafe. No hard feelings, I hope."

He gave me his yellowed grin. "I got nothing but hard feelings for you, Jane-Crazy-Bitch." He hoisted a dirty hand into his crotch and thrust in my direction a few times, grunting. "You wanna wrap your hot pussy around my hard feelings?"

"I'll pass."

He smiled. "Come back soon."

CHAPTER 28

Arnie breathed a sigh of pure contentment as he cradled his coffee cup. “Jesus, I might live after all.”

“Yeah,” Dave agreed from the back seat, slurping his own brew.

I eyed them fondly, savouring the rare moment of peace and harmony. I leaned my head back against the headrest and tried to ease the tension out of my shoulders. Breathe. Ocean waves. The smell of coffee and normalcy.

And a faint whiff of gamy clothing. Hellhound was resplendent in one of the clean new shirts, but Dave was on Day Three of what should have been a one-day T-shirt. He’d washed and borrowed my deodorant stick, but there was only so much he could do.

God, if we spent much more time together in this damn car, I was going to have to fumigate it before I gave it back to Bruce. Assuming I lived long enough.

I sighed and opened my eyes. “Now what?”

“Back to the same place, darlin’. Time to go visitin’.”

I put the car in gear with reluctance. “Maybe you should take Dave with you this time.” I wasn’t actually sure whether that would be a good idea or not, but the thought of sending Arnie back into the lion’s den alone was making my stomach twist.

"Nah. I need Dave to stay in the car an' watch out for ya. I ain't gonna be long this time."

"Arnie, I have a gun. I can take care of myself. You might need the backup."

He shrugged. "I got a gun, too."

"But you can't use it. You'll go to jail."

He snorted. "Better'n goin' to the boneyard."

"Not for me, it isn't." I shuddered. "I'd rather die."

"You're kidding, right?" Dave asked.

"God, no, I'm dead serious." I took a deep breath and let it out slowly. "I'm claustrophobic. I get panicky just thinking about jail."

"Turn here," Hellhound interjected. "There, park right there."

I pulled up to the curb, and he gulped the last of his coffee. "I oughta only be a few minutes. Half an hour, tops. If ya hear shootin', get ready to drive fast." He considered for a few seconds. "If ya hear shootin' an' I don't come runnin', call the cops an' bug out."

I knew better than to cling to him this time. I pulled him into a careful kiss, mindful of his bruised mouth, and slipped him the tongue. "See you."

I felt his lips quirk up, and he kissed me back in a way that made it clear that impending death was Priority #2.

Dave cleared his throat in the back seat. "Uh, want me to take a walk?"

Hellhound finished up unhurriedly, leaving me breathless. "Nah. I don't mind an audience." He winked and slid out of the car.

I avoided Dave's eyes until the heat left my lips and cheeks. The ones on my face, anyway. It was going to take a while to cool the others off. We sat in awkward silence, both making a show of watching out the windows for potential threats.

At last, Dave spoke. "Uh, this morning... um. Don't get me wrong, he deserved it, but... would you really have killed him? Didn't look like you were gonna stop."

I turned to meet his troubled eyes and sighed. "I don't know, Dave. I didn't even know what I was doing." I sank my head into my hands. "I'm so fucked up. Before this year, I'd never hit another person in all my adult life. If I'd killed Weasel today, I'd never forgive myself. He's just a harmless little shit. I don't know what's the matter with me."

"He's not harmless. And you're under a lot of pressure," he said.

"Lots of people are under pressure. They don't go around beating people half to death for nothing."

He reached over the seat and patted my shoulder. "Aydan, it wasn't nothing. He's a sick pervert, and he attacked you."

"He didn't attack me. He never even touched me, and I don't think he would've pushed it too far even if we'd been alone."

Dave gaped at me in disbelief. "He's a scumbag. He belongs in jail."

I sighed. "Dave, I'm pretty sure he's harmless. Trust me, I've met guys who really like hurting women, and he's not one of them. He just has some... unusual preferences, that's all. And not much sense of personal space."

"He's a sick, disgusting pervert." He scowled. "And I can't believe you thanked him."

"He's one of Arnie's contacts. I don't want to mess that up for him."

"Contacts for what?" Dave spat. "Drug deals? Stolen

cars? They're both bottom-feeders. You're wasting your time with him. Why can't you see that?"

I swallowed my annoyance. "Arnie isn't a criminal. Sometimes he needs contacts like Weasel so he can do his job as a private investigator. That doesn't mean he likes it."

Dave frowned. "Why-"

We both jerked around in our seats at the sound of two gunshots. I had just met Dave's wide eyes when a third shot rang out. Icy fear squeezed my chest, and I started the car, willing Arnie to be safe with all my might.

I'd barely begun to panic when he pounded out of the alley at a dead run. I reached across and flung the passenger door open, then put the car into gear, one foot on the brake and one on the gas.

The car lurched as he dove in, bellowing, "GO!"

I didn't waste time. The tires squealed and the Caprice shot forward as two men dashed out of the alley. The car roared and accelerated as I slapped the shifter through the gears, the tires chirping with each shift.

Another shot rang out behind us. I snapped a glance in the rearview mirror, but my vision was obscured by Dave's white face and panicked eyes.

"Aydan, train!" he shouted. "TRAIN!"

I jerked my eyes forward again, adrenaline slamming into my system like nitromethane into a top-fuel dragster. Goddamn sonuvabitch fucking train tracks in the middle of the fucking neighbourhood, what the hell was with that?

Another bang, and something thudded into the rear of the car. I gauged the speed of the train in an instant, catching a glimpse of Hellhound's white knuckles locked on the dashboard.

I could make it.

The train whistle blared and the engineer waved frantically from his window. The crossing arms were almost down.

I slapped the shifter one more time and punched the gas. The car screamed like a wild thing. Or maybe that was Dave.

At the last second I flipped the switch, and the kick of the nitrous blasted us across the tracks, the rear end fishtailing while the tires spun and smoked. The guardarm scraped over the roof and thudded on the trunk, and then we were through the crossing.

Lots of time to spare. Hell, I could've backed up and gone over again. Almost.

Hellhound let out a wild whoop and pounded the dashboard with the flat of his hand, laughing like a maniac. "Woo-hooo!" he bellowed. "I love ya, darlin', marry me now! Woo-hooo!"

I concentrated on slowing the car and headed for Deerfoot Trail, the most direct route to anywhere-but-here. The engineer had gotten a good, close look at the car. I hoped he hadn't gotten a close look at me. Or the license plate.

Hellhound was still laughing. "Jesus Christ, darlin', where'd ya learn to drive like that?"

"Bruce taught me. We used to drag a lot, back in the day." I grinned hugely, feeling the rush blooming into euphoria. "Goddamn, that was fun!" I let out a whoop of my own, and the laughter bubbled up. "God*damn*! I need to do that more often!"

I shot a grin into the rearview mirror at Dave slumped gasping in the back seat. "You still with us, Dave?"

He clutched his chest, grey-faced and sweaty. "Think I'm having a heart attack."

"Shit!" Terror flash-froze the blood in my veins. I glanced at Arnie's suddenly grim face. "Rockyview?"

"Yeah." He turned to lean over the back of the seat. "Hang on, buddy, we'll get ya to the hospital. Gimme your wrist for a sec. Just gonna take your pulse."

"No, it's okay," Dave muttered. "I was just kidding. I'm okay. Keep going."

"Ya don't look like you're kiddin'."

I shot another fearful look in the mirror. He really didn't look like he was kidding. He looked like he was in serious trouble.

Arnie gently pulled Dave's arm toward him and clamped his fingers over the pulse point. "Ya got chest pain?"

Dave took a deep breath. "No, it's gone now."

"What'd it feel like?"

"Just a sharp pain." Dave didn't sound so breathless now.

"Like crushin' or squeezin'? Any pain in your arm or your jaw? Ya feel sick? Dizzy?"

"No." Dave took another deep breath. "Just a jab. Probably just a muscle spasm. I'm okay now."

Arnie and I exchanged a look. "His pulse's slowin' down," Arnie said dubiously. "An' he's gettin' his colour back."

I turned off the street into a back alley and pulled over so I could twist around and examine Dave. He did look better. He was breathing normally, and the sickly pallor was gone from his skin.

"Have you ever had your heart checked?" I demanded.

"Yeah. It's fine. Really, I'm okay."

"When did you get it tested last?"

"Last year. Had to have the physical for my Class One

driver's license."

"Have you ever had a muscle spasm like that before?" I studied him, feeling guilty all over again.

"Yeah. Lots of times. No big deal. Let's go."

"Dave, if you're lying to me..."

He gave me a twisted grin. "What, if I die, you'll kill me?"

"Uh, yeah. Something like that. Wise guy."

"Come on, let's go," he said.

I turned back to the steering wheel. Stopped.

"Go where?" I asked.

I turned to Arnie in the silence that followed. "What did you find out?"

He snorted. "Found out those assholes had a coupla friends after all."

"Did you, um, do anything we don't need to know about?" I asked carefully.

"Nah. That was them shootin' at me, not the other way around. My guy didn't know anythin' yet, an' I was just leavin' when those two assholes showed up."

"They seemed a little testy." I took a deep breath and tried to stop trembling. It didn't work. My entire body vibrated.

"Yeah."

"So now what?" I asked. "Do you have any more ideas about how we can find Nichele? All we need to do is find out where James is holding her. Then we can pass it on to Spider and let them take care of it."

Dave leaned forward over the seat. "You mean we're not going to rescue her?"

"I think that's better left to the professionals," I said. "We're just a bunch of dumb civilians, remember? We'd probably put her in more danger than ever if we went charging in."

"But... you're not... you've got a gun. We've got two guns between us. We could..."

"Ya been watchin' too many movies, Dave," Hellhound interrupted. "That ain't the way it works in real life. In real life, the dumb civilians interfere, an' everybody ends up dead."

"But..."

We all froze at the sound of rapidly approaching sirens, but they didn't slow as they passed the alley.

"Pull in under that carport," Hellhound instructed. "They'll have the chopper up in a few minutes. We're far enough away they won't find us in a ground search, but we don't wanna get seen from the air. We can just lie low 'til they give up."

I eased the car cautiously under the sagging roof of the abandoned building and parked.

Hellhound exhaled tiredly and turned to me. "We gotta kill time until tonight. I'm set up to meet my guy again then. Different place this time," he added as I opened my mouth to protest. "Maybe ya should see if ya can talk to Webb again, see if they got anythin' new."

"Yeah, that's a good idea," I agreed slowly. "I don't want you to have to take a chance if Spider's already got the information. But I can't get in touch with him during the day. He'll be at work. He wouldn't be playing World of Warcraft."

"Shit."

We sat in silence for a few moments. Tension coiled up in my belly like a poisonous snake.

"This is stupid," I burst out finally. "What the hell are we doing? We're living out of a fucking car, for chrissakes. And why? You guys haven't done anything wrong. Arnie, I'm taking you home, and Dave, you're going to the hospital for a checkup. Then you can both get on with your lives."

Arnie's hand closed over mine as I reached for the shifter. "We had this conversation, darlin'. Dave's in trouble with the law, an' I got a contract out on me. An' neither of us is gonna leave ya. So fuck that."

"I really don't think Kane will press charges against Dave," I argued. "Not after he has a chance to explain. And we don't know for sure there's a contract out on you."

"Yeah, an' by the time we find out for sure, Dave gets arrested an' I get dead. I ain't likin' that scenario," Hellhound growled. "If I gotta die, fine, but I ain't gonna die of bein' stupid."

My tension exploded into violent irritation, and I threw up my hands. "Well, that's just fucking fine! If you refuse to show any fucking sense of self-preservation, anybody got any ideas about where we should go today? Maybe a nice trip to the zoo? Calaway Park? Or we could all get ice cream and sing fucking campfire songs. That'd be fun."

"Uh, Calaway Park's closed for the season," Dave said nervously.

"Well, I guess it's the zoo, then," I snarled. "Everybody hold hands and stay together."

Arnie broke the short silence. "Ya okay, Aydan?"

I clenched my hands around the steering wheel to prevent myself from punching something else with my already aching fists. "Fine," I grated.

Most men would have wisely shut up at that point.

"Bullshit," Hellhound said.

I loosened my grip on the wheel, one finger at a time.

"I'm going for a walk," I said very quietly, and got out of the car.

CHAPTER 29

I'd only taken a few strides when I heard the car door open and close behind me. Seconds later, Hellhound caught up to walk beside me. After a few dozen paces, he spoke.

"What's wrong?"

"Where do I start?" I growled.

"Why're ya mad at us for tryin' to help?"

"I'm not mad at you."

He caught my arm and swung me to face him. "Ya told me I could treat ya like my guy friends. So don't gimme this 'nothin's wrong' chick bullshit. What the hell's wrong?"

I bit down my first response. Then my second. On the third try, I managed speech about the same time I managed to unclench my fists. "I didn't say nothing's wrong," I said evenly. "I said I'm not mad at you, and I'm not. I just want you to be safe. I'm upset because you won't cooperate."

"I told ya, darlin', I ain't leavin' when ya need me."

Frustration burst out of me. "I don't need you! For chrissake, go away and be safe!"

I should have known better than to hope he'd get mad and leave. Instead, he eyed me soberly. "Ya keep sayin' that. Why's it such a big deal for ya to not need anybody?"

I scowled. "I didn't say it's a big deal, and I don't keep saying that, I just said-"

"Back in March," he interrupted. "Ya said, 'I don't need you or anybody else to babysit me. I can take care of myself. I always have. I always will.'" He frowned down at me. "Why's it such a big thing for ya?"

"You and your goddamn photographic memory."

He said nothing, watching me.

I blew out a breath between my teeth. "Look, every single person I ever needed is dead. The part of me that needs people died with them. I'm not trying to hurt you, I'm just saying, I don't need you, or anybody. I'm not capable of it anymore."

He took my hand in a gentle grip. "Aydan, ya know I don't want ya to need me, an' I ain't askin' ya for that. I just want ya to trust me enough to let me help ya."

I took a deep breath and met his eyes. "You know I trust you."

"I don't think ya do," he said quietly. "Ya get naked with me, but ya never let down your guard." He stroked the hair away from my face and looked deeply into my eyes. "Who beat the trust outta ya, darlin'?"

I stood a little taller. "Nobody ever beat me. I wouldn't put up with that."

"There's ways to beat people up without ever layin' a hand on 'em," he said.

The gut-punch of memory made me wrap my arms around myself to absorb the blow. I quickly pasted on a neutral expression.

"Yeah, thought so," Arnie said softly. "Robert?"

I kept my voice matter-of-fact. "No. My first husband. Steven."

"Didn't know ya were married before Robert."

I shrugged. "Wasn't worth mentioning. Look, can we

talk about getting you and Dave out of trouble?"

"How long were ya married to Steven?"

I sighed. "Too long."

"When did it start?"

"What?"

"When did he start abusin' ya?"

"I don't know, it was gradual. Look, it was just words."

Words. And silences. Sometimes I'd wished he would hit me, just so I could have visible evidence of the pain. The old coldness settled into my bones with the memory of silent endurance slowly fading to numb, deadly emptiness.

Arnie's voice brought me back to the present. "When I was a kid, I couldn't figure out why Mom stayed with the ol' man, when he was always yellin' an' whalin' on her. That fuckin' asshole. Kane's mom explained it when I got a little older, how they break ya so ya don't have the strength to leave."

I shrugged and studied my shoe while it scuffed at the pavement. "It wasn't that big a deal. I stayed because I'd promised I would, not because I was afraid to leave. When I finally found out he'd been cheating on me, I divorced him. Done deal. Good riddance."

His voice was a soft rasp. "See, that's what I mean. Ya always gotta hide what you're feelin'. Ya never let anybody in, do ya, darlin'?"

I shrugged again. "Nobody wants to hear about that shit, and I don't like talking about it. Works fine."

I could feel his eyes on me, but I didn't look up. After a moment, he sighed. "How'd ya ever wanna get married again?"

"I didn't."

I could hear the puzzlement in his voice. "But ya

married Robert. An' it sounded like ya loved him."

Weariness washed over me. "I never wanted to marry him. I didn't want to get married again, period. But he was always there, and he just kept... nudging me. Not pushy, but just always... there. After six years, I thought..."

I kept my voice steady. "I thought he must really love me. And I... after all that pain, I couldn't bear to hurt a good man. So I agreed to marry him. And I tried my best, goddammit. I loved him as much as I had left to give..." The bitterness nearly choked me. I swallowed it down and kept my tone light. "Joke's on me."

Arnie's arms closed around me. "He musta loved ya," he murmured. "Ya can't fake it for that long."

I dropped my head against his chest. "He could. He was undercover for twenty-four years."

After a moment, I straightened up and pushed away from him. "Anyway, it doesn't matter. Just because I don't talk about this stuff doesn't mean I don't trust you. If it makes you feel any better, you're one of the two people in the world who know that shit about me."

He nodded understanding. "Robert."

"No."

His mouth dropped open. "But, darlin', ya were married to him."

"It didn't come up."

He examined my face incredulously for another moment. "If ya didn't tell your own husband, who the hell did ya tell?"

"Kane." I blew out a long, tired breath. "I didn't want to, but he... I had to."

"Oh." I saw my hurt reflected on his face. "Jesus, darlin'..."

I looked him in the eyes. "So I trust you, okay?"

"Okay," he said slowly. "If ya really trust me, then trust me to stick around an' help ya."

I clutched his hand in both of mine. "Arnie, you don't get it! I stand to lose damn near everybody I care about here. You, Spider, Nichele, Dave, Bruce even, if they find out whose car we're using." I hesitated, and left Kane off the list. That was already over. "I've only got a few friends left in the world, and I don't want to lose the ones I've got. Please, just..."

"Aydan, get your head outta your ass!" he snapped. "Think about somebody besides yourself for a change!"

I gaped at him in pure shock. "I'm thinking about you, dammit!"

"No, ya ain't. All you're thinkin' about is how bad you're feelin'. How the hell d'ya think I'm gonna feel if I walk away an' let ya die? How the hell d'ya think I'm gonna live with that? I ain't lettin' that fuckin' asshole Jim kill anybody else I care about."

I eyed him with confusion. "What do you mean 'anybody else'? I thought your da... I mean, your old man, killed your mother."

"Yeah." Arnie clamped his mouth shut and turned back toward the car.

I trotted beside him and gazed up into his impassive face as he strode along. "Who did James kill?" I asked softly.

"My high-school girlfriend. It was his gang initiation."

I opened my mouth, found absolutely no words of comfort, and took his hand instead. We walked back to the Caprice in silence.

Dave eyed us anxiously when we got back in the car. "Is... everything okay?"

"Fine." I blew out a sigh. "Sorry, Dave, I just had a little too much adrenaline in my system. I'm not mad at either of you, I'm just scared for you, and I'm mad because I can't keep you safe."

He reached forward and patted my shoulder. "It's okay. You kept us safe. You got us out of there."

I gave him a smile. "Thanks, Dave." I caught Arnie's eye. "Both of you. Thanks."

Arnie winked. "What're friends for?" He cocked an ear skyward. "Sounds like the chopper's bugged out. Let's just wait a little longer an' make sure, though."

We sat in silence for a few minutes, and I turned over possibilities in my mind. At last, I turned to Arnie. "So is there anything else we need to do before tonight? What time are you meeting your guy?"

"Nine," he said. "An' no, that's all I can think of for now. I've tapped out all my sources."

My gut clenched. "What if he doesn't know anything? How long do you think James will hold Nichele before he kills her? We're running out of time."

Arnie laid a comforting hand on mine. "Don't worry, darlin', she's prob'ly got more time than ya think. Unless somethin' pushes Jim, he won't kill her 'til he's got all his loose ends tied up. He's smart, an' he won't rush it."

"So until we're dead, Nichele's probably safe."

Arnie shrugged. "Yeah. An' hell, if we're dead, we ain't gonna care anymore anyway."

"Way to look on the bright side," Dave snorted.

"Never mind, Dave, at this point, I'll take any bright side I can find," I assured him. "So... how do you guys feel about a road trip?"

Hellhound eyed me dubiously. "Prob'ly not a good idea, darlin'. It's a helluva lot harder to hide on the highway than in the city, an' the police prob'ly got a description of the car now. They'll be watchin' for it tryin' to leave town."

"You really think they'll have a description?" I argued. "The guys who were shooting at you wouldn't hang around to talk to the police. I didn't see anybody else in the neighbourhood, and the police wouldn't know to talk to the train engineer unless he called it in."

"Pretty risky all the same," he replied. "Why d'ya wanna go on a road trip? An' where to?"

"Home..."

"Aydan, that's nuts," Dave interrupted. "They'll be watching your house for sure."

"Dave's right, darlin'," Hellhound agreed. "Kane'll be watchin' the surveillance cameras, an' if Jim's hit man is any good, he'll be watchin' your place, too. Why d'ya wanna go there?"

I scrubbed my knuckles through my hair in frustration. "I can't do anything else to help Nichele right now, and I really want to see if I can find out anything more about my family. Aunt Minnie told me some things about my Dad that made me wonder. I've still got all his papers in my shed. He never threw anything away. I want to look through them and see if I can find any clues."

"Clues about what?" Hellhound asked gently. "He ain't likely to've written down 'I think they're tryin' to kill me' somewhere."

"No, you're right, but..." I shot a quick glance at Dave, trying to frame my words carefully. "Some of the things Aunt Minnie said made me think he might have known what was going on."

Hellhound's keen eyes darted to Dave and back to me. "Okay..." he said slowly. "An' ya think there might be somethin' in his papers?"

"I haven't a clue. But I'm going to go nuts if I have to just sit in this car for..." I checked my watch. "...ten hours doing nothing. I've got some people to call, too, but..."

"Callin' people prob'ly ain't too safe right now," Hellhound objected. "Kane'll be monitoring everybody ya know."

"Yeah, I know, but I don't think he'll think to listen in on the people I have in mind," I told him. "Anyway, I want to check Dad's papers first. The calls are a last resort."

"Okay, well, let's think this through, then," Arnie said. "Ya said the papers are in your shed, not in the house."

We both knew there was no way he'd forget what I'd said, but I obliged him with a yes.

"So that'd be outside the surveillance cameras."

"They're watching your house all the time?" Dave burst out.

"Yes." I turned to Arnie. "And yes."

"So Jim put the contract out on Saturday. If I was the hit man, I'd check out your place first thing, an' right about now I'd be figurin' I'm wastin' my time watchin' an empty house for two days."

I shrugged. "If he even bothered to wait that long. I've been gone for nearly a week. If he looked through the windows, he'd see wilted plants. It'd be pretty obvious I wasn't around." I straightened up in the seat as a thought hit me. "Hell, if he looked through the windows, Kane's guys would be on him like a ton of bricks."

"Good point," Hellhound allowed. "So it's prob'ly pretty safe to go to your place as long as we don't hafta go near the house where we'd show up on the cameras."

"We wouldn't have to," I said. "We could stop on the

road and come up the creek, hiding in the trees. That would give us a chance to scope out the area without being seen. Then if it was clear, I could grab the boxes from the shed and be gone before anybody ever knew I was there."

"How many boxes we talkin' here?" Hellhound asked.

"Um." I slumped a little. "Probably four or five. File boxes. Shit."

"Hafta make a few trips, then," Hellhound said.

I sighed. "Yeah. But it's almost a quarter of a mile. The boxes are too heavy to carry that far. That won't work. Dammit."

"I can carry 'em okay," Hellhound argued. "Just gonna take me a coupla trips, that's all."

"Why not just look at them right there?" Dave suggested. "We've got ten hours, and there's three of us."

"Uh, there'd be less than six hours, actually," I corrected. "It's a two-hour drive to get up there, and we'd have to start back to Calgary by six-thirty. And I don't really know what I'm looking for, so I wouldn't be able to tell you, either."

"Still, six hours," Hellhound said thoughtfully. "Hell, even if ya hadta look through all a' them yourself, ya could prob'ly still do it. That'd leave Dave an' me free to watch for trouble."

"But is it worth it?" I asked, and then answered my own question. "No, shit, it's not worth the risk. No matter what I find out, it won't change anything anyway." I slouched down in the seat.

"But, Aydan," Dave protested. "Don't you want to find out if they killed your family?"

I sighed and sank my head into my hands. "It won't bring them back, no matter what I find out. And it's not worth putting you guys in more danger. My family's dead anyway. You guys might still live through this if we don't do anything stupid."

Arnie gave me a sympathetic look. "If it was me, I'd hafta know. An' hell, we ain't doin' nothin' for the next ten hours anyway. Let's go for a road trip."

CHAPTER 30

After a few more minutes of discussion, I backed the car out of our concealment and headed for the highway. We all peered tensely out the windows as we approached the city limits, but we saw no police cars. Half an hour later, I blew out a long breath and tried to ease the knots out of my shoulders.

Dave and Hellhound both relaxed into their seats, too, and we exchanged relieved glances. Hellhound's battered face creased into a lopsided grin. "So far, so good, darlin'."

My heart lifted at the sight of the rolling country and open highway. "Yeah. So far, so good."

In Drumheller, we elected Dave as the least identifiable of our group and sent him into the small grocery store for provisions. We all munched steadily while we got back on the road to Silverside.

When we neared the turnoff, I gave in to the nerves that had been twitching in my stomach for the past twenty minutes.

"Where ya goin'?" Hellhound asked as I slowed the car a few miles before my road.

"I'm going to make a detour and come at it from the

north. I don't want to drive past Tom's place, and we'll be able to get a better view of my place if we come in from the north anyway."

Hellhound settled back in his seat. "Okay, good thinkin', darlin'."

A mile north of my land, I stopped the car and pulled on the hooded jacket, hands shaking. "Maybe this isn't such a good idea after all," I said. "Maybe we should just drive right on by and head back to Calgary instead."

Hellhound shrugged. "We just drove two hours to get here. It ain't like we had anythin' else to do, but it don't make much sense to chicken out now."

"Unless it's a really bad idea in the first place," I argued. "Then it would be smart to chicken out now."

Arnie caught Dave's eye. "Sorry, darlin', you're out-voted two to one. Drive on by, an' we'll check it out. If anythin' looks outta place, we'll keep on goin'."

I blew out a breath between my teeth and put the car in gear.

When we coasted down the hill toward the farm, everything appeared quiet. "Check out those trees at the edge of the creek," I urged. "That's where Kane had his guys stationed last time. Watch for lens flashes. They'll be easier to spot now that the leaves are gone from the trees."

Hellhound grunted. "If they're Kane's guys, ya won't see any lens flashes. They know what they're doin'." Nonetheless, both he and Dave eyeballed the woods intently as we cruised by.

I slowed to a halt opposite the creek. "Did you see anything?" I asked.

Hellhound shook his head. "Nah. Dave?"

"No, me neither," Dave confirmed. "So now what?"

"Now, I don't know," I said. "I hate to leave the car out here on the road, but I don't want to pull into my driveway. And I don't want to go any closer to Tom's place, or he'll be able to see the car parked out here."

"This's as good as it's gonna get, then," Hellhound said. "Shut 'er down, an' let's get goin'."

We left the Caprice parked at the side of the deserted gravel road and walked down through the ditch. I stepped up on the barbed wire strand beside a fence post and swung over it. When I turned to wait for the men, I caught a flash of concern on their faces.

"Don't think that's gonna hold me," Hellhound observed.

"No, probably not," I agreed. "Here." I moved to the centre of the span and parted the strands with a foot on the lower one as I pulled up on the strand above it. "Dave, can you do the same a few feet away?"

Relief filled his face. "Yeah." He copied my pose, and Hellhound stooped and stepped through the opening. Dave relinquished his position to Hellhound and eyed the fence.

"Be careful of your back, Dave," I cautioned as he bent.

"It's okay," he muttered, and stepped one foot through the opening. He jerked to a halt with a grunt as the barbs of the upper strand caught his jacket.

"Hold on." I reached to free him. "Can you bend a little further?"

"Yeah." He crouched lower and lost his balance when he attempted to pull his leg over the lower strand. His jeans caught on the barbs, and he fell with a grunt, his leg suspended by the snagged fabric.

Arnie and I both reached to help him, and Dave flushed. "I'm fine," he muttered, and jerked his pants loose. We all regarded the resultant large rip. "Shi... crap!" Dave said.

"It's okay, Dave," I said. "You really don't have to watch your language. You're not going to offend me."

Dave struggled to his feet, not meeting my eyes. "Some things you don't say in front of a lady."

Hellhound snorted laughter. "Ya see any ladies around here?"

Dave's fists clenched and I grabbed his arm as he lunged for Hellhound.

"Dave, relax," I soothed. "If he hadn't said it, I would have. I'll be the first to admit I'm no lady. There is no swear word that either of you could use that would offend me. And if I get going, I'll make your ears bleed. Don't tell me you haven't noticed."

"Doesn't matter." Dave's arm was tense under my grip. "It's about respect."

"Dave..." I touched his face, turning his scowl away from Hellhound so I could meet his eyes. "I really need you guys to get along. Please. Let it go."

"But..."

"Please," I repeated, giving him the big brown eyes for all I was worth.

His expression softened, and he touched my hand where my fingertips still rested on his cheek. "Okay."

"Thanks." I stepped away and changed the subject fast. "We can just follow the creek until we're opposite the shed. Keep your eyes open. I've posted the land for no hunting, but it's bowhunting season, and the land around a creek is technically public. And there's always the hit man, if we need some more excitement."

"Let's keep some distance between us," Hellhound suggested. "I'll lead, Aydan in the middle, an' Dave can cover our backs. Stay just within sight of each other. Then if there's a problem, we ain't all in it together."

"Good idea," I agreed with relief. "Lead on."

He nodded and strode away, pushing his way through the underbrush and skirting thickets of diamond willow. When he was almost out of sight, I followed.

Hellhound kept up a brisk pace, and I hurried to keep him in visual range. I glanced back at Dave toiling in the rear and considered asking Arnie to slow down, but I bit my tongue. No need to contribute further fuel to Dave's midlife crisis.

The next time I looked back, I couldn't see Dave at all. I was just about to call forward to Hellhound when Dave's shout sent a cold wave of fear coursing over me.

"Aydan, RUN!"

I whirled at the sound of something large crashing through the bushes toward me, and gasped relief when I saw Hellhound charging in my direction. He had just reached my side when another voice rang through the woods.

"Aydan, are you here? Are you okay?"

A very familiar voice.

Shit.

"Who's that?" Hellhound snapped.

"Tom."

Hellhound's fist clenched. "Shit!"

Tom yelled again, his voice strained. "Whoever you are, if you've got Aydan, let her go. Or I'll shoot your buddy here. You've got three seconds. Three. Two..."

"Tom!" I shouted frantically. "Tom, don't shoot, he's a friend!"

"Aydan, where are you?"

"Coming, I'm coming! I'll be right there!" I dashed through the woods in the direction of his voice, Hellhound bringing up the rear.

So much for stealth. We sounded like a herd of rhinos crashing through the bush. Assuming rhinos could yell. Christ, if the hit man was anywhere in the vicinity, we'd just made his job a whole lot easier.

I fought my way through the undergrowth, twigs slashing at my hands and face, and finally burst through the last thicket to see Dave on his knees, clutching his chest. Tom's double-barrelled shotgun swung up, and Arnie and I froze.

"Tom," I panted. "Don't shoot, okay?"

Tom's shotgun locked onto Arnie. "Aydan, are you all right?" he demanded.

"Fine, I'm fine, Tom, please put the gun down."

"Step away from her," Tom snapped, and Arnie sidestepped slowly. "Farther," Tom commanded.

"Tom, it's okay, Dave and Arnie are both trying to help me. Please put the gun down," I begged.

Dave was sweaty and ashen again, and I could see him struggling to breathe. His white-knuckled fist clenched a handful of T-shirt in the middle of his chest.

"Tom, please!" I gasped.

"Come over here," he said.

The pounding of my heart shook my entire body. What the hell was he doing? I stepped slowly toward him, keeping my movements smooth.

God, please tell me he wasn't living some bizarre rescue fantasy. Or worse, maybe he was still mad at me after the scene with Kane. It felt like forever to me, but it had only been a week. Please don't let him take out his frustrations on Arnie instead of me...

"Tom, please put the gun down." I approached him

cautiously and slowly stretched out my hand, trying to control its violent trembling. "Give me the gun."

"Stand behind me."

I followed his directions, moving carefully behind him.

"Stand closer."

Shit, what the hell was he doing? I stepped up to his back, frantically calculating angles and probabilities. Could I grab the gun away from him before he pulled the trigger?

I jerked in shock when his arm swung around to pull me tightly against his back. Normally, I would have appreciated the feel of that lean, muscular body against mine. Under the circumstances, my enjoyment was sadly limited.

"Okay, now tell me if you're really all right," Tom said.

"Yes, Tom, I'm really okay. Please don't shoot Arnie." My voice quavered with the triphammer beat of my pulse, and my panting refused to slow.

Tom's posture eased. "Really? You're not being forced to say that?"

"No, Tom, *please*!"

He blew out a sigh and his shoulders relaxed as he lowered the gun and turned to face me. "Thank God. Aydan, what happened? Where have you been?"

"In a minute." I hurried over to kneel beside Dave. "Dave! Oh, no..." I snatched at his wrist, fumbling for the pulse point with shaking fingers.

"I'm okay," he muttered. "Just another muscle spasm."

Arnie knelt beside me and surveyed Dave doubtfully. "Ya shittin' us this time?"

"No, I told you, I'm okay," Dave repeated. He relaxed his grip on his T-shirt and wiped his forehead. "I'm fine."

"I'm really sorry." Tom knelt on the other side, his face drawn. "Lie down." He pressed Dave back onto the ground.

"Are you having chest pain?"

"I'm fine. It's gone now."

"Did it feel like a heavy weight on your chest? A squeezing sensation?"

Dave sighed. "No, just a jab. I'm fine. It was just a muscle spasm."

"Do you have any pain in your arm or shoulder, or in your jaw?"

"Jeez," Dave said. "Is there an echo in here?"

Tom shot a puzzled frown in my direction.

"Tom is a volunteer firefighter. He's trained as a first responder," I explained. "Just answer his questions.

"No," Dave said. "No pain anywhere else."

"Do you feel dizzy or sick?" Tom persisted.

"No."

"Any history of heart disease? High blood pressure?"

Dave shifted uncomfortably. "No. I'm fine. I had my Class One physical just a few months ago. It's just a muscle spasm."

"You should go to the hospital as a precaution anyway." Tom pulled out his cell phone. "I'll call the ambulance."

"No!" Dave sat up. "I'm fine."

Tom sat back on his heels. "Why take a chance? You should get this checked."

"No," Dave repeated. He took a deep breath, rolling his shoulders, before struggling to his feet.

Tom rose with him, frowning. "Aydan, what's going on?"

"Um." I stared at him, my mind completely blank. "I, um... It's a long story..." I took a deep breath, trying to marshal my quivering wits.

Stall.

"Why are you prowling around my woods with a

shotgun?" I asked.

"Oh." He glanced down at the gun cradled in the crook of his arm. "I was actually riding my side of the creek. You know there was cougar in the area a while back, and I always carry my shotgun just in case. I saw, uh..." he paused. "...Dave?"

"Oh, yes, sorry. Tom, this is Dave Shore. Dave, Tom Rossburn, my neighbour."

Dave's face cleared as I made the introductions. "So he's a friend."

"Yes."

Dave stuck out his hand and Tom shook it.

"Does he know..." Dave trailed off when I gave him a fierce glare and a slight shake of my head.

I turned quickly to face Tom's puzzled frown. "So you saw Dave..." I prompted.

"Uh. Yes." Tom's eyes searched my face. "He was bent over holding his chest and I thought he might be in trouble, so I came over to see if I could help. As soon as he saw me, he yelled and told you to run, and I was afraid you were in danger."

He shot a dubious glance at Hellhound's bruises. "Then you came running out the trees with him right behind you, and I thought..."

He paused and finished, "Well, I wasn't sure what was going on, and I didn't want to take a chance. I've been worried about you. You were so upset the last time I saw you, and then you vanished..."

He trailed off and turned to Arnie. "You're supposed to be her friend. Has she told you about her problems with Kane?" His eyes narrowed in comprehension. "Did you take him on? Is that what happened to your face?"

Arnie shot me a cautious glance. "Yeah, I knew there was a problem," he said. "We're workin' on it."

Tom stood up a little straighter, his expression brightening. "Good. Finally. How can I help?"

CHAPTER 31

I assessed Tom's battle-ready posture with a sinking sensation. "Thanks, Tom, but there's nothing you can do to help at the moment. Just don't tell anybody you saw us, okay? And you didn't see the car that's parked on the road right now, either."

Tom frowned. "What do you mean, don't... Are you hiding from him?" His shoulders tensed and he swept an outraged glare at Hellhound. "If he assaulted you, call the police and report it! Don't just run and hide."

Leather creaked dangerously as Hellhound drew himself up, his fists clenching. I clutched his arm and spoke rapidly into the taut silence.

"Arnie would never run away from a fight. Kane didn't do this to him, he was fighting some other men to protect me. We're just lying low until we can figure out a plan."

Tom lifted an arm and let it fall against his side with a slap. "How much of a plan do you need? He's a dirtbag, and he's stalking you. That's illegal. Get a restraining order, and let the police enforce it." His eyes narrowed. "What other men? Protect you from what?"

I drew a breath of relief as I spotted a way to change the subject. "My friend Nichele got involved with a very dangerous man, and he kidnapped her. We're trying to find her, but this man has decided that we're a threat, so he's trying to kill us all."

Tom pushed his cowboy hat up and ran a hand over his face, fixing me with an incredulous stare. "For heaven's sake, call the police!" he exclaimed. "That's what they're there for. Assault and kidnapping and death threats. I'll call them right now."

He pulled out his phone, and I sprang to capture his hand. "Tom, no! He'll kill her if anybody calls the police. That's why we're sneaking around."

He gazed at us in frustration. "That's insane. Call the police and explain the situation to them. They're professionals. It's what they do. They'll deal with it. You're just going to get yourself killed if you try to do it by yourself."

"Tom, I can't," I said as firmly as I could. "I just need to get some boxes from my shed, and then I'm leaving again. If you tell anybody you saw us, we'll be killed. Please, just go home and pretend you never saw me."

He scowled. "You don't seriously expect me to turn my back and walk away when people are trying to kill you."

"Yes, Tom, I don't just expect you to do that, I need you to do it. I need people to believe that I was never here, and for that I need you to keep on doing what you always do. If you get involved, you're signing my death warrant."

We eyed each other tensely, and Hellhound's quiet rasp broke the silence. "Sometimes the bravest thing ya can do is turn an' walk away. This's one a' those times."

Tom shot a tortured glance at Arnie before returning his gaze to my face, his fist clenched by his side. "Aydan," he said softly. "Please don't ask me to do this."

"I'm sorry, Tom," I said as gently as I could. "If you do this for me, you'll be saving my life as surely as if you were fighting for me. Please, just go home and pretend you never saw us."

His face twisted. Then he squared his shoulders and gave me his steady, sky-blue gaze. "If that's what you need me to do, I'll do it. Just..." He caressed the sweat-damp hair away from my face, looking down into my eyes. He shot a defiant look at Hellhound, and his hand slid around the back of my head as he leaned down to kiss me lingeringly.

"Just come back safe," he murmured against my lips.

Then he straightened and glared a challenge at the other two men. "I'm holding you both responsible for Aydan's safety," he snapped. "Don't screw up. Or you'll answer to me." He strode to his horse and swung easily up into the saddle. He looked back one more time before clucking to his horse and riding away.

I stood in the short silence, my face burning while I avoided looking at Dave's open-mouthed stare and the twist of Hellhound's lips.

Hellhound snorted. "Ya got a serious problem there, darlin'."

I blew out a long sigh and massaged my aching temples. "Don't I know it."

"Uh, what... Am I missing something?" Dave stammered. "I thought you and..." He trailed off as his gaze darted from Arnie to me.

I turned to Dave, trying to manufacture an explanation while I desperately tried to remember who knew what about whom. "Tom doesn't know anything that's going on with me. He's my neighbour, and he'd like to be more than that, but I can't..." I abandoned that approach and was casting about for something less complicated when Dave spoke up again.

"Why did he know about your problems with Kane?"

"He didn't. Doesn't. He thinks Kane is a co-worker who's stalking me and trying to force me into a relationship."

"Oh." Dave fell silent.

Hellhound chuckled. "Well, darlin', how many boyfriends does it take to keep ya outta trouble? That makes what, four now?"

"None," I snapped, and he laughed.

I concentrated on peeling a couple of loose shreds of skin off a long scratch on my arm, trying to hide my irritation.

"Sorry," he added soberly. "Guess it prob'ly ain't too funny when you're stuck in the middle of it. We better get goin' before anythin' else goes to shit."

"Wait a minute." I held out a restraining hand as he turned. "We need to rethink this. Tom already saw us, so that part of the plan's down the tubes. And if our hitman's in earshot, we might as well have just sent up a flare. I think we'd better cut our losses."

"We can't just give up," Dave protested.

"No, I'm not talking about giving up," I agreed. "Let's go back to the car and drive into the yard. If there's anybody there, we're already in the car, so we'll have an escape route. If nobody's there, we can get to the shed more easily, and then we can take the boxes with us instead of hanging around."

I bit my tongue to prevent myself from adding that it also got Dave safely back in the car instead of overtaxing him in the woods.

Hellhound shot me a smile. "Good plan, darlin', let's go."

We stayed together and moved more slowly on the way back. Dave managed to get through the barbed wire without incident, though I could tell his back was hurting again after his tumble. I kept my mouth shut, and Arnie and I exchanged a glance while Dave climbed stiffly into the back seat.

I rolled into my yard and stopped the car well outside the range of the surveillance cameras. We all scanned the land and buildings in silence. At last, I shrugged. “Okay, let’s do it.”

“Hang on,” Arnie said. He turned to face Dave. “We might hafta move fast if somebody comes. Can ya stay in the car an’ get ready to drive just in case? I’ll help Aydan with the boxes.”

“Sure.” Dave eased himself out of the back seat and got slowly behind the wheel, grimacing.

I slipped an arm around Arnie as we walked toward the shed. “Thanks. That was smart. And tactful.”

He shrugged. “Dunno how smart it is to put a guy with a heart condition behind the wheel. But at least he won’t keel over tryin’ to carry boxes.”

“Mm.” I took one last look around before unlocking the shed. “You watch outside. I’ll dig out the boxes, and then we can take them all to the car.”

Half an hour later, I was caked with dust and quivering with nerves when I dropped the last box on the ground outside the shed. I wiped my forehead with the cleaner part of my T-shirt sleeve, cursing myself for not accepting Hellhound’s offer of help.

“That it, darlin’?” he inquired. “Ya really shoulda let me help ya. Ya look like ya just ran a marathon in a dust storm.”

“I know. They were right at the bottom of everything, but I really needed you to keep watch. It just creeped me out to think we might get cornered in there.”

He smiled and brushed an errant strand of hair back

from my face. “You an’ your claustrophobia, darlin’, it’s a miracle ya ever go in a building.”

“It’s not so much buildings, it’s just that I can’t stand the thought of being trapped.”

He chuckled. “I hear ya, darlin’. Come on, let’s get these boxes loaded an’ get the hell outta here.”

When the trunk and back seat were loaded, Dave shot me a hopeful look. “Mind if I drive? Need a wheel in my hands.”

I swallowed my misgivings. “Sure. I’ll sit in the back and start going through these boxes.”

On the highway, I caught a glimpse of Dave’s cheerful face in the rearview mirror.

“Better?” I asked.

“Yeah. Hate staying in one place too long. Start to miss the open road.”

“You really love driving that much?”

“Yeah.” He shrugged. “Well, no... it’s not really the driving, I just feel cooped up if I’m not on the highway.”

“Yeah, I get that,” Hellhound agreed, and I relaxed into the seat, appreciating another accord between the men, however temporary it might turn out to be.

Several hours later, I rubbed my aching eyes and slouched down in the seat.

“Nothin’?” Arnie asked.

“Nothing.” I blew out a long sigh. “All I found was his old pay stubs from when he worked for the Department of Agriculture. They started the year I was thirteen and ended the year I went to college, but I already knew that. I’d hoped to find...” I hesitated, trying to phrase it carefully in front of

Dave.

"...maybe pay stubs from somewhere else or something," I finished lamely. "Sorry, guys. That was a total waste of gas and time and nervous energy."

"Never mind, Aydan, you had to try," Dave said. "What'll we do now?"

I squinted at my watch in the dimness of the mall parkade where we'd hidden since our return to Calgary. "It's supper time, I need to make some phone calls, and I'm not planning to eat any of that potato salad that's been festering in the trunk since this morning. I'll go into the mall, get us something from the food fair, and make my calls from a pay phone."

"Not by yourself, ya ain't," Arnie said. I didn't get a chance to protest before he continued with resignation, "You're up, Dave. Don't let her outta your sight."

"I won't," Dave promised.

Inside the mall, I huddled deeper into the hood of my jacket, feeling as though I had a flashing red light attached to my head. I slouched along beside Dave, head down, hoping to look like a sullen teenage son. Jeez, please don't let him decide to cuddle up to me now.

Fortunately, Dave seemed to catch the vibe. He kept his hands in his pockets and gave me appropriate space.

The pay phones were conveniently located right beside the food court, and I made a beeline directly for them. As Dave hovered, I shot him a look from under my hood.

"Go get some food," I muttered. "I'll be a few minutes here."

He glanced worriedly over his shoulder. "I don't want to

leave you."

"You're not leaving me, you can keep me in sight while you stand in line," I argued. "Just go, okay?"

He shuffled uncertainly, frowning, before he blew out a breath and squared his shoulders. "...'Kay."

I turned my attention to the phones and swore. Three out of the four numbers on my list were long-distance. And I couldn't use my credit card.

I spotted Dave's receding back in the crowd and considered calling him back, but there was no way we'd have enough change between the two of us to make even one long-distance call.

I rolled my stiff neck and shoulders, trying to release the tension. Fine. I could make the local call, anyway. That was a start. I plugged in the coins and dialled.

Long minutes later, I clenched the phone receiver tighter in my sweaty fist. I'd grossly underestimated the logistics of phoning up one of my dad's old high-school friends and catching up on three goddamn decades. My heart leapt into overdrive at the sight of Dave's panicked expression as he forged through the suppertime crowd toward me, takeout bags apparently forgotten in his hand.

"Sorry, my call's out of time, nice talking to you," I blurted, and hung up fast.

"Cops!" Dave hissed. "Showing your picture over at the other phones!" He threw a wild glance over his shoulder. "Coming this way! Run!"

Pulse pounding, I scanned the food fair. Running would be crazy. They'd spot me instantly. I did the only thing I could think of on the spur of the moment.

"Come and get me when they're gone," I told Dave, and strolled into the men's washroom.

Inside, I kept my eyes on the floor and shuffled rapidly into a mercifully vacant cubicle. Then I sat and jittered on the toilet, trying not to listen to the noises around me.

It seemed like hours later when a tap on the cubicle door made me jump.

Dave's gruff and welcome voice came from the other side of the door. "Come on. What're you doing in there, anyway?"

I pitched my voice lower and hoped it wouldn't tremble. "What do you think, Dad? Jeez!"

"Well, hurry up. We gotta go."

"All *right*. Jeez."

His mutter receded. "Damn kid's probably doing drugs in there."

The resulting male murmur of sympathy was cut off by the sound of my flush, and I slouched out of the cubicle to wash my hands, head down. My hands were barely dry when Dave grabbed my arm and pushed me ahead of him out the door. I jerked petulantly out of his grasp and did my best surly teenage shuffle out of the mall beside him.

Back at the car, I dropped into the back seat and sprawled limply, trying to get my breathing under control. Hellhound pried the takeout bags out of Dave's fist and eyed us both with concern.

"What the hell happened?" he demanded.

Dave took a few deep breaths and massaged the centre of his chest. "Cops. Looking for Aydan. Had her picture and everything."

"*Shit*!" Hellhound swivelled a glare around the parkade. "Why aren't ya drivin? Get us the hell outta here!"

"It's okay," Dave said. "They gave up and left." His sweaty pallor was relieved by the flush that climbed his face.

"They weren't gonna look for her where she was hiding."

Hellhound glanced from Dave's face to the smile that was forming on mine. The corner of his mouth twitched up. "Where?"

I gave him the full grin. "Men's can."

He snickered. "Woulda liked to've seen that."

I heaved myself up to pat Dave's shoulder. "Nice work, Dave. You were perfect. What happened?"

Dave grinned, relaxing. "When you went into the can, I just sat down and started eating. They went around asking everybody, but it was a picture of you with your long hair, so nobody'd seen you. Cops finally just gave up and left."

I turned to Arnie. "You should have seen him playing the grumpy dad, pretending I was his no-good kid. He was great."

Dave groaned and massaged his stomach. "Just ate three burgers, though, 'cause I was afraid to just sit there doing nothing. Feel like shi... crap."

Hellhound grinned and offered him a fist bump. "Sometimes ya gotta take one for the team. Way to go."

Dave sat up straighter and beamed while Arnie and I devoured our meals.

"One thing I don't get, though," I mumbled through a mouthful of burger. "Why would they be looking for me in a mall? They can't be looking all over the city for me, can they? No way the city police would have time for that." I met Hellhound's frown. "Would they?" I asked.

"Nah." His scowl deepened. "But it couldn't be coincidence. Maybe they're tappin' the phones? Did ya say your name or anythin'?"

"Well, yeah, I had to say my name, but... they couldn't tap all the phones all over the city, could they?"

Hellhound swallowed the last of his burger and crushed the bag into a ball. "Fuck if I know. Sure as hell looks like it, though."

I sighed. "Yeah."

Dave glanced nervously around the parkade. "Now what?"

I consulted my watch. "It's eight o'clock. Just enough time to go and see if Spider's online yet before Arnie meets his contact."

"Where do you want to go?"

"I think a library this time," I said. "That internet cafe was too small. If I hadn't had Weasel with me, I'd have gotten caught for sure. At least the library gives me more places to hide."

"Okay." Dave backed the car out and headed for the exit.

I pondered while we drove.

Arnie twisted around in the seat. "What're ya thinkin' about?" he inquired. "Ya got that look again."

"I'm thinking about how Richardson showed up minutes after I made contact last time. That makes me nervous."

"Yeah," Arnie said. "Think Webb's trackin' ya?"

"I don't know. Maybe he told Kane what we were doing, and then he'd pretty well have to help them track us."

"Can't risk doing this again, then," Dave said.

"I have to."

"No, ya don't," Hellhound said. "Lemme go see my guy tonight first."

"No. That would be stupid if Spider already has the information we need. No way I want you going in again for nothing."

"Aydan..." Hellhound began, but I cut him off.

"Look, I'll be quick. Last time I dawdled around

searching those names after I talked to Spider." I blew out a sigh while we waited at the red light across from the library. "This time, I'll just get in and get out. No way Richardson will have enough time to get here."

Dave shot me an uneasy glance in the rearview mirror. "You sure?"

"I'm positive. It takes time to track an IP address," I said with more hope than certainty. "And then they'd have to get in touch with Richardson, and he'd still have to drive over here."

Hellhound scowled but didn't argue, and Dave drove into the parking lot.

"Dave, can you park somewhere where the car can be seen from a window?" I asked.

We all scanned for a parking spot. "What's your plan, darlin'?" Arnie inquired.

"This time, I want to leave you in the car, ready to drive, and put Dave next to the window where he can see you. Ideally, we find a spot where Dave can also see the entrance. Then he can signal me if there's anything funny going on, and I can have a bit of advance warning."

"But I don't know this Richardson guy," Dave said. "How will I know whether to signal you or not? And how would I signal you anyway?"

"I know Richardson an' a coupla Kane's other guys, too," Arnie volunteered. "I can signal Dave if I see anybody I recognize."

"That'll work. Dave, you can just, I don't know, sneeze or something. I won't be able to watch you because I'll have to keep my eyes on the screen."

"Sneeze?" he asked doubtfully. "Okay..."

"There." Arnie pointed. "Good spot just opened up."

Dave wheeled the car into it, and we all took stock of the sight lines.

"That'll work," Arnie said with satisfaction. "Ya sure ya don't want me to come in with ya?"

"No, you're still a little too, um, distinctive." I eyed his blackened face in the orange glow of the streetlights. The grubby bandage on his forehead added to his disreputable appearance.

He grinned, his face still asymmetrical from his swollen cheek. "Hey, my shirt's clean. Not like ol' Dave, Mr. South-End-Of-A-Northbound-Bear."

I couldn't help an involuntary glance at Dave, who flushed but kept silent, apparently recognizing the truth of the sobriquet. The trip through the woods hadn't done anything to enhance his appearance or his smell. With his torn, grimy clothes, gray-stubbled chin, wild hair, and Eau de B.O., he could easily have passed for a homeless person. And in fact, I realized, that was exactly what he was at the moment.

Hell, we all were. I regarded my own dirt-smudged jeans and T-shirt with disgust. I probably didn't smell any better. And my hair was starting to itch.

I shuddered. Definitely another trip to the gym tomorrow.

CHAPTER 32

The library staff watched us suspiciously after we entered. I could hardly blame them. I'd probably be wary of a couple of vagrants, too.

I stationed Dave near the window, within earshot of the computer terminals. "Here," I whispered, and handed him a book. "Just lean against the shelf with the book open and turn a page occasionally. Watch the door, and watch Arnie for a signal. Sneeze if I need to get out of here."

He eyed me worriedly. "...'Kay. Don't know how good a sneeze it'll be, though."

"It doesn't have to be good, Dave, just loud."

He nodded and took up his position, leaning against the bookshelf with all the casual grace of a wooden board. I considered telling him to relax, but then decided he actually looked quite authentic. Exactly like a homeless guy who was trying to look nonchalant while he warmed up in the library. I gave a mental shrug and made for the computers.

Luck was with me this time, and I slid into the chair in front of an unoccupied terminal immediately. I'd just logged into the World of Warcraft site when an explosive sneeze made me jerk around in my chair. I had half-risen, heart pounding, when Dave caught my eye and frantically shook his head. He jabbed his chin toward the table next to him, where a large man with a florid complexion was busily plying a handkerchief.

I subsided into my chair, air hissing out from between my teeth, and tried to release some of the tension from my shoulders. My hands shook while I navigated the site.

I was perusing the players when another sneeze rattled the windows. I stifled a curse and twisted around, but the angle was wrong and I had to stand again before I saw Dave's disgusted headshake.

The woman at the adjacent terminal shot me a curious glance as I settled back into the chair, clenching my teeth on the profanity that begged for utterance.

My back crawled with expectant tension, but silence reigned, and I turned back to the screen to find Spider's character.

Whisper. "Spider."

"come in now! J trying to get you!"

"Same old, same old," I muttered. "I know," I typed. "Have you found N or D yet?"

"no. come in now!"

"Is K all right?"

"Atchoo!"

I sprang to my feet again, feeling like the star of a Whack-A-Mole game and hoping the mallet wasn't about to crush my head. A brief but glorious vision of twisting the big guy's nose off evaporated at the sight of Dave's frightened face. I bit back an obscenity and made for the concealment of the bookshelves nearest the door.

My heart leaped into my throat at the sight of the two uniformed police officers striding through the entrance. I pulled my hood up over my head and loitered beside the stacks, head down while I watched from under my brows.

The two officers split up, heading directly for the two pods of computer stations. As soon as their backs were turned, I eased out the door and scuttled across the parking lot, keeping my face averted.

As I slid trembling into the passenger seat of the Caprice, Hellhound swore, and I followed his gaze to Dave, who was clearly visible with his back pressed against the library window. The two policemen loomed over him. While we watched, he shook his head vehemently, and one of the officers frowned and took him by the arm.

"Shit, shit, shit!" I chanted. "Shit! Goddammit..."

"Get down!" Hellhound yanked my shoulders toward him, and I toppled onto the seat, my head in his lap.

"What's happening?" I demanded.

"They got him." A suspenseful pause. "They're bringin' him out. We gotta go." He reached across me for the shifter, then stopped. "Wait a minute."

"What?" I hissed. "Tell me what's happening!"

"They're just talkin' to him. An' lookin' around the parkin' lot. I don't wanna drive away now, or they'll see us for sure. Just stay down."

I peered up at his intent face, barely breathing, and he glanced down at me with a leer. "While you're down there, darlin'..."

"I don't think so. Getting arrested would be bad enough. I don't intend to get caught playing the skin flute into the bargain."

His head snapped back up to watch the action outside again, and he spoke absently. "Why not, darlin', it'd make a helluva good story afterwards. An' it'd make me happy. Wait, what the hell?"

"What, what!"

He didn't reply immediately, and I clamped a hand on a sensitive area of his anatomy. "Tell me what's happening, now! Or else!"

"Easy, darlin', ya do any damage down there an' you're gonna miss it as much as I do." He paused. "They're leavin'. Gettin' in their car now."

"Oh, no, they've arrested Dave?" I wailed. "Shit, shit..."

"No, they let him go. Shit, Dave, let 'em get outta the parkin' lot first..."

"Oh..." The air whooshed out of me. "Thank God."

"That's it, Dave," Hellhound coached aloud. "Let 'em drive away before ya come over here... Just a little longer..." He relaxed. "They're gone."

The rear door opened and closed, and Hellhound wasted no time in driving away. I belatedly relinquished my hold on his crotch, and he shot a grin down at me.

"Damn, Dave, ya coulda taken a little longer. It's okay, darlin', ya can sit up now. Unless ya wanna stay down there an' play with my stickshift some more."

I sat up and twisted around to face Dave, whose blush was visible even in the semi-darkness. "What happened? What did they want?" I demanded.

Dave massaged the centre of his chest, gasping. "You. They described you. Lady at the computers told them she saw us come in together. I told them I didn't know you, you just gave me fifty bucks to watch out the window and then you left. Shi... crap, thought they were gonna arrest me, but they just gave me directions to the homeless shelter."

Hellhound laughed. "Lucky ya got that homeless look goin' for ya... *shit*!"

He seized a handful of my jacket and yanked me down again.

"Demanding, aren't you?" I mumbled into his lap.

"That was Mark Richardson. Again," Hellhound growled. "That sure as hell ain't coincidence."

My heart stopped. "Did he recognize you?"

"Nah. He was lookin' around the sidewalks an' the parkin' lot, not at the traffic."

I blew out a long breath and tried to stop shaking.

Hellhound chuckled. "If you're tryin' to blow me, you're doin' it wrong."

"Very funny. Can I sit up yet?"

He glanced around warily. "Better stay down there for a bit. I wanna get farther away from the centre of attention here."

He drove a few minutes longer, making several turns, before speaking again. "Okay, ya should be fine now."

I sat up and finger-combed the hair out of my face, peering anxiously at the passing traffic.

"Did ya find out anythin', darlin'?" Arnie asked.

"Not much. They still haven't found Nichele or Dante. I asked if Kane was still okay, but I didn't stick around to get the answer."

I blew out a disheartened sigh. "There's no way that was coincidence. There was just enough time for Spider to trace the IP address and make a call to the police. And to Richardson. I hope he wasn't lying to me about Nichele and Dante. He was really trying to get me to come in."

I slumped in the seat and rubbed my hands over my face. "We're pretty much out of luck for any more communication with Spider, I guess. The next time we talk to him, we'd better have some information about Nichele, because we're not going to be able to keep dodging him. He's too smart, and they're reacting too fast."

Arnie's hand closed over mine. "Then I guess we better get some good intel tonight," he said.

"What if your guy doesn't know anything, though?"

"Don't worry, darlin', we'll think a' somethin'."

I blew out a tense breath. Everywhere we turned, the net was tightening and time was slipping away.

"Arnie, maybe it would be better if you called Kane and told him you're coming in," I said. "You haven't done anything wrong. If you and Kane work together, you might be able to nail James and find Nichele, and you'd be protected just in case James has a contract out on you, too."

"I ain't gonna leave ya," he said with a touch of irritation. "When're ya gonna get that through your head?"

"But, Arnie, you'd have a better chance of saving Nichele that way."

"I ain't tradin' your life for Nichele's," he growled. "Lemme talk to my guy tonight, an' we'll take it from there." He consulted his watch. "Better get goin'." He pulled off into a strip mall parking lot. "Aydan, ya better drive, just in case I gotta make a fast getaway." He grinned. "I might just fake it so ya stand on it again. That was a blast."

"A little hard on all our hearts, though," I pointed out. "Let's aim for boring, okay?"

"Yeah, darlin', I hear ya."

Back on the road again, I followed Arnie's directions to the Foothills Industrial Park, and we drove the deserted streets in silence.

"Park over there." Arnie indicated a spot under a burned-out streetlight. "This shouldn't take any longer'n last time. Same thing, get ready to run."

He leaned over to kiss me, and I trailed my lips around to his ear. "Come back in one piece," I whispered. "I want to stroke your stickshift and rev you out to redline later."

He chuckled and turned to nuzzle my ear in turn, sending shivers down my neck. "Wouldn't miss it for the world, darlin'," he rumbled. He swung out of the car and vanished between two buildings.

Dave and I sat in silence while my shoulders slowly climbed toward my ears. I drew in a deep breath and tried to release the tension, but to no avail. I shifted to yoga breathing, slow and deep.

Dave's voice made me jump. "Are you okay?"

"Fine." I blew out another long breath, trying to convince my heart to slow down. "I'm just doing some breathing exercises to keep calm."

"Does it work?"

I twisted around to survey his tense face in the semi-darkness. "Yeah. Just breathe from your belly. Long and slow. Think about ocean waves rolling in... *Jesus!*"

A tap at my window made me snap around in the seat, adrenaline pumping. My heart achieved panicked-gerbil rate when I recognized the source of the sound. A gun barrel. 9mm. Pointed right at me.

"Shit!"

CHAPTER 33

"What do we do now?" Dave's voice cracked.

I realized there were two shadowy figures outside the car. I couldn't make out the faces, but the gun barrels against the windows were crystal-clear. One for me, one for Dave.

"You. Out." The gun barrel rapped against Dave's window. "Slow. Or she gets it."

"Okay," Dave quavered.

Another tap on my window. "Don't try anything, or you're both dead."

Frantic thoughts rocketed half-formed through my head. Why hadn't I left the car in gear? I could have stomped on the gas...

The rear door clicked open and I felt the car's suspension lift as Dave got out.

The driver's door opened from outside, and the gun barrel stared me down. "Now you."

"I just have to tie my shoe..." I started to reach for my ankle holster and pain exploded in my head. I vaguely heard a scuffle and Dave cried out. A hard yank on my hair made me stumble up and out of the car to avoid being half-scalped. The ground heaved under my feet. I clutched at the car for balance.

Suddenly, I was sprawled facedown over the hood while rough hands groped me intimately. My head throbbed and sour bile rose in my throat. Dave yelled again, but I couldn't tell whether it was pain or defiance.

The hands were efficient. In seconds, both my gun and my waist pouch were gone, and another jerk on my hair indicated that I should stand.

This time the world stabilized, and I focused on Dave's drawn face. He was clutching his chest.

"Dave!" I reached for him, but was yanked back by my hair, pain shooting through my head again. "He's having a heart attack!" I shrieked, pure terror pumping through my veins.

Dave's knees buckled and he sank to the ground. His breath came in shallow gasps while his fist clenched over his heart.

"Yeah, I think he is." My captor sounded amused.

"Help him!" I plunged toward Dave again.

"Hold still." A jerk on my hair accompanied the command, and the cold gun barrel jabbed under my chin.

"Dave!" My breath caught in my throat, my heart galloping as if it would beat for both of us.

It wasn't enough. Dave crumpled, head bowed. At the last second, his trembling hand reached out to the leg of the man beside him. The arc of the stun gun flashed in the dimness, and both bodies collapsed to the ground. One twitched and quivered.

The other lay still. So still.

"*Dave!*" My throat tore with my scream and I lurched forward, heedless of the gun under my chin and the hold on my hair. I swung wildly with one arm and my captor swore when I connected with his nose. His hold released, and I flung myself to my knees beside Dave's motionless body. My throat burned, and I realized I was still screaming.

I was reaching for Dave when electricity sizzled through me. I only vaguely registered my impact against the ground.

A confused jumble of activity. By the time a measure of comprehension returned, I was slung over a hard shoulder in a fireman's carry while my captor strode along. Moments later, the breath jolted out of me when he dropped me.

"You didn't kill her, did you?" a male voice demanded.

"I'm not stupid," my captor growled. A foot nudged me none too gently. "Had to stun her. Dumb bitch acted like she didn't give a shit whether I shot her or not."

"Where's the other one?"

My captor grunted. "Dead. Hit Larry with a stun gun and then croaked. Heart attack. I left them both there. Larry can deal with the body when he wakes up."

"That's convenient. One less body to dispose of. We can just prop him up in the car, and it'll look like a natural death."

I tried to marshal my twitching muscles into some useful movement, and failed. My breath came shallow and fast while my heart thudded in my ears. Come on, for shit's sake, get it together. I struggled for control.

Too late. A rough grip jerked my hands behind me and the cold click of the handcuffs sent despair trickling through my veins. At least they hadn't tied my feet. Yet.

I lay unmoving, trying to get a sense of where I was by peering through half-closed eyes. My face was mashed into the floor, so my view was limited to a blurry dark object barely inside the range of my peripheral vision.

I was beginning to get control of my breathing when I was grabbed by the shoulders and pulled upward.

"On your knees," commanded the second voice.

My muscles refused to cooperate and I fell. The back of my head smacked against the floor, sparks dancing behind my eyes in fireworks of pain. A hard blow to my shoulder wrenched an inarticulate cry out of me, my tongue still not working well enough to form words.

"Cut it out! She can't! The stun ain't worn off yet!" Arnie's bellow made me pry my eyes open, and the mystery of the blurry dark object was solved. He knelt on the floor a few feet away, his feet tied, hands bound behind his back.

"Man up, little brother, you always were a whiner." James's precise diction would have made me shudder if I'd had sufficient muscle control. He crouched beside me and turned my head to look into my eyes. "Hello again, Aydan. How nice to see you."

My uncooperative lips formed the words, "Fuu... u."

"How uncivil." He stood, and I lost sight of him as he moved away. "I have private business here. Go and wait for the buyer."

There was a mumble of agreement, and I heard the door open and close.

He spoke again from outside my range of vision. "These are two lovely gifts you've brought me, little brother. Nichele has been very useful, and now you've given me Aydan, too. How can I ever show my appreciation?"

"Ya could choke on a dick an' die."

"Now, now. Is that any way to talk to your big brother? I was thinking of a different kind of reward. I'll let you live, and I'll set you up in the family business. You'd have to work your way up the ranks, of course, but there are many opportunities for advancement."

Arnie snorted. "Ya ain't my fuckin' family, an' I'll take a

fuckin' bullet to the brain before I'll get in your line a' business."

James burst back into my field of view as his arm scythed through the air. The blow that hit Arnie's face sounded like a rifle shot, and he pitched over to land heavily on top of me.

"Arnie, oh, God," I mumbled, realizing how incredibly painful that had to have been after all his earlier injuries. I managed semi-controlled movement at last, craning my neck in an attempt to see him.

James seized Arnie's shoulders and jerked him to his knees again. Arnie made no sound, his nose misshapen while blood poured down. His eyes burned with hatred.

"Why aren't you crying, little brother?" James taunted. "Little baby Arnie, always crying about something."

When it became clear he'd get no response, he spoke again into the silence. "Think about it, little brother. This is your chance to make something of yourself."

He shot a contemptuous look at Arnie's jeans and leather jacket. "You're pathetic. All your life, people have bent over backward to give you special treatment, and look what you've done with it. You're a loser. Nothing but a biker wannabe, riding around on your Harley. You can't even string together a grammatically correct sentence. You live in a tiny apartment, and you've got no money to speak of. I had to fight for everything I got, and I made something of myself."

"Yeah," Arnie mumbled thickly. "Ya made a fuckin' asshole a' yourself. 'Course that ain't no stretch. Ya always were a fuckin' assho..."

His last word exploded into a grunt when James drove a fist into his stomach. Arnie doubled over, gasping, and James grabbed a handful of beard and yanked Arnie's chin up to glare into his face. "I started out as a sleazy little gangbanger, and I taught myself to speak and act like a businessman. Now the gangbangers answer to me. I got where I am today through my own brains and balls, not through handouts and coddling."

He bent closer, snarling. "I have money and respect and power, and I damn well deserve it. I can crush you like a bug, little brother."

Arnie spat in his face.

I saw the kick coming, and heaved my uncoordinated body in James's direction.

His foot struck a glancing blow to the same shoulder he'd kicked before, and the pain lanced through my bones. I clenched my teeth on a cry that jerked out anyway.

James smiled down at me. "Well. You're back with us, I see. On your knees, then." He hauled me up by the shoulders, and I managed to balance precariously. "So you're fond of him, are you?" he asked.

He turned to Arnie. "What is it with you? All you have to do is cry, and women give their lives for you. Aren't you getting tired of hiding behind pussy yet?"

Arnie's eyes burned holes in him and his shoulders strained his jacket while he fought the ties on his wrists.

James returned his gaze to me. "Didn't he tell you, sweetheart? That's how our mother died, too. Trying to protect little Arnie."

He snapped a glare back at Arnie. "Poor little Arnie. He cried and cried. Why couldn't you just shut up and take it like a man? Like I did. Like Don and Cathy did. She wouldn't have died if you hadn't been such a snivelling little shit."

"He was five!" I burst out. "Half the bones in his face

were broken! How can you expect -"

I tried to duck the blow, and partially succeeded. Instead of hitting me in the face, his fist struck above my temple with such force that the floor rushed up dizzyingly and the breath slammed out of my body when I landed.

I blinked tear-blurred eyes as Arnie lunged awkwardly to his feet, bellowing. I heard an impact and a hoarse grunt, and Arnie crashed to the floor beside me. Blood spattered across me and the floor, and terror clutched me.

An instant later, he was struggling up again. He had made it to his knees when James planted his hands on Arnie's shoulders and pushed his face up close.

"Look at her," he said, and the edge in his voice turned my spine to ice. "Lying there. Suffering. You did that. Just like you killed our mother. Remember her lying there, bleeding out? Remember that, baby Arnie?"

He slapped Arnie viciously in the face, sending another shower of blood flying. "Why aren't you crying, baby Arnie?"

"Stop!" I knew it wouldn't help, but I couldn't prevent the word from jerking out of me.

James smiled down at me. "He's not worth it, you know. He's just a pathetic loser."

"You're a pathetic loser. Arnie is twice the man you'll ever be."

His face twisted, and Arnie threw his body in front of the kick that was meant for me.

James kicked him savagely again, grinning. "That's more like it, little brother. Show some guts for a change."

He straightened and took a deep breath. "Well." He shook out his arms and shoulders before stooping to wipe his blood-smeared hands on Arnie's shirt. "I feel so much better now. Those prison shrinks knew what they were talking about after all. That was quite cathartic."

He grabbed my shoulders and hauled me onto my shaking knees again. Arnie lay unmoving, but I could still see the rise and fall of his chest. Despair bowed my shoulders. There was no way James would let us live. Dave was already dead. I wondered why James was wasting time. Why not just shoot us and have done with it?

What the hell. Get this over with.

"Arnie said you were smart, but I guess he was wrong." I tried to hold my voice steady without much success. My heart thudded violently in my chest. "Your hit man couldn't get the job done, so why not just kill us now and get on with life?"

James laughed. "Little brother thinks I'm smart. Isn't that nice. He doesn't have a clue how smart I really am." He stooped and patted my cheek. "Aydan Kelly."

He straightened and crossed his arms, smiling down at me. "Yes, about the hit man. Do you have any idea how few professional hit men there really are? It's not like you can just look them up in the Yellow Pages."

He shrugged. "Of course, you can always find some stupid little thug who'll kill somebody for you if you offer enough money, but the true professionals? Almost nonexistent. You have to have connections."

"Which I do." He smiled. "But do you know, all my connections have connections, too. And when I let the contract out, I discovered something very, very interesting."

He stooped again and stroked my cheek, his touch repulsively gentle. "Remember Fuzzy Bunny?"

The bottom dropped out of my stomach.

CHAPTER 34

"I see you do," James purred. "They were quite eager to find out whether you're the same Aydan Kelly whom they thought was dead. And it appears you are."

"I haven't a clue what you're talking about," I quavered. "Who or what is Fuzzy Bunny?"

"Please don't play dumb. It's unbecoming."

I tried a derisive snort. "I'm hurt."

"Not yet, but you will be." He bent to pull Arnie onto his knees again. "Sit up and pay attention, little brother."

Arnie straightened slowly, his eyes glittering dangerously through the mask of blood.

James patted him briskly on the shoulder. "Now that I've exorcised my demons, I'm going to give you another chance. Your little Aydan here is a very valuable commodity. She probably hasn't told you exactly how valuable. Let's just say that Fuzzy Bunny was more than happy to compensate me for the deposit I lost when I cancelled the contract on her life. And in fact, I'll make a handsome profit when I hand her over."

Arnie said nothing, and James frowned at him before continuing. "You're not being very gracious about this, but I forgive you. After all, blood is thicker than water, as they say." His lips quirked up as he regarded Arnie's smashed face and the blood-spattered floor.

"Aydan is so valuable they agreed instantly to the price I asked. Which is sad, really." He frowned and tapped his lips thoughtfully. "I must have left quite a bit of money on the table. Most unfortunate. However."

He squatted in front of Arnie, out of range. "I'm prepared to offer you a generous finder's fee. In exchange for keeping your mouth shut. Confidentiality is quite important to my contacts. And I'd hate to have to kill my own brother."

"Fuck off," Arnie growled.

James's face hardened, and I thought he would hit Arnie again, but he stood instead, staring down for a few moments.

"You're really beginning to irritate me with your holier-than-thou attitude," he said at last, his tone conversational. "I've tried and tried to reach out to you, but you just keep pushing me away. That's quite hurtful, you know."

"Prison shrinks teach ya that touchy-feely shit, too?" Arnie grated.

"Touchy-feely shit." James sighed. "Aren't you the tough man? Little Arnie takes a beating and never sheds a tear. But I'm terribly hurt. And do you know, despite what the shrinks say, I find vengeance is much more healing than forgiveness."

He leaned closer. "I still know how to make you cry, little brother."

Arnie glared back in silence and my heart pounded into overdrive. He'd already taken so much punishment. Rage and nausea climbed the back of my throat at the thought of having to watch James beat him more.

"Leave him alone!" My voice came out harshly between

clenched teeth.

James turned a beatific smile on me. "Oh, I will. You see, I already knew little Arnie had grown up. He was the toughest kid in the whole school. It didn't matter how much of a beating he took, he'd never show pain or back down. Then he hit puberty and started to pump iron, and nobody ever messed with him again."

He sneered at Arnie. "Isn't it ironic. You got bigger and stronger than your big brother. But I found out how to really hurt you." He paused, his eyes measuring me. "Didn't I, little brother?"

"Don't." Arnie's rasp held immeasurable pain.

James chuckled. "Oh, don't worry, I won't kill her. She's much too valuable. Not like that little slut you knocked up in high school."

He frowned down at Arnie. "You never did thank me for solving that little problem for you. If not for me, you'd have been saddled with a wife and kid at eighteen. I really don't know why I keep trying to help you when you're so ungrateful."

He shrugged philosophically. "At least she provided hours of entertainment before I finally killed her." He made his voice high and squeaky. "Don't hurt the baby, oh, don't hurt the baby."

His fine diction slipped as he pushed his face close to Arnie and snarled. "By the time me an' the boys were done fuckin' her, she was beggin' to die."

Arnie roared and dove at him, and James dodged sideways, lashing out with a kick that dropped Arnie to the floor.

"Watch carefully, little brother. Maybe you'll learn some new techniques." James turned his feral smile on me. "It'll be a treat for you to get fucked by a real man for a change."

Adrenaline hit my bloodstream in a burning rush. As he stooped over me, I lunged out of my kneeling position and head-butted him in the face. He rocked backward and I stumbled for the door, jerking at the handcuffs behind my back.

I spun to grapple behind me for the doorknob and saw Arnie and James both struggling to their feet. Arnie bellowed, "Run!" and dove clumsily to strike James with his shoulder, already falling when his bound ankles left him hopelessly off-balance. James staggered, but returned a sweeping punch to Arnie's face.

Arnie crashed to the floor again and the knob finally turned under my slick, shaking hands. I caught a glimpse of James turning in my direction as I wheeled to run out the door.

I hadn't even managed a full step before I slammed into Mark Richardson.

Recognition and relief made me light-headed, and my knees threatened to give way as I collapsed against him.

Richardson gave me a hard shove that sent me staggering. He shot a look around as he followed me into the room, gun in hand. "What the hell is this?" he demanded.

James straightened, holding his shoulder. "You're early."

"Looks like I'm right on time," Richardson countered. "What the hell's going on?"

"A family dispute. It's been resolved. Nothing to concern you."

"It concerns me if my merchandise is disappearing out the door," Richardson snapped.

James drew himself up. "My merchandise. It's not

yours until it's paid for."

"It's paid for." Richardson's face was impassive. "I just finished the transfer to your offshore account."

"Check it with Nichele." James glanced past us to the gunman who had followed Richardson in. I'd only gotten a confused glimpse of him earlier, but I was pretty sure it was the same guy who'd gotten me out of the car. I didn't recognize his face, but the brass buttons on the cuffs of his jacket were burned into my brain.

Brass-buttons nodded and withdrew, and faint relief penetrated my brain. Nichele was still alive. Thank God. I stood trembling in the middle of the room, trying to grasp what was happening. My mind crawled at the pace of a crippled snail.

As I gaped around me, Arnie rolled over slowly and struggled back onto his knees.

Richardson's gun jerked up and he sidestepped to place his back against the wall beside the door.

James shot Richardson a scornful glance. "Don't worry, he can't hurt you."

Arnie dragged his drooping head up to glare at Richardson with the one eye he was still capable of opening. He shook his head like a wounded bear, crimson droplets pattering onto the floor.

"What the hell?" he mumbled thickly.

"Howdy, Hellhound," Richardson said breezily. "You're looking worse than usual."

Arnie spat blood. "An' you're lookin' more like a traitor than usual."

Richardson shrugged. "Loyalty isn't very profitable. Fuzzy Bunny pays better."

My knees gave way and I hit the floor hard.

Richardson eyed me coldly, his gun held unwaveringly between Arnie and me. "What are you looking at?"

"I..." My voice shrivelled to a whisper inside my dry mouth. "Mark, you're not..."

"Sorry," he said. "Nothing personal."

Brass-buttons returned to mutter into James's ear. James turned an expansive smile on Richardson. "It's been a pleasure doing business with you. The merchandise is yours to do with as you please. I do hope you'll keep me in mind if you have any further needs."

Richardson's mouth quirked up in a grim smile. "I certainly will."

His gun jerked up, and he fired two rapid shots. James and Brass-buttons both crumpled to the floor.

Hellhound's teeth gleamed fiercely through the blood as he regarded James's body. "Asshole," he grated. "Burn in-"

Richardson fired again. Arnie's body jerked, his face slackening into shock. "...hell?" he finished faintly, and toppled to lie motionless on the floor.

CHAPTER 35

Time stopped. I couldn't draw a breath. The empty shell casing spiralled slowly through the air. It struck the floor and arced gracefully up again, turning end over end. The bell-like clink came to my ears long seconds later. I watched, transfixed, while the casing bounced and pirouetted across the concrete. Its silvery tinkle sounded like fairy bells.

At last, it settled into the deafening silence.

My heart beat once, a sledgehammer blow that rocked my entire body.

Then again.

Thud.

Richardson was already beside me.

I tried to move, to speak, before realizing my mouth was already open and a high-pitched, wordless keening was filling the room.

Richardson grabbed my arm, his lips moving.

The syringe in his hand looked enormous. A crystal-clear droplet clung to the tip of the gleaming needle.

Still paralyzed, I could only watch it slide into my arm.

The room faded, and Richardson's voice spoke from a great distance, deep and slow like a record played at the wrong speed.

"N-o-t-h-i-n-g p-e-r-r-s-s-s-o-n-n-a-a-l-l-l..."

CHAPTER 36

I groaned and tried to raise my pounding head. Pain pulsed through my skull in resonant waves that matched my heartbeat. I managed a brief glimpse of spinning whiteness before the whirlpool sucked me under again.

Several attempts later, I managed to pry both eyes open and lift my head simultaneously. My stiffened neck and shoulders protested fiercely, and I groaned again. A hand slapped my cheek firmly.

With an effort, I focused on the face hovering in front of me. The handsome features with the dimpled chin and the thin scar slicing across the cheekbone.

I recoiled with a cry and began to struggle in earnest when I realized neither my hands nor my feet would move.

Richardson slapped my cheek again, just hard enough to sting. "Settle down. You're not going anywhere."

I gasped a couple of panicky breaths while I continued to jerk at my bonds.

"I said, settle down." Another brisk slap.

I held still and panted, heart hammering while I snapped my head around, taking in the details of my prison.

A featureless white room. Small table with a laptop on it in the corner. My chair in the middle. The chair Richardson had recently vacated was a few feet away, with a small black canvas satchel beside it. His was a standard rolling desk chair. Mine, not so much.

It looked and felt like a dentist's chair, but the sturdy leather restraints at the arms and feet would have sent any dental patient screaming in terror.

It was definitely doing it for me.

I bit down hysteria and regarded my white face and enormous eyes in the reflective panel on the wall. One-way glass, obviously. Nothing like an audience.

I hadn't realized I was crying until I saw my tears in the mirror.

"You didn't have to kill him." My quavering voice barely broke the silence of the room.

Richardson shrugged. "I like a tidy site. No loose ends."

I was pretty sure it was hopeless, but I had to try. "Mark, why are you doing this? I know there's money in it for you, but think about the good people you're betraying."

His lips curved in a sardonic smile, activating the cute, elusive dimple in his cheek. I'd thought it was adorable the first time I met him. Now it wasn't doing much for me. I fought down terror and rage.

"Good people like you?" he asked. "How modest."

I held my voice steady with more success this time, the anger strengthening me. "Hell, no, they were going to kill me anyway. People like Webb, Germain..." I paused. Yes, he was a good person. "...Kane."

"Whatever." He leaned close. "I'm doing you a favour. You know they'll kill you if they catch you. I'm offering you a new life. Working for Fuzzy Bunny has its perks. You'll get a luxurious place to live, piles of money, anything you want. And all for a few hours of work a day."

I shrugged. “Sounds great, but I’m no use to you. I can’t access any networks without...” I paused, not wanting to give away any classified information just in case. “...help,” I finished.

“You mean this kind of help?” He lifted the satchel onto the chair and extracted a small object.

I tried to hide my horror when he dangled the amethyst crystal in front of my eyes.

They had another network key.

He appraised my face, smiling. “I’ll take that as a yes.” He placed the thin chain around my neck and patted the amethyst into place between my breasts. “There you go.”

I said nothing, and he frowned. “You’re not going to go all goody-two-shoes on me now, are you?”

My thoughts stampeded, driven by panic. I had no hope of escape or rescue. I’d hidden my tracks from Kane’s team too well, and there was nobody left to contact them. Dave and Arnie both dead, my worst nightmare come true...

I jerked my mind away from the memory of Arnie’s slack, blood-covered face, all his humour and keen intellect wiped away by the indifferent hand of death.

“What’s the matter, cat got your tongue?” Richardson asked. “Come on, Aydan, wise up. Kane’s team will kill you at the drop of a hat. There’s nothing there for you except an early grave. Work with me, and you can live happily ever after.”

I managed to pry my tongue loose from the roof of my mouth. “Except you’ve killed most of my friends.” My voice was so hoarse I barely recognized it as my own. “And except if I work with you, I’ll be helping you kill the rest of them.”

Richardson snorted. “Friends. Hardly. Stemp ordered your husband killed, Webb ratted you out to the team, and

Kane's been ready to put a bullet in your head ever since you ran. Hell, he was ready to shoot you last summer. With friends like those, who needs enemies?"

He leaned close again and gave me his attractive smile. "I'm the best friend you've got. I saved your life."

I blew out a long, unsteady breath. This was where it was going to get ugly.

"Fuck you." I trembled in the chair, fighting to hide my fear.

He stepped back. "Think this through, Aydan. You and I both know how this will end if you don't cooperate. You and I both know that nobody's going to miraculously rescue you this time."

He crossed his arms over his chest and leaned a shoulder against the wall, flashing his dimple again. "You're very resourceful. You caused no end of consternation to a team of highly professional agents. Left everybody standing there looking stupid. It would be terribly disappointing to have to waste your talents."

My heart hammered, attempting to escape my body before it was too late. I swallowed once, twice, trying to summon up enough saliva to speak. Deep breath.

"Life's full of disappointments," I growled. "Fuck you, and fuck Fuzzy Bunny up the ass with a dead chicken. Twice."

He sighed and heaved himself away from the wall. "I was afraid you'd say that." He paused. "Well, not that, exactly. I have to admit, I wasn't expecting the dead chicken." He dimpled again. "Come on, Aydan, be a sport. Don't make me get my hands dirty."

I couldn't trust my voice to speak again, so I summoned up my best glare and sat as still as I could. The entire chair vibrated with my tremors.

"All right." He reached into the satchel again. My heart stuttered to a halt at the sight of the small butane torch in his hand. I had one just like it in my kitchen. I used it to melt the sugar on my crème brulée. I was afraid dessert wasn't on his mind.

He clicked the button and the clear blue flame whistled evilly. He eyed me seriously, no sign of the dimple. "Aydan, the fun's over. Let me make this really clear. Just access the virtual network. It's all set up. You have the key. All you have to do is go in and decrypt a few files. You can agree to do that now, and be amply rewarded."

He leaned in, the torch hissing spitefully in his hand. I couldn't help straining away from him despite my best attempt at bravado. I clenched my teeth to stifle the whimpers that wanted to come out on each shallow breath.

"Or," he said softly, "You can end up doing what I want anyway, after hours or days of excruciating pain." The torch moved a little closer. "Frankly, I expect you'll break in less than an hour. I'm very good at what I do. But you may surprise me. Sometimes women are much tougher than men."

The flame approached my arm slowly, and I froze in sheer terror. Heat mounted. I knew the tip of the flame was invisible. It would burn me before I ever saw it touch my skin.

"Stop!" My voice came out in a shriek. "I'll do it. I'll go into the network now."

Richardson patted my cheek. "That's my girl. I'll monitor from here." He rolled his chair over to the small table while I gulped down hysterical sobs.

He pressed a few keys and eyed me levelly. "Oh, and I

hope you're not trying to bluff." He placed the laptop on his knees and rolled back over beside my chair. The torch whispered its threat as he brought it within inches of my arm again.

He smiled, his dimple peeking out coyly before vanishing again. "Whenever you're ready."

I bowed my head in defeat. "What do you want me to do?" I quavered.

"Visualize the virtual corridor. The files are in the first room on the left."

I stepped into the white void of virtual reality and put my hands to my head. "My head hurts."

Hold onto control now. I concentrated with all my might. Don't give them any warning. My hands shook.

"Get on with it," Richardson snapped.

"Okay." In the instant between one heartbeat and the next, I materialized a gun, pressed it against my temple, and pulled the trigger.

CHAPTER 37

I'd thought a bullet to the brain would be relatively painless.

I'd been wrong.

Agony tore through my head. My body convulsed, jerking frantically in a useless attempt to escape. The cool blue flame of the butane torch would have been a welcome relief from the roiling white-hot lava that seared my veins. My throat ripped under the lash of screams I felt rather than heard. A nauseating vortex of colour sucked me down and I tumbled like a rag doll, blind and sick, suffering unspeakable, unending torment.

At last, the spinning slowed and the colours faded.

The gut-churning smell of burned flesh filled the air.

Comprehension arrived with a hammer-blow of despair. He'd pulled me out of the network before I died.

I'd failed.

"No." My voice came out a raw whimper.

I couldn't open my eyes, but I didn't want to anyway. I could feel the burn sizzling on my arm. I didn't want to see the flame approaching. I didn't want to watch my skin bubble and blacken under its heat.

"No," I repeated. My body trembled helplessly, soaked in sweat.

I clenched my fists and dove for the network again. They wouldn't be able to stop me every time.

I barely glimpsed the void before hell's volcano erupted inside my head and the agony began anew.

Consciousness returned abruptly, but I kept my eyes closed. Waves of pain coursed through my body, and I held myself still and silent, trying to stifle despair.

"I thought you said she'd be awake by now." A vaguely familiar male voice almost made me betray myself with a start. I concentrated hard on my breathing, trying to calm the sudden pounding of my pulse. Who had spoken? Richardson? I wasn't sure.

"I said she *might* be awake by now." The second male voice was definitely not anyone I knew. "When you drag in an unconscious body, you can't expect me to predict things down to the minute."

"Why isn't she restrained in the chair?"

"We need her to believe she's safe, from the first instant she wakes up. If she wakes up tied to the chair, she'll never believe us."

A pause.

"Very well. But this is against my better judgement. Be on your guard. Don't underestimate her. If she feels threatened, she won't hesitate to kill."

"What's she going to kill with? We have her clothes, so I know she doesn't have any concealed weapons. Besides, if she wakes up feeling safe, it won't be an issue. She'll know she doesn't have to fight. And anyway," the voice continued. "She'll be weak and disoriented, and in pain."

Another pause.

"Don't say I didn't warn you. Stay alert. Let me know as soon as she wakes up."

"Right."

The quiet click of a door closing.

I took stock as best I could with my eyes closed. I was lying on a soft surface, apparently a bed. I could feel fabric touching me, so if they had my clothes, I must be covered with a sheet. No restraints. That was good. And now I had the element of surprise, and the knowledge that they were going to try to mess with my mind.

I kept breathing evenly, gathering my strength and trying to ignore the pain. The burn on my arm was still stinging, but nothing else hurt as badly as I'd expected. I must have passed out before they really got going.

I counted the rapid beats of my heart.

Nine hundred and seventy-three beats later, I heard the quiet click of the door again. This time, I eased my eyelids open the tiniest crack. Only one blurry figure bent over me.

Now or never.

I grabbed my captor's wrist and yanked him toward me as I jerked up from the bed. My fist smashed into his nose, and I followed up with a vicious knee to his stomach. He doubled over, and I hit him as hard as I could at the base of his skull with my two hands locked together.

Pain ripped through my left hand as he fell, and an IV pole toppled to the floor with a clatter. My legs felt like rubber when I staggered to my feet. A wave of dizziness swamped me, the edges of my vision darkening. My pulse pounded in my ears, painfully loud. In a couple of stumbling steps, the dizziness began to abate and I was able to raise my head. A hand closed around my ankle, blasting adrenaline through my veins. I kicked free with a cry and fled.

I hadn't even made it to the doorway when a large black-clad figure blocked it. Nowhere left to go.

I lowered my head and charged with a berserk roar.

It was like tackling a brick wall. Pain slammed through my shoulder into my neck and back. I staggered. Hard arms crushed me. Screams tore from my throat while I jerked and twisted frantically.

A jab in my butt.

Then nothing.

I woke in mindless terror, thrashing uselessly against the restraints while pain hammered my body.

"Aydan, stop, you're safe." Kane's voice. I froze, blinking and squinting, trying to focus while my panicked panting whistled in my throat. I was back in the dentist's chair. Wearing a hospital gown. Helpless. Kane sat beside me on the chair Richardson had occupied.

"Aydan, it's all right, you're safe," he repeated.

In an instant, I understood. Kane had once told me effective torture was mostly psychological. They must have placed me in a sim while I was unconscious. I had expected them to try to mess with my mind, but I hadn't expected this.

I lay whimpering and trembling, unable to control either my voice or my body.

"Aydan." He brushed my cheek with his fingertips, and I jerked away, shuddering.

It was a sim. Only a sim. I concentrated desperately on making the chair and the restraints insubstantial.

Nothing happened, and panic overtook me again while I

fought wildly, beyond rational thought.

"Stop! Aydan, stop!" The avatar that looked like Kane grabbed my shoulders. "Aydan, listen to me, it's over. You're safe. You're not with Fuzzy Bunny."

"Liars!" I shrieked. "Filthy fucking lowlife murdering liars!"

"I'm not lying. You're safe." He held my face between his palms and I twisted, trying to bite him.

He clamped down, pinning my head to the chair, and leaned over me. Completely incapacitated, I glared up at the avatar, distilling all my despair and horror and loss into a concentrated beam of hatred. If I could have killed through sheer force of will, he would be nothing but a heap of crumbling ash.

"Nice sim," I snarled. "How are you doing it?"

"Aydan, it's not a sim. This is real. You're really safe."

I gasped a couple more breaths, grappling for control. "Yeah. I feel really safe. Tied to a chair with your handy-dandy torch all ready to go."

He followed my gaze to the torch that lay on the floor in the corner. I jerked my head loose to try to bite him again, and he yanked his hands away.

"No," he said urgently. "Nobody will hurt you, I promise."

"Well, thanks, now I feel all warm and fuzzy." I heaved at my bonds again. Had I felt the faintest bit of give? I wrestled them some more, sweat trickling down my body, heart pounding.

"Aydan, if you'll stop struggling, I'll undo the restraints. Please, just stop fighting."

A tiny flame of hope kindled. I went limp, gasping for breath. "John," I quavered. "Oh, thank God, John, is it really you? Please... hurry... get me out of here..."

"It's all right, Aydan," he repeated as he rapidly undid the straps. "I'll have you out in a minute-"

He broke off abruptly when I put all my strength into a violent lunge, fists swinging. The force of my attack sent him staggering back, and I spun toward the door.

I hadn't even taken a step when his massive arms wrapped around me. His weight pinned me against the wall while I thrashed and screamed.

I knew I couldn't win. There was no strength left in my muscles and no hope left in my heart. My attempts grew feebler until I was completely immobilized. I would have spat at him, but I had neither the spit nor the energy.

"Aydan, please! It's all right! It was a setup. You're safe. Everything's okay."

"Okay?" My voice rose. "Bullshit! The real Kane would never, ever tie me to a chair! The real Kane would never, ever try to tell me everything was okay when his best friend..."

The last shreds of control slipped away and a raw shriek burst from my throat. "Arnie's dead and you're trying to tell me it's okay, you... you..."

Suddenly I was crying and screaming and beating my head against him, the only part of my body I could still move.

Richardson ran in, and a jab in my arm made the room dissolve.

CHAPTER 38

In my dream, Arnie's raspy voice growled gentle nonsense while his hand stroked the hair away from my face. I squeezed my eyes tightly closed, willing the dream to continue. Tears prickled the backs of my eyelids and I held them in with fierce concentration.

He brushed a kiss across my forehead, a familiar touch of warm lips and prickly whiskers.

"Hey, darlin', wake up."

I lay still. As long as I could hear his voice and feel his touch in the dream, I could pretend I was safe and he wasn't dead.

The bed dipped as he sat on it, and I felt his arms around me. "Hey. Aydan. Come on, darlin', I know you're in there."

My eyes flew open despite myself, only to be confronted by a nightmare face.

"Sorry I ain't much to look at." He chuckled. "But, hell, I never was. It ain't that much worse'n usual."

I gaped at the bruises ranging from deepest black through purple to a delicate though unflattering shade of yellow-green. His left eye was swollen completely shut, and his nose was so heavily packed and taped that the rest of his face was barely visible.

I jerked back, wrapping my arms over my head to curl

away from the monstrosity they'd created.

"Stop!" I tried to yell, but my voice came out in a broken rasp. "I won't! I don't care what you do, I won't. I know this isn't real. I know he's dead."

"It's okay, darlin'," he said. "I ain't dead, an' you're safe."

I flinched away from his gentle touch. "Aydan," he persisted, "It's okay. Ya gotta believe me."

I coiled up tighter. I couldn't bring myself to hit the injured construct that looked and sounded so much like him.

"Aw, darlin'," he said, and I tried to close my ears to the rough-edged rumble I'd never hear again.

"Ya think this's one a' those mind control things, don't ya?" he asked softly. "This's real, darlin', an' I'll prove it to ya. I'll tell ya somethin' only I could know, same as ya did for me this summer."

I froze. My heart listened with desperate hope even while my mind tried to block out his words.

"I know Steven abused ya. I know ya won't let yourself need anybody, ever again. An' I know how to put a smile on your face in the passenger seat of a highway tractor."

A single sob leaked out as I uncurled to stare at him. His arms closed around me and I touched his swollen, split lips with trembling fingers.

"Arnie?" My voice was nothing but a husky whisper.

"Shhh, darlin', ya just about blew out your vocal cords." He pulled me closer, stroking my hair.

"But... I saw Richardson shoot you."

"Yeah. Trank gun. Bastard. I owe him one for that."

I started to shake as reality flooded in. "You're not dead." My eyes welled up despite my best efforts.

"Not last time I checked. Hey, darlin', don't cry. Didn't think you'd be that disappointed I'm alive an' kickin'."

I flung my arms around him, battling the tears that squeezed out anyway, and he cradled me in his strong arms, muttering comfort and stroking my hair.

I fought my way back to control and pulled away, turning to discover a convenient tissue box on the small table beside the bed. I blew my nose and took stock of my surroundings for the first time.

There was an IV in my hand, although it wasn't connected to the pole that stood in the corner. The bed looked hospital-issue, and a panel in the wall contained various knobs and fittings. There was a small white dressing on my arm. The burn underneath still throbbed.

Arnie's voice was soft behind me. "Ya okay, darlin'?"

"Yeah. Sorry about that," I quavered.

"Aydan, ya got nothin' to apologize for. You're amazin', darlin', an' a few tears don't change that."

"Thanks." I didn't turn to meet his eyes. "Did they tell you..." I gulped as my fragile composure threatened to shatter again. "Arnie, Dave..."

"Dave's okay, darlin'. They checked him out, stress test an' EKG an' everythin', an' he's fine, 'cept for his back still hurts. Nichele's fine, too. Everybody's fine."

I gasped a couple of shallow, ragged breaths, and Arnie's hands closed on my shoulders. "Take it slow, darlin'. Just breathe with me. Nice an' slow."

I turned to burrow into his arms again. To hell with not needing anybody. I needed to feel his familiar bulky body against me, his powerful arms around me. Needed to hear his gravelly voice muttering tenderly in my ear.

At last, I took a few deep breaths, then pulled away and straightened.

"Thanks," I whispered. Another long breath. "I'm okay

now. Where am I? How did you get me out? What time... no, what day is it? Was it... How much of it was real?"

My numb mind staggered in circles, unable to believe this was reality. Maybe it was still a sim. But it couldn't be. Arnie was the only one who could know about the passenger seat.

Arnie held up his hands. "I dunno much myself. You're in a private room in the secured part a' the Silverside hospital. It's about three o'clock, Tuesday afternoon. I dunno about anythin' that happened to ya after I got tranked. I woke up here in the hospital, too. Guess they brought us in by chopper."

"Where was I? Who got me out? Did they catch Richardson?"

"Richardson ain't a traitor, darlin', it was a setup. An' I dunno about any a' the rest, you'll hafta ask Kane."

I gulped. "Is he here?"

"Yeah, but I only saw him a few minutes ago when he grabbed me an' said ya needed me."

"What about James? Is he dead?"

Arnie scowled. "Nah. No such luck. Richardson tranked him, too."

I ran a shaking hand over my face. "I completely forgot about those damn ballistic trank guns. I heard the shots and saw the casings, and I just believed..." My voice shook and I clammed up.

"Hell, I did, too, darlin'. I really thought I was free a' that fucker this time." He brightened. "But the good news is, he ain't gonna go through the public legal system this time. No fancy lawyers an' plea bargaining. This time that fuckin' asshole's gonna pay his dues."

I took his hand, wincing at the sight of his injuries.

"Arnie, I'm so sorry."

"Darlin', what the hell for? Ya ain't done anythin' wrong."

"I'm sorry you had to go through this because of me. I'm sorry for what James did to you. Now, and... earlier."

He brushed a kiss across my lips. "No big deal, darlin'."

I held his face gently as he pulled away. "You never let anybody in, do you?"

He went very still, and then one corner of his bruised mouth quirked up. "It's different when I do it."

I laughed.

A tap on the door startled me. I shot Arnie an uncertain glance, and he nodded reassuringly.

"Come in." My voice was still a hoarse whisper.

"Come on in," Arnie called.

I tensed instinctively when Kane stepped through the door. He stopped immediately. "Did you tell her?" he asked.

"As much as I know," Arnie said coolly.

A spasm twisted Kane's face. "I'm sorry," he said. "I didn't have time to say it before, but I owe you a huge apology. I wasn't thinking straight. I know you'd never stab me in the back. Or you wouldn't have, anyway. I don't deserve your trust now, but..."

"Aw, shut the fuck up," Arnie rasped. "Ya dumb shit, ya really think a little misunderstandin's gonna fuck things up between us? You're the only fam'ly I got." He stood. "Lemme know when you're done debriefin'. I wanna talk to Aydan again later." He limped out, slapping Kane's back on his way by.

The relief on Kane's face made me smile despite myself.

He smiled, too, the taut lines easing from his face. "There's nothing like almost losing something to make you realize how important it is," he said quietly.

"Amen," I agreed. "Speaking of which, um... am I going to live to see tomorrow?"

His smile widened. "Yes. Lots of tomorrows. Stemp's rescinded the order. Everything's fine."

"Maybe for you it is," I said, and watched his smile fade. "Was that really you, earlier? When I was in the chair?"

He eyed me unhappily for a moment, and took a deep breath. "Yes. Aydan, you have to believe I was trying to help you. The restraints were Stemp's orders. I couldn't convince him otherwise. I really thought you'd believe me. I thought you knew I'll always come to rescue you-"

"And Richardson torturing me," I interrupted. "That was a setup, too? I was here all along?"

"Yes, Aydan, I'm sorry..."

"Save your breath. Let's just get the debriefing done, okay?" I rose carefully, and he took a step toward me, hands half-reaching.

"Do you need help?" he asked tentatively.

"No." I grabbed the robe that hung on the back of the door and shakily donned it. "Lead on."

CHAPTER 39

After a short, silent trip down the hallway, Kane opened a door for me and I stepped through. The three men around the table rose, and I froze at the sight of Mark Richardson.

His handsome face twisted as if in pain. "Aydan, I'm so sorry, I..."

"Save it," I interrupted. "First I want the whole story."

He nodded and shut up, muscles rippling in his jaw.

My gaze skimmed over Spider's pale, drawn face to meet Stemp's reptilian eyes.

"So you set me up. Again. That's getting old." I preferred to think my hoarse whisper lent menace to the words.

Stemp shrugged, impassive as always. "Please sit, and we'll begin debriefing."

The sound of his voice sent a shock of recognition through my body. "You. You were the one who wanted to keep me tied to the chair."

He eyed me coolly. "So you were awake then. I warned the good doctor not to underestimate you. Now he has a tangible reminder of the wisdom of that advice, in the form of a broken nose. Please, sit."

Rage spread its heat through my blood. It would have been wonderfully defiant to remain standing, but my quivering muscles had other ideas. I sank into a chair before my knees could drop me.

Kane swung the door closed and joined the others as they took their seats around the table.

Stemp nodded in my direction. "Ms. Kelly, we'll begin with you. What, exactly, have you been doing since last Tuesday evening?"

"Hitched a ride to visit my aunt in Victoria. Spent the rest of my time trying not to get dead."

After a brief silence, Stemp's eyebrows rose fractionally. "Succinct."

I shrugged.

He eyed me for a few seconds, then exhaled audibly. "In detail. Day by day." Another pause. "Please."

I blew out a breath of my own and began to recount my activities. When I mentioned setting up the meeting with Arnie at Hotel Village, something about Kane's immobile posture made me study his face. His eyes widened almost imperceptibly, and I trailed to a halt in my narrative and faked a cough.

"Sorry," I croaked. "Need a drink."

Spider sprang up to fill a glass, and in the momentary confusion, I met Kane's eyes. He gave me the tiniest of headshakes.

I sipped my water, stalling and considering. Maybe he hadn't reported our run-in at the hotel. If he hadn't, that meant Dave's possession and use of an illegal weapon against a government agent would never come to light unless I brought it up.

It also meant Kane was covering his ass. Lying and concealing his actions. Sick disappointment dragged at my heart. He might have betrayed me on a personal level, but I had believed implicitly in his professionalism and dedication to duty.

I straightened and swallowed the bitterness. Just more lies. That shouldn't surprise me anymore. At least I could get Dave off the hook.

I took a deep breath. "I met Arnie at the hotel, and we decided it would be smart to lie low. We were sure you'd be looking for me, and I wanted to do everything in my power to help Nichele. We all got in Dave's truck and got out of the city."

I opened my mouth to continue, but Kane interrupted, his gaze steady. "I'd like to add some detail, if I may."

Stemp shot an unreadable glance at him, and raised a questioning eyebrow at me. I nodded slowly. What the hell was he up to?

"I didn't realize Aydan had been communicating with Webb," he began.

"Sorry," Spider muttered miserably, his eyes fixed on the table.

"It's all right, you did the right thing," Kane said. He spoke directly to Stemp. "Aydan told Webb I'd killed her husband, and he decided to investigate further before telling me about Aydan's communication, in case I was compromised. It was the right decision."

Stemp nodded once. "Noted."

Spider's strained expression eased, and Kane continued. "I had been in contact with Hellhound without telling him any details, and I led him to believe I'd lost touch with Aydan and urgently needed to speak with her. As soon as he got her message, he called me. I was hiding at their meeting place when Aydan arrived."

Kane's steady grey eyes met mine and held me. "Aydan

and I had... had words... before she left. I let my personal feelings get in the way, and I acted unprofessionally. As a result, I botched the operation, and Aydan escaped. I take full responsibility."

Stemp nodded again. "Noted. Ms. Kelly, please continue."

A flood of unidentifiable emotion held me speechless for a second. Relief and gratitude and who-knows-what-else. He hadn't covered his ass. He'd told as much of the truth as he could without incriminating Dave. I sipped some more water, recovering.

After another moment to gather my thoughts, I carried on with my story, pausing at the point where I'd reported the potential hit on Kane. "Is that when you told him?" I asked Spider.

"Yes." He met my eyes imploringly. "I'm sorry, I didn't know what else to do."

"It's okay. I expected you'd have to. Was James actually trying to have everybody killed?"

"Yes," Spider replied. "It took us a while to dig it up, but he had contracts out to kill everybody but Hellhound. They were just supposed to capture him."

A jolt of fear made me jerk up in my chair. "Dante! Did you ever find him? Is he..."

"He's fine," Spider comforted. "He wasn't even in the country. He was at a photo shoot in Milan."

I let the air leak out through my lips as I sank back. "Thank God. So he doesn't know a thing about this."

"And he never will," Kane said.

"Thank God." I sipped some more water, trying to ease my aching throat. "Is that when you started tracing my IP addresses?" I asked Spider.

He flushed. "Yes. Well, no, actually, I was tracing you right from the start, I just didn't..." He trailed off.

"It's all right," Kane encouraged. "It was still the right decision."

I gave Richardson a hard look. "So you were looking for me at the internet cafe. That wasn't coincidence."

His eyes darted to Stemp, and a muscle jumped in his jaw as a faint flush climbed his neck. "It was coincidence that I was the one closest to the cafe. As soon as Webb sent the word out, I got over there. Where were you?"

"Hiding in the corner with my hood up and my head down. When Weasel started making a commotion, I slipped out behind you."

His flush deepened. "I noticed a skinny teenage boy in a baggy sweatshirt slipping out. I was looking for long red hair. That was pure incompetence on my part."

I wasn't harbouring any charitable feelings toward him, so I let the silence lengthen for a moment before moving on.

"And at the mall? Did you have the phones bugged? Is that why the police showed up?"

Richardson's eyes darted to Stemp's impassive face. "Not exactly bugged..." He trailed off.

"But you knew I was there."

"Yes," Stemp said.

In the silence that followed, I realized he wouldn't elaborate, and clenched my fists in momentary frustration before letting it go to move on. "So at the library, you just happened to be in the vicinity again?"

"Not close enough," Richardson replied. "By that time, we'd discovered the hit on you had been cancelled, and James was trying to capture you alive at all costs. We knew that meant he'd discovered you were more valuable alive than dead, so we immediately made the connection to Fuzzy Bunny. We were desperate to bring you in before they could get to you, so we sent the police on ahead and I came as fast as I could."

He shot me a frustrated glance. "And missed you again."

I shrugged. "How did you find us in the industrial park? More to the point, how did James find us in the industrial park? We were just supposed to be meeting Hellhound's contact."

Kane grimaced. "James had ears on the street trying to track your whereabouts, and he found out you'd set up the meeting. He *convinced* Hellhound's contact to tell him where and when. The contact is in the hospital now, but he's expected to survive."

He shot a look of approval at Spider. "Webb was digging for anything he could find on James the whole time, and once we realized the connection to Fuzzy Bunny, he had more to go on. At that point, we gave up on finding you and focused on finding James instead. You were too hard to catch, and we expected you'd end up in the same place eventually, since we knew you were searching for him, too."

He nodded to Spider, and he took up the tale. "James is smart, but I eventually unearthed a connection through one of his aliases in a shell company, and found the cell phone number he was using. We tracked him using his cell phone."

"So we were able to put people in place at the industrial park waiting for you," Kane finished.

Fury bubbled up. "And you let Arnie go in anyway. Did you see what James did to him?" I jerked forward, my voice grinding my flayed throat. "Do you have any idea how much pain he went through? For nothing?"

Kane's eyes reflected the full knowledge of that pain.

"We had originally planned to intercept you and extract you."

Stemp's cool voice cut in. "But then Webb discovered James had arranged a trap for you, and a transfer to Fuzzy Bunny's buyer. The opportunity was too good to pass up."

His dispassionate gaze raked over me. "I required some assurance of your continued loyalty. So we captured the buyer and sent Richardson in his place. It's unfortunate that your friend had to suffer, but the ends justified the means."

The air choked out of my body. "The ends... justified...? You... What if James had killed him?"

"It was an acceptable risk," Stemp replied. "We knew James wanted to capture him, not kill him. I would have avoided collateral damage if I could, but my priority is the security of this country, and the millions of innocent lives that would be at risk if you were compromised. A few bruises and broken bones are a small price to pay for that."

"Yeah," I grated. "As long as they're not your bones."

Stemp met my gaze with his flat eyes. "I've sacrificed my share of bones. I have nothing to prove."

I shut up, seething. In my heart of hearts, I believed him. I knew he'd been a field agent for years, and I knew the risks that came with that role.

When I could trust my voice, I spoke again. "So you set me up to believe I'd been taken by Fuzzy Bunny."

Stemp shrugged. "It was the only way we could be sure you were still loyal."

"So how long were you going to torture me before you could be *sure*?" I spat. My eyes strayed to the bandage on my arm before I glared at Richardson.

"Aydan, I'm so sorry," he implored, his voice raw with emotion. "I..."

"We never intended to torture you at all," Stemp cut in.

"I expected the captivity alone would be enough to break you eventually. The threat of torture was just icing on the cake. I was hoping to speed up the process." His clinical tone made my skin crawl.

He continued, "When you agreed to enter the network, I wanted to see if you would accurately decrypt the files, or whether you would lie about their contents. We made sure the files contained information that would be disastrous in Fuzzy Bunny's hands, and we knew you'd realize that as soon as you decrypted them."

He shot a glance at Kane. "We thought you might have an anxiety-driven loss of control inside the sim, and Richardson had been briefed that he might have seconds to extract you if that happened."

For once, Stemp allowed expression to creep onto his face. A flash of wry humour transformed him briefly into a human being before the mask closed down again.

"None of us expected you to blow your brains out," he said.

Richardson leaned forward, hands flat on the table, his expression beseeching. "Aydan, I'm so sorry. I'd been told that you usually visualized suffocating or getting trapped, so I thought I'd have a few seconds to get you out. When I saw the gun, I panicked. I knew a pain stimulus would yank you out of the network instantly. I didn't have time to drop the torch and pull the crystal off you."

"It's only a small second-degree burn," Stemp said.

Richardson spared him a single hostile glance before meeting my eyes again. "I didn't realize how horrific it is for you to be pulled out of the network like that," he said. "That was just..."

He shook his head and continued, "And then you went in

again so fast. I yanked the crystal off you, and you started to go through hell again, and I..." He met my eyes wretchedly. "I shot you with the trank gun. It was the only thing I could think of to make you stop suffering. I'm so sorry. I never wanted to hurt you."

I took a moment to process that, letting my whirling mind adjust from loathing the man who'd tortured me to having sympathy for a good agent forced into an untenable position. God, talk about a mindfuck.

I restrained myself from slumping forward to rest my aching forehead on the table for about a year, and settled for a long sigh instead.

"It's okay," I told him. "I know you were doing what you had to do. I wish you hadn't been so convincing, but it's okay."

"Thanks," he muttered.

"So then when I woke up and overheard your conversation with the doctor..." I shot Stemp a glare. "...I assumed I was still with Fuzzy Bunny. So I tried to escape."

"It was an excellent attempt," Stemp said. "Both attempts were quite impressive, actually, under the circumstances."

I met his eyes across the table. "So, are you satisfied? How many times do I have to prove myself to you?"

He sighed. "Unfortunately, the answer is 'over and over'. You've seen for yourself how agents can be turned."

I slouched in the chair while I absorbed the truth of his statement. Heavy exhaustion oppressed me. This was my life now.

The rest of the debriefing dragged interminably.

CHAPTER 40

At last, we emerged from the meeting room, and I massaged my aching temples. I glanced up at Kane as he paced beside me. "Can I get out of here now?"

He gave me a sympathetic glance. "Yes. Linda is waiting back at your room. She'll take that IV out of your hand and do the discharge paperwork with you. I'll meet you down in the lobby."

I nodded thanks and trailed back to the small room. Linda met me with a compassionate hug, my backpack, and a bottle of orange juice. "Don't worry," she whispered. "It's over now, and everything's going to be okay."

"Thanks, Linda." I let her naive reassurance comfort me a little.

When I stepped into the lobby, I was greeted by a familiar smiling face.

"Dave!" I hugged him fiercely. "Goddamn, Dave, you scared the shit out of me! I'm so glad you're okay!"

He patted me on the back and pulled away to meet my eyes. "Sorry I scared you. I got another muscle spasm, and then when I tagged that guy with the stun gun, he fell on me and wrenched my back. Couldn't even move, it hurt so bad.

Tried to tell you I was okay, but I couldn't catch my breath."

"I was so sure you were having a heart attack."

He smiled. "Told you I was okay. Think I've had my fill of excitement, though. The chopper ride was cool, but I'm ready to go back to driving now."

I gave him an extra squeeze before I released him. "That's really good to hear."

"Hey, get your hands off my man!"

I jerked around at the sound of Nichele's saucy voice. I caught a glimpse of her bruised face before she flung herself on me and hugged me half to death.

"Thanks, Aydan," she whispered.

I extracted myself from her embrace to frown at her. "What do you mean, your man?" I glanced from her grin to Dave's flushed, smiling face. "Uh, congratulations...?"

I dragged her a few steps away and bent to whisper. "What the hell, Nichele?" I shot another look at plain, overweight Dave in his nondescript jeans and T-shirt. "Don't mess with him. He's a sweet guy and you'll break his heart."

"I'm not messing with him. I know he's a sweet guy. We've been talking non-stop since last night."

"Nichele, he's not drop-dead handsome, and I'm pretty sure he doesn't own a suit. I know you. You're just going to screw him and then get tired of him and dump him and break his heart. Just don't, okay?"

"Aydan, I swear I won't." She grimaced. "I've developed a sudden allergy to men in suits. And when I found out what a hero Dave is, I realized maybe I've been looking in the wrong place. I'm going to give him a chance."

I sighed. I knew Nichele. She had a heart of gold, but a 'chance' would probably last a few weeks at best.

"At least let me give Dave fair warning," I begged.

"Okay. But I'm going to surprise you this time."

I couldn't help smiling at her. "You do that."

I walked over to Dave. His smile dissolved at the look on my face.

"Dave, we need to talk," I said.

He eyed me worriedly. "...'Kay. About what?"

There was no way to be tactful about this. I rubbed my headache. "Dave, I'm sorry, I need to say something that's going to... that you're not going to want to hear."

He squared his shoulders. "...'Kay."

I suppressed a groan. "Dave, Nichele is... um, flighty. She changes her mind really easily. Um..."

He relaxed and grinned. "Aydan, it's okay. Look at her." We both looked, taking in her tasteful, expensive clothing and impeccable hair, nails and makeup. Dave chuckled. "A guy like me with a woman like her? Maybe for a couple of weeks, tops. But I'm ready to celebrate life a little. I'm just going to enjoy this for as long as it lasts."

I squeezed his hand. "Dave, you're an amazing guy."

He flushed. "Thanks. You're pretty amazing yourself."

"Come on, Dave, let's go." Nichele bounced over and hugged his arm to her impressive cleavage.

They made their way to the door, arms locked around each other. Dave's beaming face could have lit up the entire town of Silverside.

I was standing there smiling and shaking my head when a familiar gravelly voice spoke from behind me. "Looks like a happy endin' for Dave."

I turned to see Kane and Arnie approaching. I grinned. "Yeah. He gets the girl, and he gets away with a small indiscretion involving an illegal weapon." I met Kane's eyes. "Thanks for leaving that part out."

He smiled back, but his eyes were serious. "I owed him after all he did for you."

"Will he get his truck back?" I asked.

"Yes. And he'll be getting more than the truck, although he doesn't know it yet," Kane said. "Sirius will compensate him for his lost load this week, and I've recommended him for a Medal of Bravery for risking his life to save you."

"That's wonderful." I savoured a glow of pure happiness for Dave. This probably marked the end of his mid-life crisis.

I shot a look at Hellhound's bandaged face. "There's somebody else here who deserves a medal or three."

Kane turned to regard his friend seriously. "I wanted to recommend him, but he wouldn't let me." His lips quirked up. "He's already got a drawer full of them anyway."

Arnie shuffled his feet and cleared his throat. "Yeah, well, anyway..." He gave Kane a look. "I gotta talk to Aydan."

He laid an arm across my shoulders and guided me toward a couple of unoccupied chairs. I looked up at him. "Drawer full of medals. I believe it."

He shrugged, not meeting my eyes. "He's exaggeratin'. Listen, darlin', we need to talk."

"Uh-oh."

He didn't smile. "Let's sit."

Once settled, he reached for my hand and gave me a steady look from the eye that wasn't swollen shut. "Aydan, there ain't a good time to say somethin' like this, so I'm just gonna say it. I'm gettin' too attached to ya."

I blew out a breath as my heart contracted sharply. "I was going to talk to you about that, too," I interrupted. I was glad my voice had been nothing but a hoarse whisper to begin with. It couldn't betray me now. I continued quickly before I lost my nerve.

"It's too dangerous for you to be around me. Every time we're together, you end up suffering. Sooner or later, luck will run out, and your death will be on my hands. I won't take that chance. Thanks for everything you've done. You'll never know how much it's meant to me."

I squeezed his hand, wanting to hold on for all I was worth. "Goodbye, Arnie. Thanks."

I made myself let go of his hand and stood, turning away quickly so he couldn't see my face.

I'd only taken a couple of steps when his rasp stopped me. "Hang on. Did ya just dump me?"

I sighed and turned to face him as he rose. "I'm pretty sure it doesn't qualify as a dump when we were never together in the first place. It's just a goodbye."

He scowled. "An' you're thinkin' ya gotta leave so poor little baby Arnie doesn't get beat up anymore."

I winced. "No, Arnie, I-"

"Ya think I'm scared of gettin' a few bruises? We talked about this. I thought ya said ya trusted me."

"No, I do trust you, you know I do, I just..."

"Ya just what, darlin'?" His voice softened as he stepped closer. "Ya tryin' to protect yourself again?"

I held my head. *This is why you don't let people in. It only hurts too much when you lose them.*

I straightened. It was for his own safety. Like Kane said. Don't get too close in our line of work.

"No. I'm thinking of you. I know how you feel about getting attached, and I'm getting too attached to you, too."

I knew exactly what to say to end it forever. I forced the words out of my mouth. "Arnie, I love you."

He rocked back a step and the unbruised parts of his face

paled. He spoke uncertainly into the silence. "You're just sayin' that so I'll run."

I sighed as the weight of loss threatened to crush me. "No. I'm saying it because it's the truth. I love you. And we both know you don't want that. So goodbye." I turned away.

"Aydan," he said hoarsely.

I stopped without turning, closing my eyes to shut out the pain. I opened them again when I felt his arms around me.

He tilted my chin to look down into my face, and his voice was a rough velvet rumble. "Aydan. Darlin', ya got no idea how long I been waitin' to hear ya say that. I love ya, too." He kissed me gently, and then sank down on one knee in front of me, clasping my hands between his own.

"I joked about it often enough, but this time I'm serious. Aydan, will ya marry me?"

CHAPTER 41

My breath went out of me in a hiccup. I stared down at Hellhound's battered, earnest face in sheer horror for a few long seconds before my panicked gaze darted around the lobby, searching frantically for an escape route.

Kane and Spider were staring at us, Spider's mouth hanging open in an 'O' of shock. Activity in the lobby ceased and conversations hushed while everyone turned to watch.

"Arnie, get up! You're attracting attention!" I hissed.

"Not 'til ya gimme an answer," he said. "I been waitin' a long time for this. I knew ya were the one the very first time I met ya, when ya slammed my head into a wall an' made a crack about my stayin' power. If ya love me, too, then let's make it official."

My legs gave way and I dropped to my knees beside him. "Arnie," I choked. "I can't. I'm sorry, I just can't."

"So ya were lyin' when ya said ya love me," he said quietly.

"No, I was telling the truth. I do love you. I love you for your big heart and your courage and your dirty sense of humour and your brilliant mind..."

"An' I'm good in bed," he reminded me.

"And you're mind-blowing in bed. And in truck seats. And everywhere else."

"But ya won't marry me."

"No. I'm sorry. I don't want to marry anybody, ever again."

He searched my face. "Will ya move in with me?"

"No." I dropped my gaze, unable to watch what I was doing to him.

He raised my chin again and eyed me gravely. "Will ya go steady with me? Not be with anybody else?"

"Arnie, I don't want anything more than we have right now, and I never will. I'm sorry."

He bellowed out a laugh and swept me into his arms. "I love ya, darlin'!" He kissed me soundly, and I pulled away, staring at him.

"W-what...?" I stammered.

He grinned. "I knew ya were shittin' me."

Comprehension dawned. "You... you... tricky bastard! You faked me out!" I gaped up at him, not knowing whether I was going to laugh or cry or smack him.

He roared laughter again. "Christ, ya shoulda seen your face!"

I was starting to laugh in spite of myself. "You lousy bastard! You scared the shit out of me! What would you have done if I'd said yes?"

He chuckled. "Ran like hell, what d'ya think?" He stroked the hair back from my face and took my hand. "Okay, let's try this again, darlin'. I gotta say this, 'cause we promised not to lie to each other."

I sobered, watching him, but he smiled. "What I was gonna say was, I'm gettin' too attached to ya. I been down this road before, an' it always ends up ugly, 'cause chicks think that means goin' steady or movin' in or whatever, an' that'll never happen. But if ya don't want that, if we can keep what we got..." He met my eyes, serious for once. "Long as you're still good with our original deal. No commitments, an' no lies."

I tried to swallow the bubble of joy and relief, but it burst out on my face in a huge grin despite me. His face lit up, too, and his shoulders relaxed.

"Arnie," I said. "That is exactly what I want." I threw my arms around him, and he held me close in a sweet, lingering kiss.

Applause and whistles made me jerk away to see everyone in the lobby clapping and smiling, patients and hospital staff alike. A couple of women dabbed at their eyes.

I turned back to Arnie. "Oh, for shit's sake."

He burst out laughing and stood, reaching a hand down to me. As I rose, he tucked an arm around me and waved graciously to our audience, smiling. "Hell, darlin', they'll never know any different," he growled out of the corner of his mouth. "Let 'em think they're seein' a happy endin'."

I grinned up at him. "They are."

"That they are." He pulled me closer and kissed me again, and the crowd began to drift back to its normal rhythm and flow.

After a moment, he pulled away, his expression serious again. "Aydan, I know what ya been through, so I'm gonna cut ya some slack this time. But don't ever pull that shit on me again. If ya wanna be rid a' me, look me in the eye an' say so, but don't play mind games, okay?"

I swallowed hard. "Okay. I'm sorry."

"It's okay, darlin'." He kissed me gently before pulling back with a wicked grin. "An' I promise not to fuck with your mind by pretendin' I wanna get married." We both laughed and turned to face Kane and Spider as they made their way over.

Spider was grinning from ear to ear, practically bouncing up and down. Kane wore his unreadable cop face.

"I take it congratulations are in order," Kane said evenly.

Hellhound grinned and squeezed my shoulders. "Yeah. I'm the luckiest guy in the world."

Spider flung his lanky arms around both of us. "Congratulations! Wait 'til I tell Linda, she'll be so sorry she missed the big proposal! When's the wedding?" he bubbled.

Arnie and I exchanged glances. "Dunno, darlin'," he said thoughtfully. "What d'ya think, February 31st?"

I pretended to consider it for a few seconds. "Yeah, that'll work. Hell should be frozen over by then. We could go there for a skiing honeymoon."

We turned to face the other two. Spider's expression of consternation almost made me feel sorry for pulling his leg. Kane exploded in a bark of laughter.

"But... but... what...?" Spider stammered. "That looked like..."

Hellhound chuckled. "Hell, ya spy on people's private conversations, ya get what ya deserve."

I relented. "Sorry, Spider, I know what it looked like, but it wasn't that. Arnie and I are happy the way we are, and that's the way we're going to stay."

"But..." His disappointment was almost palpable. "But you're not... anything. You're not even together."

Hellhound clapped him on the shoulder. "Now you're gettin' it." He turned to me. "I gotta go. I gotta see a client in Calgary tonight. Ya need a ride, darlin'?"

"Uh, yeah, I guess I do. I'll have to get my car."

"No need," Kane said. "We impounded it from Nichele's the day you left. I had it delivered back to your farm last night. I'll take you home."

I surveyed him in pleased surprise. "Thanks!"

Arnie began to drift toward the door, his arm still around me. "Damn, darlin', I was hopin' we'd have time for a little celebration later. I wanna see ya put some drag-racin' moves on my stickshift."

I linked my arms around his neck and pressed close. "Yeah, my slushbox needs some work, too, and you've got just the right tool. Too bad you're leaving."

He grinned. "I might be back."

I kissed him. "Better be."

CHAPTER 42

Kane and I got into his Expedition in silence. We had driven for several minutes before he spoke abruptly. "Webb said you were wondering if your family had been executed. Did you find the information you were looking for?"

I stared out the windshield. "No. Spider said all information on me had been redacted, and I couldn't find anything on my own."

"What will you do now?"

"Nothing. I have no place left to look. And you don't need to ask what I'm going to be doing, because I have to give you a notarized report every time I sneeze or go to the bathroom from here on in. Stemp made that pretty clear. Either that or I get locked up."

He shot a sidelong glance at me, which I ignored. "You understand it's for your own safety, don't you?" he asked.

"Yeah."

We rode in silence for a few more minutes.

"Your father and your uncle both died natural deaths," he said. "The circumstances around your mother's car accident were... unusual, but our government didn't kill any of your family, directly or indirectly."

I jerked around in the seat to stare at him. "How did you find that out?"

He kept his eyes on the road. "I called in some favours. There's more, too."

My hands trembled as I folded and unfolded the seatbelt over my chest. "What?" My voice cracked, and I cleared my throat and swallowed hard.

"Back in the mid-sixties, the idea of the brainwave driven network was conceived. A few years later, Sirius began widespread testing of school-aged children, looking for specific brainwave patterns."

My heart hammered. "And I was one of them."

"Yes. You were one of only six in the entire country who fit the parameters. Dr. Kraus developed a system of exercises designed to develop and enhance those patterns. Over the years, the other children's patterns stagnated and eventually deteriorated despite the exercises. Yours didn't."

"Testing three times a year. And the exercises that he called games."

"Yes," he confirmed. "You weren't supposed to remember them. The others didn't. But you were different. By the time you reached junior high school, it became apparent that you were the best hope for what Kraus had in mind. It was then that Sirius recruited your father."

"Who began to work for the government. Carrying a gun. And teaching me to shoot." I squeezed my eyes shut briefly, willing away the dizziness and nausea. "You're telling me I've been manipulated my entire life."

Muscles jumped in his jaw. "They tried. You were supposed to be recruited into the computer program right out of high school. Your father was supposed to encourage you in the right direction. That didn't happen."

I tried to suck oxygen out of air that seemed suddenly too thin. "When Mom died, we just... shut down. Just going through the motions. I couldn't deal with the thought of an academic program, so I went into drafting instead, got a quick certificate, and started working."

"And met your first husband," Kane said tightly. "That's when they deployed Robert, but it was already too late. You were too damn loyal, and you wouldn't break it off with Steven, even though you should have."

"Hindsight's twenty-twenty," I said faintly.

I had already suspected what he was telling me, but the confirmation was almost more than I could bear. I stared blindly at the highway lines dashing by outside the SUV. One at a time, too quickly to count, like wasted years slipping away.

"I can't believe they made Robert hang around all those years," I said finally. "No wonder he went rogue at the end."

"They didn't make him," Kane said gently. "He volunteered. Year after year. He took over the mission to manipulate you into working for Sirius. For years, he sent in reports describing his efforts. When your first marriage finally ended, he said he would have to marry you in order to apply more pressure, and the department approved it. He was still sending in reports detailing his plans and efforts to bring you into Sirius the week before he died."

Confusion stirred up clouds of silt in my brain, and I turned to frown at Kane. "He never even mentioned Sirius. And he never wanted me to do anything with computers. When I took those computer courses, it was almost like he was discouraging me."

Kane continued, still watching the road. "By that time, Stemp was in the director's position, and he asked some hard questions. When the analysts really dug into it, they couldn't verify any of Robert's reported activities. Then they discovered he was secretly making plans to take you out of the country and give you a new identity. Stemp ordered me to eliminate him before he could complete his scheme. He had airline tickets for both of you, for the evening he died."

"He said he had a surprise for me, and I was so looking forward to it. He came home early that day to celebrate." Cold sickness tunnelled into the pit of my stomach. "So he was working for Fuzzy Bunny all along."

Kane slowed to turn into my lane and stopped at the gate. He turned to meet my eyes. "No, he wasn't. He was protecting you. He loved you, Aydan. He knew the kind of life you'd lead if you worked for Sirius, and he was willing to do whatever it took to prevent that. Even if it meant making you vanish. Even if it cost him his life."

His words slowly penetrated my brain, and I stared out the window, blinking hard.

Kane got out and unlocked the gate, and by the time he returned, I had my voice more or less under control. I'd also had a chance to consider what he must have done in order to get this information. Even Spider's super-hacker skills hadn't been able to unearth it.

I swallowed hard and met his eyes. "Thank you. This means... more to me than you can imagine."

"You're welcome. I owed you that, and a lot more besides."

Another thought hit me.

"So..." My voice quavered, and I stopped and tried again. "So when the perfect farm came up for sale here in Silverside... My dream farm... That wasn't coincidence, was it?"

"No. It took them almost two years to get it set up. They had to acquire the house and land, get your requirements from your real estate agent, update the property, and then list it and make sure it went only to you." He shot a wry smile at me. "You made it easy. All they had to do was build that deluxe garage. They didn't even have to renovate the house."

Hurt and anger burst out of me. "Why didn't you just tell me?"

"Please believe I would have told you if I'd known," he said quietly. "If I had known this from the start, it might have changed... a lot of things. Stemp doesn't believe in providing any more details than what's absolutely necessary to accomplish what he wants."

He parked beside the house and turned to face me. "I still owe you that apology. Aydan, I can't tell you how sorry I am. If you'd been able to trust me enough to come to me with these questions, this latest disaster could have been averted. And I took a bad situation and made it worse."

His steady gaze faltered, and he turned to stare at his whitening knuckles on the steering wheel. "I was angry and... hurt. And I let that get in the way. It wasn't just unprofessional, it was childish, and I'm sorry-"

"John, it's okay," I interrupted. "You had orders. You were doing your job. I've always admired your sense of duty, and it's not your fault that I don't always like what your duty demands."

"To hell with duty!" He turned and took my hand, searching my face. "Aydan, I wouldn't have killed you. Not even under a direct order." He swallowed. "I didn't know you'd been communicating with Webb. I didn't want to believe it, but I was starting to think you'd betrayed m... our team and gone rogue. And when I thought you'd turned Arnie against me, I... did and said some things I regret."

"We both overreacted. I'll forgive you, if you'll forgive me for taking off and leaving you holding the bag. And I hope you'll forgive me for saying some things I didn't mean, too. Can we just put it behind us?"

His face softened, and he drew in a deep breath. "Yes. Thank you. I... yes."

He shifted in his seat, his clear grey eyes serious. "Aydan, there's something else I have to say. I... you won't want to hear it."

My shoulder muscles coiled into slow knots, and I held my voice steady with an effort. "Add it to the list of things I didn't want to hear. Spit it out."

"Aydan..." He stopped as if gathering his strength. "You know I've never lied to you."

"So you said."

He flinched. "I've never lied to you," he repeated firmly. "I can't make you believe that, but it's the truth."

I sighed. "John, you're a spy, and spies lie as easily and convincingly as they tell the truth. I'll never know who you really are, and I'll never know whether you're lying to me or not."

I looked up to read the pain in his face. I paused, uncertain, then took a deep breath and made the decision. "So, this is probably stupid, but I'm just going to trust you unless you give me a reason not to."

I hadn't realized how rigidly he was holding himself until he relaxed. "Thank you," he murmured.

"You're welcome." I made my voice as casual as I could. "If we can, I'd like us to be friends again."

His voice was very quiet. "Always."

"Thanks." I gave him a smile as I opened the door and slid out.

"Aydan."

I leaned into the truck. "Yeah."

"Remember when I said earlier that you sometimes don't realize how much something means until you think you've lost it?"

"Yeah." I glanced up at the sound of a vehicle turning into my driveway. Tom's truck. Shit.

"I thought I'd lost you." He took a deep breath. "I've spent the last few months trying to ignore how I feel. Telling myself that what I want can't happen. But when I saw you and Arnie together, I..."

Tom's truck rolled up, gravel crunching behind me. Kane's fist clenched on the steering wheel and he spoke quickly, staring out the windshield. "I know you don't want to hear this, and I won't bring it up again. But I have to say it, because I obviously didn't say it clearly enough this summer."

He turned at last to meet my eyes, his hand reaching out between us. "Aydan, I love you. I'm not saying that because I have orders. I'm saying it because I can't help it. I love you," he repeated.

His words hung in the air.

A door slammed behind me, and I turned to face Tom. His gaze raked Kane before turning to me. "Aydan, is everything all right?" he asked dangerously.

I sighed. "Everything's fine. And John was just leaving."

I gently closed the door of the Expedition.

A Request

Thanks for reading!

If you enjoyed this book, I'd really appreciate it if you'd take a moment to review it online. If you've never reviewed a book before, I have a couple of quick videos at http://www.dianehenders.com/reviews that will walk you through the process.

Here are some suggestions for the "star" ratings:
Five stars: Loved the book and can hardly wait for the next one.
Four stars: Liked the book and plan to read the next one.
Three stars: The book was okay. Might read the next one.
Two stars: Didn't like the book. Probably won't read the next one.
One star: Hated the book. Would never read another in the series.

"Star" ratings are a quick way to do a review, but the most helpful reviews are the ones where you write a few sentences about what you liked/disliked about the book. Thanks for taking the time to do a review!

Want to know what else is roiling around in the cesspit of my mind? Visit my blog and website at http://www.dianehenders.com. Don't forget to leave a comment in the guest book to say hi!

About Me

By profession, I'm a technical writer, computer geek, and ex-interior designer. I'm good at two out of three of these things. I had the sense to quit the one I sucked at.

That's how I currently support myself. To deal with my mid-life crisis, I also write adventure novels featuring a middle-aged female protagonist. And I kickbox.

This seemed more productive than indulging in more typical mid-life crisis activities like getting a divorce, buying a Harley Crossbones, and cruising across the country picking up men in sleazy bars. Especially since it's winter most of the months of the year here.

It's much more comfortable to sit at my computer. And hell, Harleys are expensive. Come to think of it, so are beer and gasoline.

Oh, and I still love my husband. There's that. I'll stick with the writing.

Diane Henders

Since You Asked...

People frequently ask if my protagonist, Aydan Kelly, is really me.

Yeah, you got me. These novels are an autobiography of my secret life as a government agent, working with highly-classified computer technology... Oh, wait, what's that? You want the *truth*? Um, you do realize fiction writers get paid to lie, don't you?

...well, shit, that's not nearly as much fun. It's also a long story.

I swore I'd never write fiction. "Too personal," I said. "People read novels and automatically assume the author is talking about him/herself."

Well, apparently I lied about the fiction-writing part. One day, a story sprang into my head and wouldn't leave. The only way to get it out was to write it down. So I did.

But when I wrote that first book, I never intended to show it to anyone, so I created a character that looked like me, just to thumb my nose at the stereotype. I've always had a defective sense of humour, and this time it turned around and bit me in the ass.

Because after I'd written the third novel, I realized I actually wanted to publish them. And when I went back to change my main character to *not* look like me, my beta readers wouldn't let me. They rose up against me and said, "No! Aydan is a tall woman with long red hair and brown eyes. End of discussion!"

Jeez, no wonder readers get the idea that authors write about themselves. So no, I'm not Aydan Kelly. I just look like her.

Bonus Stuff

Here's an excerpt from **Book 5: How Spy I Am**

"We need to do damage control."

I suppressed an exhausted yawn along with my urge to say, 'No shit, Sherlock', and eyed the civilian director of clandestine operations with distaste.

Charles Stemp returned his usual impassive stare from across the table, and I let my gaze slide off his reptilian features to the much more rewarding sight of John Kane beside him.

Stemp's flat voice continued, "Fuzzy Bunny came too close to capturing you this week. That would have been disastrous to our national security, not to mention to you personally."

"Wouldn't have been much worse than being captured by you," I snapped before I could stop myself.

Stemp met my eyes levelly. "We needed you to believe you were in enemy hands. And I don't need to remind you that Fuzzy Bunny will not stop at a small burn to force your cooperation if they capture you."

I swallowed the sudden dryness in my throat and willed myself not to hug my bandaged arm. Hell, no, he didn't need to remind me. The only thing cuddly about Fuzzy Bunny was their name.

God, what if they were hunting me again? My gaze flicked toward the doorway despite the knowledge that we were in a secured building.

Jeez, woman, relax.

I drew a deep breath and attempted to follow my own advice. I was safe. Kane was probably Canada's most lethal weapon, and after our conversation yesterday, I was pretty sure he'd protect me with his life. My mind sidled away from the memory of his lips framing the words 'I love you'. I'd spent half the night worrying about that.

Deal with it later.

Stemp's voice dragged my tired brain back from its rambling. "We need to convince them you are dead. And Kane informs me your cover here in Silverside is not as," he hesitated. "...Robust," he said finally, "...as we would prefer."

I met Kane's steady grey eyes, wondering exactly what he'd reported. My gaze strayed lower without my permission to admire the massive chest and bulging biceps straining his black T-shirt. Lethal and unbelievably hot, goddammit...

"Aydan?"

"Ms. Kelly?"

Kane and Stemp both spoke my name, and I herded my mind back to the meeting table yet again. "Sorry, what?" I asked, massaging the ache in my forehead.

"Do you have any ideas to contribute regarding your cover identity?" Stemp repeated.

I forced myself to appreciate his attempt to include me in the process. "Not at the moment, I'm sorry." I didn't bother to add, 'I've been a little busy trying to stay alive lately'.

"It's all right," Kane said. "We can work on it today."

I shot him a grateful look.

Stemp rose. "Very well. Have a proposal ready by end of day." He fixed me with his expressionless gaze. "Please check the network first thing for any chatter regarding yourself. Our analysts haven't picked anything up from the public channels, so you'll need to breach Fuzzy Bunny's firewalls and check their systems directly."

He strode out, and I sighed and sank my forehead onto the table, cushioned by my crossed forearms. I grunted and quickly repositioned my arms at the jab of pain.

"Are you all right?" Kane's velvet baritone was quick with concern.

"Fine. I just bumped that burn," I mumbled into the table. I hadn't even heard him stand, and his touch startled me. "It's fine," I repeated, but he was already lifting the dressing away from my arm, his powerful hands deft and gentle.

We both contemplated the angry-looking wound. "I thought Stemp said it was just a small second-degree burn," Kane growled.

I shrugged and retrieved the bandage from him, smoothing it back down onto my skin. "Richardson panicked. I guess he held the torch on me a little longer than he meant to. It'll be fine."

"Aydan, I'm so sorry you had to go through that. I know it doesn't make it any less traumatic to know it was faked." His face darkened. "Except for that burn."

"You've got nothing to apologize for." I stood and drifted toward the door. "Stemp, on the other hand, owes me a buttload of apologies, which I'm highly unlikely to get. Let's go."

Slouched on the small sofa in my office a few minutes later, I scowled at the tiny piece of circuitry in my hand. Why the hell did it only work for me? And why the hell hadn't its unknown inventors created something that wouldn't drive flaming spikes through my brain every time I used it?

I drew a shallow breath through my mouth.

"Are you okay?" Clyde Webb's voice made me concentrate on putting a more pleasant expression on my face. It wasn't difficult when I looked up to see the concern on his youthful face.

"Fine, Spider, thanks." I flicked my eyes in John Smith's direction, and Spider's expression cleared in comprehension.

I had hoped to work with Kane and Spider as usual today, but apparently Smith had orders to attend as well. I took another shallow breath, trying not to inhale his stench. Somebody really should tell him to change his shirt more than once a month. You'd think he'd get the hint when its pattern of food stains started to resemble a particularly creative Jackson Pollock canvas.

I shook off my mood with a sigh and waited for Kane to pull up a chair before eyeing my team. "Everybody ready?"

Spider nodded, his fingers already flying over his laptop keyboard. Smith concentrated on the desktop computer, and Kane gave me a nod and a smile, fingering the fob that would give him painless access to the brainwave-driven simulation network.

Painless. Huh. I wish.

I banished my self-pity with another sigh and gripped the network key, concentrating on stepping into the white void of virtual reality. A second later, Kane's avatar popped into existence beside me.

The network was a busy place. Kane stepped protectively in front of me when a couple of researchers' avatars approached in the virtual corridor. They exchanged wary glances and gave us a wide berth.

I patted Kane's hard shoulder. "Don't scare the locals. I'm pretty sure we're safe here."

"I'm not taking any chances," he rumbled.

I smiled up at him. "Thanks."

His strong square face softened into an answering smile, activating the sexy laugh lines around his eyes, and we made our way to the virtual file repository in comfortable silence.

Inside, I surveyed the towering stack of virtual files with dismay. "Shit, they really piled up."

Guilt prodded me. If I hadn't run off last week...

I tamped it down. Too late to be sorry, just fix the problem. "Have the analysts flagged anything in particular?" I asked.

"Nothing that's a higher priority than hiding your identity," Kane said. "You need to check Fuzzy Bunny's network first. You can worry about these other files later."

"Okay. This will probably take a while." I created a virtual chair in the sim and sank into it, and Kane pulled one out of thin air beside me, reaching toward me as he sat.

I took his extended hand and gave it a little squeeze. "Thanks for being my anchor." I glimpsed his smile one more time as I faded into invisibility to seep into the data stream, feeling my consciousness stretch from his grip like a rubber band.

Hitching a ride on data packets, I shot through a roller-coaster of connections, following the delicate tracery of markers I'd left behind in my earlier surveillance. When I reached Fuzzy Bunny's first firewall, I paused for a deep virtual breath before trickling through the pinhole I'd left open in my previous visit. Their intrusion-detection software passed harmlessly over me, and I continued my stealthy progress, nosing around invisibly in their file system.

If I'd had a stomach in my current form, it would have clenched at what I discovered. I willed calm. Search it all out.

I sifted their data with the finest filter I could create before moving on to the next server. And the next.

And the next.

By the time my exhausted consciousness oozed back into the file repository, it was all I could do to recreate my avatar. When I faded into wavering existence, Kane reached carefully for my shoulders.

"Stay with me now," he encouraged. "Come on, let's get you out of here."

"Okay..." I whispered, concentrating fiercely.

He gathered me up and guided me to the exit portal, the warm strength of his arm holding my virtual form together.

My momentary relief at getting to the portal was erased by the familiar explosion of pain when I returned my consciousness to my physical body.

"Aaah-God-dammit-sonuva-fucking-*bitch*!" I spat, clutching my temples.

Kane's hands gently pushed mine away to close around my head, and I whimpered gratitude while his massage eased the worst of the pain.

At last, I slumped back on the sofa. "Thanks," I mumbled.

Kane stooped to look into my face as I sprawled limply. "Are you all right?"

"Fine. Thanks." I wedged myself into a corner of the couch in an approximately upright position. "God. Shit." I ran a hand over my still-aching face.

"What?" Kane demanded. "What did you find?"

I blew out a long sigh. "Lots of chatter about me, unfortunately. They're not positive I'm alive, but they're sure as hell stirred up about finding me if I am."

End of How Spy I Am, Chapter 1 excerpt